THE HUNTER'S COMPANION

Lori Powell

Copyright © 2014 Lorraine Powell

This is a work of fiction. Names, characters, businesses, places, events and incidents are either the products of the author's imagination or used in a fictitious manner. Historical information has been researched thoroughly but used with artistic licence. While The Witch Finder General, Matthew Hopkins, was indeed a real person, the events in this story are entirely fictitious.

Copyright © 2014 by Lorraine Powell
All rights reserved. This book or any portion thereof may not be reproduced or used in any manner whatsoever without the express written permission of the publisher except for the use of brief quotations in a book review.

First Printing, 2014
Second Printing, 2016
Third Printing 2024
ISBN: 9781500644918

ISBN-13: 9781234567890
ISBN-10: 1477123456

Cover design by: Art Painter
Library of Congress Control Number: 2018675309
Printed in the United States of America

*For Big G, Isabel & Callum, the most special lights in my life.
The Hunter's Companion has been a long time in the making. What started off as a dream developed and went through multiple transformations before the book, as it is now, was created. It is a fact, that without the encouragement, advice and help from my sister Lynda this would still be lingering on my computer, a half-written story. Thank you, Lynda, — you know how much you've done, not least in believing in me and giving me the belief that I can do it and for my beautiful cover.*

Thank you to ALL my family, because without you I wouldn't be me and this story would not exist. You know you are the best family a girl could have.

Since the first publication of The Hunter's Companion as an e-book I have some special people to thank. The UM, because they brighten each day. (Natasha, your feedback — thank you). A huge thank you also, to Lynda Lamb, editor extraordinaire; thank you.

One
1645

The fen fog rolled off the marsh, curling its damp fingers around Lora's limbs as she hurried along. Eyes squinting against the impenetrable grey, she tried with growing desperation to keep her feet on the narrow path without losing speed. The blackness of the bog lay in wait all around, patiently seeking its next meal. Yet for Lora, fear of the hungry bog paled in comparison to her terror of that which pursued her. Her ears strained to hear any indication it was still behind her over the wailing North Sea winds. *It*, the thing, the creature. Her heartbeat quickened; she forced herself not to think of it.

Her foot slipped from the invisible path and muddy water seeped into her boot. Balance lost, she reached forward, found something solid and heaved herself back up, her frantic mind worrying what her mother would say about the state of her new gloves. She scrabbled along the path on hands and knees, realising with dread that above the sound of her own heaving breaths and thumping heart she could hear its breathing. The sound was not human. Each intake of breath rasped as though its chest was thick with phlegm; each breath out oozed with malevolence. Lora didn't know *what* was following her, but she knew it was evil. She knew it as sure as she knew her own name.

The fog grew denser. She tried to claw it out of the way, to free her eyes to see the path ahead. Standing again she searched, seeking a way through the fog. But she stood too long and her boots sank into the mud. She pulled them free, fearing the sucking noise they made was loud enough to indicate her presence. If it didn't, the noise of her thumping heart or her ragged breath was sure to. Or maybe it would be the scent of fear itself, radiating from every pore, that would lead the monster to her.

With each step she took, she prayed. She prayed that the Father God would forgive her sins. She prayed for the sight of the town's lamps, burning through the fog. She prayed she would make it through the night.

As the way became harder to pass and fright seemed to steal her mind completely, warm tears trickled from her eyes, the saltwater leaving tracks in the icy mist that caressed her face. She tried to stifle the sobs she felt rising in her chest as each step became more difficult to take. A glimmer in the fog gave her hope; the town was nearer than she'd dared dream. Then all hope died.

As the rasping behind her grew louder, nearer, a shape appeared in front of her. A tiny glint of silver caught her eye, and Lora knew then she had a choice to make. Death by the creature gaining behind her, or by the knife of the man standing before her.

Her prayers for forgiveness grew more frantic as she sank to her knees in the waterlogged mud. Cold slime slipped over her legs and through her skirts as she prayed for her soul. With her last rational thought, she prayed that the end be quick.

Two
2013

Regan stepped out of the car and arched her back to release the kinks the long journey had knotted there. Tuning out the excited chatter of her mum and sister, she surveyed her new home. The endless flat fields in varying shades of yellow, gold and green swayed in the breeze like soft ocean ripples, as alien to her as if she'd landed on another planet. The rays of the high sun gleamed on the swathes of crops; sparkles chased each other playfully over them, yet Regan felt a coldness the sun couldn't chase away. She shivered, trying to quell her horror at her new life before her mum emerged from the car.

'It's beautiful, isn't it?' asked Katherine White as she joined her eldest daughter, leaning against the old Saab. Regan smiled, trying not to notice the dark circles and fine lines that had appeared around her mum's eyes in the last few years.

'Home,' said Katherine. 'There's no place like it.'

Smiling again, Regan attempted to appear excited, knowing how perceptive her mum was of her moods; she didn't want the small spark that had recently ignited in her mother's eyes to flicker out because of her.

'It's certainly how you described it, Mum; I didn't know anywhere could be so flat!' She kept her tone level as her own eyes swept once more across the fields in front of her, coming to rest on the large, rundown house that was now her home. She took her sunglasses from where they nestled in her expensive blonde hair and slipped them on to hide the fear she knew was creeping into her eyes.

'Wow, Regan, it's like looking at a yellow sea!' Her sister, fed up with waiting in the car, bounded out like an eager puppy. 'This is way better than Brighton, I bet there's loads of stuff I can do here. It's not just shops, shops, shops!'

Regan smiled. 'Sure is different kiddo!'

The fact there were no shops for miles was not quite as appealing to Regan as it was to Ashleigh. In fact, she was trying hard not to think about it. She was also trying hard to forget the fact that there was no beach, no nightclubs, no nail or hair salons, and no Marcus. She stopped her train of thought as she caught her mum's anxious expression and forced herself to smile again.

'This is going to be the best move we've ever made,' she said, pulling her sister in for a hug. 'East Anglia had better watch out cos the Whites have arrived.' Grabbing the biggest suitcase, she headed towards the ancient house. 'Come on then Mum, show us into our new home.'

'Finally you arrive!' As they approached the door, a small woman with an indescribable accent rushed out, talking nineteen to the dozen to Regan's mum. 'I have train to catch, I thought you would be here earlier.'

'I'm sorry; we were late leaving and the traffic …' Katherine trailed off, seeing the woman wasn't interested.

'No matter but I must go now, Mrs Tate's tablets is on the side, I have written note so you know when she is next to have them. Her favourite to eat is chicken and she does not like the fish.' Before anyone could say anything further the lady who had been caring for Katherine's aunt for the last five years picked up a bag and hurried out of the driveway, disappearing from sight almost instantly.

'I've got a feeling we've just been dropped in at the deep end,' said Katherine, the cheerful note in her voice dipping a little, 'I guess I'd better go and see if Aunty Vi remembers me! Why don't you two explore a little; I'll find you when I need you.' And she made her way into the house to find her aunt. Regan shook her head. She still didn't understand why her mum wouldn't put the old lady in a nursing home. She'd been born before World War 1 had started; she was nearly a hundred years old.

'I'm going to explore the garden first,' said Ashleigh, a huge grin splitting her face in two, 'I think I can see where we could keep some chickens.'

'Okay but be careful.' Regan stood for a minute taking in the overgrown yard and the cracked grey rendering that must surely have started off white. Resigned to the fact that this was now her home, she made her way up the path and tried to ignore the ache in her chest. She *must* look happy; she must pretend she wanted to be here as much as they did.

Entering through the door her mum had taken, she found herself in the kitchen. A yellowed Formica table stood in the middle of the space with two worn stools tucked under it. The ancient fridge whirred noisily in the corner and the oven looked as though it had been dragged here from the seventies and not used since. Dumping the suitcase in one corner Regan stretched over the sink and tried to open the window. As she pushed against the filthy glass pane paint flaked into the sink, disturbing a huge spider. Shuddering, she pushed harder. Another shower of paint later the window was open and fresh air was battling with the mustiness of the unused room.

A small microwave in the corner appeared to be the only concession to the 21st century. Regan turned her nose up in distaste at the bin overflowing with plastic trays which indicated what the carer had classed as suitable tea for Aunty Vi. This house had obviously been quite beautiful once but had been neglected, just like its owner. Guilt at the overwhelming urge to run straight back to Brighton gnawed at Regan. After checking that Ashleigh was still all right in the garden, she made her way out of the kitchen into the long hallway. The stone tiles that lined the floor were worn and faded with years of footsteps, but Regan could still see the quality in them; with a bit of care, they could look quite spectacular again.

Her mum's muffled voice came from behind one of the doors in the hallway; deciding to avoid her — and the inevitable introduction to Aunty Vi — until she'd explored the rest of the house, Regan made her way up the stairs.

She found four bedrooms in all on the first floor, two completely beyond use due to damp and mould. The other two, though musty and dusty, could be perfect for her mum and sister. It would only take a little bit of vision and a whole lot of cleaning. Passing a large bathroom with a cringe-worthy avocado suite — yet another relic from the seventies — Regan discovered a small wooden staircase and things started looking up a bit. Ascending the five stairs, she entered an attic room. Cobwebs hung from the ceiling and dust motes swirled and danced in the sunlit skylight. A single bed was pushed into one corner, and the rest of the space seemed to be taken up with boxes and books, suitcases, old pieces of furniture, and a hanging rack of antique clothes. She crossed the creaking wooden floor and tugged at the skylight, letting in some air before she choked on the dust. This would be perfect as her space, Regan thought. Private, tucked away from the rest of the house — a place she could truly make her own.

Ignoring the urge to make the bed and sink straight into it, Regan knew she had better get back downstairs to find her mum. One thing was certain: this house was going to need some serious cleaning before she would let any member of her family sleep in it, and unfortunately it wasn't going to clean itself.

And, the voice in her head reminded her, *you still have to meet Aunty Vi.* She decided to get that over with first; she loved her mum, but potty old ladies she'd never met before were really not her thing. She planned on staying as far away from her aunt as possible; she wasn't sure she could get away with not meeting her at all though. The idea was tempting … but no, her mum had enough on her plate without Regan adding to it. A quick introduction, a few minutes of polite conversation, then back to cleaning. *Brace yourself*, she thought, making her way back downstairs.

'Mum, I've found the perfect room for me, up in the attic,' she said when she found her mum.

'That's nice, dear,' Katherine answered, her voice distracted, 'are you sure you're comfortable, Aunty Vi? I can find another pillow if you need one.'

'Oh do stop fussing, it's fine. Mother will bring me a pillow if I need one.'

Regan raised her eyebrows. Aunty Vi was older than Father Time; there was no way her mum was still alive. Great, another plus to add to the move to the backside of nowhere — cuckoo relatives. She sighed, then noticed her mum watching her. Plastering the smile back on her face, she moved towards the old lady and leant forward. 'Hi Aunty Vi, I'm Regan, Katherine's daughter.' She was surprised at how frail the old lady looked. Her thinning hair was bone white, her skin softly wrinkled like an old T-shirt, her fingers bent and gnarled. She swallowed, then took one of the fragile hands in hers. She really, really, needed to make an effort for her mum. 'It's lovely to meet you Aunty Vi.'

The old lady lifted her milky eyes to meet Regan's, and as she did a look of shock came onto her face. 'No, you can't be one — Lizzy was the last, there can't be any more of you —' Suddenly the grip became tighter. She pulled Regan closer; the strength in the old lady's arms was surprising. 'You be careful, don't go out, don't do it. They took Lizzy and they'll take you.'

Fear ran through Regan and she pulled her arm away and backed off. Feeling her heart beating just a little faster, she looked nervously at her mum who was trying to calm the old lady down. 'Don't worry darling,' she said to Regan, over the top of Aunty Vi's head, 'dementia is a cruel illness.'

Regan rolled her eyes and, as soon as she was out of hearing range, wound her fingers beside her head and muttered, 'Bloody cuckoo, I knew it.'

Three

Glad to escape from the dust fest that was her new home, Regan checked the sheets that were drying on the line. The blazing summer sun had dried them in record time, so at least they could all have clean bed linen tonight. Hours of cleaning that afternoon had given her something to focus on, but as she un-pegged the sheets, Regan found herself with time to think and she felt an overwhelming urge to get out of there. The happy, smiley Regan she was presenting to her mum and sister was wearing a bit thin, and she needed to find some space to think properly.

'Mum, I'm going into the village to see if I can find the shop, we need more bleach and some milk,' she called as she carried the dry linen inside. She decided against asking her mum if she could use the car. After all, she didn't *technically* have a licence, though she knew perfectly well how drive. Even on these quiet, endless roads, her mum would never agree. Besides, walking would give her more time alone and the opportunity to ring Marcus.

'How long are you going to be love?' asked her mum, walking into the kitchen. The long day was starting to show on Katherine too. Only Ashleigh was still excited about their new life.

'Not sure. I'm going that way,' she pointed down the track they'd driven up that morning, 'we passed a shop in that direction, didn't we?'

'Yes, that's the way. It's a couple of miles though — I'll go, I can drive in half the time.'

'Betty? Where's Betty?' Aunty Vi's confused voice came from her bedroom down the hallway. Regan smiled sympathetically at her mum.

'Looks like you're needed here. I'll go, the walk will do me good. Besides I've got to learn the way there sooner or later.' Grabbing her phone, she prayed she would get signal; she wouldn't be surprised if mobile phones were an alien concept in this part of the country. As she walked, the sun blazed down, the breeze doing little to cool her. She'd walked just a few feet when rivulets of sweat starting trickling down her back. God, she missed the sea breeze. With horror she noticed her brand new white and silver sandals were covered in dusty streaks. *Damn*, she thought. They might not be Jimmy Choo's but they'd cost £60 and, currently jobless, she couldn't afford to ruin nearly-brand-new footwear.

Taking deep breaths to calm herself, she glanced back towards the house — still in sight despite the distance — and took in the surrounding views. The verges were overgrown with tall grasses, poppies, and other wildflowers that Regan couldn't name. A long, thin line of birch trees, like soldiers standing to attention, edged a field. A distant river sparkled gold and silver in the sun, meandering towards the horizon. Blue sky surrounded her but despite the vastness of the space Regan felt it was somehow suffocating her, trapping her beneath its dome. A roaring noise suddenly cut through the air, spoiling the silence. Moving to the verge, Regan looked around for the source of it; it took only seconds for a motorbike to come into view. Zooming past Regan, it sprayed dust in the air before disappearing into the distance.

'Idiot,' she yelled after it, then turned with a sigh and resumed her walk towards the village. Enveloped in silence again, she pulled out her phone and was elated to see she had a signal. Flicking through her phone book she found Marcus's number and pressed call. It rang endlessly and just as she was about to hang up Marcus answered with his usual, 'He-ello.'

'Hi Marcus, it's me,' she said, her heart jumping at his familiar voice.

'Regan. I take it you're now safely in the back of beyond?' he didn't bother to hide the distaste in his voice.

'Yes, we made it safely. Sorry I didn't have a chance to ring you earlier,' she said, 'we've had to have a bit of a tidy up to get some rooms ready for us to sleep in …'

'Good,' he said shortly and she flinched. Then he tried a different tact, 'Come on babes, come back home, we could find you a flat or a bedsit nearby. There must be something you can afford.'

'On what I was earning, in Brighton?' she asked, not really wanting to go over this ground again. So much of her last weeks had been spent arguing with Marcus about her decision to make the move, she felt exhausted by it.

'You could've found something if you'd wanted to. Or you could've moved in with your dad.' His petulant voice sounded like a five-year-old who'd been told no and didn't like it.

'You know I can't live with him,' she said. At least, she couldn't live with Trish, the twenty-two-year-old bimbo he'd left Mum for.

'Or I could have moved in with you,' she said, squeezing her eyes shut tight the instant the words left her mouth.

'You know why you couldn't move in with me, Regan,' Marcus said, though actually she had no idea. His endless list of reasons had been vague and inconsistent.

'Yes, I know why, Marcus. Because you are afraid of commitment,' she said before she could stop herself.

'*I'm* the one afraid of commitment? That's rich coming from *you*. We've been together six months now and you're the one who won't show me you love me.'

'Your idea of it and mine are quite different then, Marcus.'

Maybe she was old-fashioned, wanting some sort of assurance before she gave him the kind of *commitment* he wanted. Maybe at the end of the day that's what it all boiled down to: Marcus was putting his parts on because she wouldn't sleep with him.

Marcus's voice turned ice cold; despite the blazing sun Regan felt shivers run down her spine. 'Perhaps, since you're not willing to show me you love me, and you've decided that moving halfway across the country is the best thing, we should just call it a day.'

As much as she'd been dreading this, it wasn't exactly a surprise. The horror she'd been expecting didn't materialise; instead, a feeling of relief washed over her. An end to the continual arguments, the pressure to sleep with him — maybe this move *was* the best thing that could have happened to her.

'You're right, Marcus. Maybe that's exactly what we should do,' she said as she hung up on him.

She tucked her phone into her bag as the grassy verges gave way to manicured lawns. A higgledy collection of homes lined the one and only street in this tiny fenland village. Regan could see the banks of a river, built up high, higher than the roofs of the bungalows in front of it. She wondered briefly if it was the same one she'd seen glinting in the distance. As she headed towards the shop, which was clustered together with a pub and another more modern building at the end of the row, she wondered if anyone actually lived here. The emptiness of the village was eerie.

In the middle of a hot summer's Saturday, Brighton would have been bustling. Families would be fighting with the sun seekers for space on the beaches, town would be alive with shoppers all looking for the perfect outfit for the clubs later, or the best bottle of wine to drink al fresco with family and friends. The cafes and coffee shops would be filled with the young and the hip, those who wanted to see and to be seen. The contrast with Old Scytheton was spooky. With the exception of the idiot on the bike, she'd seen no other signs of life since she'd left home.

Regan soon found herself outside the small village shop. By God, if there was ever a local shop for local people this was it. It sat side by side with a pub (The Hunter's Rest), and the modern building, which according to the words etched into the stone above the door was *Old Scytheton Village Hall 2006*. A bell rang as she entered the store; the lad behind the counter looked up from his magazine. Regan watched, amused, as he suddenly realised he didn't know this stranger who stood in the doorway; he shoved the mag below the counter, smoothing his hair down casually.

'Can I help you love?' he asked, his fen accent much stronger than her mum's, his choice of words suggesting time usually spent with those much older.

'Yep, I'm just looking for some bleach and milk. Oh, I see them,' she said, grabbing some bleach from the shelf and four pints of milk from the fridge where they nestled beside the beers. She glanced round the shop; it seemed to stock everything one could possibly run out of in a week. At the back was a small post office counter, just a window with a plethora of official-looking forms behind it. As the boy rang up her purchases, she spotted a community message board; handing over her money, she asked if he knew if any of them were jobs — anything to relieve the tedium of endless days in this back of beyond hole she'd ended up in. The prospectus from the local college had several beauty courses she was interested in, but she couldn't even enrol for another month and the courses didn't start until September. Besides, taking her driving test and owning a car were very high on her priority list and the meagre amount she had in her bank account was not going to stretch very far.

'I doubt it, but if you're looking for something local, Tina's just walked out so Nick'll be looking for someone next door.' He jerked his head in the direction of the pub.

'Thanks,' said Regan, collecting her goods. Now was as good a time as any to enquire about it, she supposed. Glancing down at her now somewhat scruffy and dusty looking clothes, she shrugged. It was doubtful a Gucci suit would be required for getting a job in this lifeless village anyway.

Taking a deep breath, she pushed against the heavy oak door of The Hunter's Rest. It creaked reluctantly open; the two men sitting at the bar looked up at the noise and then carried on with their pints, not at all interested in Regan's appearance. The man behind the bar, however, smiled at her and stepped forward.

'Can I help you, miss?' he asked in the broad fenland accent she realised she would get used to very quickly. She liked the look of him at once. Receding brown hair, smart moustache; he was probably approaching middle age, and warmth spilled from his hazel eyes as he smiled. In a way, she realised, he reminded her of her father. At least, how he should look if only he would act his age.

'Hi, yes, I heard that there was a job going here? I'd like to apply for it?'

'Er, sure, come in. I'm Nick, the landlord. Have you tended bar before?' He asked, straight to the point. Regan wondered if the stint she did waitressing at her cousin's wedding last year counted. She decided probably not.

'No,' she said, 'but I'm a fast learner.' She smiled her brightest smile.

It seemed to work — Nick asked her some basic questions then gave her a form to fill in. He glanced at it and said, 'Okay, well can you start tomorrow? At about half four?'

'Sure,' Regan replied, wondering if she'd heard right. Well that was easier than she'd expected. 'I'll see you then, then …' With a smile she left, swinging the door shut behind her before he could change his mind.

It seemed that actually getting the job was the easy part, as Regan found out when she told her mum later.

'The Hunter's Rest! Regan, are you serious?' Katherine said when Regan told her.

'It's a job, Mum. I'm not sure what else is going to be available around here. It doesn't have to be a permanent choice, but it'll give us a little extra money each week.'

'Does he even know you're not eighteen yet? And how are you going to get there?'

Looking her mum in the eye, Regan used her responsible face, the one her mum relied on when times were tough. 'It'll be fine mum, I promise. He didn't ask my age, I didn't tell him, my birthday is only a couple of months away anyway. And I can walk there for now, it's not far and it's hardly the middle of the city. I don't think there's going to be danger lurking around every corner, do you?'

Katherine sighed, 'I don't know Regan, what about …' a loud rapping on the open back door stopped her mid-sentence.

'Hallo? Anyone home?'

Katherine looked at Regan and raised her eyebrows. Regan shrugged; she watched as her mum re-arranged her features into a wide smile. It didn't fool Regan, though; she could still see the exhaustion underneath.

'Don't get up, I'm making my way through,' the voice called, getting nearer and nearer. Regan looked around for something heavy in case she needed to bash someone. True, whoever was coming down their hallway didn't sound like a threat, but what kind of person makes their own way into your house? She soon found out. An explosion of vibrant colour burst into the lounge in the shape of a tiny blonde woman in a bright orange maxi dress, holding a fuchsia pink box that was emitting delicious smells.

Regan looked at her mum, waiting for the polite but quick *welcome and get rid of.* Instead, she saw the fake smile her mum had plastered onto her face turn into a genuine grin.

'Cyndi Palmer, as I live and breathe!' Katherine scooted across the box-strewn room and threw her arms around the visitor. 'I can't believe it's you!'

'I know, I couldn't wait any longer to see if it was my Katherine come home. I hoped it was, but I wasn't sure.' Cyndi grinned at Regan, 'And who is this gorgeous girl?' she said to Katherine.

Regan couldn't stop herself from grinning at the effervescent visitor, 'I'm Regan. I take it you know my mum?'

'From way back; we were the best of friends,' she scowled a little, 'until she disappeared to the bright lights of Brighton, never to be heard from again.'

'Until now,' Katherine said. 'It's a long story that definitely needs to be told over a glass of wine Cyndi, but could you wait until we're a bit more settled?'

'Of course I can Katherine. I can't tell you how pleased I am to have you back! My daughter Toni's about your age Regan, I'll tell her to call round and she can show you the sights, though they're probably a bit tame for you if you're used to Brighton.' She handed the box she was holding to Katherine.

Regan grabbed it. 'Mmm, smells delicious,' she said, taking it into the kitchen to the fridge. She made a pot of tea and took it through to them, then tackled the out-of-date packets in the larder. Twenty minutes later, she was dumping a full bin bag beside the overflowing wheelie bin when Katherine and Cyndi came out.

'Anyway I won't keep you a second longer,' her mum's friend said, enveloping them both in a jasmine-scented hug, 'I only popped round to say hi and drop off the bolognaise I made. It was great to meet you, Regan. See you soon Kat.' Then, in a whirl of brightness, she was gone.

Regan looked across at her mum. ''She seems nice Mum!'

Katherine chuckled, 'She is — the best. I can't believe she hasn't changed a bit in, wow, nearly twenty years.'

'Well you'll have loads to catch up on then,' said Regan, turning away from her mum. Calling Ashleigh in, she hoped the longing she felt for the only home she'd known wasn't showing on her face.

Four
1645

'Please let it be quick,' Lora prayed as she closed her eyes to the man in front of her, and her ears to the creature behind her. Her legs were numb from the icy water; the rest of her was numb from fear.

She'd never really wondered what the end would be like. Death surrounded her often; disease took the poor, excesses and greed took the rich. Men were killed by wars. Women died in childbirth. And children just died. Yet still, she had never thought of her own mortality. If she had, she wouldn't have imagined the end being like this.

'Get up!' The voice was firm, but not frightening. Almost without thought, Lora complied.

'Run child, I'll deal with this creature.' Though Lora wanted to obey, to welcome this reprieve that had been granted by death itself and run into the town, away from these fenland fogs and the evil they hid, her legs refused to comply.

She watched in silence as the man's attention shifted; no longer worried if Lora was there or not, his whole being focused on the rasping in the mist. She watched as he pulled aside his short cloak and unsheathed another knife. He slid forward into the mist, his movements covert and soundless. The unyielding hold the bog had on Lora did not seem to affect him the same way. Her eyes strained to keep him in view, his dark shape just visible in the haze though he was barely a few feet in front of her.

Suddenly his arm swung out, a knife silhouetted against the grey. She watched it swing forward again, slicing through the mist. A thud then an unearthly scream pierced the air. Icy fear wrapped its fingers around her heart and she knew any chance of escape had passed. The only hope she had now was this stranger. This hunter.

Movement focussed her as the creature retaliated, its arms shooting forward. Lora imagined the claws that were its arsenal. It was like nothing she had ever seen before; surely such a creature could only have been made in hell? Tall and thin with long limbs that ended in sharp talons, it moved with rapid, almost dancelike movements.

It swayed to and fro before striking; the hunter fought back, a knife in each hand, every movement flawless. Even in the grip of fear, Lora found herself mesmerised by the grace with which the man moved, each sweep of his limbs almost an art form in itself.

With practised ease, he swung around; his foot lifted high and met the creature's torso, pushing it off balance. The blade in his left hand sliced at the creature's skull; moments later, he used all his strength to swing the second blade up into its gut.

The return attack had none of the hunter's precision, but the creature did move smoothly, with great speed and obvious strength. Growling, its head darted forward, hungry for the hunter's flesh. Claws ripped at clothes. They fought equally until the hunter misplaced his move, his arm jolted by the creature's own peculiar limb, and his knife shot into the air to be swallowed at once by the greedy mist.

Unbalanced, the hunter turned and tried to bring his remaining knife around to strike the creature's head, but it outmanoeuvred him. Its claws slashed, and even through the fog Lora saw five angry lines of blood spurt instantly across his face.

The hunter lost his sight as blood seeped into his eyes. She watched with increasing horror as he wiped at them with his empty hand, jabbing blindly ahead with the knife he still held. Her mind raced — if the creature won would she be able to outrun it? Would she find her way in safety through the hungry fen, or would she be better off feeding the marsh herself? Choosing to die seemed the better option. More controlled, somehow.

In that moment of surrender, the fear let go its hold on her legs and she started to edge forward step by step, her feet finding their way towards the marsh with more silence than she thought was possible. Where the gloopy mud was swallowed by the murky swamp water, she resolutely stepped forward and sank slowly down.

Five
2013

'Another one in there love, when you're ready.' The hand that pushed forward the empty pint glass was weathered and scarred by years of work on the land. Regan filled the glass with the dark ale she already knew Jim preferred.

'Ta love,' he said in his thick Norfolk accent, and Regan relaxed a miniscule more. Thirty minutes into her new job, and she already felt as though she was getting the hang of it.

'I hope you're gonna keep hold of this one Nick,' Jim added before slurping at his pint.

Nick winked at Regan, 'Don't worry Jim, Regan here is twice as good as Tina and she's only been at it half an hour. Besides, if the Barney lads keep drinking as quickly as they are so they can come and chat her up, I'll have doubled my profit by the end of the evening!' Regan smiled a polite smile and, with relief, moved down the bar to the next waiting customer. Apart from the unwanted attention from the group of young lads in the corner, Regan was surprised at how naturally she seemed to have taken to bartending. It had taken all of two minutes for Nick to establish that he had known her mum when they were kids, and she'd been welcomed in as if she'd lived there all her life.

She groaned as a youngster from the group of seven in the corner made his way up to the bar. She wasn't quite sure which ones were the Barneys, they surely couldn't all be, but three of them had already tried asking her out. She'd knocked them all back, but by the looks of the skinny lad in front of her they were still intent on trying.

'Did it hurt when you fell from heaven?' he blurted out before Regan could speak. Resisting the urge to roll her eyes, she decided ignoring his attempts to chat her up would be the best way to spare both their blushes.

'What'll it be, another Bud?' she asked, reaching into the fridge where the bottles were kept.

'Ta,' he said, taking it quietly back to his group. Thankful that he hadn't tried harder, Regan used the now-empty bar as an excuse to grab a cloth and start wiping down the tables.

It was only then that she noticed the man sitting by himself in the corner. She did a double take, and then averted her eyes fast — he was staring straight at her. A blush started to creep up her neck and she was thankful the pub was so dim, because — *hot damn* — he was gorgeous. His short, dark hair was dishevelled and Regan would bet a week's wages it looked that way naturally and wasn't the result of half an hour in front of the mirror.

The darkness of his hair was rivalled only by the darkness of his eyes, two deep black pools framed by impossibly long lashes. She leaned forward to clean the other side of the table and glanced up at him from under her fringe. His worn leather jacket and faded T-shirt did little to hide his broad chest and developed muscles. She didn't think she'd seen anyone so beautiful in her whole life.

Noticing the empty glass on his table, she headed towards him, pausing to wipe half-heartedly at a couple of tables on her way. *Act natural,* she told herself as her heartbeat quickened.

'Have you finished with this?' she asked, tipping her head a little so she was peering up at him, an angle she knew made her lashes look longer and her blue eyes wider.

'Yes, thanks,' he said in an American accent. *Intriguing*, thought Regan as the timbre of his voice sent shivers down her spine. She pinched herself to check she wasn't dreaming and then waited on tenterhooks; was he going to be the only person in the pub who didn't want to know her entire history? His eyes finally seemed to meet hers again, after sweeping across the room and taking in every detail in one fell swoop. Eyes so dark they were almost black.

'Hi, I'm Regan,' she said, when the silence became somewhat awkward, 'I've just moved here. I take it you're not local either?'

'No,' he said.

Regan turned up the wattage on her smile and flicked her blonde hair over her shoulder. *Cliché*, she thought, but she'd seen it work in the bars of Brighton a hundred times. 'So can you recommend anywhere for a good night out?' she asked, starting to feel a bit embarrassed.

He smiled at her and she took a breath to try, one last time, to engage him in conversation. He interrupted before she could start.

'You're very beautiful Regan, I'm sure you're aware of that, if not only because of the number of times you've been asked out tonight. I'm not the person you should be flirting with though. If you want to see the sights around here, I'm sure any one of them,' he tipped his head towards the Barneys, 'would be glad to show you. Maybe you should get back to work before Nick starts questioning the age of his staff.' A flush of heat burned through her and she knew her face would be glowing like a beacon. Turning, she walked away as humiliation swept through her body, followed closely by a healthy dose of anger. Who was he to talk to her like that? How the hell did he know she was underage? And what business was it of his anyway? She threw the glasses she held into the sink so hard she was surprised they didn't shatter on contact.

Pulse racing, she prayed no-one else had noticed the exchange. Taking deep breaths to try and calm down, Regan checked that Nick wasn't watching her; she couldn't afford to lose this job less than an hour after she'd started it. *Focus Regan*, she told herself. Smiling brightly at the two girls waiting at the bar, she asked, 'Can I help?'

'Vodka and orange, and a Bacardi Breezer please Regan,' said a bubbly blonde girl. At her name Regan looked up from the shot of vodka she was pouring. 'You must be Toni,' she said as she took in the girl's grinning expression and bleached blonde hair, 'you look just like your mum!'

'I know,' Toni rolled her eyes, 'when we're out together she makes me call her Cyndi and tell everyone that she's my sister!' Regan laughed; she'd only met Cyndi for a few minutes, but she could quite believe it.

'I just wanted to say hi — I'll call you sometime and we can meet up perhaps?' Toni said, then raised her voice slightly and looked over at Nick, 'I won't get you into trouble on your first day at work, I know what a slave driver your boss is!' Nick looked over and Toni stuck out her tongue at him. 'Don't worry, he's going out with my mum so I can get away with it,' she muttered under her breath to an amused Regan.

'Don't be so sure young lady,' Nick called over, his wide smile showing he was joking, 'I'll ban you if you keep my staff from working!'

'Yeah right!' Toni called back, 'Nice to meet you Regan — oh, and this is Ella.' Regan smiled at the dark-haired girl standing quietly beside Toni. The smile wasn't returned, and Regan felt embarrassed again; Toni didn't seem to notice anything, though, as she pulled Ella away to the beer garden. Regan wished Toni could have stayed talking to her, especially when she found herself looking unwittingly back over towards the awful American. Her heart pounded as she noticed him watching her.

Turning back to the bar she served yet another one of the Barneys. This time she used all the humiliation she felt at the Yank's earlier brush off to turn up the flirting. She'd show him. She leaned over the bar, talked in such a sugary way that it actually made her feel sick, and flicked her hair about as if she was in a shampoo advertisement. Joe Barney, the youngest of the group of lads — who were apparently all brothers — grinned up at her. The poor lad looked as if all his Christmases had come at once. She almost felt guilty, but anger at the stuck-up Yank suppressed the guilt and she just tried a little bit harder.

As Regan chatted, laughed, and flirted with Joe, she was barely aware of him actually being there. Every inch of her was trying to show that American exactly what he was missing. As careful as she was to avoid looking in his direction, she was aware of every move he made. And, when he stood up and quietly left at quarter to eleven, she felt physically drained. Being an animated Barbie doll half the evening was more exhausting than it looked; she wasn't sure how all those It girls and celebrities did it. Letting Joe down was easier than anticipated — the look on his face told her he wasn't entirely sure he could handle her after all. A quick mention of her pro-wrestler boyfriend did the trick.

She realised she'd spent the entire evening trying not to notice the Yank. Her new job, ex-boyfriend and new life had barely entered her consciousness.

Six

Regan was thankful that while the rest of the country had embraced the twenty-four-hour drinking laws, The Hunter's Rest still stopped serving at eleven. By ten minutes past, the pub was empty, and by quarter past Nick had sent Regan on her way.

She grabbed her bag, said goodbye, stepped out of the pub and stopped short. While she'd been working the bright summer's day had disappeared, and instead of the clear, starlit night Regan was expecting, Little Scytheton was blanketed in thick fog. Her confidence faltered; for once, she didn't know what to do. Ring a cab? As she leaned against the pub wall, the fog started to curl around her, its dampness finding its way quickly into the thin denim jacket she wore. She rang directory enquiries for the number of a local taxi firm. Bob's Cabs seemed to be the only one nearby, so she gave them a ring.

'Oh no love, Bob's out I'm afraid,' said Sal, who'd answered the phone. 'He can get to you in about an hour and that's the best I can do.' Regan debated for about half a second before she said no. In an hour she could be home. Next, she rang her mum; Ashleigh picked up.

'Ashleigh, you should be asleep! Where's Mum?'

'Aunty Vi had a bit of trouble, Mum's bathing her so I answered the phone. It woke me up,' Ashleigh accused.

'Okay, sorry Ash — will you just tell Mum that I'll be home in about an hour? I'm just leaving off.'

Using the torch function on her phone, Regan made her way cautiously back through the one road of Little Scytheton. She shivered. How could such a hot day turn into this kind of night? Pulling her jacket tighter, she gripped her bag and peered into the fog. Her straining eyes were giving her a headache and she was trying not to acknowledge her jangling nerves. It wasn't the walk home under a dark sky decorated with stars and a beautiful glowing moon that she'd imagined.

When she finally left the pavements of the village, she could feel her heart beating faster. She placed one foot in front of the other tentatively, each step deliberate and careful. The fog was getting thicker. Not being able to see made the way seem longer; she had no idea where she was. Trying to distract herself from the gnawing fear that was creeping into her stomach, she started to sing to herself silently, humming a tune in her head where only she could hear it.

A noise behind her made her heart jump into her throat; she spun round, her thin torch beam reflecting weakly back at her as it bounced off the wall of fog. She listened, straining to hear above the blood rushing in her ears. Nothing, not even the sounds of nature that Regan expected to hear at night. Finally, as she shivered once more against the damp that pervaded her clothes, she started off again; she was barely five footsteps ahead of where she'd stopped when she heard the sound again. It was hard to identify, just a quiet rasping noise. Regan wasn't sure she'd heard any animal make that sound before.

Another sound, like a muffled footstep; Regan reached in her bag for her keys, jamming the heavy front door key between her fingers as a makeshift knuckle duster.

'Who's there?' She tried to keep the fright she was feeling out of her voice. She vaguely remembered from her self-defence classes that it was best to sound confident if possible. Nobody answered, although as she listened the hoarse, heavy breathing sound seemed to get louder. Closer.

'Is that you?' she called, 'One of the Barneys from the pub?' She suddenly felt certain it would be. She'd turned them all down one by one; it would be their idea of a laugh to frighten the snooty, townie girl who thought she was better than they were.

'I'll be back in the pub tomorrow evening,' she fervently hoped this was true, 'maybe we can talk about things then. It's just, I, er, have a boyfriend …' she trailed off. There was no reply; she couldn't hear anything above her own voice.

She spun around as she heard, again, a noise like breathing underwater. Finally, in the fog, she could see the vague outline of someone tall and thin. She started talking again as she pulled her arm up, ready to punch with her hidden weapon; it wasn't a lot, but it was all she had. As she drew her arm back, she heard an engine echoing over the fog-filled fields. The shape that was looming stopped, then, in an inhumanely quick move, turned and ran. The headlight of a bike appeared and swept through the fog. As Regan watched, it picked up the shape disappearing in the gloom and took off after it.

Regan didn't have a clue what had just happened, but she knew she needed to get the hell home. Tomorrow she would hand in her notice; until she could drive there was no way she was going about in these strange, terrifying fens alone. She pointed the weak beam of her torch in the direction she hoped was home. It wavered a little as her hand shook. She started walking. With each step she felt calmer, and she noticed as she looked around that the fog was starting to lift. Patches of it lingered, thick and blinding, but in between was clear black night, stars visible in the heavens.

Her confidence grew and the fear faded. She hadn't too far to go when she heard the roar of a motorbike engine getting closer again. She tensed, ready to run, to take flight — the house was so near now. The bike drew up beside her and a familiar American accent sounded.

'Are you all right?'

'Fine, thank you,' she said. She didn't allow her surprise at the identity of the mystery biker to show in her face or voice, and she certainly wasn't going to thank him for what he probably thought of as his *heroics*. For some reason he got her back up, and her pride marched into place. 'I was doing fine. I am perfectly capable of handling a drunken teenager!'

'It isn't safe to be walking along these roads on your own at night,' the American said, 'things are not always as they appear to be.'

Regan tensed as anger lashed through her body — who the hell was he to tell her what to do?

'Look … Yank …'

'Nate,' he muttered.

'Look Nate, where I go and when I go there is my business and nothing to do with you. You are not responsible for me in any way.' Regan ran out of steam. 'I'm going home now', she turned and walked with intent in the direction of the house. The night was as clear as day now, each star twinkling like a jewel in the sky, the moon high and bright. The anger had faded and had cleared the fear out of her system. In fact, it was hard to remember why she'd been so afraid. Had the fog really been that thick? Regan didn't think it could have — it had been a long couple of days, she was exhausted and it was all new to her. She was used to the bright lights of Brighton, a town that seemed to be lively 24/7. She'd let tiredness frazzle her brain and she wouldn't let it happen again.

'What are you doing?' She stopped abruptly, turning to confront Nate who was pushing his bike behind her.

'Just seeing you safely home,' he said, his sentence short and sweet as usual. Taking a deep breath, ready to argue, Regan paused, then changed her mind. She didn't have the energy. Besides, having an escort the rest of the way wouldn't be the worst thing she could imagine, though she wouldn't have admitted that to anyone. Shrugging, she turned and carried on down the road. As soon as she'd made in through her front door, she heard the bike roar off. Heart pounding, she went to bed.

* * *

To say she hadn't slept well was the understatement of the century. Regan woke the next morning to the sound of her mum telling Ashleigh that she *did* have to start her new school today, whether she liked it or not. An early morning was the last thing she needed, but she ignored the urge to crawl back under her covers and instead stormed down the stairs like a bitch with PMT.

'Do you have to make such a racket?' she stormed at her sister. 'Some of us were working until late last night, is it too much to ask that I'm allowed to have a little bit of sleep this morning?'

'Regan, don't speak to your little sister like that!' said her mum, 'she's nervous enough about starting a new school as it is!'

'So why can't I wait until after the summer holidays? They're only a few weeks away.' Ashleigh said, picking up the thread of the argument that had woken Regan up.

'Because it's illegal and they'll send mum to jail or something,' Regan said, then, seeing the nerves on her sister's face, lightened her tone a bit. 'Besides kiddo, you're going to be fab! There's not a person on this planet who doesn't want to be your friend as soon as they meet you!' It was the truth. Ashleigh was special; she had a glow of goodness about her that Regan had never possessed. There was no jealousy though. It was impossible to keep up negative feelings around Ashleigh; her kindness spread to those she was near like a beacon, inviting only feelings of love towards her.

'I know,' said Ashleigh as she sat down and spooned the Weetabix in front of her into her mouth, 'I just love it here and there's still so much to see. Oh well, after school I guess,' she decided, finishing up her breakfast.

'So, Regan, are you sure you're going to be okay if I nip to the day care place after dropping Ashleigh off?'

'Mum it's fine, honest. I mean Aunty Vi's probably just going to sleep or something isn't she?'

Katherine looked at her daughter and raised an eyebrow. 'Well, possibly, but she may wake up and need something. I tell you what, I'll go another time.'

Feeling guilty, Regan shook her head, 'No Mum, you go — I'll be fine, honest. It'll do you and Aunt Vi good if there's a place at day care.'

As soon as her mum and sister had left and Regan was Aunty Vi-sitting, her bad mood returned. And ninety percent of her anger was aimed at Nate. *Who did that arrogant American think he was*, she thought, banging drawers and cupboards shut as she tidied away in the kitchen. What gave him the right to act like her saviour, as if she couldn't handle things herself?

She was still fuming about him as she gathered up the clothes that she had worn last night ready to wash. Frowning, she wrinkled her nose as an unpleasant odour wafted off of the clothes. *Great,* she thought, *that had better wash out*. Stomping down the hallway, she caught herself before she strode past the old lady's bedroom. She was meant to be looking after her aunt, so she supposed she'd better stick her head in on her before she got caught up doing the laundry.

Remember to be civil, she thought as she poked her head round the door. 'Hi, Aunty Vi, do you need a cup of tea or anything?' she asked.

'Oh Katherine where have you been, I've been alone for hours!'

'It's me Aunty Vi, Regan. Mum's taken Ashleigh to school, she'll be back soon.' Regan tried really hard to resist the urge to roll her eyes. It wasn't Aunty Vi's fault she was so confused, but Regan found her very trying. Katherine had been a nurse for years and possessed the patience of a saint, a gift that had skipped Regan completely and bestowed itself generously on Ashleigh. Care of the elderly most definitely hadn't made it onto Regan's shortlist of possible careers.

'Well if you're okay, Aunty Vi, I'm just going to do some laundry,' Regan said as she retreated into the hallway.

'That's it,' the old lady's weak voice bleated, 'just leave me alone. I haven't seen anyone in days and now you're leaving me again.'

Regan took a deep breath. Leaning her back against the wall, she counted to three. She plastered a huge smile on her face and, arms full of dirty clothes, entered the bedroom.

'Ah Katherine, I knew you wouldn't leave me again.' Her voice trembled and Regan watched as the old lady clutched at the bed covers. Slipping her hand inside her aunt's, she noticed with shock the contrast between the old lady's gnarled fingers and her own long tanned digits, decorated with perfect manicured nails. The skin was soft and fragile under Regan's reassuring touch; it felt like tissue paper that might easily tear, and Regan was saddened by the realisation of her aunt's frailty. She decided not to correct her assumption.

'Yes, I'm here. Why don't you try and have a sleep Aunty Vi,' Regan asked, leaning forward to tuck in the bed covers. As she moved, the washing shifted in her lap, and the odious smell she'd noticed earlier drifted up and invaded her nostrils. *Please go to sleep, I really need to get the laundry done*, she thought, smoothing out the pillow as best she could.

Regan paused as Aunt Vi started to shrink back into the bed covers. Her frail voice was barely above a whisper and it took Regan a second to realise she was even speaking.

'No, get them away from me. They're gone, they're meant to be gone.' Aunt Vi scrabbled at the bedclothes with her hands and seemed to disappear even further into the bed.

Leaning forward, Regan tried to calm her aunt down. 'Nothing's here, just you and me, Aunty Vi,' she said soothingly, trying to stroke the old lady's hair.

The voice was barely audible as it said again, 'Please, get away from me. I can smell them here, they've come and no one is here to fight them.' Regan watched helplessly as a tear trickled down her aunt's chalky white cheek. She leaned forward again, hoping that a soft voice would help calm her. It had the opposite affect and Aunt Vi grew more agitated.

'Familiar. Familiar. I know what you are, I've read about you. Taking lives, that smell was always on her clothes. Then you took her.'

'Ssh, Aunty Vi, it's just me, Regan — Mum will be back soon.'

'Mum is back now,' came a voice from the doorway. 'What have you been doing to get Aunty Vi so upset?' Katherine came into the room and glared at Regan, pulling her daughter off the bed then sitting and talking calmly to her aunt. Realising she was only in the way, Regan took the pile of clothes to the washing machine, her mood not improved one iota.

Seven
1645

Crouching down, Lora ripped off her glove and felt around in the oozing mud with her fingers.

Of course, she thought as she grappled for the lost knife, *there was always a third option*. She could always fight. Her fingers closed around the weapon she was searching for, feeling the metal, solid and real. It was a glimmer of hope. Taking a breath, she rose, her slender figure hidden by the mist that shrouded her. Hope sparked again, then faded as the hunter, a mere arm's length away, fell.

Death seemed inevitable, but at least she could die fighting. It was surely nobler than running away, and more honest than taking her own life. Turning towards *it*, she used all her weight to slash forward, not caring what she hit — only that when she died, she would die fighting.

Stabbing blindly in the fog, she didn't know whether to pray that she hit or missed. Its phlegmy breath echoed in the otherwise silent night and Lora couldn't tell which direction it was coming from. Controlling her own breathing, she listened. There was a movement on her left and she swung the knife in a silent arc. With a swishing sound, the metal cut through the air. With a thud and squelch the sharpened edge connected with something. It. An inhuman wail pierced the air and Lora stabbed forward time after time with a strength she hadn't known she possessed, connecting with the monster again and again.

She felt its blood seep through her gloves, and the air filled with a strange metallic odour. Then its sharp claws pierced her skin. She screamed in pain but didn't falter, prayers spilling from her lips as she kept up her battle.

Her dress was soon in tatters as its claws shredded the material, each mark burning her skin as if it had been branded by the devil himself. Still she fought on. Still she refused to give up. Death was going to have to drag her to hell screaming and shouting. Each time she slashed, stabbed and swung the knife, the creature's keen filled the air. It took Lora's mind away from her own pain.

Soon Lora realised she was bearing far more damage than it was. Her arms felt like lead; her body burned, her brow fevered despite the clammy freezing fog that surrounded her. Her eyes were straining so hard to see that they ached in a way she hadn't known was possible. Just as she was beginning to fade, beginning to feel the fight drain from her, a deep voice spoke from beside her.

'We can do this. Keep fighting and we will win,' it said. Lora wasn't sure if it was the hunter or an angel, but she did as she was told. She shook the ache from her arms, ignored the burning, and started fighting again. Maybe the night didn't have to end in death.

Eight
2013

Thankfully Regan's mood had improved by that evening, when they were once again invaded by the Palmers. Cyndi and Toni had bustled into the house, a riot of colour and noise, bearing bags full of cartons from the local Chinese takeaway. As the delicious smell of chow mein, fried rice, barbecued ribs and other delights wafted enticingly around the full kitchen, Regan tried not to notice the tall, blond guy lurking in the doorway.

'Oh come in and sit down, Sam,' said Cyndi, 'Kathy doesn't mind do you Kath?' Regan's mum — who had never been called Kath or Kathy as far as Regan was aware — shook her head and gestured for him to come in.

'Grab a plate. Come on, the more the merrier.' He did as he was told and in a long, loping stride made his way across the kitchen to pile food onto a plate.

'Regan, just pull the door shut, I'm sure we won't disturb Vi but it's better safe than sorry.' Katherine smiled at her eldest daughter and Regan got up and pulled the kitchen door closed. She turned to sit back down and noticed that Sam had nicked her place on the small settee.

'Come on gorgeous, don't be shy, plenty of room here,' he grinned at her and patted his knee.

Regan smiled back as Toni cuffed her brother. 'Don't worry I'm fine here,' she said, sitting cross-legged on the floor, 'I know what it's like when you get old, more difficult getting up from the ground …'

Sam's jaw dropped before he grinned again. 'Cheeky!'

Toni shook her head and sighed. 'God Sam, can't I have one friend that you don't try and flirt with?'

Her brother shrugged, 'Dunno Toni, it's your fault for being pals with gorgeous birds!'

'SAM!' exclaimed Cyndi, Katherine and Toni all at once. Regan just sniggered; Sam, she guessed, was going to be as much fun as his sister.

The takeaway was a treat, and as she spooned down forkfuls of egg fried rice, she realised that she was actually starving. Aunty Vi's old house had been neglected for years; there was dust on top of the dust, and as Katherine already had enough on her plate Regan was trying to get as much of it cleaned as possible on her own. It meant her every spare second had been taken up by cleaning. Between the three of them, they had just about got the main living rooms habitable, so today Regan had scrubbed the entire hallway. Now she just had to get round to sorting out her attic room. It was a veritable treasure trove of stuff (most of it, she was sure, was going to be good enough only for the bin).

'Ok, ok, is everybody listening? I have an announcement to make?' Katherine tapped the side of her wine glass with a biro, smiling at all of them. 'Firstly, thank you Cyndi for the dinner, it's just what the doctor ordered! It is so nice being home —

nothing has changed, it's like I walked away from here yesterday. Now, I know not all members of the family feel quite as enthusiastic about this move to "The Back of Beyond" as —'

'Aw Mum, that's not fair, I've not complained,' interrupted Regan.

'I know you've not honey, but I know you too well. You've been amazing, and look, you're already making friends and have a job, I'm sure the charms of the fens will grow on you in time.'

'I like it, it's really cool here,' said Ashleigh from where she was squashed beside Toni on the couch.

'It is pretty cool here,' said Sam, 'I know it must seem pretty tame after the bright lights of Brighton, but honestly I don't know what a city has got to offer that we can't give you here.' He winked at Regan, 'I mean, if it's attractive guys you want, look no further!'

Regan blushed. A picture of Nate flashed into her head, swiftly followed by one of Sam, cheeky grin and all. It was true, the percentage of cute blokes did seem to be in her favour …

'I must be looking in the wrong places then …' she said, keeping as straight a face as possible. Sam looked at her in mock aghast.

'I don't know Toni, maybe you'll have to take me out a bit, show me some of the talent …' she added and Toni smirked, a loud snort of laughter escaping from her nose.

'Oh this is going to be fun. I'm really going to like you being here, Regan. A lot!'

Katherine tapped the biro on the side of her glass again. 'I'm sorry everyone but I haven't finished.'

'Sorry Mum,' mouthed Regan.

'As I was saying,' Katherine glared at her daughter, the crinkling of her crow's feet a tell-tale sign that she was joking, 'I have some news. Today when I took Aunty Vi to the day care centre, I ended up getting myself a job.'

'A job! Where? What, at the centre? Who'll look after me?' Ashleigh asked one question barely before another had been formed.

'Whoa, steady up Ashleigh.' Katherine put down her glass and turned to both her daughters to explain. It was perfect for her — truly she was overqualified, but as she would work at the day care centre when Aunty Vi was there it sorted out several problems at once. Money had been the main cause of worry for Katherine, Regan knew, and she was pleased that it was seemingly solved so easily. If it meant a little extra baby-sitting, who cared? Most of her shifts were evening ones, and it wasn't as though she had a full social life at the moment. A look at the siblings sharing their dinner though made her hope that this would change soon. Maybe this move wasn't going to be the worst thing that could happen to her. And looking at Toni and Sam, it did appear as though both of them would be right at home anywhere.

'That's fantastic Mum, just the bit of good news that you needed.'

'It certainly is Regan,' Katherine sipped from her glass. 'And the daycentre is going to be so perfect for Aunt Vi. It is a super place; they have nostalgia days and all sorts, better than her sitting around here every day waiting until her time is up.'

It was nearly midnight when Cyndi, Toni and Sam left. Sam had lifted Ashleigh up to bed when she'd fallen asleep on the sofa. Then the rest of them had sat around chatting. Cyndi and Katherine had reminisced about their childhoods in this very village, and Regan was surprised at the sudden attachment she felt to the place. It was no longer some place in her mum's past — it was very much a place in their present. It was real. She found herself wanting to see the different places her mum spoke about, to put images to the descriptions.

And she found she quite liked chatting with Sam — she'd found out he was a postie, a fantastic pool player and had a wicked sense of humour. She liked the interest he had in her. Regan wasn't stupid enough to think the interest stemmed from anything other than the fact that she was an unknown quantity to him. A fresh face. A new challenge. It was obvious from both Toni's and Cyndi's remarks that Sam was one for the ladies — in fact, he'd had at least three texts from girls in the little while he'd been there. But there was something about his easy-going manner and jokey attitude that Regan liked, and when he casually suggested they go out for a drink sometime she was more than willing to say yes. After all, at least he spoke to her like an equal and not in the annoyingly patronising way the Yank had yesterday.

Nine

Polishing the bar for the hundredth time since the start of her shift, Regan could feel her traitorous eyes straying in Nate's direction. Again. She was exhausted from avoiding him and even more cross with him than she'd been a week ago, yet she couldn't stop glancing his way. And he knew it; he'd caught her peeking at least three times.

'God, I wish you'd go home,' she muttered under her breath as she rearranged the contents of the drinks' fridge, one place from which she couldn't involuntarily peek at him. Chatter hummed in the background in that fenland accent she was fast becoming used to. It was funny how at home she felt in the pub, as if she'd worked there for years.

'Two orange juices please, and I hope you're not talking to me!' piped up a familiar voice, and Regan turned to see Toni and Ella standing at the bar.

'As if,' she replied, 'No-one could accuse you of getting on their nerves.'

'I'm not too sure about that, Mum says she could cheerfully strangle me sometimes, especially first thing in the morning!' Toni said, handing Regan a five-pound note and Ella one of the drinks.

'Yeah well, you're so goddamn chirpy all the time — *nobody* needs that first thing in the morning.' Toni just grinned at her and she beamed back, pleased to see her new friend again. Not wanting Ella to feel left out, Regan offered her a smile. It wasn't returned. *Awkward.*

Toni didn't appear to notice. 'How'd your mum get on today? Any first day nerves?'

'Do you know, she had a fantastic time,' Regan said, wiping the bar down while she chatted, 'It's brilliant — not only is Aunty Vi getting out of the house for the first time in goodness knows how long, but Mum is able to work as well. She was really worried she'd be so stuck looking after Aunty Vi that she wouldn't be able to get out herself. That's one of the reasons why I moved up here to help.'

'Works out perfectly for you then,' said Ella, 'maybe you can go back to your old friends now.' She sipped her drink, her clear green eyes unsmiling.

'Oh she wouldn't do that Ella — would you Regan? — not when you're just starting to get to know everyone.'

'I have no plans to go back to Brighton just yet. Besides, it's nice getting to know you all.'

'Yeah, and I know someone who wants to get to know *you* better,' said Toni, 'he may be my brother, but just watch yourself with him; he does think he's god's gift sometimes. Doesn't he Ella?' The other girl flashed a sarcastic smile at Toni and shrugged in reply. Regan deduced that Ella had once been the target of Sam's affections — remembering where she was, she glanced at Nick, 'I suppose I'd better get back to work or I'll be the jobless one!'

'We're not going to be long, I want to get back in time for *The Only Way is Essex!*' Toni said. Regan raised her eyebrows — she liked Toni but honestly, sometimes she was a little chavvy. Toni waggled her fingers and they took their drinks to a table filled with villagers Regan only knew by sight. As she sat down, Ella turned and glared at Regan; she was sure she wasn't being paranoid and imaging the sneering looks Ella was sending her way, but frankly, she didn't really care. They weren't in primary school any longer; Toni was quite capable of having more than one friend.

Scooping up some dead glasses, Regan found herself glancing over towards Nate again. His jacket was abandoned on the chair next to him and his T-shirt was just too well fitted to be good for her blood pressure. He was talking to one of the old farm boys who spent as much time in the pub as at home. It hadn't escaped Regan's notice that Nate was much more comfortable in the company of the older generation than those his own age. The men who yapped your ear off if you let them often stopped and chatted to him, but the young ones seemed to leave him alone.

'A large glass of Merlot, please,' said a voice from the bar. Regan poured the wine and handed it over, 'That's £2.40 please.' Glancing up, she did a double take, 'Oh, wow, is that a Stella McCartney top?' she asked, eyeing the bright pink satin Matsu top with envy.

'It certainly is! You can't be from around here if you recognise a Stella McCartney piece!' the girl in front of her answered with raised eyebrows. Shaking her head, Regan looked the girl up and down. Toni was great, but maybe here was someone more similar to herself. That would please Ella, she was sure.

'Nope, just moved in — from Brighton,' she answered. 'I'm Regan. Do you live in the village?'

'Temporarily,' the girl said with a feline smile, 'don't think I could live here permanently, I'd go stir crazy! I've heard that spending more than £10.00 on an item of clothing is practically a criminal offence!'

Regan found herself smiling and selfishly hoped that temporary wasn't too temporary — maybe she'd found herself a shopping partner. 'So, where's the best place for a girl to go buy some bargains?' she asked, 'if they weren't into £10.00, nylon, wash at 30, can be tumble dried tops?'

'King's Lynn is the nearest, but for more choice Cambridge and Norwich are just over an hour by car. Of course London isn't too far by train,' she leaned in and whispered conspiratorially, 'it's public transport, but anything to avoid £10.00, nylon, wash at 30, tumble drier-proof tops, hey!'

'Absolutely! Anytime you need a shopping partner, well, you can find me in here!' Regan smiled and — with reluctance — moved up the bar to where Howie Barney was waiting, empty pint glass in hand.

'I'll take you up on that. By the way, I'm Maeve. Nice to meet you, Regan!' Turning effortlessly, she took her drink to a quiet table where a dazed-looking twenty-something sat, obviously not quite able to believe his luck. Talk about out of his league!

'Don't know what Smithy did to pull her,' said Howie, plonking himself on a bar stool and settling down to chat. 'Mind you, gives hope to the rest of us,' he winked at Regan. She glanced over at the stunning girl and her date and understood what Howie meant. Ignoring the wink, she realised he might be a good source of information.

'So where does Maeve live then?' she asked, leaning forward, widening her eyes and switching to flirt mode.

'Oh, not far from you love. In a big house in the middle of Potters field. Why a pretty girl would want to be living there on her own I don't know. Still, no doubt she'll be gone again soon; we've never had so many strangers around here!' It took Regan a second to realise that she was one of those strangers. Howie turned away suddenly and, following his gaze, Regan watched as Maeve and Smithy left the pub. Smithy was pretty easy on the eye, Regan decided; the manual work that was most common in Scytheton did leave the bodies of the younger generation pretty fit. Of course, they were soon spoiled by years of beer guzzling, as evidenced by the guts of most of the men in the pub.

Smithy turned and winked at his mates; cringing, Regan decided his toned body couldn't compensate for his goofy grin, bad haircut, and serious fashion faux pas. What Maeve was doing with him was beyond her. *Maybe she's just a nicer person than I am,* she thought, pretty sure she wouldn't be able to go on a date with someone so yokel and keep a straight face.

The summer's day was turning into a clear summer's night. Regan noticed, as the door swung open to let Maeve and Smithy out, that there was no sign of last week's fog. In fact, Regan was pretty sure she'd imagined it; each day since had been hot and humid, and each night bright and clear. The thought made her glance in Nate's direction again and she couldn't help but draw a comparison between the untalkative, irritating American and the villagers. She groaned as she caught his eye yet again. He might be gorgeous, he might look cool, but he was still annoying. So why was her heart beating just that bit faster than it had been a minute ago?

Ten
1645

Just as Lora thought that she was able to fight no more, the hunter raised his arm high and bought his blade down on the creature's head. Its skull cracked in two, the sound echoing across the fenlands like a pistol shot. The creature withered to the mud below, seeming to shrink to the size of a mere weasel before being swallowed by the unendingly hungry bog.

Relief and exhaustion washed over Lora and she sank to the ground, her body limp and trembling, unable to bear even her own weight a second longer. Immune now to the penetrating iciness of the fog and the murky wetness of the marsh, she lay, each breath a marvel, the absence of violent noise a gift to be treasured.

'Child? Child, are you all right? Have you been hurt?' The now-recognisable voice forced Lora's eyes open, and for the first time she got a look at the man alongside whom she had fought. He was dressed plainly — breeches and waistcoat, simple and unadorned — unlike the men Lora was used to seeing about the town. Indeed, unlike that decorative attire favoured by her intended, James. His eyes were darker than any she had encountered, and now that his hat was lost, she could see his long hair was tied back, his moustache trimmed in a simple manner.

'I am well, sir,' she answered with surprising calmness, 'I am alive, and this surely was not supposed to be, earlier this afternoon.' She opened her eyes and looked up at the hunter.

'The devil's-own creature is gone now — it will not return, but there are more like it. It is not safe to walk these paths alone. Indeed, why do you have no escort?'

'I must confess I gained some hours to myself this afternoon, and it had been such a lovely morning that I thought a walk through the countryside would be pleasant.' It sounded naive even to Lora's own ears, but the day had started beautiful — the kind of September day that makes you forget that autumn is on its way. 'I did not realise the devil himself would be taking a walk today too.'

'He takes many walks on these paths, I am afraid; he has bent these creatures and their mistresses to do his will.'

Lora sat up, her exhaustion waning as her interest was piqued. 'And pray tell me, what was this creature I happened upon today?'

The hunter looked her straight in the eye. 'It is something that need not concern you. Go home, carry on your business and forget about the malevolence of this afternoon. I only ask that you heed my warning: do not walk these paths alone, especially if they are shrouded in mist.'

The stubbornness in Lora reared. Mother deplored this aspect of her character and told her countless times it was un-ladylike. *Why,* she thought, *am I considered incapable — just a pretty decoration — simply because I am female?*

'Did I not fight alongside you? Am I to be denied knowledge of that which I fought?' she said. But looking at the steadfastness of the hunter's face, she realised this tactic would yield no fruit. She tried another. 'Shall I go back into the town and tell them of what I have seen? I could bring a fighting party out to the marshes.'

His expression did not change. Lora, who considered herself a rather good manipulator, was beginning to feel uncertain. She had one play left; it would be a cheap move, she realised, but the urge inside her to know about the creature was stronger just then than her sense of right and wrong.

'Of course, sir, when they see the state of my face and clothes — the blood, the tears — they might not believe in the creature but think it is you who is responsible for it.' She glanced up at him, almost afraid of the words as soon as they had left her mouth.

'I should have let the creature finish you off!' he replied, his dark eyes sparking. Then, as if seeing the state of Lora for the first time, he said, 'Let me escort you to a safe place. I will tell the tale of the evil we fought; we will need to concoct a believable explanation for your appearance.'

'Thank you. Please, take me to my sister's, she will supply clean clothes and will be faithful with our secret. My name is Lora Smith,' she introduced herself boldly. Under these exceptional circumstances, no rules of etiquette applied as far as she was concerned.

Holding out a hand to help Lora up, her saviour bobbed his head forward and said simply, 'Rafael Nathaniel Hunter, though commonly I am known as Rafe.' Clasping the proffered hand, Lora eased her way up from her muddy bed and said, 'It is a pleasure to meet you, Rafe,' before turning towards the town.

Eleven
2013

The box was deceptively heavy, Regan discovered as she attempted to heave it towards her bed. The cardboard was weak and misshapen; evidently damp had seeped into it at some point, and then it had re-dried in the heat of the summer. Mould spores and dust settled in her lungs and she started hacking for the umpteenth time since she'd decided to reorganise the attic room that was her home for the foreseeable future.

Rubbing a filthy arm across her sweaty forehead, she blinked away the tears that her coughing had brought on and wondered why this had seemed like such a good idea. Tugging at the box, she hoped it would slide across the wooden attic floor. Fate, which she was discovering seemed to particularly dislike her at the moment, had other ideas; the side of the box split, the contents spewing out onto the floor. Cursing under her breath she gave up and sank down onto the wooden boards. It was as good a place as any to sort through the box.

She had questioned the morality of going through stuff that technically belonged to Aunty Vi but, she reasoned, not in a month of Sundays would Aunty Vi be ascending these stairs again. Morbid as it may seem, it would be down to her and Katherine to sort through the stuff when she'd gone anyway — what was wrong with getting a head start? It wasn't as if she was stealing the crown jewels, or even any family heirlooms. Just sorting through piles of moth-eaten clothes, rusted junk, and — looking at the pile spilling out of the box in front of her — mildewed books.

Black bin liner by her side, Regan picked up the first book. It was so that rotten it mushed under her hand in a stinking mess. Gagging, she dropped it straight into the bin bag. Resisting the urge to just scoop the whole lot straight into the rubbish, she decided to put them in piles: completely unsalvageable, possibly okay, and good condition. Then she could see if Katherine wanted to keep any. The next couple of books weren't even nearly salvageable, but after that the 'possibly okay' pile gradually started to grow. With titles like 'Don'ts For Husbands' and 'Don'ts For Wives', Regan wasn't entirely sure that Katherine would want to keep them, but she felt she should give her the choice.

She wiped her hands on her jeans, trying to get rid of the mouldy, dusty feeling, and reached into the box for the last pile of books. It was a small stack, bound together by a faded red ribbon. They were little — about A6 size Regan guessed — and had hard, cracked leather covers in a plain navy blue. Intrigued, she slipped the top book out from under the ribbon.

Feeling strangely compelled to look inside, she opened the front cover gently and then jumped, a little squeal escaping from her as something fell on her lap. Convinced it was a spider, she flicked at it with the back of her hand. It landed in a disintegrated heap in a muted pool of sun that filtered through the skylight. On further inspection, Regan realised it wasn't a spider, disintegrated or otherwise, but a dried plant. Squinting, she peered at it and wondered if it had started off life as a sprig of rosemary.

Turning her attention back to the book held delicately in her hands, she turned the aged, yellow pages with care. It was a diary, she realised with awe as she tried to make out the faded inscription on the front page. The writing was unfamiliar, and the ink so discoloured she could hardly read it, but one date caught her eye: 1645. *Impossible,* she thought, bringing the book right up under her nose and scrutinising it closely. Holding her breath against the vaguely yeasty smell that rose from the book, she tried hard to make out the numerals. Astonished, she was still convinced it said 1645. Underneath the date she noticed a name, but try as she might, she couldn't read the writing in the weak light of her dingy attic room.

Stretching her cramped legs out from beneath her, she picked up the next diary. It was so similar to the first, only close inspection revealed the minute differences. Carefully, she tried to open the book, but it was impossible; damp had penetrated the cover and swollen it, clumping the inside pages together. The third volume had fared the same fate.

The last one, though, seemed to be holding up better than the others. She picked it up eagerly; again it was slightly different in style, and she ran her fingers over the hardened leather, letting her thumb trace a small crack. She eased open the cover and saw that the date was relatively recent: 1922. The name was clearly written in beautiful italic script — Elizabeth Maureen Simpson. *Elizabeth*. The name rang a bell; Regan racked her brains trying to think where she'd heard it ...

The writing was elegant and the prose archaic, but it was legible; she could definitely read this one. She wasn't really a big reader — in fact, other than her stash of gossip magazines, she barely read at all — but her hand trembled in anticipation as she examined Elizabeth's journal. Once again, she admired the beautiful slope of Elizabeth's handwriting, then, with just the tips of her fingers, she slowly turned the page.

Regan felt her pulse quicken slightly as she gently leafed through the pages. More of Elizabeth's elegant script flowed across the paper, each letter formed perfectly, each word exquisitely crafted. Grabbing the torch she kept by her bedside, she aimed its powerful beam at the page and started reading.

21st June 1922.

This journal is intended as a record of my encounters with the malevolent creatures that roam these lands. People in these parts deny their existence, but at the setting of the sun doors are quickly bolted — when mists shroud the land, fathers keep home their daughters, and husbands closely guard their wives. Old Scytheton is a large village which I am proud to call home. The people are friendly. Most men work on the land, though some are fishers who work through the night catching the eels that are so bountiful in local waters. Despite their hardworking nature, neighbours have time for each other. Cross words are so rare it would be accurate to say disagreements never happen. Strangers are made welcome, be they just passing through or dwelling locally.

Yet, for more than two months now, since the mists started frequent visits, things have changed. Neighbours fight neighbours. Farmers accuse their workers of theft; fishermen barely talk to each other. Strangers are not welcomed, even friends are not welcome in each other's homes. Yet I seem to be the only one who has noticed. Even Father says I am letting my imagination get away from me, but I heard him fighting with Mrs Roberts about the milk jug she had accidently broken — the first time I have ever heard Father raise his voice in anger.

I can tell Violet senses something is amiss, but she is too young. I must protect her — my sister is pure of heart; she attracts warmth and love to her like a candle lures a moth. I WILL protect her.

I have seen creatures in the mist, I know they exist and my eyes are not deceiving me. I do not know yet from where this malevolence originates or what it is, but I will uncover these facts. I will not close my eyes to the truth; I will refuse to be blinded by fear ...

Regan paused — for a second, she was back in the thick fog, blinded and deafened by its density — then she shook her head. Despite the hairs standing up on her arms and the shiver that ran a cold finger down her spine, her natural scepticism took over. *Elizabeth was obviously a fantasist*, she thought. For a start, no village or town — or even city for that matter — was that perfect. People were always going to argue. It was human nature.

And, creatures in the fog ...

'Ridiculous!' she said out loud, startled at the sound of her own voice. She yelped with fright as something thudded against the skylight above her. *Just a bird*, she realised, watching a fat blackbird as it pecked at the glass and then flew away. The diary had made her jumpy. For reasons she could not define, a nagging doubt tugged at her. Those creatures. The fog. Maybe there *was* something to it.... Putting her normal cynical self in charge, she re-read the words, then rested the diary on her knee and closed her eyes. The account *had* to be fantasy, but the way Elizabeth had written it, she'd clearly believed every word.

'Okay,' Regan said, her voice echoing slightly around the room. 'Let's think about this logically. Malevolent creatures-in-the-fog do not exist. Simple. End of.' She got off her bed and paced across the floor. 'So why is Elizabeth so certain they do?' She asked out loud, and ignored the voice in her head that responded, '*Why do you care so much?*'

The mist. I know from experience that it's thick and disorientating. Maybe a wild creature, glimpsed through the mist, could appear to be something more. I don't know, a fox or something.

Memories of the foggy walk home after her first shift in the pub started worming their way to the surface. The fog *had* been unnatural — maybe it *had* been a 'what' that was following her and not a 'who'. Could it have been a fox? Or even a stray cow or something. She closed her eyes and tried to summon up the image of what had pursued her. Tall and thin was all she could remember; if she'd had a chance at a proper look before that damn American chased it off, she might have been able to solve the mystery of Elizabeth's creatures. *I have no idea what it was, but I'm pretty sure it was no fox*, she admitted to herself.

Sighing, she opened the pages again and started to read on. But her reading was too slow, and the old-fashioned handwriting too confusing to skim. Frustrated, she shut the book again. Needing to do something but not knowing what, her brain at last remembered something; as he'd left that night, Nate had said something about 'things not being what they seem'. There was one other way to find the answers — one other person who knew.

Jumping up from the floor she ran a quick comb through her hair, for once not really caring what she looked like. She left her mum a note, made her way out of the house into the rapidly darkening night and headed off towards the pub.

If Nate wasn't there, someone would know where she could find him.

Twelve
1645

'Lora!' Mary gasped, 'What has happened child?'

'Let us in Mary and I will explain,' said Lora, 'at least, this man will.'

'Man?' said Mary, then caught sight of Rafe standing behind Lora. 'Forgive me, sir, I did not see you there.'

'I am sorry to inconvenience you on this cold evening, but I fear Mistress Lora needed help.'

'It is no inconvenience sir — come in,' Mary turned and they followed her into the hall, where she preferred to receive visitors. A fire was glowing, its warmth felt all through the grand room. 'Lora, come, Harriet will draw you a bath …'

'Mary please, I have not time for that, some water and a change of clothes is all I need to restore me.' It was unfortunate for Lora that Mary was not as carefree as her younger sister; she insisted Lora have a proper bath and her wounds tended to. By the time Lora was ready, she feared that Rafe would have left. To her delight he was still there, drinking some of the household's best French brandy, when she was shown back into the hall,

'I was not sure that you would have stayed,' she said.

'I am not sure why I did, Mistress Lora, but I feel that if I had not, I would surely live to regret it.'

The strange looks her sister was giving her discouraged Lora from saying any more. She wished fruitlessly to have time alone with Rafe, to find out what had been pursuing them in the marshes. She knew better than to expect Mary to leave her without an escort. Mary was a good sister, but there was a limit to that which Lora could expect her to accept. Unaware she was pacing across the room while she thought, Lora was startled when Mary demanded an explanation.

'You come to my house unannounced, in the company of a stranger, without an escort. I believe I have a right to know what is happening.' Lora wasn't the only one in the family who had inherited a stubborn nature. No matter that Mary managed it in a more ladylike way; it was a trait they both shared. Glancing at Rafe, Lora decided that telling the truth was the only choice. She trusted her sister without reserve, and for her own sanity she needed to know from Rafe what had happened to her.

She settled herself into the fine oak chair in the corner and began to speak. She told Mary of the encounter she had had that afternoon, of her walk along the path, of the fog that had suddenly appeared and of the creature that had pursued her. 'It is the truth, dear sister. I did not expect to see the end of this day; I thought I was being called home. Then Master Hunter appeared through the fog. The Lord himself must have sent him.' She allowed herself a glance at Rafe; he was holding his head high, but Lora fancied she could see some discomfort in his features. 'It is entirely Master Hunter's doing that I am here now,' she said, staring straight at her sister.

Mary raised an eyebrow — not much, just enough that Lora knew she didn't believe the tale. Before she had a chance elaborate, Mary had turned to Rafe.

'I'm afraid my sister isliableto exaggeration, Master Hunter. I wonder how you would tell the story of this afternoon.'

Rafe coughed, his uneasiness hanging about him like a cloak. 'Yes ma'am. Mistress Lora is telling the truth.' Lora smiled at Mary; it would do her sister good to believe her in the future. Unfortunately her smugness was short lived. 'It was very foggy this afternoon out in the fens, as if the clouds themselves had come down. Any young lady out unattended at such a time is bound to become fanciful of mind.' Rafe took a breath, 'When I came along the path, I found Mistress Lora frightened and lost. She'd fallen in the bog and was terrified, talking of a creature from hell. It took me but few moments to realise that the creature she spoke of was nothing but a footpad, out to thieve what he could.' Lora gasped and anger flared through her; she opened her mouth, ready to protest. At the gasp Mary turned and frowned at her, and while Mary's attention was directed away from him Rafe looked Lora in the eye and gave a small shake of his head. Honesty glinted in his eyes and Lora let the protest die before it reached her lips.

'I did my best to fight the thief — I was lucky that I knew the paths through the marshes and he did not; he lost his footing and was seized by the mud. It was then I was able to bring Mistress Smith to the place in which she felt safest.' There, he stopped — enough heroism to appeal to Mary; the footpad, more believable than the truth of what they had seen; and just a little flattery — the perfect story was told. Of course, Lora herself wasn't shown in the best light and she was, as yet, none the wiser as to what she had encountered on the marsh that afternoon, but there was something about Master Hunter that she trusted. He would tell her the truth, when he was able.

Thirteen
2013

The setting of the sun was doing nothing to ease the humidity of the day. Each inhalation of the cloying air felt like trying to breathe through a sponge, every muffled breath not quite satisfying enough. Swatting off gnats and spitting out midges, Regan longed for the cool breeze that blew in over Brighton from the English Channel.

The setting sun was a brilliant red and cast an orange glow over the fields like fire. In spite of herself Regan couldn't help but notice how beautiful the low-lying land looked this evening. Despite the humidity, despite the flies, despite the questions clawing for attention in her brain and despite the corner of her mind that had been completely occupied with Nate since she'd first met him, Regan actually noticed the surrounding countryside and managed to compare it favourably to Brighton.

Swinging open the familiar brown door of The Hunter's Rest, Regan wiped a sheen of sweat from her brow with the back of her hand. God, she hated summer. Despite the huge fan Nick had perched on the side of the bar, the pub offered no relief from the stifling heat and she decided to get out of there as soon as possible. Glancing over to Nate's usual corner, she felt a small tide of disappointment wash over her when she saw it was empty.

'All right Regan love? Didn't expect you in tonight,' Nick's cheerful tone rang across the pub.

'I'm just looking for Nate — has he been in this evening?' she reached the bar and, slipping behind it, helped herself to an ice-cold Coke, depositing the money into the till.

'Nate? I don't think I know a Nate,' Nick said, looking puzzled.

'The American …'

'Oh right, the Yank! He's not been in tonight. I didn't know you knew him.' Nick gave her a questioning look as she glugged down her frigid drink.

'Nah, I don't — not really — I just need to see him about something.' She smiled at Nick — a smile that warned him against asking too many questions. 'I don't suppose you know where he lives, where I could find him, do you?'

'Hmm, yeah, he's renting from the Greens, er, turn left out of here …' he proceeded to give Regan directions to Nate's place.

'Regan, you're not thinking of going there alone, are you? It really is in the back of beyond, makes your place look like Piccadilly Circus!' Regan tried to ignore the look of concern on Nick's face. After all, he wasn't her dad. Still, an uncomfortable feeling of guilt tugged at her as she shook her head and told him she'd see him tomorrow when her shift started. Snagging herself another cola, she waved goodbye and left the pub. She stood on the pavement outside and sipped her drink until the heavy door had swung shut behind her. As soon as she was out of sight of her boss, she turned left instead of right, and walked out of the small village in a direction she'd never been before.

It wasn't long before the village pavement petered out and Regan found herself walking with crops she couldn't identify rustling head height beside her. She walked quickly, her brain occupied with remembering the directions Nick had given her, not allowing herself to think about exactly what she was going to say to Nate.

Watching carefully for the next turning right, Regan was starting to understand why her boss had asked her not to go this way alone at night. The single track was hidden between two fully grown fields and she felt insignificant, almost non-existent, among the towering crops. The sun had disappeared completely now and the sky was a strange hue of navy. The moon that lit the way was almost as bright as the sun, but its eerie glow left long shadows in the darkness. Nothing was the colour it should be and Regan's eyes strained to see the way.

Resisting the urge to turn back, she searched as far as she could see for any indication that she was heading in the right direction, her eyes and ears on full alert for any sign that Nate may actually live out here — a building, a light, an engine or radio. Anything would do. But the night air carried only the sounds that belonged in the night; insects buzzed, the crops rustled and somewhere in the distance a mouse squeaked. Regan kept walking, her shoulders hunching up to her chin. Constantly scanning the horizon, she jumped every time a piece of corn, or wheat, or whatever the hell was growing in this field moved. Thoughts of the diaries had almost left her as her eyes searched for any sign of *anything*, and she was nearly ready to admit this may be her stupidest idea to date.

Just as she was starting to give in to the panic slowly simmering inside her, she picked out the shape of a house in the moonlight — just a darker square in an already dark horizon. As she stretched her eyes and they became used to the dimness, she began to make out a higgledy roof and slightly sloping walls.

She sped up as she made her way to the house. Its windows were blank; not one showed any sign of a light inside. *Typical,* she thought, *I've trekked all this way and I bet he's not even bloody here.* Resisting the urge to stomp like a put-out toddler, she finally came up to the house. The yard was empty except for a broken-down old motor wedged against a wall. Ignoring it, she finally stepped out of the field and onto the drive. As soon as Regan saw the deep ruts of sun-baked mud that ran up the drive, she felt convinced she had found the right place — she was certain that these tracks came from the bike Nate had shown up on the other night. Nerves started to set in as she wondered what Nate was going to say when she found him. The burning desire to ask about Elizabeth's diary had diminished, and now she was wondering if she was about to make a prat of herself. She brushed her hands through her hair, wishing she'd stopped to brush it properly before rushing out. Tucking the loose strands behind her ears, she followed the tracks round the side of the house and was greeted by a distant light and a faint but repetitive pulsing sound.

A tumbledown stone barn stood adjacent to the house. Only a couple of walls were intact; the roof was barely more than a few beams. Ivy seemed to be holding the building together, starry night sky twinkling through the gaps. A small light hung from a beam, vaguely lighting the place. Its glow didn't reach the corners of the barn and the shadows stretched out, almost daring Regan to investigate them.

As she moved closer, the thumping sound grew louder and was interspersed with grunts. Relieved to have finally found Nate, Regan stepped forward. 'Hey …' she stopped as she caught a glimpse of him. Unaware of Regan standing there, he carried on, rhythmically pounding a huge punch bag suspended from the beams. Half in the shadows, the dim light caught the sweat running in rivulets down his bare back. As he punched, Regan's breath caught in her throat; each movement was like poetry. He punched, ducked, spun and kicked. Every single move hit its target. Every single move made Regan gasp for breath. Mesmerised, she couldn't take her eyes from him; even a bat swooping in front of her failed to distract her.

'Are you going to tell me what you wanted, or did you just come to see a workout?' The sound of Nate's voice made Regan jump out of her skin. Instantly she felt her hackles go up.

'I came to ask you something,' she said, then bit her tongue. It would do no good to ask him how long he'd known she was there; she was sure she'd only get a smug smile in return.

Aiming one last kick at the punch bag Nate turned and grabbed a towel to rub himself down with, looking expectantly at Regan. Suddenly this seemed like a really dumb idea. Wishing she'd thought it through before she left the house, Regan tried to think of a good excuse, a valid reason for turning up in the middle of the night at the house of someone she barely knew.

As a light breeze blew the sweet smell of oilseed rape past Regan's nose, she racked her brain. Nothing came to her. Feeling Nate's burning gaze she decided to settle for the truth. 'What did you mean when you said things weren't always what they seemed?' She looked at him, watching for his reaction.

'Nothing,' he said. But he shifted his eyes — just a tiny bit, but enough to show he was lying. It was almost enough for Regan to believe that Elizabeth wasn't actually completely bonkers. Her cynical inner voice seemed to be dying quietly in the corner.

'So what were they then?'

'Nothing, I told you,' flinging the towel down, he turned to continue his workout.

'I don't believe you,' said Regan, moving into the dim light of the barn. 'If it was a person you'd have said no-one, you didn't flinch when I said "what" not "who".' She moved into his line of sight, refusing to give up. He wasn't going to just brush her off as if she was some silly schoolgirl.

Moving across the barn Nate picked something up from an old cart. Ignoring Regan he went to the far end of the barn, to a corner nestled in blackness where the dim light didn't reach. The pounding sound started again, only this time there was something different about it. Determined not to be put off, or to be the first to give in and talk again, Regan moved closer. As her eyes adjusted to the darkness, she realised what the strange sound was. Nate was using knives, and every move was entrancing. She was aware that she should be afraid of this man she barely knew who was wielding two hunting knives, but she wasn't. As she watched him move she was unable to take her eyes off him. Each time he swung the knife in an arc, her heart swung too. Something was stirring inside her.

Fascinated, she continued to watch, every move seeming more and more familiar to her. She knew when he was going to duck, when he was going to swing high, when he was going to stab with his left hand, attack with his right. She found herself swaying in the rhythm too. *Left, right, duck. Twist, stab left, duck, back stab right.*

Nate stopped, looked at her then tossed her a knife. She caught it effortlessly; silently, the two of them attacked the punch bag, each knowing instinctively where the other was, how to attack, when to aim high, when to aim low. Nate sped up, Regan followed, switching the blade easily between hands as she fought an invisible foe.

Her heart was racing, the hairs on the back of her neck stood up. How could something she'd never done before feel so familiar? How could she know what she was doing? Five minutes passed, then ten.

She matched each of Nate's moves perfectly; something was stirring in her and she felt whole for the first time ever. Whole and she hadn't even realised that part of her was missing. Eventually, Nate stopped and said, 'I didn't know any of you were still alive.'

As sweat trickled down the side of her face and saturated her flimsy top she bent forward, fists on knees. Gasping for breath she still clutched the knife tightly, refusing to let go of it.

'Any of who were still alive?' she asked when she'd regained the ability to speak.

'Any of *you*. The companion hunters,' Nate said. Regan gave him her best withering stare, a look she'd spent hours practising last year. She felt like she'd just found herself, hell she didn't even know what she meant by that, and Nate was talking in riddles.

'You really don't know?' he took a deep breath, 'I guess I owe you an explanation then.'

Following Nate into his house, Regan accepted the bottle of water he pulled from the fridge. She quashed the burning questions she had — Nate did things in his own time; after two brief meetings with him even she'd managed to work that out. Sitting herself at the small table in the corner, she wobbled for a second until the rickety chair regained its balance. She let the icy bottle cool her forehead and the back of her neck before glugging down the water. Nate's naked torso was something of a distraction and Regan forced herself not to stare at it. Wiping the back of her hand across her mouth, she looked around the kitchen; to say it was sparse was bordering on an understatement.

As well as the table and chair there was a tiny fridge and a microwave. A bare bulb hung from the ceiling, its 40 watts scarcely spreading any light at all. It was all spotlessly clean though; a mug and plate lay drying on the draining board, a tea towel hung from a drawer. Curiosity got the better of her and she didn't even bother to hide the fact that she was looking around. Nate was an enigma.

'Sorry, it's not much,' he said from where he leaned against an old butler's sink, 'I'm not used to company.'

'No, its … uh, I like it,' she said truthfully. 'I know, doesn't really go with my image, but I do like it. What's with the aversion to lights though?' She pointed to the dim bulb hanging in the middle of the ceiling. Nate finished his drink and pulled on a plain white t-shirt that hung on the back of a chair. As he tugged it down, Regan couldn't help but notice a row of marks across his chest: puckered white and red scars in five bar gates on his left side, and similar black tattooed tally lines on the right. Looking away, her eyes paused briefly as she noticed for the first-time long weal marks on his left arm. Wondering how he had got them, she stared at the floor — being caught looking would be just too embarrassing.

'It helps if my eyes don't get too used to the light in the evening. I may need to go at any time and night blindness is not going to help me at all.'

'Help with what? What is going on around here? I don't understand a thing that has happened since I moved to this damn place.' Regan turned and looked

Nate straight in the eyes, only just managing not to be distracted by their hypnotic darkness.

'Why did you move here?' he asked, returning Regan's gaze. Unable to stare into his eyes any longer she glanced to the floor. 'I don't see that it's any business of yours.' she said as unwelcome goose pimples crept up her arm. Why did he have to be so gorgeous?

'Please Regan. I'm not prying, but I need to know.' He caught hold of her hand. A warm tingle started in her fingers and she could feel her pulse racing. *It's just the exercise, you're not used to it,* she thought, forcing herself to look at him again. 'Why here?' he repeated.

'Because my mum moved here. To look after her aunt. Mum grew up around here, so when Aunt Vi needed some help it seemed only natural she move back home.' Nate straightened his back and frowned, his deep eyes not once straying from Regan's face.

'Your mom is from around here, in the fens? How long ago did she move? How long have the family been in this part of England?'

'Um …' Regan tried to think, 'Mum moved away when she was my age. Her and Dad got married and moved down south. The family's been here forever I think — Dad always used to joke about Mum coming from Norfolk, said the family had been here that long she must be inbred and he was surprised we weren't born with six toes or something.' She turned and stared out the window, 'I think it was the one thing that really got to Mum. She loves it here.'

She concentrated on a small moth fluttering pathetically against the window so she didn't have to think about the arguments her parents had had, before they finally separated a few years ago. Every time the moth moved, trying to reach the dim light inside, it reminded her of how she'd felt when her mum announced they were moving back to Norfolk. She'd desperately wanted to stay in Brighton, but every time she thought of another way to possibly do so she remembered how much her mum needed her. She could see what she wanted but was not able to get to it. Family was too important; her mum needed her too much.

Moving to her side Nate said, 'Look Regan, it's clear we really have to talk but I need to check some stuff out first. I'm going to take you home now; I'll come and find you when I know some more.'

'Nate! You are not just going to leave me! I'm sick of you talking in riddles, talking down to me — tell me what's going on!' She moved away from him, aware that — as annoying as he was — he was managing to get round her this evening. 'Don't treat me like a child.'

Nate laughed, 'Well if you're going to act like one, I shall certainly treat you like one!'

'Aaaarrrggh!' Regan barely resisted the urge to stomp her foot. Taking a deep breath she turned and smiled her best, well-practised killer smile, 'I haven't even had a chance to ask you about the diaries yet.'

'Diaries?'

'I found a pile of them in my room — they're old, like *really* old. I've started reading one but it's so slow going. Elizabeth Simpson her name was, she was writing about ...' Regan paused, searching for the right words — 'about round here, about the fog. I didn't imagine it, did I?'

Nate shook his head, 'No Regan, you didn't. I promise I'll explain. Just not tonight.'

Taking a deep breath she resigned herself to the fact that, no matter how hard she pleaded, Nate wasn't going to tell her any more now.

'Okay, well I guess I'll go home and I'll see you when I see you.' She got up and made her way to the door.

'Where do you think you're going? It's the middle of the night.'

Regan was confused. 'Home, like you just told me to ...'

'I'm taking you,' he said in that commanding tone that got Regan's back straight up. Before she could argue he added, 'You'll have to borrow my helmet, I've not got a spare. You'll be fine on the back of my bike, won't you?'

A ride on his bike! Since she was a child she'd been longing to go on a motorbike but until now she'd never had the opportunity. *Suddenly*, thought Regan, *the day's looking up.*

Climbing aboard, Regan put on the crash helmet he handed her.

'Are you okay?' he asked and Regan nodded, her head feeling clumsy and heavy with the weight of the headgear. 'Hold on to me and relax — just let your body move with the bike. I won't go too fast, you'll be perfectly safe.'

Doing as she was told, Regan wrapped her arms around Nate's waist. A chill of excitement ran down her spine. She didn't want to admit it, but it felt so natural to hold on to him. His body was warm beneath his thin t-shirt and she could feel each contour of his defined stomach with her fingers.

'Hold tighter,' he said, and Regan found herself more than willing to do so. *Goddamn you Regan, don't you dare develop a crush on him,* she thought as he started up the bike.

It powered to life and sped down the drive. The actual driveway out of Nate's place was a long winding dirt track that led from the opposite side of the house. Disorientated at first, it didn't take her long to figure out where she was; the road was the same one she'd left Old Scytheton on, the driveway was just about four miles further along.

As they passed The Hunter's Rest, Regan instinctively turned her head towards the pub — just in time to see Maeve leaving with another of the hapless village boys in tow. Wishing she'd been working so she'd had a chance to see Maeve again, Regan made up her mind to invite her on a shopping spree when she was next in the pub. Whatever else was going on, she'd still need some new clothes and a proper girly day out might just help clear her head.

All too soon, Nate slowed down and pulled the bike to a stop. Regan climbed off reluctantly and undid her helmet.

'I wasn't sure how your mom would feel about you turning up on the back of a motorbike, so I thought we'd walk the rest of the way,' Nate said, hanging the helmet on his handlebars.

'I'll be okay, I can walk from here on my own,' said Regan, not really wanting to give up Nate's company just yet.

'Regan, I don't know what's in those diaries but whatever it is, trust me, you need to believe it. Walking alone here at night is not safe. *Not ever* safe, so please don't.' Quelling the inner rebel that usually appeared every time she was told she could or couldn't do something, Regan nodded.

Walking along the lane to her house, Regan found she was enjoying Nate's company. He wasn't exactly talkative, but his presence was reassuring.

'So when are you going to tell me what's going on then?' she asked.

'I'll see you after work tomorrow. I'm going to make sure you get home safely from now on — no more wandering on your own in the dark.'

Glad she was finally going to get some answers, Regan didn't even bother to protest. Tomorrow she might be able to make some sense out of the situation. As she lay in bed trying to sleep, she couldn't help wondering about this mysterious American in the heart of the English fens.

Fourteen
1645

Lora glanced around, searching as far as her eyes could see and praying that she wouldn't be seen; the scandal, the shame it would bring to her family, would be more than she could bear. The fens spread before her, quiet and desolate of any other human life. The air was fetid and gnats formed moving halos above their heads.

Finally, satisfied no one else was around, she turned to face Rafe. 'Master Hunter. A week has passed, and I am still awaiting an explanation.' She looked at him in anticipation, her hazel eyes never leaving his face.

Rafe sighed. 'I could tell you, Mistress Smith, that I was concerned about the lies you would spread about me. I could tell you I was worried about the danger you would be in if I did not share with you the truth. I *could* tell you that I am an honourable man and I keep my promises. All of which is the utter truth, all of which are very good reasons,' he stopped and stared at Lora, hesitating a little. 'You have been very patient, but it is not too late to change your mind. You could go away, promising not to go out in the marshes alone — live your life as you had planned. Marry your gentleman and forget about last week. Forget about me,' he halted again as Lora's eyes flashed.

'So you are just like everyone else, sir, and do not keep your promises at all. I assure you I am quite capable of handling the truth — I am not just a simple girl, interested only in gossip and marriage, I —'

'You deserve an explanation,' Rafe bowed his head. 'I know. Never before have I seen such courage, such determination. You, Mistress Smith, have an iron will, and *that* is why I am here. Let us walk.'

Gathering her skirts, Lora matched her stride to Rafe's. She wanted him to think of her as an equal, and she wasn't sure if he was going to get beyond the fact that she was a girl.

'I wonder, have you heard of a publication named the *Malleus Maleficarum*?' Lora frowned and then shook her head slightly; she was reluctant to appear ignorant, but the name meant nothing to her.

'I do not think so; it does not sound familiar to me,' she said. Rafe slowed, causing Lora to bump into him; he put out his arm to steady her. She started, her arm burning as though it were aflame. Feeling the blush creeping into her face, she moved abruptly aside.

'It tells us about witches and their powers,' Rafe turned and continued walking; Lora took a deep breath and followed him again.

'Oh. Well, that is why I haven't heard of it then. My father believes such things to be nonsense; I have oft heard him say, "If evil occurs it is solely the work of the devil, he needs not humans to help him."'

'Then, forgive me, but your father is a fool!'

Lora felt herself blush again. She alone had ever felt that her father may be foolish — generally he was well regarded, his opinion respected. She batted away a fly that buzzed too close to her face and waited for Rafe to continue.

'Such folk are very real; they move among us, live among us and it is likely that neither you nor even I would know who they are. Most of the time we do not need to bother with them; they have abilities and knowledge that we don't, that is all. Some, though, are pure evil and *have* made a pact with the devil. The devil knows how to deal with those whose hearts are already black; he bargains with them until whatever little bit of soul they did have is gone.'

As a chill ran through her she pulled her shawl tighter. Though the weather had been kind for September, now October was creeping closer the wind that grazed her skin was definitely cooler. Gathering her thoughts she delayed replying to Rafe, busying herself with lifting her skirts to avoid a patch of mud, aware of Rafe watching her as she deliberated.

Taking a breath, she said, 'So was this creature we encountered a witch?' *A witch. Could she believe in such things?* After years of listening to her father her head said no, but her heart knew that whatever they had met a week ago was inhuman. Why couldn't it be a witch? She frowned. 'No Master Hunter, I do not believe it was. A witch would surely have used magic and curses to defeat us, not clawed and fought like some monster.'

Rafe smiled at her perceptiveness, 'You are right Lora, *it* was not a witch but one of their creatures, their familiars.'

Lora snorted, she couldn't help herself. Lifting her skirts with one hand and tightening the shawl further with the other, Lora strode off. Why had Rafe bothered to meet her if he was going to fill her head with nonsense?

'Mistress Smith,' Rafe strode to catch up with her, 'Mistress Smith! Lora!' he soon caught her and reached out, his fingers encircling her wrist. Her hand felt small in his and she was glad when he dropped it; she did not want him to think of her as delicate and incapable. 'I speak nothing but the truth. They may appear as normal creatures when with their mistresses but they too hunt and fight, seeking blood and flesh — food, human if they can get it. It keeps them strong so they can assist the witches with their dark magic. And here, in this part of the country with its fens, bogs and salt marshes all eagerly awaiting the stray traveller, nobody notices those that go missing.'

Lora realised this was the truth. Oh, if she hadn't come home the other day her family would surely have mourned her, but nobody would have questioned her death. Death was no stranger to these parts. She turned to look at Rafe, taking in his plain clothes, his tidy but unfashionable hair. He spoke as if he were well bred, but he had no adornments; his look was simple.

'And this creature's mistress?'

'The creatures come to feed to gain strength; the more strength they gain the stronger the witch to whom they belong becomes. The stronger the witch, the more power she wields. And if there is one thing a witch craves, it is power.'

She took in his strong jaw and aquiline nose; when her eyes met his, she didn't turn away but saw in their deep cornflower blue nothing but the truth. However incredible it sounded, she believed Rafe was in earnest. Her thoughts raced and half-formed ideas started to flicker into her mind. Knots settled in her stomach as she let herself formulate the unthinkable. A sense of purpose enveloped her as she had never known before. With steely determination she said, 'So what are we going to do about it?'

Fifteen
2013

The hum of conversation in the pub was louder than usual. Nick had managed to hook a TV up and the local footie derby was showing. Today in The Hunter's Rest it was standing room only.

Regan leaned over the bar a little so she could hear the next customer's order. 'A pint of lager and your phone number love,' the green and yellow clad twenty-something said, holding out a pen.

'One lager coming up, but I don't hand out phone numbers on days with a vowel in them. Sorry,' she said, passing the pint across the bar and accepting a fiver.

'He'll be a while working that one out — I'm afraid Jonesy doesn't know what a vowel is,' Sam said, pushing the lad up so he could squeeze in near the bar. His green and yellow t-shirt matched Jonsey's, and he unwound his scarf before adding, 'Besides, Jonesy, I saw her first. She's going out with me!'

Regan raised her eyebrows, trying desperately hard not to smile. 'Oh I am, am I?' she asked, 'I don't recall that being part of the conversation the other night.'

'I don't need to hear you say the words, I know you want to …'

'SAM! Leave poor Regan alone, haven't you got someone else you can be hassling?' Toni pressed them all up a few centimetres further as she squashed in along the bar as well, pulling Ella in alongside her.

'Keep your nose out little sis'. It's my duty to take out all the good-looking girls, show them a good time. In fact I consider it a moral obligation in this case — I don't want Regan thinking that Little Scytheton and these glorious fenlands can't keep up with town life!' He glanced at Ella and a gleam entered his eyes, 'Anyway, Ella will vouch for the fact that I know how to show a girl a good time, won't you Els?'

'Shut up, Sam,' said Ella through gritted teeth, the colour rising up her neck nearly matching the deep red top she was wearing.

'Aw Sam, give it a rest. You know Ella has gained a sense of taste recently,' said Toni.

'If only you knew, little sis'.' Ella blushed even deeper and turned away, but not before Regan noticed the uneasy look in her eyes. Sam himself was grinning from ear to ear and had a slightly self-satisfied look on his face. Regan was intrigued; there was definitely something going on there and she was pretty sure Toni was oblivious to it.

'Unfortunately,' said Regan, 'I don't have time to sort out a date with anyone at the moment *and* if I don't serve some more customers, I won't be earning any money to go out anywhere, ever!'

'True,' said Toni, 'even Mum won't come in when a match is on, she knows Nick gets his knickers in a knot!'

At that Regan moved down to the next customer in line, glancing down the bar to see if she could gauge Nick's mood; he returned her glance with a tight smile. Stressed, but not aimed at Regan yet.

Finally the match started; the line at the bar diminished as the sea of yellow and green crowded round the flat screen on the end wall. The sound levels went from nearly silent to full volume chanting every time Norwich veered the ball near the goal, but Regan didn't mind. It gave her time to collect dead glasses, wash them and give the tables a wipe over. After chatting to her friends she really wanted to try to keep in Nick's good books.

Sam, she noticed, was singing along with the rest of them, only slightly outdone by his sister. Never had she met two people so full of zing. She picked up another handful of empty pint glasses and snuck another peek at Sam. As she looked away, an uneasy feeling crept over her; Ella was staring straight at her, an undisguised look of dislike on her face. She turned away as soon as she saw Regan looking. Regan carried on collecting glasses but she couldn't shake the feeling of disquiet that had settled on her. Damn Ella, Toni was allowed to have more than one friend. *Although,* she thought as she filled up the dishwasher, *I would give my eye teeth to know what had happened between Sam and her.*

'Vodka and orange please, Regan.'

Looking up, Regan couldn't help grinning when she saw Maeve there. Remembering, just a fraction of a second too late, to try and keep cool she toned down the smile, 'Would you like ice in that?'

'No thanks,' Maeve said, leaning forward conspiratorially, 'I wouldn't want to water it down too much now, would I?' Regan grinned back and gave an exaggerated glance around the room, 'Not if you're on the pull in here you wouldn't,' she said. Maeve opened her brilliant green eyes wide in mock horror. 'I like you Regan,' she said, 'I'm glad you've moved in.'

'Me too,' Regan said, 'I was wondering if you fancied that shopping trip we were talking about before? I haven't been for ages and much as I love my mum, when it comes to clothes ... let's just say we have slightly different tastes.' *Sorry Mum.*

'Sure honey, that sounds like fun — how about Monday?'

'A shopping trip? I am so up for one of those,' Toni appeared beside Maeve at the bar. Her bright scarf trailed in the dregs of beer spillage on the smeared surface but she seemed not to care. Regan worked hard to quell the horror that she was sure must be showing on her face. She liked Toni, she really did, but ...

'A Primark has just opened up in town, honestly you can get such a bargain, can't you Ella?'

'Yeah, a real bargain,' Ella echoed quietly from just behind Toni. She glanced at Regan, a triumphant spark in her eyes, 'I don't think Regan wants us to join her on this shopping trip though Toni — I'm not sure Primark's really her ... style.' She sneered the last word and Regan flushed.

'Of course you're welcome to join us, aren't they Maeve? I love Primark,' she added, flinching at the lie, 'but we *were* thinking of going slightly further afield.'

'Oh well Cambridge is fantastic for a day out. Come on girls, who's up for it?' Toni looked round the three of them, a grin plastered across her face. She reminded Regan of how Ashleigh looked when she wanted something, and she felt really guilty. She was being a huge snob, she knew — Toni had been nothing but kind to her since they'd first met. She raised her eyebrows at Maeve, 'What do you think? Cambridge sounds good to me.'

'Sounds fun! See you Monday, then,' said Maeve. She grinned at Toni and then swung her hair over her shoulder; face hidden from all but Regan, she raised her eyebrows and smirked. 'Should be loads of fun!' she reiterated before taking her drink and settling down amid a group of laughing twenty-somethings, immediately becoming the centre of attention.

Regan waved to Toni and Ella as they sat back down, before serving the halftime queue that had formed.

Three hours later and the smell of stale beer was finally starting to make Regan feel a bit queasy. Toni, Sam and Ella had left, her feet ached and if she heard one more time what a fabulous team the Canaries were she'd scream. Football at the best of times was boring — a football team named after a caged bird? That she just couldn't figure out.

Plastering a false smile on her face, she agreed with the hundredth, billionth customer that yes, it was the best goal ever seen. Pulling a pint of real ale, her attention strayed as she noticed Maeve standing up with a small crowd getting ready to leave the pub. Great, they were probably going clubbing or something. Tired as she was, the idea was suddenly appealing and she hoped for a second that Maeve would come and ask her to join them when her shift ended. No offer came though, and as soon as the door swung closed on the group Regan felt tired and irritable and blamed Toni for the lack of invitation. God, she bet Maeve cancelled on them, then she'd be stuck going to Cambridge with Toni and Ella — the bitch — looking in cheap-as-chips shops. She could have screamed.

'Regan, stop staring into space and wipe down some tables,' snapped Nick, his famously endless patience seeming to have found its end tonight.

'Yes sir,' she mumbled, grabbing a cloth and rubbing the nearest table so hard she nearly took the top layer of polish off it. Expertly scooping up the dead glasses that crowded the next table, she dumped them on the bar and proceeded to strip another table of its polish. Turning to repeat the act with a third, she stopped short when she saw Nate sitting there.

Huffily wiping her cloth over his pristine table she said, 'How long have you been here?'

'A while,' he said, 'you may want to watch what you're doing with that cloth.' She yanked it back from where it was dangling nearly in his drink. 'I'm perfectly capable of wiping a table, thank you!' Stomping back to the bar she put the empties she'd collected in the wash, the clatter they made barely audible over the noise in the pub.

A glance at the clock told her she had only a quarter of an hour left at work and she purposely ignored Nate for the rest of her shift. As much as she wanted to know about the diaries, she wasn't going to be treated like a six-year-old. Whatever the hell was going on she'd learnt last night she could match Nate move for move, so if anyone did try and attack her, she was sure she would be more than a match for them. Besides, she had her phone and a can of body spray in her bag — she could call 999 after blinding any assailants with a blast of Lily Mist. What she didn't need was a babysitter.

Quarter of an hour flew past and Nick came to tell her to go. 'Here,' he said, handing her an envelope, 'a bonus. Thank you for tonight — it was a bit busy, wasn't it? And I'm sorry for being an old grump.'

'Thanks Nick, you weren't too bad,' she said, shoving the money in her bag, 'it *was* a bit manic though!' Swinging her bag over her shoulder, she said goodnight and left the pub.

Relieved to be out in the fresh air after the stale alcoholic fumes that permeated the pub, Regan paused as she stepped out the door and took a deep breath. The air smelt sweet. A cool breeze tickled her face and she smiled to herself as she breathed in deeply again. This time the air was tinged with a musky, masculine smell; eyes still shut she said, 'Hallo, Nate.' She turned and opened her eyes to see him leaning against the wall, so cool it was as if the word nonchalant was invented just for him.

'My escort service has arrived I see,' she said, with just a hint of sarcasm lacing her voice.

'Ready and waiting, Ma'am,' said Nate, coming up alongside her. 'I think we need to talk.'

'So what do you know about witches?' asked Nate as they strolled out of Little Scytheton.

'Witches,' replied Regan, 'what, evil old hags who come out on Halloween, broomsticks at the ready? Hubble, bubble, toil and trouble, that kind of thing?' She looked at Nate, 'I'm not wasting an evening walking home with you for you to feed me a load of crap,' she said. She was starting to feel irritated again and she was not hanging around for him to take the piss out of her. Before she could stomp off, Nate spoke.

'No I mean witches, as in the great witch hunts of the seventeenth century.'

Swallowing, Regan looked at Nate; with his hands in his pockets he looked perfectly relaxed. She would have been fooled if she hadn't noticed his eyes. Eyes so alert that every movement in the surrounding fields was noted. Every shrew that ran across the road, every bit of corn blowing in the breeze, every owl that hooted overhead. Eyes that betrayed the truth he was telling; even a two-year-old would be able to see he wasn't mocking her.

Wracking her brains, she tried to remember the little they'd learnt about the witch trials at school. She recalled what she could and then Nate told her what he knew about them. The thought of those innocent men and women tortured and humiliated made Regan shiver.

'Do you want my jacket?' Nate asked.

'No, I'm fine. But what have witches got to do with anything?' She paused and raised her eyebrow in disbelief, 'You're not seriously trying to tell me they really exist, are you?'

Snorting, she started walking again. The hardened mud road crunched beneath their feet as they walked, breaking the silence while she waited for Nate to answer her.

'Not now, but they used to. They just weren't the ones caught by the so-called witch hunters.'

'Ok-ay. So this is not about witches, right?' Even saying the words she felt ridiculous, yet when Nate mentioned them, he sounded as cool as ever.

'No, not about witches, not exactly. Have you ever heard of a witch's familiar, the creatures that used to help them with their magic?'

'Weren't they black cats or something?'

'Sometimes they were cats, but they could be any creature at all — dogs, sheep, frogs, weasels. Anything. Well, witches needed their familiars, but familiars needed witches too. And the more powerful a witch became the more powerful the familiars became.' He stopped and looked at Regan; she nodded to show she was following him.

'About two hundred years ago witches seemed to die out, yet their creatures still exist. Over time, though, they've evolved to become creatures of the dark. They live only to kill, and the more they kill, the more powerful they become.'

She hesitated. Most of her brain was telling her this was the best bit of fabrication she'd ever heard, but some small part of it — and, if she was brutally honest with herself, most of her heart — wanted to believe Nate was telling the truth. Unfortunately her cynical side always had been strongest.

Turning, she stared at him in disbelief, 'You're good Nate, I'll give you that,' she said. 'No wonder you didn't want to say anything last night — needed the entire day to make up this fabulous tale, did you?'

Regan strode ahead, a million thoughts running through her brain. Familiars, witches' pets — how could they exist? Yet the fog she'd witnessed … it had been thick and unyielding. A wall of solid grey mist. How could that be anything but supernatural? Even the sea mists she'd witnessed in Brighton were nothing in comparison to this fog and the way it had wrapped itself around her.

And did she truly believe that whatever had been pursuing her that night was human? Its elongated shape was taller than that of any human she knew. Saying that, cats, frogs and dogs were all smaller than humans were and she wasn't aware of any giraffes wandering around the fens. Coming to an abrupt standstill, she swivelled round to face Nate.

'Okay Nate, say I do believe you. Explain what happened the other night. There's no way that whatever you managed to frighten off was in any way a domestic pet.'

He shook his head. 'No, it wasn't a pet. The familiars around here have evolved; they started off as stoats and are now just an evil parody of what they were.'

'So what do they want? What are they after and how do they get it?'

'They want *us*. Humans. Unlike the witches, they have no desires other than living, and in order to live they have to have human blood.'

Regan stopped again, trying to process this. 'So why aren't there constantly reports of people going missing then? How come the people from the towns and villages don't put up warning signs and missing posters?'

Stopping beside her, Nate explained patiently, 'People do go missing, but it's those that live on the outside, that don't belong to anyone. Most people use cars to get about these roads; there aren't many who walk here now. Not at night anyway. And familiars have a survival instinct — they won't attack a group of people.' As Regan opened her mouth, he put up his hand.

'Look, I understand you have a million questions right now, but it's not the time or place to answer them. What I need to talk to you about is who *you* are.'

Regan frowned. 'I'm Regan White,' she said, 'you know that. Recent occupant of the fens, barmaid and … well that's about it really.' She shut up, slightly ashamed of her lack of accomplishments.

'Regan. When I saw you mirroring my moves yesterday, you were so in sync with me. You knew exactly how I would move next; it made me realise there may be more to you than meets the eye.'

Regan raised her eyebrow at that remark. Nate ignored it and continued, 'Way back in 1645 an ancestor of mine saved a girl from certain death on these very paths. Of course the fens were very different back then — they were yet to be drained and villages were isolated dwelling places among the marshes. Rafael was a witch hunter, but not the kind that have been documented in the history books. He truly knew how to find witches, and their familiars. We know that from the day he saved her she fought beside him, and then through time descendants of her bloodline fought alongside mine. They were the hunter's companions.'

'So?' Regan asked patiently.

'So, I think you're one of her descendants. I can't prove it, not without a look at your family tree and tracing it back a bit, but no-one else could mirror me so instinctively, I'm sure. I wanted to check back home with my father. He thinks you could be too; he's very excited.'

Crunching along the lane, Regan was surprised when she realised they were already at the turning to her house. The downstairs windows were lit up and she could see the silhouette of her mum in the front lounge with Aunty Vi. Ashleigh, she was sure, was safely snuggled up in bed for the night.

'Nate I've got to go, that's a lot to think about. Will I see you tomorrow? I may have more questions then.'

'Sure,' he said, 'I'll come and see you. I'd really like a peek at those diaries too — they may be really useful to me.'

Regan nodded and made her way up the path, tired but knowing she wouldn't sleep. She may not have a computer in the house but, this being the 21st century, she could access the internet on her phone. It wasn't perfect, but tonight she was going to do a little research into the so-called witch-hunters, and the witches and familiars they pursued.

'Who was that?' her mum asked as soon as she walked through the door. Shrugging off her jacket she hung it up, resisting the urge to say 'no-one'.

'Oh, his name's Nate; he walks me home because he doesn't think it's safe for me to wander around on my own.' A conflict of emotions flicked across her mum's face: guilt that she wasn't the one making sure her daughter got safely home; suspicion that he was after more than just Regan's safety; relief that someone was taking the time to make sure she got home in one piece.

'You'll meet him tomorrow, Mum. He's nipping over to have a look at some books I found upstairs. He's very interested in history.'

'Oh,' said Katherine, 'well, it will be a pleasure to meet him.'

* * *

When tomorrow eventually arrived, the weather had finally changed. Gone were the hot sweaty summer days they'd had for the past several weeks; in their place was swirling grey. Rain lashed down at Regan's attic window, huge drops that bounced off the glass and down again. The muted light distorted the colour in her bedroom and everything looked drained. It reminded Regan of when the colour button had gone wrong on the television; everything was familiar yet strange at the same time.

Despite her tiredness the night before, she'd still lain in bed unable to sleep. She'd left her phone on charge overnight so she was hoping to get some Googling done that day. She'd attempted to read Elizabeth's diary again, but her eyes were too sleepy. Her body needed to sleep, but her brain was churning over a thousand or more questions. And sleep, when it finally did arrive, was haunted by strange dreams of mists and witches and evil creatures, all after her, all wanting her blood.

For once Regan didn't jump straight out of bed to help her mum with Aunty Vi, or to help locate Ashleigh's lost maths book or shoe or whatever it was her sister had misplaced today. This morning she lay in bed, watching the rain as it splattered onto her skylight, trying to make sense of what Nate had told her the previous evening.

No matter how much she wanted to think that he was talking complete rubbish, no matter how hard she tried to believe he was pulling her leg, she couldn't. More fool her if she was wrong, but however unbelievable it may all sound, she trusted every word Nate had said last night. She wasn't sure what she was meant to do with the information and she had about a gazillion questions, but there was no doubt in her mind that it was all true.

And for some reason that knowledge made her feel more alive; she was *someone*, not just a seventeen-year-old barmaid with no foreseeable prospects. Something inside her buzzed. Something inside her was stirring.

'Are you getting up today, missy?' her mum's voice called up the stairs, 'I've got to take Ashleigh in a minute and Aunty Vi hasn't had her breakfast yet.'

'Yeah, coming Mum,' she yelled back, finally finding the energy to get out of bed. Wrapping herself up in a housecoat and putting her slippers on she wandered down the stairs. 'Morning, kiddo,' she greeted her sister, ruffling her hair.

'Morning Regan,' said Ashleigh, 'have you got a boyfriend now?'

Regan creased up her forehead in an exaggerated frown, 'No Ashleigh, where did you hear that?'

'Mum said that a very kind young man had walked you home and as you hadn't stomped out of bed like a bear with a sore head yet this morning, you must have a crush!'

'Ashleigh …' blustered Katherine, a slight blush tingeing her cheeks as she tried to deny it. Regan laughed, 'No Ashleigh, I do not have a boyfriend, and if I did it most certainly would not be Nate. He's the most annoying person I have ever met and he wouldn't be my boyfriend if he was the last man on earth.' *Besides*, she thought, *looking like that he probably has his pick of women and I highly doubt I'd be his type. Not that I'd want to be, obviously.*

'Don't say it Mum,' she warned, knowing her mum was itching to say "I think she doth protest too much." 'Anyway hadn't you two better be going or Ashleigh will be late to school? I'll take this through to Aunty Vi,' she said, picking up the plate of toast her mum had left on the side.

Aunty Vi was having a good day so Regan left the tray for her to feed herself while she tidied up a little. The bedroom smelled stale with lavender overtones. It was cluttered with knick-knacks and floral patterns and gave Regan a headache. As she dusted, a collection of photos on the dressing table caught her eye. She went over for a closer look.

Most of them were either black and white or sepia prints, and showed formal groups of prim, miserable looking people. One stood out though — two young girls sitting together on a lawn. The older one was making a daisy chain, the younger one wearing another ring of flowers in her hair. At first glance both girls looked happy, as if they hadn't a care in the world. Drawn to the picture, Regan picked it up and looked closer. The younger girl, the one with flowers in her hair, did indeed look happy. Her smile reached from ear to ear and her eyes sparkled.

They bore such a strong resemblance to each other, there could be no doubt they were sisters. But the older girl was sad. Even though her mouth was stretched into a smile, her eyes held none of the younger one's sparkle. They were drained, tired looking. And wary, as if the camera had managed to catch the girl mid-way between looking at her sister and looking around. Regan couldn't stop staring at her.

'Aunty Vi, who's in this picture?' she asked, taking the photo across the room. The old lady put down her toast and held out her hand.

'Let me have a look Katherine my dear,' she said. Regan had given up on correcting her. Twisting the photo in her gnarled hands so that the light from the table lamp lit it up, she peered at it.

'Why Katherine, you know who it is — it's me and Lizzy.' Regan was shocked to see her aunt's eyes fill up with tears; she tried to take the picture back, but Aunty Vi held onto it with surprising strength.

'Poor Lizzy, my poor lamb,' she said as her hands trembled. Regan placed her hand over her aunt's and then gently eased the photo out of it. Today was a good day so far; she wasn't going to be the one who upset her.

'I'm sorry Aunty Vi.' She passed her aunt the next slice of toast, hoping — this once — that the disease that was stealing the poor lady's mind would take away the pain the picture had caused.

Sixteen
1645

Lora agreed with Rafe wholeheartedly; it was unladylike for a lady to fight. If it became known, she would become a pariah; her family would disown her. But it felt so *right*. For over a week, her whole body had been buzzing. She felt alive, purposeful — as though there was a reason for everything, a reason for *being*. This made no sense to her, even though she spent every available second thinking about it.

Her mother and father had lost patience with her several times in the last week; James had left in a fury after an evening during which she had barely listened to a word he had said. His conversation was never particularly inspiring; over the course of their courtship she had endured some mind-numbing conversations with him. Though, as she'd told Mary, *conversation* was not really the right word. The time she spent in his company consisted mainly of his monologues, with the occasional fawning interjection from her. The engagement was an arranged one; James was a banker with good prospects and would ensure that Lora had a comfortable future. While her father was in a stable situation financially, he could not afford to look after a spinster daughter forever. So she was betrothed, and the wedding was to take place in eleven months when she was eighteen. The way

Lora saw it, she had a year left to live. Thankfully he had left for Cambridgeshire earlier in the week, to join Oliver Cromwell as he gathered men to fight with parliament against the crown. Her father and uncles were to join with the Eastern Association soon also; Lora relished the idea of the freedom this would give her.

But now ... now she had a more important purpose, a meaning. She just had to convince Master Hunter; today, she fully intended to change his mind on the matter. As soon as her mother left the house, Lora tucked the knife she had stolen from the kitchen safely into the top of her underclothes and slipped away.

Less than half an hour later she was out on the fen where she had first encountered Rafe. It was her best chance of finding him; she had no idea where else to start looking. She pulled her shawl tightly around her and ventured onto the path that wound through the boggy fenland. The marshy ground filled her nose with its pungent, earthy scent. Even this late in the year she could hear insects all around, buzzing, rubbing, clicking, humming.

The day was grey and dull but Lora found her way easily enough. An instinct that seemed somehow sharper than two weeks ago kept her away from the mud that was quick to swallow unwary travellers. The same instinct helped her decide which way to go when the path forked in two directions. As she made her way along the left divide, mist started to gather into a thick shroud. Her heartbeat faster and her hand reached for the knife she had tucked away. It felt comfortable in her hand and she quickened her pace,movingwith the speed and silence of a cat. The mist continued to thicken into a fog and a frisson of excitement shivered through Lora's body. Right or wrong, with or without Rafe, she was supposed to be here.

The smell of the bog was suddenly overpowered by a putrid, rotting stench that Lora had smelt only once before. Fear trickled cold down her spine and then anticipation took over her senses; her sight seemed clearer, her hearing sharper, her reflexes quicker. She raised the knife in her hand and let her eyes search through the fog.

Her ears alerted her to the demon on her right first.She swung round with confidence, making a slash through the matted fur of the creature behind her. An otherworldly shriek filled the air but she didn't let it stop her. She lashed out again, and then for a third time. Energy rushed through Lora's body as she twisted and turned.

She sensed Rafe was there before she saw him; without a word they fought side by side. Lora recalled the moves Rafe had used before and mimicked them to the best of her ability. Within minutes, Rafe delivered the fatal blow to the creature and its death wail filled the air. It fell and shrivelled. Immediately the vile smell started to fade and the fog began to lift.

Lora stood still and tried to catch her breath. Her heart was pounding but she had never felt better in her life. Rafe looked at her and she thought she caught a glimpse of admiration in his eyes. After a moment he said, 'We will have to find you some better attire to fight in.'

Seventeen
2013

As rain tapped out a regular pattern on the window behind her, Regan did her best to surf the net. Sitting on her bed in an oasis of cushions, she sighed for the gazillionth time as the typically British weather interfered with her web connection.

Malleus Maleficarum/Witch Hunter's Bible, she scribbled down, adding it to the bunch of scrawled, half-written words that she hoped would still make sense when she read them back later.

Just as her online connection started to work again, she heard the muted tone of the front doorbell echoing up to her attic bedroom. Knowing there was no way Katherine was going to resist meeting Nate, she quelled the urge to race down the stairs to let him in and tidied her notes into a pile while she waited for her mum to call her. Within half a minute her mum had yelled up to her and, after making sure that the old rocking chair she'd found at the back of the room was free from junk, she slowly went downstairs. Hopefully she'd given her mum enough time to interrogate Nate. It was catching that perfect point between allowing Katherine to gather enough information to feel satisfied, and the moment she would start to embarrass either Nate or Regan. Actually, thinking about it, she didn't really care if her mum did embarrass Nate; it might take him down a peg or two.

By the time she'd got into the kitchen, her mum was heating up hot chocolate on the hob and Nate was settled very comfortably at the table. His leather jacket hung on the back of the chair and he was wearing his usual uniform of jeans and a plain t-shirt. Today's was marl grey and fitted him perfectly, the short cuffs defining his biceps. Not that Regan noticed. Much.

'Wow Regan, you look just like your Mom!' he said as she walked into the room.

'So I've been told,' said Regan, trying not to grit her teeth at the cosy domestic scene in front of her. 'Shall we go upstairs? It's where the stuff is you wanted to look at.'

'Sure,' said Nate, looking more at ease and less mysterious than she had ever seen him. They each grabbed a mug of hot chocolate from Katherine and Regan showed him back out to the hallway.

'Here, take some biscuits,' called her mum. Rolling her eyes, Regan pointed Nate to the stairs and went back to grab the plate. 'He's gorgeous, I want your door left open,' her mum hissed under her breath. Refusing to even try to respond to her mother's assumptions, Regan took the biscuits and left.

At the top of the small flight of stairs to her attic room, Regan kicked a big box over to hold the door open. When she saw Nate looking she muttered, 'Don't ask,' but could see by the smirk on his face that he got it.

'Your mom is lovely, Regan. You're lucky to have her.'

Nate pulled the rickety old rocking chair from the back of the attic to under the skylight and sat down, long legs stretched out in front of him to steady it. He seemed to feel pretty relaxed in her home, Regan noted with irritation.

'I know,' she sighed as she put down her drink and flopped onto her bed, 'okay Nate, where do we start?'

'Well, I wrote down last night everything that I know about Rafael and his story and as much as I know about the Hunters' stories, right up to me.' As he spoke, he wiggled a thick wodge of papers from his pocket and handed them to Regan. 'How about you start with this and I'll look at the diaries?' Regan agreed and grabbed the papers out of his hand, showing him the box which contained the journals. Settling back into her cushions, she lifted up the first page of Nate's beautiful script and began to read.

The words flowed from the page; the writing was descriptive, but not flowery. Nate's description of the fens was unlike anything Regan had read or could imagine. She shifted a little, uncomfortable that this man from an entirely different country knew more about the history of the place her own mum had grown up in than she did.

The rain beating down on the skylight overhead made it easy for her to imagine the cold, foggy night he had described when Rafael first met her supposed ancestor. The flat, colourful fields outside, with their endless sky, were a world away from the boggy, hungry salt marshes that Nate had described. Even given Nate's straightforward style, Regan found she could vividly conjure up the world that he was describing.

Pausing only to sip from her steaming mug she read about Rafael's training as a hunter, about the dark paths he wandered at night. About the fogs he feared as he knew they meant more than just a change in the weather. It read almost as if Nate was speaking from experience.

Then she read about his encounter with another female on the path — of how she, Mistress Smith, had stopped to help him fight. How her pluck and courage had in fact saved Rafael's life; how together they had fought the familiar and killed it.

She read, *"Rafael was placed in a position that he felt he had to share the secret of what they had fought with Mistress Smith. His journal tells us he tried to evade her, but she insisted on joining him. He taught her how to fight; he wrote that she soon mastered the art of knife fighting, that she was able to wield weapons with both hands and fight with cunning and agility. Unfortunately Rafael's journal was badly damaged and it is only the first half of it that remains."*

'Oh wow,' said Regan, rubbing eyes that were blurry from focusing so hard. 'Rafael sounds very interesting; it's a shame that you only have half of his story.'

Nate paused in his reading and looked at Regan, 'Yes, it is. He was the first of the Hunters we have any information about; all the others since have concentrated on writing about technique. About how to hunt, how to fight. How to seek out familiars — and obviously, in the early days, witches. It's useful, but Rafael had a way of helping you understand it all better.'

Regan nodded and returned to Nate's account. From what he'd written, she understood that the unnaturally thick fog she had seen on the fields was exactly that — unnatural. It was something to do with the familiars, how they'd evolved. They created the mist to help with their hunting. By shrouding their hunting ground, they were able to confuse their prey — and hide — until they pounced.

She shuddered at the thought. Stretching out her cramped legs she said, 'Why do these creatures want us? If all the witches are gone, why do they still carry on?'

Nate looked up. 'We're not entirely sure, to be honest. I think, like any animal, they have a survival instinct. In the days when they were still controlled by their mistresses, they killed to drink blood for themselves but also to help the witches find what they desired.' Shifting in the hard rocking chair, he carried on, 'These diaries are fascinating; I would really like to work out a way to read this older one. Do you mind if we try and make it more legible?'

'How would you do that?' asked Regan uneasily — after all, it wasn't really her diary to fiddle about with.

'I'm not sure, to be honest. I think I might try to copy it, if you don't mind,' he glanced up at Regan, 'it's really old and stuff like this deteriorates quickly; it ought to be preserved properly, really.'

'I hadn't thought about that,' said Regan, shuffling the information about Rafael into a neater pile, 'you don't think we should donate it to a museum or something, do you? It is really old, and doesn't really old stuff belong to Queen and country?'

Nate raised his eyebrow at her, 'Well, being a citizen of the good old US of A, I wouldn't know about that — maybe try to get any information out of it ourselves and then report it to your National Heritage people?'

'I suppose,' said Regan. 'I mean if I hadn't decided to unpack this box then it would still just be laying in there.' She tucked a strand of hair behind her ear. 'Okay, let's get it copied and then I'll pack it back away, it's survived this long.... Even a copy is going to be hard to read, isn't it?'

'I was thinking I'll maybe scan it onto my computer and fiddle around with contrast — I should be able to make some of it out. As long as you don't mind, of course?' She nodded; there could be no harm in that as far as she could see.

'Okay, I'll bring a magnifying glass back with me tomorrow, if that's okay?'

'Cool,' said Regan. 'So, are we going to do some training now?'

Nate looked puzzled for just a second, and then realisation drew his face into a smile. 'Oh no Regan, there is no way you are coming out fighting with me!'

'Excuse me?' said Regan, her eyebrows arching in disbelief, 'I'm the companion hunter, you told me so yourself. It's my destiny to fight!' Inwardly she cringed — could that sound any cheesier?

'You may well be, but there is no way you are going to fight. There has been no need of a companion hunter for several decades. I've fought alone since I was 16 and for two years before that I helped my dad. I don't need your help.'

'Fine,' said Regan, 'have it your way.' She kept her face blank, but inside she fumed. What an arrogant, selfish son-of-a-bitch. Well, she'd show him — she'd proven last night that she was capable of fighting the same as he was. Well, capable of the same moves at least. She could handle a knife; if you'd said that to her two days ago she wouldn't have believed it, but she'd proven it to herself.

'Okay Nate,' she said, her voice as sweet as honey, her jaw working overtime to keep her teeth from clenching, 'I'm afraid you'll have to leave now. I have stuff to do.'

'Of course! I'm sorry, I didn't mean to hold you up, but these are fascinating.' He held up the oldest volume, 'Is it okay if I take this one? I'll bring it back tomorrow, and some printed copies for you?'

Regan bit her lip. She wanted to tell him where to go, but she also wanted to find out what was in the journals and it would take her forever by herself.

'Fine,' she said, 'I'll see you then.'

'I'll see you tonight after work,' reminded Nate, 'you'll need a lift home.'

'Fine,' Regan repeated, getting up and showing him the door.

Eighteen

As soon as Nate had left the room, Regan rummaged through her chest of drawers and fished out her old gym clothes. After slipping on a tracksuit and sleeveless t-shirt, she pulled a pair of trainers onto her feet and made her way out of her bedroom. If Nate wasn't going to help her be a hunter's companion, she would have to do it herself. First, though, she was going to have to get her fitness levels back up to scratch.

After doing a few quick stretches to warm up, Regan jogged down the stairs, groaning at the sight of her mum attacking imaginary cobwebs with a huge feather duster right at the bottom of the staircase. She knew they were imaginary as she'd dusted the very same spot yesterday, after she'd spotted a big black spider scuttling across the floor and a huge fresh web strung across the ceiling from the coving to the light rose.

'I'm just going out for a run, Mum,' she said and made for the back door, trying to escape without interrogation. She was unsuccessful.

'Nate's a lovely boy, isn't he Regan?'

'He's hardly a boy Mum, he's twenty-one!' Katherine ignored her.

'But he's very handsome, and chivalrous. Look how kind he is to see you home every night. I wouldn't be surprised if he has a crush on you, you know — between him and Sam you're becoming quite the popular young lady!'

'He doesn't have a crush on me, Mum, it's just the way he's been brought up. And Sam fancies any female over the age of sixteen with a pulse as far as I can work out.' It was really hard not to roll her eyes heavenwards.

'Well, I think he's lovely, and I think it would do you good to ask him out, you know. Maybe go out for a nice meal or to the pictures or something.' Her mum tucked a stray strand of hair behind Regan's ear and smiled enthusiastically. Trying not to dampen her mum's spirits too much, but wanting to set her straight, Regan said, 'I'm not going to ask him out Mum, we're just friends.'

'Whatever you say, dear,' Katherine replied, finally letting her daughter go.

The rain that had been pouring down since early that morning had finally taken a break; this had not, in any way, eased the endless gloom or the dark grey sky. It hadn't done the roads much good either, Regan discovered as she started to run. Her stubborn pride, however, wasn't letting her turn back; it may be thick with mud and covered in puddles the size of ponds out here, but if she wanted to prove that she was just as capable as Nate of defending this area she knew she needed to get fit. So, running it was.

It took a while but slowly Regan got into a cadence, her feet pounding through puddles, her breathing regulated, her arms moving rhythmically by her side. She emptied out her head and refused to think of Nate. She jogged to the village and out the other side, her head turning involuntarily to look at the turn-off which led to his place. Out here the road was even muddier and full of water-filled potholes; Regan found she had to watch her feet to avoid twisting her ankle in one. Allowing her lungs to fill up with air fully each time she breathed — in, out — her feet pounded — one, two.

When the road smoothed out a bit, she looked up again and noticed the leaden sky darkening even further. Not wanting to get caught in a downpour, she decided to cut across the fields. Aiming in the general direction of her house, she leapt across a ditch and ran along the edge of a field filled with the bright yellow oilseed rape so common in this area. A gate closed this field off from the next, and as she climbed over the wet metal bars the thought that this could possibly be her worst idea to date entered her head.

Rust from the gate and splashes of mud covered her white jogging bottoms; gasping for breath, she decided to walk the rest of the way. A huge wet dollop of rain fell on her, followed by the opening of the skies and a torrential downpour rivalling the one they had had that morning. With nowhere to hide in the open landscape, Regan looked around in despair. Through the gloom she could see a house in the distance and was relieved to find herself on a road — of sorts — again. Clods of clay earth stuck to her trainers and refused to let go no matter how hard she shook her foot. Regan's patience was fast evaporating; if it weren't for that bloody Nate, she wouldn't be in this situation.

The sound of an engine vibrated just above the pounding of the rain. Regan moved onto the verge, just avoiding a Windermere-sized puddle, and edged as close to the water-filled dyke as possible. Unfortunately the navy-blue Renault that sped past wasn't so careful and drove straight through the puddle. A tidal wave of water cascaded over an already dripping Regan. It took every ounce of strength she possessed not to start bawling. *Damn Nate Hunter, this was all his fault!*

A few seconds later the sound of another car approaching had Regan swearing softly under her breath. She climbed onto the verge again and balanced right on the edge of the ditch. At this point in time she almost didn't care if she went in or not — after all, she couldn't get any wetter. To her surprise the car passed her and slowed down, then stopped and reversed slowly back down the road. A splash of bright yellow in the unremitting grey, Regan didn't know whether to laugh or cry when she saw Toni's head sticking out the wound-down driver's window.

'You look like you need a lift!'

Regan held her arms out, letting Toni see just quite how sodden she was. 'There's no way I'm getting in your car like this, I'll ruin it!'

'You obviously haven't seen in my car — Sam calls it the e-coli mobile,' she flashed her trademark grin, 'come on, I'm not taking no for an answer. I'll wrestle you in if I have to!'

The idea of 5'2" Toni wrestling her own 5'8" frame into the car nearly made Regan laugh out loud.

'Come on, Regan,' said Toni, and Regan, fed up with the rain dripping down her neck, decided to take her up on her offer. Hell, if she made too much mess, she would just help clean the car out later.

Toni was not joking about the state of her car, Regan realised as she eased herself into the front seat. Magazines, take-away cartons, chocolate wrappers, empty drinks bottles, all littered the seat and passenger footwell.

'See, I told you,' said Toni. 'Just shove it in the back,' she grabbed a handful and chucked it over onto the backseat. Regan followed suit, feeling vaguely guilty about the extra mess she was making.

'Don't worry, I'll clean it out tomorrow,' said Toni, 'it's kind of a once-a-month thing so I'll do my June clear-out now!' She pulled away from the edge of the road and started chatting incessantly.

'It was a good job I recognised you, I nearly didn't in all that rain — and I don't think I've ever seen you so casual. Ella couldn't have recognised you or she would have stopped, she was just ahead of me.'

Regan remembered the blue car that splashed her. *Yeah, I'll bet she didn't know who it was.*

'We've just been to the college looking at courses, but Ella had to go get changed for work.'

'Oh, what ones are you looking at?' Regan asked, remembering her own plans to look into the beauty course. She leaned forward and rifled through the pile of Toni's CD's sliding in an untidy heap at her feet. Most of them were downloads recorded onto blank discs; a surprisingly elegant script flowed across them naming the artist.

'Cyndi Lauper, Debbie Gibson, Madonna, Taylor Dane …?' She held one up to Toni, a mock questioning look on her face.

Toni laughed as she pulled the indicator stalk down and turned left. 'Aahh, yes, I have a confession — I have two requirements from my music, it's either 80's or cheesy. Preferably both. If you rummage long enough, you'll find an Angry Anderson download in there somewhere!'

'Angry who?' asked Regan, her face breaking into a smile despite her uncomfortably sodden clothes.

'Anderson. You know, "Suddenly"? The song that played at Scott and Charlene's wedding?'

'I literally have no idea what you're talking about.'

'Neighbours … never mind, it was well before our time. Unfortunately as well as a short stature and a snub nose, I also inherited my lame taste from Mum. She makes me watch old recordings!' She glanced at Regan, 'No, don't pity me, I actually enjoy it. I'm doomed!'

Regan couldn't help it, she laughed. She couldn't imagine a dull moment around Toni. It must be nice to be so cheerful all the time.

'Anyway I was looking into an art course, and there are still places for that, but the beauty course Ella wanted to do is fully booked. She's well peeved about it!'

'Oh, really? Damn, I was hoping to enrol in that too. Mum is going to be so annoyed — she did tell me I needed to look into applying earlier but it kind of …'

'Ended up at the bottom of a long list?' suggested Toni. Regan nodded. 'Yeah, I know that problem! I've got a brochure at home if you want to take it and see if there's anything else you fancy.' Without waiting for an answer she pulled the car up, did a U-turn and followed the road back the way they'd come. Regan already knew better than to argue.

Soon the fields and grey edges gave way to the small collection of houses at the far end of Old Scytheton. Regan had only been out this way once, the first night Nate had given her a lift back from his place. Toni turned onto a small side road and then into a nineties housing development. The red brick houses with their dark timber window frames weren't visible from the road and Regan had not seen this part of the village. Old Scytheton, she realised, was not as tiny as she had first thought. It made sense, really — the pub regulars all had to live somewhere.

Toni pulled into a drive behind a modern sporty mini. 'I can't stay long Toni, I've got to get ready for work soon.'

'Don't worry, why don't you get ready here? I'll ring your mum if you want?' Toni pulled the keys out of the ignition and climbed out of the car.

'I don't have any clothes — or any make-up!' Regan argued; she looked down at her drenched clothing and knew her make-up must be smeared across her face.

'Not a problem, I've got something that'll look perfect on you!'

Not quite sure how it happened, Regan found herself in Toni's bedroom rummaging through the wardrobe with a phone under her ear, explaining to her mum that she'd be fine getting to work, it was literally 'round the corner.

'Here it is,' said Toni, pulling a blue dress from a hanger and handing it to Regan.

'Oh my god Toni, I can't wear this. It's gorgeous!'

'Wear it — you can have it. The darn thing nearly reaches my ankles, it looks ridiculous! It was an impulse purchase — I know I should stick to the petite ranges, but I was seduced!' She continued poking around, 'I've got some perfect sandals in here somewhere that go fab with it.'

'Toni,' said Regan, 'if I wear it, you can't return it.' She handed the expanse of blue silk back.

'It's a bit late for that, I don't think they give refunds after six months have passed.'

'Six months! You could have changed it for one in your size!'

'Oh, Regan,' Toni shook her head, her eyes gleaming, 'you really don't know me very well, do you? Organised I'm not. But that works out very well for my friends. Just ask Ella, honestly, I'm sure at least a quarter of her wardrobe started off as mine!'

Regan finally grasped the dress as Toni thrust it back into her hands, along with a towel and a bag of cosmetics and creams. She pointed Regan in the direction of the bathroom, promising her the water was always hot, and went downstairs to make them both something to eat.

Regan clutched the stuff to her chest and padded across the landing to the bathroom. The door was shut but as she reached for the handle it pulled away from her, opening inwards. Regan shrieked and barely managed to hold on to the bundle of possessions in her hands. Standing in front of her, in only a towel, was Sam. His sun-bleached hair was glistening with water droplets and his lean torso had rivulets of water dripping down it.

'That's right, baby, you get a good look. Don't worry, I'm not shy.' Mischief glinted playfully in his eyes and Regan felt her pulse race and the colour rise in her face.

'I'm so sorry, Toni didn't tell me you'd be in there.'

'Don't be sorry babe, I never mind meeting gorgeous girls when I'm half naked!' Fire burned from Regan's face and for a moment she was lost for words. Then she remembered what a mess she looked. *Gorgeous*? Yeah, right. Pushing past him, she slammed the door shut behind her and made sure the bolt was shot into place.

Standing in the shower, using Toni's mandarin-scented shampoo, Regan tried to shake the image of Sam's naked body from her head. Somehow, she just couldn't rid herself of the picture. To make matters worse, as she scrubbed the runs of mascara from under her eyes, she realised she was comparing his long, lean body with Nate's scarred, toned one. Sometimes being seventeen and full of hormones could be a real pain in the arse.

Back in Toni's room Regan slipped on the sheath of silk that constituted the dress Toni had given her. She looked in the mirror and gasped; even without make-up on she liked the look, and it matched —

almost exactly — the colour of her eyes. Thin spaghetti straps crossed lightly over her shoulders and the top was fitted, following the contours of her body as if it had been designed especially for her. The skirt just skimmed her knees, falling in soft folds from her waist and somehow, combined with the sandals, making her legs look longer.

'Oh wow Regan, I knew that this was the dress for you! It makes me glad I didn't get to take it back!'

'Thanks Toni, it's lovely. Do you think it's a bit dressy for the pub, though?'

'Oh, who cares? It'll give the place something to chat about!'

Not entirely sure she wanted to be the focal point for the village gossips, Regan still somehow let herself be persuaded to keep the dress on. She convinced herself it was because she had nothing else dry to wear and didn't really want to ask Toni for a lift home. Besides, at least it would show Sam that she could scrub up, thank you very much!

As if reading her mind Toni passed over a sandwich and said, 'You've made Sam's night I'm afraid. That boy is such a diva; he thinks the world revolves around him. I'm afraid the fact that you and him rendezvoused in the bathroom with him undressed is going to be a point of gossip with his friends' tonight anyway!'

'It was hardly a rendezvous! I didn't know he was in there; we just passed in the doorway.' Regan blushed at the sudden thought of entering the bathroom a few minutes earlier and truly catching him naked. She choked on her sandwich.

'Careful,' said Toni. 'Don't worry, I gave him an earful ... unfortunately knowing Sam it went in one ear and out the other.' She shrugged, 'Never mind, it'll be forgotten by tomorrow.'

Regan wasn't entirely convinced.

* * *

Climbing out of the car, Regan waved good-bye to Toni and walked through the doors of The Hunter's Rest to a low wolf whistle from Nick.

'Too dressy?' she asked, somewhat embarrassed that she'd kept the beautiful dress on. It was too gorgeous to waste on a wet journey home, though. They'd decided to go all out and Toni had helped her twist her hair into a chignon and lent her a simple silver chain for round her neck. It may have been only Saturday night in the local — and she was technically working — but that didn't mean she wasn't allowed to get herself dressed up. Or so she'd managed to convince herself. Sam's reaction when she had made her way downstairs had almost been worth the effort. The loudmouth was for once silent, with only a sincere 'You look amazing' passing his lips. Toni swore she had never seen him so dumbfounded. It certainly made up for the smeared make-up and drenched jogging suit.

'You look cracking love, just what this miserable old pub needs!'

'Thanks Nick,' Regan put her bag away and started getting the glasses out of the dishwasher ready for the evening clientele, most of whom had been chucked out a couple of hours previously while Mavis whizzed round the place with a duster and vacuum.

As was usual every Saturday night, the place rapidly filled up with groups of people from the surrounding villages. Mostly men, young and old, but a few women graced the place in small groups. Regan knew most of the punters who came in pretty well now. She genuinely enjoyed her job and found the regulars a pretty amusing bunch. Far from the simple 'locals' she'd labelled them as when she first moved here, they were a nice group who had managed to make Regan feel welcome.

'Dressed up for anyone nice?' asked old Howie, from his usual spot at the bar. 'I've seen you talking to that American a few times, he's not a bad looking chap.'

'Howie! I just felt like a change,' said Regan, managing to blush a little at the thought of getting dressed up for Nate. She moved to the side bar to serve the queue waiting there and her blush deepened at the sight of Nate. Standing just the other side of the post to Howie's seat, he *must* have heard his comments.

'The usual?' she asked, still peeved with him. It was totally his fault she'd got so soaked earlier.

'Thanks Regan. You do look absolutely beautiful, by the way,' he said as she turned to get him a pint of ice-cold cola. She knew now why he never drank alcohol; if he needed to fight it was obviously best not to be inebriated at the time.

'Thank you,' she said, knowing she was crimson by now. Once he'd sat himself at his usual table, though, a warm glow settled in the pit of her stomach. She ignored the feeling. It had nothing to do with who'd paid her the compliment, she told herself — her ego just liked to be stroked from time to time.

* * *

As usual, the evening passed quickly. Nate had left a couple of hours earlier, but Regan knew he'd be waiting for her when her shift finished. Like clockwork, he was sitting on the bike outside The Hunter's Rest by the time she walked out the door.

The wet, miserable day had turned into a foggy, miserable night. A frisson of excitement ran down Regan's spine. Tonight was the night. It was foggy, the creatures were about. Tonight she would start the fight that destiny had decided was hers. Hitching her dress up, she climbed on the back of Nate's bike and wrapped her arms around him. Despite the coat she'd slung on, her outfit wasn't really the best choice for either the weather or the bike ride. Pressing her head into his leather jacket, she could feel the adrenaline already coursing through her veins.

They pulled up outside Regan's turning, hopped off the bike and walked the short distance to her front door. Regan asked, 'So are you going out hunting tonight, then? I mean, this isn't a natural fog, is it? It's created by *them*?'

He looked at her sharply, 'I am going out tonight. Alone.' Regan shrugged, 'I couldn't do a lot dressed like this, could I?' She waved her fingers in a goodbye and let herself in through the front door.

Nineteen
1645

A rotten stench filled the air. The smell, familiar to Lora from her hunting jaunts, was more potent than she had ever encountered it. Reminiscent of rotting vegetables and curdled milk, the odour wafted across the barren yard and made Lora wrinkle up her nose. Crouched low behind a crumbling wall, she shifted her weight as her legs cramped and the needle-sharp spines of the holly bush to her left caught and scratched her bare arms. She didn't need the warning glares that Rafe was sending her from where he was wedged under the offending bush to know to keep quiet. She knew that the scratches, though painful, were a small price to pay to catch a glimpse of the witch — the mistress of the creatures that haunted the fens and waterways.

A shadow moved across a dimly lit room at the back of the house they were observing. Silhouetted in the window was the form of a young woman, flickering and jumping as the candle guttered behind her. Lora watched silently as the occupant moved around the room gathering things from jars and baskets. Even straining her eyes, Lora couldn't see what was being collected.

As she crouched waiting, an icy cape of cold night air gathered around her and each breath misted out in front of her. She rubbed her hands together for warmth, her gaze straying to the smoke that spiralled from the chimney of the cottage, beckoning her with warm fingers.

A low hiss from Rafe concentrated her attention again, and she watched as the raven-haired occupant of the house stood, head bowed, in front of the window. The moon appeared from behind the clouds and Lora saw the woman staring with fixed concentration at what she was doing. Peering across the yard, she wished could get closer and see the menace she was dealing with more clearly.

Wishes sometimes have a disconcerting way of coming true. As she watched, the woman in the house slowly lifted her head and with emerald eyes surveyed the area outside. Lora found she was unable to stop watching; the beauty of the woman was compelling. Moonlight glinted off perfectly coifed black hair, elegant cheekbones that could have been sculpted from ivory, and lips stained as red as the juice from summer cherries. Never had she seen anyone more beautiful. Entranced, she stared and goose bumps covered her body that were nothing to do with the cold. Disappointment washed over her as the face turned away and the woman disappeared. Seconds later she returned, this time silhouetted in the doorway. Lora watched as the lady took one step onto the stone path. Her bosom heaved above a scarlet dress; her stays pulled so tight that Lora felt sure she could encompass the tiny waist with even her small hands.

Then time stopped. The woman turned her head and, though Lora knew she could not possibly be seen where she was hidden, seemed to look right at her. Lora froze, but her heart pounded and a thrill ran through the core of her. With unnerving slowness, the woman curved her lips up into a smile that spread to a grin and then into peals of laughter. The sound was like honeyed water. Then it stopped. The woman winked and turned back into her house. Dread lay in Lora's belly like lead.

Twenty
2013

Which is exactly why I am going to get changed first, Regan thought as she murmured a low goodnight through her mum's bedroom door. Slipping on a pair of loose khaki trousers and a fleecy, fitted long-sleeved top, she shoved her feet into her spare trainers.

She walked quickly but silently downstairs, remembering just in time to avoid the creaky step third from the bottom. Regan knew there was no way she could go out to fight without some sort of weapon. Not having the hunting knives that Nate did, she raided the kitchen. At first, she pulled out the long carving knife from the knife rack on the side, but she couldn't decide how to wear it. Unsheathed, even tucked into her belt, it was dangerous to herself. Frustrated, she opened the drawer with Aunty Vi's silverware in it and, rummaging around, was about to give up when her hand fell on a leather pouch at the back. Pulling it out she saw a short wooden handle protruding from it and, wrapping her hand around it, she pulled out a knife. The blade was about 5 inches and came to a sharp point. The wooden handle, as long as the blade, nestled in her hand perfectly.

Believing that fate obviously intended her to go out tonight, Regan tied the leather pouch around her waist, making sure she could draw the knife free when she needed to. Grabbing a powerful torch and ensuring her phone was safely in her pocket, Regan snuck out the back door.

Now she was out here, she wasn't exactly sure where to go. But she was damned sure she wasn't letting Nate do this on his own; she wasn't a hunter's companion for nothing.

After a second of thinking she decided to make her way back towards Little Scytheton, where she had encountered the familiars before. Using the torch to penetrate the fog as much as possible she headed back down the lane where, less than fifteen minutes ago, Nate had dropped her off. She'd not gone very far when the icy dampness of the fog managed to penetrate through to her skin; despite her fleecy top, she shivered. A quiver of fear entered her heart that she was just stubborn enough to ignore.

The road was still muddy from the day's downpour and it was really hard going in the opaque grey. She strained her eyes, trying to see beyond the swirling mists, searching for any sign that she wasn't alone out here. Nervous tension was building up inside her and the eerie silence was somehow more deafening than any noise she'd encountered. The purplish light from the LED bulb in her torch bounced back at her, its beam just revealing more endless grey.

Her ears strained, trying to catch any sound in the incessant silence, but apart from the beating of her own heart and the panting of her own breath, she could hear nothing. Refusing to admit to herself that this was one stupidly dangerous idea she carried on, each step taking her further and further into the blanket of fog. As she rubbed her hand across her eyes to try and relieve some of the strain, her ears suddenly caught a distant sound. She paused, listening. A second later and it came again; a low, phlegmy rasp.

Moving stealthily in the direction of the noise, she reached around and felt the worn wooden handle of her knife in the palm of her hand. She flicked off her torch and hooked it on her belt, waiting while her eyes adjusted to the darkness. More alert than she had ever been, she crept along. A whiff of stench wafted under her nose and Regan was reminded of the stink from the pile of clothes she'd worn last time she'd encountered the creature. It was the day Aunty Vi had gotten so upset with her … something was trying to connect in Regan's head, but she pushed it aside for another time; right now, she was here to fight.

A grating sound came from her left and she turned, the outline of *it* suddenly visible through the grey. Adrenaline surged through her body, eradicating her fear. It felt as though she was superhuman — her vision was clearer, her hearing more acute. Drawing her knife she watched the shadowy shape, never taking her eyes from it. Bouncing a little, she let her knees flex, somehow remembering that which she could not have known.

The creature moved forward with unnatural speed until it was alongside Regan. It swiped out a limb, needle-like claws extended. Pulling her blade free she swung it up, silently taking aim at the thing. The creature leapt back and Regan's blade sliced through nothing but air. Turning, she had the knife up again in an instant, this time making slight contact with the creature's flesh.

An unearthly scream echoed across the fields, its pitch so high it hurt Regan's ears. Taking advantage of her momentary distraction, *it* had time to swipe at Regan again, this time catching the long sleeve of her top and shredding it like silk under a knife.

For the first time, Regan felt properly afraid; it was as if her brain had finally cottoned on to the fact that she could end up hurt — or worse — tonight. Grabbing her fear with both hands, she ducked as the familiar's claws came at her again, then turned, jabbing her knife upwards and stabbing into her prey. She was ready for its shriek this time and used the pause to regain her balance and move away from the creature. Switching the blade between her hands, she got herself into a comfortable stance and jabbed with her right hand, changed hands again and stabbed with her left.

A vile smell filled the air and Regan couldn't stop herself from gagging. She was unprepared as the creature lunged forward, its claws just skimming her head, managing to do no more damage than pulling her chignon out. Off balance, she stumbled backwards in the mud. Her heart raced as she tried both to regain her balance and to get a better grip on her knife so she could attack again. Steadying herself, she was able to jab forward once but was stopped by a sideswipe from the creature. With her fingertips only, she managed to keep hold of her weapon.

Her mind raced, trying to decide the best strategy. Her body moved backwards, the creature's swinging claws an arsenal of weapons swiping continually in front of her face. She swung her knife forward again, her left foot stepping backwards, and stumbled as the ground seemed to disappear from under her. Righting herself, she realised that she was on the edge of a ditch with nowhere to turn. The ditch could be a small jumpable one, or one of the many deep, water filled ones that lined these fields. She turned to face her foe, panic hovering somewhere around her larynx, ready to take hold if she let it. The creature's attack was relentless. She kept swiping the knife in front of her but its long, loose limbs fought wildly back at her.

Unable to retreat she kept blindly stabbing forward, each piercing scream telling her she was managing to do some damage. Damage or not, the creature returned every swipe and Regan started to give in to her rising panic. She realised that she wasn't going to be able to do this. Stubbornness insisted she kept fighting, but she was about to let go of hope when the distant sound of an engine filled the air. Knowing it was Nate she screamed his name, hoping he could hear her above the engine.

'Nate,' she shrieked again, a new vigour filling her body. As she stabbed forward this time she also moved forward, forcing *it* to back up. She copied herself and did the same again. Striking out, she was aware of Nate's bike swinging up onto the field, its light breaking through the grey and illuminating the creature enough for Regan to recognise its stoat-like appearance, and also see the black, sticky blood-like substance oozing from the cuts she had given it.

The bike and its rider were soon beside her and, jumping off as soon as he had stopped, Nate pulled out his knife and started to fight with her. All fear drained out of her body and she matched Nate's rhythm. He swung low, she swung high. He stabbed left, she dug right. A strange sense of relaxation came over her and it was almost with a sense of enjoyment that Regan continued to fight.

They battled without a sound together for at least ten minutes, wordlessly predicting each other's moves. Their skills combined proved no match for the creature and, with one last ear-piercing scream, it fell, withering away to nothing.

'Get on,' said Nate, picking up his bike where it had fallen and straddling the seat. Without question she obeyed and he started the engine and sped across the fields, the way becoming clearer by the second as the fog evaporated. Regan's arms stung like crazy where she had been swiped by the creature's claws, but she knew she couldn't complain; even with her stubborn streak, she would have to admit that had Nate not turned up she would be dead. And she could tell by the tension in Nate's body that he wasn't going to let her foolishness lie.

'I knew you were silly, but I didn't know you were a complete idiot,' he began as soon as they got off the bike. 'Why would you do something so foolish? How would your mom and sister feel when they got up in the morning and you weren't there?'

Regan shrugged, not knowing how to reply; tears burned at the corners of her eyes, threatening to spill over at any second.

'How can you be so nonchalant?' he asked, 'This is not a game, Regan. This is life and death!'

Swallowing the tears down, Regan took a breath and said, 'I know, I'm so sorry, I wasn't thinking. I'm an idiot.' She looked up at Nate, 'It felt so different when you were there fighting with me — it gelled. It worked,' she paused, 'or did I imagine it?'

Nate tensed and she thought for a second he was going to refuse to reply. Then he sighed. 'No, you didn't imagine it. I've not managed to fight like that for years, not since I've been fighting alone. That doesn't mean you were right to go out by yourself. It was really the most foolish thing I've ever seen anyone do.'

'I know,' said Regan, 'Thank you.' She turned to make her way back to the house.

'You'll need your arms seeing too,' said Nate; he turned to the storage box on his bike and pulled out a first aid kit. Gingerly Regan pulled back her sleeves and watched as Nate soaked a swab in disinfectant. He wiped it carefully over Regan's scratches. It stung like hell but Regan refused to utter one sound. Closing her eyes tightly, she squeezed back the tears the pain had brought on.

'You're brave, I'll give you that,' said Nate, 'I know how much those scratches hurt.' Putting the bottle away and bagging the swab for rubbish he peeled back his own sleeve, revealing the scars she had noticed before. 'Don't worry, I got caught particularly badly the first time I decided to go out alone. If my father wasn't so relieved to see me alive, I think I would have had matching scars on my ass from a beating. I guess he thought I'd learnt my lesson.' Regan nodded understanding.

'I'll pick you up tomorrow before work and we'll practise some moves together, okay?' With that he turned and pushed his bike away. Letting herself back in the kitchen door she raised her hand briefly, knowing Nate would not go until she was safely in.

Twenty-One

The rain had completely disappeared by the next day and Regan was glad when Nate came to pick her up. She'd chosen a light but long-sleeved summer blouse to wear with her favourite floral skirt, hoping that by covering her arms she would avoid explaining her wounds to her mum. Unfortunately, as it was nearly 25 degrees C, her mum had spent most of the morning asking her if she felt all right, was she coming down with something? 'It's not like you, Regan, to be wearing sleeves in this heat! Are you sure you feel okay?'

'I'm fine mum, stop fussing. I told you, I caught too much sun the other day and don't want to make it worse.'

'Hmm, I'd find that more believable if I hadn't been there the year you and Ems basted yourselves in baby oil and sat out for hours in the burning sun!' replied Katherine.

'Mum! I was thirteen years old, I'd like to think I've managed to grow up a little since then.'

Sighing in the way that only a parent could, Katherine pointed to Nate walking up the path, 'Nate's here, Regan. Why doesn't he bring his car up the driveway?' Regan swallowed; while her mum was more than happy for Nate to escort her home each night, she wasn't entirely sure she'd be so happy if she knew it was a motorbike and not a car they were riding around on. Feeling guilty at her lie of omission she shrugged, kissed her mum goodbye and skipped out the front door.

'Let's go,' she ordered Nate; he waved a greeting to Katherine and then to Ashleigh, who was watching from the swing in the garden, before following Regan.

As they made their way to where Nate had parked the bike about a quarter of a mile down the road, Regan stripped off her shirt, revealing a plain white vest underneath; the relief she felt was instant. Nate smiled, 'Didn't feel up to explaining the scratches to your mom, huh?'

'Not exactly,' Regan said, grinning back, 'I find at times that what she doesn't know can't hurt her.'

Nate's smile widened as he handed her a helmet. Wrapping her arms around him Regan leaned into his broad back, enjoying the cool breeze as it blew soothingly over her stinging arms.

At Nate's she slipped into a pair of shorts and followed him round to his workout area. Today, in the bright sun, Regan was flabbergasted by the amazing view he had. The endless sky was azure blue, a colour more beautiful Regan didn't think she'd seen before. The oilseed rape growing in the fields was bright yellow, the sickly-sweet scent of it wafting over from time to time on small puffs of breeze. The river she'd noticed before shone and sparkled in the distance and a bright green tractor chugged up and down a few acres away.

'Oh wow,' said Regan, 'If I could paint I would be out here capturing every inch of this scene! I've never seen anything so beautiful in my life!'

'I know,' said Nate, 'it takes your breath away, doesn't it? I've seen several countries, and several parts of this country, but this is still one of my favourite views ever.' Regan nodded.

'I mean, it may not have the grandeur of the mountains, or the Grand Canyon or something, but it is absolutely beautiful in its own peaceful way.'

'I agree; I suddenly understand why mum loves it so much here.'

'Enough procrastinating, let's get on with our workout. To be honest I don't think there's too much I can show you but practice makes perfect, right? So let's just work out together and if I see anything I need to help you with I'll let you know. Okay, follow me.'

Within seconds Regan had found her rhythm and was able to match Nate's pace and style perfectly. She felt she could almost close her eyes and do it. With only a couple of minor corrections to her stance from time to time, the pair worked out for half an hour, till they were both pouring with sweat and gasping for a drink.

While she towelled herself down, Nate grabbed some fresh bottles of water from the fridge; its icy sweetness was like the nectar of the Gods to her parched throat. Flinging her towel onto a pile of washing, she followed Nate down the garden to a huge old oak tree. The branches made a vast area of shade in the otherwise blazingly hot back garden, and they both lay down thankfully in the grass. As the gentle breeze cooled their burning skin, Nate started to tell Regan all he knew about the familiars.

'As I said before, these ones are originated from stoats, and like stoats they like to hunt alone. Their method of killing is to entrance their prey, hypnotise it as such, by …' he paused, 'well, the only way I can describe it is as a sort of dance. Then when the victim is under their spell, they bite the back of the neck and, well, that's it really. The victim is dead. The familiars then drain all the blood out of the body and leave it somewhere to be eaten by wild animals.' Regan shuddered at the thought.

'They sound like vampires to me,' she said, 'biting and draining the blood!'

'I'm pretty sure it's where the vampire myth came from; these familiars were very active in Romania for a long time.'

'Urgh!' was all Regan could think to say.

'Of course other familiars fight in different ways; those evolved from dogs fight as a pack, those from rats work together to feed the head "rat".' Regan nodded, trying to process everything.

'So are there other hunters then?' she asked.

'There were. A few still fight — we all have our own 'breed' of familiars to fight and for some reason the only ones that have stayed really strong are these ones. I've chased them all over the world; I think I've killed them all and then another spate starts somewhere else. They seem particularly fond of the fens though.'

Lying back in the soft grass, Regan let herself think.

'Okay, you say you follow them all over the world, but how do you know where they're going to be? Is it some kind of instinct or something?'

Nate chuckled, 'I'd like to say so, but for me it's very easy. I just check internet weather sites.' Regan frowned, trying to figure out how that could help.

'Oh, I see,' she said after a while, 'if there have been unusually foggy conditions, right?'

'Exactly,' said Nate, 'you know Regan, you're not half as dumb as you look!' She threw her empty water bottle at him and laughed as it bounced off his forehead.

'Not a bad shot either, am I?' She rolled over and, careful to avoid her wounds, lay her head on her arms, the combination of the warm sun and her late night making her sleepy.

'Did you bring the diaries?' Nate asked before she could drop off.

'In my bag,' she replied, stifling a yawn and closing her eyes, 'I'll help you look through them in a minute.' She heard Nate fish out the volume he wanted and listened contentedly to the birds singing overhead. Slowly, slowly, she began to drift off to sleep.

* * *

She was awoken, after what seemed only seconds, by a cold cascade of water on her back.

'Aaagh!' she jumped up screaming and turned to see Nate smirking. 'Sorry, I couldn't resist,' he said, arching an eyebrow.

Glowering at him she said, 'I'll get you back one day!'

His grinned only widened and Regan couldn't stop herself smiling back at him. 'Do you need a shower before I drop you off at work?' he asked. A shower was just what she needed and seconds later she was enjoying the cool spray of the water. Dressing again she made sure her cut arms were covered by her long-sleeved blouse; the sting, she noticed, was already starting to ease a little.

'So did you find out anything more from the diaries?' she said once she'd found Nate in the garden again.

'A little,' he said, 'the older one was written by a Lora Smith and in it she mentions a Rafe Hunter. I suspect this Rafe may be our Rafael.'

Regan's eyes widened, 'No way!'

Nodding, Nate continued, 'The first passage — from what I can make of it — describes how they met and it pretty much concurs with Rafael's account. It's hard going though — not only is the writing faded, but it's hard to read and the terms are very old fashioned.'

'Look Nate, I know they're not strictly mine, but how about I leave Lora Smith's diary with you? You can read it when you have the time then. I'll carry on trying to understand Elizabeth's ...' she paused, something stirring in her memory. 'There's something I need to check out,' she said as she half captured a thought, 'I'll fill you in tomorrow.'

'Okay. Now if you're going to get to work on time we'd better get going.'

'Yes, sir,' she saluted, 'anything you say sir!'

Nate dropped her off at the front of The Hunter's Rest and sped off on his bike; she knew he'd be back later though. The pub was as busy as ever that night and Regan didn't have time to tug at the nagging thought that kept evading her. The sunny day had made everyone extra cheerful and chatty, and by the time she left off she was almost hoarse from talking. And she'd agreed to work Monday evening as well.

'Please, Regan,' Nick said, 'I know it's short notice and I'd definitely owe you one, but you would really be helping me out.'

'Okay Nick, but I wouldn't do it for just anyone!' She mentally reconfigured her plans; she may have to cancel the nightclubbing, but she was still going to go shopping — she needed new clothes and had been looking forward to some proper girly time with the girls.

'Did you find anything else out?' she asked Nate as she stepped out into a beautiful clear night.

'A little. Shall we walk for a bit and I'll tell you?'

'Sure,' said Regan; it was a perfect night for a walk.

'Well, from the bits I've managed to read, Lora persuaded Rafe to let her fight with him. But she became more and more obsessed with finding the witch that was controlling the familiars.'

'And did she?' asked Regan.

'I don't know, the ink has faded so much even with adjusting the image I had to give up trying to read it for the time being.'

Regan gave a disappointed 'Oh.'

'Don't worry, I'll keep trying tomorrow,' Nate said. They walked home in a comfortable silence, Nate pushing his bike. Regan started to wonder how she had ever thought Nate annoying; she was really enjoying his company and found she couldn't wait until it was time to meet up with him again.

Twenty-Two
1645

A roar of laughter echoed down the table as Uncle Tom told a tale of a vicar and a serving wench. 'Thomas Hammond, I will not have you telling such tales at the table. If you do not fear the good Lord's punishment, that will be between you and He on judgement day, but I will not have such talk in front of my daughters.'

'My apologies, sister,' Tom replied, lifting his flagon; the ale-induced twinkle in his eye suggested he wasn't sorry in the least. Some of the guests laughed, others glared at the exchange. Aunt Marjorie's lips were pursed tight, a bible quotation barely suppressed.

Lifting the fork to her mouth, Lora tried to swallow a mouthful of eel pie. Usually her favourite, it choked in her throat and only a swallow of water helped it slide down. Sleep had evaded her all night and exhaustion racked her body. Every time she had closed her eyes a pale, beautifully carved face had slid into her mind. As she'd started to drift to sleep, a vision of full lips the colour of crushed berries caused her heart to beat a little faster. Eyes like clear green bottle glass had penetrated her thoughts. In that blissful plane between consciousness and sleep, she had felt her soul lift; she'd wanted to sit beside the owner of this beauty, whisper in her ear, confide all her secrets. She'd wanted to make her smile, to own that smile. Then the berry lips *had* smiled and hopes and dreams she hadn't even been aware of were realised.

She'd relaxed and waves of sleep had washed over her, each dragging her further towards blissful slumber. A berry-red smile, green, green eyes ... then those eyes had flashed and one had slowly, sensually closed. The smile had disappeared, replaced by a scarlet sneer, a parody of a smile, and Lora had at once awakened, heart pounding in her chest, bedclothes damp with sweat despite the chill autumn night.

This had happened time after time through the night. She had maybe managed ten minutes here and half an hour there, but each dream was haunted by white, green and red. The purest skin, the clearest eyes, the fullest mouth. Lora had been glad when she was roused from her bed, glad of the chores she had to do — clearing the fire, sweeping the hearth. Distraction was what she needed.

Truthfully, what she really needed was to talk to Rafe, but there was no chance she would escape today. Her day had been filled with chores — the house had to be dusted and scrubbed ready for the guests this afternoon. Her Uncle Peter, who lived two weeks ride away, had come to visit. Tomorrow the brothers Peter, Stephen and Thomas were to ride with the Eastern Association, as had James, to join Cromwell in his cause. The last time her uncle had been to stay, Lora had been but a child herself, and her Mother, his sister, was very much looking forward to this visit. Though Peter was staying in town with Thomas, Mother had insisted on hosting festivities tonight and had taken care to ensure cook had provided the best food they could afford. Nothing too fancy, though, she had assured Father — plain fare was to be served, food befitting those that served the good Lord. No amount of plain fare and piousness, though, was going to stop Thomas Hammond enjoying his flagon of ale. Aunt Marjorie could quote all night from the bible and he would still make lewd remarks.

Mary was also here, her rounded, growing belly visible beneath her best gown, with her husband Oliver and daughter Eve. Lora had spent half the afternoon trying to keep Mother and Mary apart, fearful that Mother would question the amount of time she was apparently spending at her sister's. Or that Mary would request that Lora come more often to aid her during her last months of being with child.

The lies she had told were like a poorly threaded loom, likely to come undone at the merest tug. Head pounding and nerves fractious, Lora was only just keeping it all reeled in. Further down the table, Father looked at his timepiece and declared that they start eating while they were still waiting for Uncle Stephen and his wife, renowned for their tardiness to everything, to arrive. Stephen could eat the cold leftovers when he deigned to get here. Lora was looking forward to their arrival; she'd always got on well with Uncle Stephen and Aunt Louisa. A modern couple, they treated her with respect. Aunt Louisa was not constantly exasperated at her poor embroidery skills and lack of genteelness. They didn't laugh when she said she wanted to learn to read and write. In fact they had given her a diary and taught her how to form her letters. She wrote in it every night and hid it under a loose floorboard, away from the eyes of her mother and father.

Finally they were on the last course; the conversation crashed around her, her head aching more with every shrill laugh, every debate. She had withdrawn from the company, managing to answer questions politely but otherwise sitting quietly, pushing the food around. Mary had frowned at her, the only person who didn't quite believe her plea of a headache. The sound of horses from outside distracted Mary and everyone waited while her Uncle Stephen and Aunt Louisa were shown in.

'Welcome Stephen, you will forgive that we have started without you — dear Louisa — we have kept some fare for you,' Lora's mother rose to welcome her brother and sister-in-law.

'We have brought a friend with us; I trust you do not mind, sister dear. This is Cecily Kashshaptu, Louisa's dear friend and companion.' Stephen beamed at his sister, beckoning his wife and her friend forward. Lora's mother frowned slightly before welcoming the two ladies. Lora ignored her Aunt Marjorie when she muttered, 'Highly irregular,' just loud enough for the entire party to hear. It *was* highly irregular, but she liked Stephen and Louisa more than Aunt Marjorie and enjoyed the fact that her staid old aunt was put out.

'Lora, go and fetch your uncle's food please,' her mother ordered quietly before she had a chance to welcome her favourite aunt and uncle. 'Now Stephen, there is a space here for Louisa and Mistress Cecily …' Lora left the room as her Mother rearranged the seating to fit in the new guests.

Bringing the saved food back she was amazed that the entire table seemed to be enraptured by her aunt and uncle; all eyes were turned to them, all other conversation muted. As she made her way to where they were sitting, she realised that it was in fact her aunt's companion who was holding the conversation. 'It is only an old gown and not nearly as handsome as yours,' Lora heard Cecily telling Aunt Marjorie in a voice as soft as the wings of a butterfly. Lora was astounded when she heard Marjorie simper in reply; in all her years, she had never heard anything resembling a laugh pass her aunt's lips.

'Lora!' said Stephen, 'Let me look at you.' Uncle Stephen looked her up and down, amusement in his eyes, 'You certainly are not my Little Lora anymore; how your mother dares to let such a ravishing beauty out of the house I do not know.' Lora blushed as all the eyes around the table turned to look at her. She could feel steely disapproval at Stephen's remarks radiating from Father and Aunt Marjorie; if the men were not leaving in the morning, she knew Father would never have permitted Mother to have such a large gathering of people.

As her face heated up and her insides squirmed, a butterfly-soft voice, quiet but clear, said, 'Now let me see this beautiful niece of whom I have heard so much!' Lora's blush deepened as the gentle tones caressed her; stepping forward, she put down the food and turned to her Aunt Louisa and her companion. Ignoring her favourite aunt, she smiled and lifted her eyes to the gentle voice that seduced her.

All thoughts of tiredness and her aching head disappeared as her eyes took in a crimson dress of soft silk, laced up to a milk white bosom as inviting as a gently plumped pillow. A flash of ruby red glinted in the candlelight, a delicate chin. Lora shyly lifted her eyes further and took in scarlet lips, porcelain skin and emerald eyes. Suddenly she was glad that she had to be here — there was no other place she wanted to be. In fact, she found it hard to imagine ever being anywhere else at all.

Twenty-Three
2013

Tentacles of sunlight crept in through Regan's skylight and caressed her sleeping form. The early warmth of a late May day broke into dreams of dark creatures that she wouldn't remember after waking. Not even a lingering thought, especially today as the much more anticipated — and, she would insist, important — shopping trip was looming.

As soon as consciousness was fully upon her, she flung back the quilt and stretched. Toni and Ella were going to meet at hers in about three quarters of an hour, and she wanted to be showered, depilated and clean haired before they arrived. The balance of all things could be sorted out with a decent outfit and pristine hair, she felt. At least it had always worked for her and Ems in Brighton.

The straighteners were just heating up when Toni burst into the room, her cropped hair a dramatic shade of hubba-bubba pink today. Wide eyed, Regan grabbed Toni by the shoulders and twirled her round, 'Oh wow Toni, I love your hair! It really suits you.'

'I know, isn't it brilliant? Ella did it - she's so clever, isn't she.' Still unsure of her standing with Ella, Regan just offered her a smile in reply as she came in behind Toni.

'Let her do yours Regan — she's a genius, wasted in King's Lynn. She should be in one of those big salons in London!' As Ella rolled her eyes and grinned at her friend, Regan glimpsed for the first time a friendly girl behind the snide remarks. Someone she could understand the effervescent Toni being friends with.

Not knowing how to turn down this offer without offending ... well, anyone, Regan found herself perched on the edge of her bed, Ella deftly sorting her long blonde hair into sections. Taking advantage of her immobility, Toni had rummaged through the open make-up bag and started on Regan's nails. It seemed pointless protesting. Besides, not since she had stopped chewing her nails aged ten had they looked so ... ragged. Fortnightly gel nails were a thing of Brighton past; they somehow didn't suit the hunting lifestyle she was leading these days.

'Whatever do you do to your fingers?' Toni asked, 'It looks as if you've been gardening with them. I didn't realise bar work was so tough on the hands!'

'It's all the glasses I have to scrub clean. Nick is a terrible boss!'

Toni snorted, 'I might believe that if I hadn't been dragged round the shops with him and Mum looking for the dishwasher. Hey, it's looking great, Ella,' Toni said, stopping what she was doing and watching her friend.

'Let me look,' said Regan, twisting her neck around a little to see in the mirror. A searing pain caught her just below her ear.

'Aahh, fuck,' she said, jerking away and pulling the hair still clamped in the straighteners Ella was holding.

'Regan, what the hell ...' said Ella, only just firming her grip on the irons in time. 'You idiot,' she said, releasing the hair and standing back.

'You what?' said Regan as she clamped her hand to the pain in her neck, 'You're the one who's just burnt me!' She strode out of the room to the bathroom and stuck a flannel under the cold water. Once it was drenched and icy she applied it to her neck. In all honesty it took only a couple of minutes for the pain to ease, and when Regan looked the mark was miniscule. Her temper took a little longer to cool, though. She just couldn't shake the feeling that Ella had done it on purpose. 'Damn it,' she swore softly to herself. Today was not the day for it. Today was meant to be the day she started to feel like a normal girl again. A day out with new friends, shopping, clothes, watching the boys.

She swallowed hard, trying to force her anger back down her gullet and form an apology for swearing at Ella. It wouldn't be *so* hard to do. She breathed deeply, knowing that she *had* moved her head. But still, Ella made her living as a hairdresser — surely, she was used to clients not keeping entirely still. 'Stop it, Regan,' she told herself in the mirror before going back to the bedroom. Ella was sitting by the window, Toni's arms around her shoulders. It didn't look as if she had been crying, but even Regan could see she was upset. Or at least pretending to be, she wasn't entirely certain. Biting her lip she said, 'I'm sorry Ella, it was all my fault, I moved my head. I shouldn't have shouted at you.'

'It's fine; I'm sorry too,' said Ella, words that did not match the glare on her face.

'See Ella, I told you it was Regan's fault. Don't worry Regan, I move my head all the time when I'm having my hair done, I bet Ella has nearly chopped my ears off a hundred times!'

This pulled a smile from Ella, 'Dope,' she said as Regan sat back down and offered the straighteners back to her.

* * *

'So what first girls?' asked Maeve as they stretched out of her car. 'Shopping for clothes or window-shopping at the students?' A gleam entered her bright green eyes, brows raised suggestively.

'Clothes,' said Regan and Ella. Toni just giggled.

'Girls, girls,' sighed Maeve, shaking her head theatrically, 'clothes it is then. How about we hit the Grand Arcade first and then we'll make our way back into town.'

'Honestly, I don't really care as long as I get some new clothes. I'm going to start looking like a local soon!' Regan bit her tongue as soon as the words were out of her mouth; a quick glance told her that only Maeve had heard the barb — she flashed Regan a grin.

'Don't worry, I won't let you resort to the discount shops,' she whispered, and a warm feeling of satisfaction burned inside Regan. Calling the other two, Maeve about turned and led them to St Andrews street. In under twenty minutes Regan was in the changing rooms of All Saints, trying on a leather dress that was way more Maeve's style than it was her own.

She shifted uncomfortably, glimpsing herself in the mirrors. Pulling at the hem to see if she could stretch it just a little bit further over her thighs, she tried to ignore the angry red cuts on her arm and, for a brief moment, contemplated buying the dress. It was gorgeous; it would look fantastic with knee-high boots and a choker. But, she conceded to herself, she would never feel comfortable in it, and feeling confident in what you were wearing was half the key to looking gorgeous.

'Oh wow you look hot!' said Toni, as she emerged from behind the dressing room curtain, 'but what the heck have you done to your arms?'

'Oh Regan, honey, they look really sore.' Maeve swept up one of her arms and inspected the long scarlet scratches.

Regan pulled her arm away, 'An abject lesson on cutting back brambles in a vest top,' she lied, 'the conclusion was, don't do it. So what do you think?' She drew attention back to the dress. 'My own feelings are, the dress is fabulous but unfortunately not for me. One of you should try it on.' She slipped back into the changing room and out of the dress. Toni stuck her hand in and grabbed it from her, 'Here, you try it on Ella, you're the same size as Regan.'

Regan struggled into the second outfit and emerged just in time to see a flushed Ella being admired by Toni. The dress looked gorgeous on her but she looked even more uncomfortable in it than Regan had, her face burning brighter at every one of

Toni's compliments. Ignoring them, Regan turned to Maeve. 'What do you think?' she asked, twirling in a skimpy floral dress that managed to look innocent and sexy at the same time. 'I love it,' said Maeve, echoing Regan's thoughts; she put it straight in the 'to buy' pile.

A couple of hours later — with a purse much lighter — Regan walked along the river chatting easily with Toni and Maeve. The day was going exactly as she had hoped it would; she felt normal again, all thoughts of Nate and familiars pushed firmly into the corner of her mind. She was just about able to keep them there. The bright sun helped — no creatures of the fog could be lurking here — and even Ella was acting, if not friendly, pleasant.

By mutual agreement they found a pub with an appealing (and affordable) lunch menu down one of the city's narrow streets. The bonus — mostly for Maeve judging by her widened eyes — were the boys huddled around the pool table. Toni grinned at the sight of them; only Ella seemed as uninterested as Regan.

Settling down on the plush covered bench in one corner, Regan grabbed a menu. Despite smoking being banned from pubs for several years now, a faint odour of cigarettes hung in the air layered with the recognisable smell of spilt alcohol. The pub was dimly lit, the bright sunshine from outside not following them in, and the tables were slightly sticky. In spite of all this the small tavern had a vibe that Regan liked. Though not full by any stretch of the imagination, there were enough people in there ordering meals on a Monday afternoon to suggest it wasn't a complete dive, and the friendly banter batting back and forth between the girl behind the bar and the customers added to the affable atmosphere.

'Regan, you are going to look so cute in that dress!' said Maeve once they'd all surveyed the menus and placed their orders. 'The question is, when you are going to wear it? You need to have someone to impress — other than us, of course!'

'I have no idea,' Regan sighed, 'other than work, seeing you guys and Nate, I've done nothing since I moved here.'

'Nate?' said Maeve, leaning forward and raising her eyebrow, 'Who's Nate?'

'Oh, just a friend,' said Regan, kicking herself for bringing him up. *Way to go Regan. Now explain your way out of this one. Without, of course, mentioning supernatural creatures and hunting with knives.*

'No way Regan! You don't get to mention an unknown male to me and then say he's just a friend! Does she Toni? Help me out! First off, is he good looking?'

Regan shifted in her chair a little, 'Well yes, he is, but he's also very irritating!'

'Tell us more — where did you meet him?' Toni asked, a teasing look in her eyes. Maeve shot her a look of approval. Ella had a smirk on her face, looking oddly comfortable at Regan's unease.

'At work,' said Regan sheepishly, 'I tell you, I haven't been anywhere other than work for weeks!'

Maeve opened her eyes wide, 'Oh my god, you're not talking about that really gorgeous bloke who wears the leather jacket?' Regan nodded sheepishly.

'Oh wow,' said Maeve, 'I've always wanted to talk to him but haven't had the guts yet!' Regan raised an eyebrow; no way did she believe that. Maeve seemed at ease talking to anyone and in any situation.

'You foxy little madam, so how did you get him talking to you?'

She squirmed a little, yet was slightly proud of the fact that Maeve thought she'd managed something amazing. 'He offered me a lift home one night when it was foggy; he didn't like the idea of me walking alone in the dark.'

Maeve and Toni squealed in unison, 'Oh Regan, he must fancy you, he wouldn't do that if he didn't. What a gentleman!' she stared out of the window with a dreamy look in her eye, 'you are so lucky!' Ella shook her head, seemingly unimpressed by Nate's supposed chivalric behaviour. Somehow this raised her in Regan's esteem.

'Well I think it's brilliant,' said Toni, a glint in her eye, 'I know a certain older brother who could do with a bit of a rival. He seems to think you and him are just a matter of time!' Regan just shot her a look, not deigning to even try and reply to *that* statement.

Thankfully she was saved by the waiter delivering their meal. As she surveyed her plate Regan didn't think she'd ever seen such delicious food in her life. Her steak was cooked exactly right; the new potatoes and salad appeared almost fake, they were so perfect.

The first forkful melted in her mouth and she had to stop herself from swooning at how delicious it was. Not bad for a back-alley pub.

'This is scrumptious Maeve,' she said, glancing over at her friend. 'How's yo— Oh, Maeve how could you eat it like that?' Her friend's steak was rarer than any Regan had ever seen before; a trickle of blood oozed from the middle, making Regan want to gag.

'It's an acquired taste.' Her friend grinned. 'But once you've acquired it you never want to go back!'

'Oh yuck,' Toni wrinkled up her nose and Ella pulled a face.

Maeve laughed, 'Oh come on girls, all the T.V. chefs serve it like this!'

'True,' said Regan, 'but still eurgh.'

They ate in silence for a bit, each enjoying her own dinner, then Maeve brought up Nate again, 'So does he know you fancy him?' Regan almost choked. Swallowing some of her water to try and stop coughing, she eventually replied, 'I don't fancy him, we're just friends.'

'Yeah, right. I've seen that look before; I know when someone has a crush!'

Regan blushed, 'Okay, my traitorous hormones might have an incey, wincey crush! I'm seventeen, I can't help it. My brain's saying, "sort it out", my hormones are saying "cute guy"! What am I supposed to do?'

'Oh Regan, you kill me!' said Maeve, laughing. 'There's nothing wrong with fancying someone! If I were you, I'd just tease him a bit though, you are way too young to be getting serious.'

'I think I'm going to leave us at the just-good-friend's stage and hope that my hormones get fed up before I disown them completely!'

Regan pushed her plate away and glanced at her watch. 'I'm sorry to rush you, girls, but I'm going to have to be going soon if I'm gonna be back in time for work. I can't believe it's as late as it is.'

They all gathered their bags and headed back to the car. 'We'll definitely go clubbing next time,' said Regan, 'it's been a fab day.'

Twenty-Four

'I'll stay with Aunty Vi if you want to go shopping,' said Regan, blowing on her nails to dry the pearlescent varnish she was applying.

'Are you sure, love?' Katherine ran her fingers through her hair, a sure sign she was feeling harassed. 'There are no spots for delivery left until the end of the week and we need to stock up the cupboards before then!'

'It's not a problem, Mum, promise. Now scoot and don't forget to get some cookie dough ice-cream!'

'All right bossy, I won't be long,' said Katherine, 'Come on Ashleigh, you can come and help me.' She raised her eyebrows at her eldest daughter. Regan smiled; she knew her mum worried about Ashleigh, who loved being at home so much it was difficult to get her to go anywhere other than school. She watched as her mum and sister drove away, wishing for her mum's sake they were going somewhere more exciting. Even taking her job at the day care centre into account, in Regan's opinion Katherine didn't get out enough.

Alone at last, Regan had the perfect opportunity to put her plan into action. Filling the kettle up and putting it on to boil, she tossed a couple of tea bags into the china teapot and then searched out Aunty Vi's prettiest porcelain cups and saucers. Loading them on a tray, she filled up the teapot; while it brewed she searched through the cupboards, trying to locate a packet of biscuits. In luck, she found a packet of custard creams that Ashleigh hadn't touched, put some out on a plate and added it to the tray.

After pouring the tea, she carefully carried the tray through to Aunty Vi's room and balanced it on the sideboard.

'Aunty Vi, would you like a nice cup of tea?'

'Oh Katherine dear, that would be lovely,' her aunt replied. Regan was pleased to see she looked quite bright and cheerful today; it was definitely one of her better days. Carefully she manoeuvred the wheeled bed table over to the old lady and placed a cup of tea in front of her, adding the plate of biscuits as well.

'So how are you today, Aunty?' she asked, not entirely sure how she was going to start this conversation.

'Oh I'm having a good day dear, it's quiet today and that's nice.' Regan wasn't sure what noise Vi imagined there usually was. The house was always fairly quiet as far as she was concerned.

When her aunt was settled, Regan picked up the photo she had been looking at the other week. Once again, she was struck by the difference in the girls' faces — the happy, carefree smile of one and the guarded, wary look of the other.

'Aunty Vi, you said this was a photo of you and your sister Lizzy? Was Lizzy short for Elizabeth?'

'Of course Katherine, that is me, Violet Jane Simpson, and my elder sister Elizabeth Maureen

Simpson, brother Jack and Elsie aren't in the picture. I think Jack was at work and Elsie was just a baby.'

Regan had never met Jack or her Nan, Elsie. Katherine had lost her mum to cancer long before Regan was born. But it wasn't either of them she was interested in; it was Lizzy, or Elizabeth Maureen Simpson, writer of the diary.

'What happened to Lizzy, Aunty Vi?' asked Regan. She'd been toying with different ways of wording her query but decided that she might as well just come out with it. Bringing up Elizabeth's death was not going to go down well with her aunt however she asked the question. At least bringing it up so soon after her mum had left might mean she'd have a chance to calm Vi down before Katherine returned if needs be.

'Oh Lizzy, she was a good girl, a brave girl …' Aunty Vi sounded proud of her sister, 'she disappeared in one of the nastiest fen fogs I've ever seen. 23rd September 1922. We said goodnight to her,' she looked up at Regan, 'she'd gone to bed very early you know, said she had a headache, but it was a lie. Then when we checked her bed at just after nine that evening, she was gone.'

'Are you all right Aunty Vi?' asked Regan, slightly surprised at how together her aunt sounded.

The old lady ignored her. 'Of course Father never knew why she'd gone out, but I did. I knew why she slipped out into the night. I knew what took her.' The old woman was staring through Regan as if she was seeing the ghosts of her and her sister from decades ago.

'She'd gone out to fight the creatures, the ones that brought the fog. The ones that took all those foolish enough to step out at night. I don't know why she didn't make it back that night, though. I'd seen her fight, she was good.

'I'd snuck out once, to see where she went at night. I thought she was meeting a boy, that she had a secret liaison. I followed her into the fog and I was so frightened — I hid and watched, then they smelt me and came to where I was hiding. I was so scared. But Lizzy … she was brave. She fought them, she killed them. She wouldn't let them get me.' Vi sighed, the memory of that night clearer than today was to her. 'She told me off so bad but I didn't care, I knew I would be dead if it wasn't for her. She made me promise to never tell anyone what she did. She said that I had to keep it a secret forever, and I have. For ninety years I've kept it to myself but it's okay to tell you, dear, because you're like her Regan. You're special.' Placing her teacup back on the tray she said, 'I need a nap now, dear.'

Regan said goodbye and left quietly, taking the tea tray with her. Head spinning, it was only much later that she realised Vi had called her Regan and not Katherine.

* * *

'So have you found out anymore?' asked Regan between punches, 'how did Lora and Rafe get on, hunting familiars?' She volleyed some hits at the punch bag and then paused to catch her breath. Nate finished his workout and Regan tried not to admire the way his muscles rippled under his t-shirt. She grabbed a drink and chucked it to Nate before sinking beside him in the grass.

'She does mention them; she always refers to them as "The Creatures"—'

'I can understand that,' Regan interrupted, 'it's how I think of them too!'

'Anyway,' Nate glared at her, 'she's writing mostly about hunting witches. She was a very feisty young lady — I can see why Rafael had a hard time saying no to her. She's written an entire passage on why Rafael thought the Witchfinder General was such an idiot.'

'Who?'

Nate grinned, 'Don't worry, I had to Google it too — the Witchfinder General, or to give him his real name, Matthew Hopkins. He and his little band of witch hunters spent 1645 and '46 seeking out and killing witches.'

'I thought that's what they wanted,' Regan said, furrowing her brow.

'Well, yes, but Rafe apparently said that our Mr Hopkins wasn't actually killing *witches*. He'd just latched on to the fears of the population at the time. Lora wasn't so sure she agreed with him.' Nate drew out his hunting knife and started to sharpen the blade, 'The Witchfinder General was making a lot of money from towns and villages to rid them of their witches.'

'So he took money and just haphazardly picked women to kill?'

'Oh he didn't have to pick women at random; neighbours and friends were more than happy to offer up suspected victims. Any minor disagreement — a bad crop, the slightly eccentric woman from down the road, a lady seen talking out of turn to a gentleman — any reason would do for people to report their friends and neighbours as witches.'

'I am so glad I didn't live then!' said Regan, watching the late sun glint off Nate's knife. 'You men always get the easy end of the deal!'

'Oh, don't be mistaken Regan, men were tried as witches too. Not as often as women, but they were.'

Happy with the keen edge of his blade, he cleaned the knife until it gleamed and then put it away. 'Anyway, that's as far as I got.'

'Well, I have some information for you too,' she opened her eyes wide, 'You know Elizabeth Maureen Simpson, our diarist? She is none other than my Aunty Vi's big sister!'

Nate looked at her, interest written all over his face.

'Apparently, she disappeared one night when there was a bad fog. Aunty Vi knew what she did, but no-one else did. Vi has kept it a secret all these years.' She paused before adding, 'And, get this, apparently she can tell *me* as I am one of the creature-fighters like Elizabeth was!'

Nate looked surprised, 'She knew that? Did you tell her?'

Shaking her head, Regan said, 'No I didn't tell her, but apparently she knows it anyway.'

'When did Elizabeth die then?' asked Nate.

Regan thought for a moment, 'September 23rd 1922. Well, that's when she disappeared.'

'I think it's safe to assume that it's also when she died,' said Nate, 'you've seen first-hand now what she was up against.'

'I know,' said Regan, stretching out her legs, 'I can't help thinking, what was different that time, though? Aunty Vi said she was a good fighter; what was different about this occasion?' She shrugged, unsure really what she was trying to ask.

'It doesn't matter how good you are, Regan. One error is all it takes,' Nate said earnestly, 'if you are doing this 'job' then you have to accept that. Every fight could possibly be your last.'

Regan smiled, refusing to let the terror of Nate's words penetrate her brain, 'But we're all right — we fight together as a unit now, which has to more than halve the risk.' Nate looked at Regan, then raising his eyebrow said, 'I truly hope you don't believe that. The familiars are supernatural creatures. It helps that there are two of us, but it doesn't mean we are any less at risk.' He changed the subject back to Elizabeth. 'So, I think we should try and find out more about that night, more about what happened.'

'How are we going to do that?' asked Regan, 'it's not exactly going to be written in her diary, is it!'

'But if there were suspiciously thick fogs that year and if Elizabeth and maybe others disappeared, then it probably made it into the local newspaper. Maybe we ought to check the archives.'

'No time like the present,' said Regan, hopping up and heading for Nate's bike.

It took about fifteen minutes for them to get into King's Lynn, and then they had to find the library.

Half an hour later they were searching through the archives of the Lynn News and Advertiser.

Knowing the date of what they were searching for was a godsend, but it was still a time-consuming job. Three cups of coffee and a trip out to the cake shop later, Nate suddenly gave a small cheer.

'Here, I've found it — "The Disappearance of Elizabeth Simpson".' Together they pored over the paper and Nate read,

The Disappearance of Elizabeth Simpson
Yesterday, when the fogs descended over West Norfolk, eighteen-year-old Elizabeth Simpson disappeared. Her father Alfred Simpson maintained a stiff upper lip when he said "Elizabeth had gone to bed early, saying she had a headache. When her younger sister, Violet, checked on her she was not in her bed. I have no idea where she has gone but I believe that she will return home soon."

Mr Simpson claims there had been no family disputes and that Elizabeth was a happy girl who willingly looked after the rest of the family since the death of her mother in childbirth. The police will continue their search of the area. An inside police source has told us he feels that Miss Simpson may have left of her own accord and has maybe taken up with a young man.

'Oh wow,' said Regan, 'do you think she did? You know, just run away with someone? I mean if her mum — my great-grandma — did die when Nan was born and Elizabeth was expected to bring up the entire family maybe she just got fed up and ran away.'

Nate pushed the paper carefully away from him and considered this for a moment. 'It's possible. It's always possible, but don't you think she would have taken her diaries with her? And now you know about all this, could you just run away and leave Ashleigh in danger? Do you think Elizabeth would have left knowing that Violet and your Nan were still here?'

Regan shook her head slowly, 'Probably not, but what if she really loved him, found someone she couldn't bear to be away from?'

Nate looked at her scornfully, 'You think she'd just leave her family at risk for the sake of lust? If she truly loved someone, she would have made it work right where she was! No, I think that your aunt is right. Elizabeth finally lost a battle, had one bad night of fighting. Hell, it wouldn't even have to be a bad *night*, just one bad move …'

'You're right,' sighed Regan, 'I know it, I can feel it in my bones. But wouldn't it be nice to think she had survived, that she had simply loved someone too much to carry on without them.'

'Regan,' said Nate, his dark eyes penetrating, 'you've really got to stop watching chick flicks. Real life just isn't like that you know. No matter how much you love someone, duty and responsibility comes first. It simply has to.' With that he replaced the old paper in its file and returned it to the librarian, leaving Regan miffed by his remarks.

It was comments like that that made Regan realise the differences between the two of them, reminded her of the obnoxious American that had formed her first opinion of Nate. Nothing would ever come between her and true love — she could guarantee that!

'Do you want to look at anymore, sir?' the librarian asked.

'I don't think so thanks, we found what we were looking for. Ready, Regan?' he asked, grabbing his helmet. He'd finally invested in another one — taking Regan so frequently on his bike, he was just asking to be stopped by the police if he wasn't wearing it. Of course, he didn't wear it on the nights he was out fighting. He needed to be able to get straight off his bike and fight; being stopped by a police patrol vehicle was the least of his worries those nights.

Twenty-Five
1645

Lora tried to watch Cecily from under her half-closed eyelids. Every move she made was delicate and feminine. Even the way she nibbled chicken from a bone, her straight white teeth taking small, ladylike bites. Whenever Lora ate chicken, she would be wiping grease from her chin. Sometimes it wasn't just mother who despaired at her lack of delicacy.

Slowly, she became aware of a conversation taking place at the end of the table.

'I think twenty shillings is more than a fair price to rid the town of witches. If Matthew Hopkins is able to see through their cunning, then we will all sleep more easily at night,' Peter looked around the table, trying to gain support from the other guests.

'I disagree, sir. If Hopkins is able to perform this, then why should our purses pay for it? Edward Hyde is happy to take our money and put it into the government's coffers — ridding the country of the plague of witches should be taken from that money. Money we have already paid!' Thomas took a long drink from his goblet of wine, satisfied that he had made his point well. The conversation lulled as those around the table started to listen.

'Brother, I find myself unable to agree with you. The country is in enough trouble at present. While

Cromwell marches against Charles, that money is not going to be spent on keeping witches from our midst.'

'That fool Charles is what is wrong with the country at the moment — mayhap I suggest that money from the *crown* should pay for the removal of witches!'

Thomas snorted rudely. 'You may indeed suggest it; it won't mean it is likely to happen.'

'It matters not who we think should pay for it,' Stephen's quieter voice joined the debate, 'the matter is, if we want to be rid of these temptresses, then Matthew Hopkins and John Stearne, good fellows that they are, offer us a workable solution. I suggest that if a town is not willing to find payment, then maybe there is something they are looking to hide!'

'Buffoons, the lot of you!' Father spoke with such command that everyone else fell silent. 'There are no such things as witches. The devil is quite able to cast his evil work without using harlots to aid him. There are plenty of sinners ready to do the devils work without potions and magic playing a part. If more people were to listen to the Lord's word and be less sinful, the devil would not be able to spread his evil.'

Lora frowned, distracted momentarily from Cecily as she absently raised a piece of creamy cheese to her lips. Her Father was strict but also ignorant in this matter; he could be as righteous as he liked, it would not aid him against the creatures and their mistresses. He scorned the men making suggestions of witches and magic, so she knew he would not listen to her. After all, she was just his daughter, a female; her place was purely to make a good marriage.

'I am so sorry, Sir, to disagree with you at your own table,' Cecily's soft voice somehow managed to be heard loud and clear, 'but I have seen for myself the consequences of a disbelief in witchcraft. It is only a fool or a brave man who truly believes the devil needs no help, that magic is not used. I fear, Sir,' Cecily looked straight at Lora's father, 'that those who work at his command are all around; it is wise not to trust too widely. The evidence is there if you care to look, and most saddening, I find, is that all witches are somebody's wife or daughter. A difficult truth to acknowledge, for any but the strongest of men.'

Twenty-Six
2013

Regan's shift at the pub was nearly over when Nick commented on the thick fog that hung over the area once more.

'I don't know what's going on with this weather at the moment. These fogs are bad for trade — people aren't turning out. Nobody wants to walk in weather like this, and not many of these fellas want to come to a pub and drink cola all evening. Not like your American,' he winked at Regan.

'He's not my American, Nick. We're just friends and yes, thanks to him, I don't have to walk home in the fog.'

If only you knew, she thought, *exactly what I do when the fog descends.*

'No, he's not her American — for now!' said Toni, pushing her empty glass across the bar. Regan glared at her.

'Don't worry, she hasn't told Sam. *Yet,*' Ella mocked.

'What does it matter if she does tell Sam? We're not dating!' Regan said defensively.

Toni just grinned. 'I'm waiting for the perfect moment, that perfect take-him-down-a-peg moment.'

'Hey, don't use me as a weapon in the sibling rivalry war,' Regan warned.

To her surprise, Ella agreed with her, 'Toni, that's not fair, Sam's a good guy!'

'When did he get such a fan club?' grumbled Toni, 'Oh, I know, when he hit puberty and turned into a self-confessed Lothario.' She downed the last of her orange juice and pushed the glass towards Regan.

'Come on, Toni, I want to go. I hate driving in this weather,' said Ella, pulling on her jacket. Regan waved as they left, wondering for the first time where Ella lived.

'I hope Toni lets her stay at theirs, Cyndi won't mind,' said Nick, 'it makes more sense than trying to drive on these narrow by-roads in zero visibility.' Regan nodded her head in agreement. She knew exactly what it felt like to be driven about the narrow, winding fenland roads when it was virtually impossible to see the hand in front of her face. Thankfully in her case Nate did all the driving.

'Anyway Regan, can I ask a favour? I know it isn't part of your job but would you mind doing the mantle for me? Mavis is off sick and I thought I'd managed to clean everywhere earlier but I just noticed all the dust atop the fireplace.'

'Not a problem,' she said, fetching the polish and duster from the cupboard in the little kitchen. The mantelpiece was covered in old horse brasses and other knick-knacks, including, Regan discovered, a string full of stones with holes in the middle. Stones with holes in the middle, she realised, were nigh on impossible to get dust-free with just a duster — they would need a soak in some water. *Or better yet,* she thought, *chucking out.*

'Nick, why do you have a mantelpiece with holey stones on it?' she asked her boss. 'Can I throw them in the bin?'

Nick looked over and chuckled at her. 'Only if you want to let the witches in,' he said.

Her heart stopped for just the tiniest beat until she looked up at Nick's beaming face.

'Got ya!' he said. 'It's an old tradition in the fens, goes back centuries. A stone with a hole would save you from the witches. Willow 'round the doors and windows keeps them out too! Oh, and the wonders of an old woman's toenail clippings if you wanted to cross the fen at night …'

'Eurgh!' Regan screwed up her nose, 'that's gross.'

'Ah,' said Nick, 'but if ya wanted to get across the fen you needed your safekeep, else a davil will have ya.'

'Or the Bogart,' piped up Howie from across the bar, 'or even worse the Hookey man!'

'Well I am quite glad I live in the 21st century, then,' said Regan, 'I'm not sure I'm up to dealing with the Hookey man, especially not if it requires any sorts of toenail clippings!'

She gave the stones a clean with some washing up liquid and a cloth, then she carefully carried them back to the mantelpiece — if they kept out witches, they might work on familiars too, and any help in that area she would accept gratefully.

The door opened once more and Maeve came in from the grey gloom outside.

'On dusting duty today?' she asked, unwinding a beautiful silver scarf from around her neck.

'Staff shortages,' said Regan, smiling at her friend. 'That is a gorgeous scarf!'

'Thanks honey. So how are the hormones behaving just lately?'

Regan shrugged, 'They're okay,' she said, a little fed up with having to explain her friendship with Nate.

'Well you've got admit, not many men run around every night if they want to be *just friends.*'

'Honestly, Maeve, he's just a nice guy and we both enjoy looking into these old diaries.'

'If you say so honey,' Maeve said as Regan turned back to the mantelpiece. She re-arranged the ornaments and made a space for the newly cleaned stones.

'Ha, no witches will enter here tonight!' she said with a flourish.

'Well if they do, I'm sure that gorgeous hunk of yours will protect you,' laughed Maeve.

'Maeve,' said Regan, turning round again, 'he's not—' she stopped short. Standing directly behind Maeve was Nate, his face unreadable.

'Hallo,' said Maeve, turning, 'we were just talking about you!'

'Oh, were you?' Nate directed this to Regan.

'No, I … I was just cleaning the stones that'll keep the witches out …' *God you sound like a jerk, Regan,* she thought to herself, *now not only does he think you've been telling people you fancy him, he thinks you're slightly nuts too.* She started to get Nate his usual soft drink when a thought struck her … she hoped he didn't think that she'd told anyone about the familiars.

'So what can I get for you, Maeve?' Regan asked, her stomach clenching at what thoughts could be going through Nate's head.

'Nothing really, I was just passing and thought I'd pop in and see you. I had a fantastic time shopping, let's do it again soon!'

'It was great, wasn't it,' Regan leaned on the counter, letting Nick get Nate his usual Coke. 'I am so up for another trip any time you like!'

'Great, I'll text you then, see what we can sort out.' She waggled her fingers goodbye and left.

* * *

'Wow that certainly is sharper,' said Regan as she reached Nate's bike and he handed over her knife. Even in the fog the newly sharpened edge was visible. The blade she'd found in Vi's kitchen drawers must have been Elizabeth's, but its worn handle fitted her hand as if it had been crafted for her.

'As I said,' Nate told her, 'it's important that the knife is sharp, it's all there is between you and death when you're fighting.' Supressing an urge to answer him back, she nodded her head; she knew he was right, but boy did she hate being told what to do.

Climbing on the bike, she felt the familiar thrum between her thighs as Nate started it up. Tonight was going to be a fight night, she could feel it in her bones — there was no way the fog outside was natural.

Their increased frequency was worrying Regan. She remembered that first night when just the sound of Nate on his bike had frightened the familiars away. Now, they were both fighting a couple of times a week.

Anticipation buzzed in her stomach as they rode down the narrow byroads. An intuition that Regan didn't understand led him. The dank air clung to Regan, but she was becoming used to it and didn't give it a second thought. Nate slowed the bike; Regan was unsure where she was, but dark shapes of trees were just visible, indicating a wood or copse of some sort. They jumped off and Regan unsheathed her knife, her eyes darting back and forth, scanning the grey for any sign of the creatures. The sound of a twig cracking echoed like gunfire in her ears and she turned sharply, knife at the ready. Her heartbeat rose and every sense felt on high alert, sound and smell heightened as vision was so limited.

Nate recognised the sound of human voices before she did, and he lowered his knife, sheathing it quickly before making his presence known.

'Hi there, folks,' he said and a young female voice uttered a small shriek; her companion — a hopeful boyfriend, Regan guessed — comforted her. 'Sorry, I didn't mean to alarm you ma'am. I'm from the forestry commission and we are making sure that these woods are uninhabited tonight. There's been a sighting of a wild cat in this area and in the fog, you might be easy prey. We're recommending that you stay out of these woods in the dark,' he said.

How anyone could get away with such rubbish Regan wasn't sure, but he had an authority to his tone that meant he was believed. At least, no-one had argued with him yet, though it could just be the dread the familiars emitted; dismay and panic rolled off them in waves like the fog itself did.

'Was it just them do you think?' she asked as the young couple clambered into an old mini and drove out of the woods to safety.

'I think so.' Nate's knife was at the ready again; he searched the fog for the creatures they both knew were nearby. 'I can't imagine many people staying out in this. A young couple — well they might think a nice dark deserted wood is all the privacy they need.' Regan was glad he couldn't see her blushing.

A pungent stench wound its way into her nose. Its familiarity did nothing to lessen the vileness of it, but it was a useful warning. Wordlessly she stood back-to-back with Nate and unsheathed her knife, the wooden handle reassuring in her hand. Around her the fog thickened to a deep and murky soup, grey on grey, swirling and condensing; she peered into it until the even greyer shadow of the familiar was almost visible.

Instinct told her there was more than one, a phenomenon that scared her witless but she pushed the fear away. She circled slowly, never taking her eyes from the shadowy shape in front of her. She felt Nate move forward and heard his grunt as he started to fight. Still her eyes remained focused. Then *it* struck, its long, twisted limb stretching forward so fast she only just leant left in time. She brought up her knife — it brushed against the slick, oily skin of the creature, enough to nick it, to release the tar-like substance that oozed through it. Not enough to slow it down.

A wail filled the air and pain shot through Regan's ears. Both of its limbs came forward, stiletto-like claws scratched the air where her head had been half a second earlier. She straightened her knees, leg extended. Kicked. Ducked. Swung forward, weapon stretched, grazing. Another piercing screech filled the air. She stabbed and bent forward. Too slow; a searing pain flashed down her shoulder; heat throbbed and she stumbled. Fear spiked in her chest and her breath came in short bursts. She found her footing and ignored the panic; her hand thrust up, straight into the gullet of the thing. A scream of icy breath smothered her; sound and ice and ichors, all as black as pitch, covered her. Then a painful silence as the scream faded, the deafening aftermath echoing only in her ears.

Once she was sure it had gone, she turned to help Nate; her heart stilled as she saw two belligerent creatures slowly backing him into a corner. *Three* familiars tonight. A shiver ran down her spine that was nothing to do with the cold. Nate was fighting with hunting knives in both hands yet he was only just managing to parry the creatures' blows. Strategies flashed through Regan's head as she crept forward; should she scream? Run? Join Nate? She dismissed each one as quickly as she thought of them, they were all too flawed.

Then an idea slipped into her mind. It was preposterous, it was dangerous, but it was the only idea she could see that may have a chance. As the thought formulated, she kept stealing forward; Nate was fighting hard but the familiars were pushing him back further and further into the dense trees. She gained ground quickly and sensed rather than saw the moment he realised she was there. She moved closer and closer to the nearest creature, half her mind praying that Nate would realise what she was about to do, the other half praying it would work.

Eventually one of the creatures was directly in front of her, less than an arm's length away. Like a stoat entrancing its prey, it wavered on its hind legs. A super-sized, malignant stoat. The greasy back of it was unprotected in front of her and she lunged forward, her weapon aiming up — straight into the area that would be its kidneys, if its anatomy resembled a human's in any way. 'Come on,' she muttered,then a scream issued from its throat as it flailed momentarily against the pain in its back. Regan pushed forward with the full force of her body until she was leaning against the creature, her knife embedded to the hilt. It shrieked again before imploding, gore and smell the only parts lingering.

Seconds later Nate sent the other creature the same way. The matter that was left seeped slowly into the ground, feeding back into nature. Nate made his way to where Regan stood leaning forward with her hands on her knees, trying to catch her breath. She lifted her head and saw fear etched in his face before he rearranged his features to their usual calm.

'Well done, Regan. I wasn't sure we were going to make that.'

'I'm not sure we did,' she replied, absently scraping the goo off her arm as she took stock of the cuts and slashes to his clothing. His thick leather jacket was shredded down one side and — 'You need that seeing to,' she said, indicating the deep scratches that made track lines across Nate's neck.

'It's just a nick,' he said, 'downside of the job.' He shrugged, but Regan knew it had to hurt a hell of a lot more than he was making out. 'That was a stupid move you did back there,' he said, 'perfectly ridiculous, it could have killed you, so close ...'

'It saved your life!'

'It saved my life,' Nate agreed, 'it was still a freakin' stupid thing to do.' But the gratitude in his eyes didn't match the words he uttered. 'Let's get home,' he said, rubbing her arm, a friendly gesture that sent chills through her.

'I do need a shower,' she agreed. 'It wasn't that dangerous, really,' she said as they made their way to his abandoned bike, 'after all, I knew it couldn't reach behind itself — you were in more danger from it than I was.' A slow smile crept across Nate's face and he thrust her helmet towards her before fastening his own and climbing on the bike.

Twenty-Seven

Regan fidgeted in her chair and rubbed her eyes. After an hour and — she glanced at her watch — twenty-seven minutes of staring at the computer screen, the thin padding stretched across the seat might as well have been no padding at all. She was getting severe arse-ache.

She scrolled down the seventh Google search page. The word *fen* caught her eye in the sixth article and she paused, her mouse hovering, ready to click on it. A quick scan of the first sentences showed her that it would be no more use than any of the others she had already investigated.

'How many pages of this rubbish is there?' she muttered, clicking on the page numbers at the bottom of the search engine. Nineteen, twenty-three, thirty-five, forty-two, fifty-five. Fifty-five pages, with ten suggestions on each page. 'Oh crap,' she let her head fall into her hands.

'It's a good job you're not going to university,' said Nate, making her jump, 'you'd have to spend way more time researching than this!'

Regan turned in her chair and stretched, 'This is the most boring thing I have ever done in my life,' she moaned, 'did you realise that any moron with access to a computer can spout off into cyber-space about whatever they want? This one guy, he wrote an entire two-page blog post about the fog he could see from his bedroom window, I mean, get a life …'

Nate gave her a look and, before he could tell her that everybody was entitled to their own hobbies, she stuck her tongue out at him.

'So, did *you* manage to find anything?' If she was honest, when she'd suggested Nate trawl through the newspaper archives again while she searched the internet, she'd thought that he was getting the short straw. But judging from the satisfied look on his face, he'd actually managed to find something out. All she'd managed to achieve was a wasted hour and a half of her life.

'Actually, I did,' he said, placing his notepad full of scrawled notes in front of Regan. 'And it was very helpful. Do you want the long or the short version?'

'The short, please,' she said, 'I've spent enough time in here already this morning!'

'Okay,' he said and pointed to his notes. 'I searched back through the papers and decided to ignore the ones from the last three decades for a start. These fogs, they're a real talking point, especially in the pub. You've heard old Sid sit there and moan about them, even Nick's grumbling about them keeping business away. I guessed they'd be comparing them to the ones of the eighties if they'd been happening that recently.' Regan nodded; it made sense, though to her the eighties were ancient history, well before her time. Before computers and mobile phones.

'Okay, so when did you start looking?' she asked.

'Well, I nearly started with the seventies but I didn't —'

Regan rolled her eyes, 'I thought this was the short version!'

'Sorry. I changed my mind and started at the beginning of the last century and there it was, ten years in, a report of thick, unnatural fog. The reporter actually used that word — *unnatural*. And,' his eyes gleamed, 'the reporter was thorough. He mentioned in the article that fogs like that had not been seen for nearly a hundred years. So I went back and there were reports of them in the autumn of 1813, then further and there was a mention of them also in 1713....'

'So it's every hundred years,' Regan interrupted him.

'It would seem so,' Nate said, 'one thing struck me as different though, the fogs had been recorded as daytime and night-time occurrences, but we—'

'Seem to only be seeing them in the evening,' finished Regan, 'hmm, that is odd.'

'Yeah, I wonder if it's just good old evolution again,' said Nate. 'Maybe survival of the fittest includes those with a self-preservation gene. Modern habits simply mean that the evening became the time it was easiest for these creatures to hunt.'

Regan, who just about followed his logic, nodded.

'It's worth thinking about,' he added, 'but we can't just jump to conclusions; we need to research it further, but at least we have a starting point.'

'*You* need to research further,' Regan said, 'I need to go to work.'

Twenty-Eight
1645

To Lora's amazement her Father had conceded Cecily's point. But then, why would he not? The visitor had been speaking the truth. There was something so familiar about her aunt's companion — and something so … compelling. Lora wished with increasing fervour that she was interesting enough to catch Cecily's attention. It seemed the Lord was listening.

'Lora,' Cecily smiled at her and Lora felt herself falling, oblivious in an instant of all others around the table. Shyness struck and she found herself incapable of speaking, a thousand thoughts ran through her head as she tried to think of something to say. It was impossible, but she wanted all of Cecily's attention to be on her alone. 'I have heard so much about you, Lora,' Cecily continued, her green eyes holding Lora's pale ones in their gaze, 'you are a very interesting young lady.'

'Oh, she is,' said Aunt Louisa, eager to regain her companion's focus, 'she is very *modern.*' The uncharacteristic scorn in her aunt's voice was palpable. Lora ignored it; she didn't care.

'I know, very *modern.* Wandering around the marshes with young Master Hunter and not a companion in sight!' Lora smiled at Cecily, glad to be the subject of her regard. Then, slowly, the meaning of her words penetrated. Lora gasped, the sound of guilt echoing in her ears. She tore her stare away from Cecily; her eyes darted to the left, to Aunt Louisa and Uncle Stephen, sure she would see outrage on even their most tolerant faces. When she realised that they had paid no mind she looked 'round further, certain that everyone else around the table would be aghast. Slowly, she realised that in fact the other guests had all resumed their own quiet conversations and were oblivious to Lora and Cecily.

The feeling of want and comfort that had cosseted her since Cecily had arrived slipped off like a silken shawl in the wind. Her head ached, dull and leaden; she found thoughts hard to formulate. Panic tightened its fist on her. The air felt thick and she struggled to draw in breath as the full implication of Cecily's words slowly filtered through to her brain. She knew about Rafe. But how? It was impossible — they had been so careful. Sluggishly, she raised her eyes to meet Cecily's again. The green eyes had lost their beauty; coldly they stared at Lora, the ruby mouth sneering now.

'You should be careful, little Lora, when prowling around at night. It is a well-known fact that those who get too close to the fire end up burnt. I will give this one warning — to you and dear Master Hunter — do not carry on your *quest*,' she spat the word out, 'or I promise you, you will both regret it.' Lora stared at Cecily anxiously, trying to think of an excuse, a reason to offer up. As she tried with desperation to think of something to say, the images that had haunted her sleep flashed into her mind, swiftly followed by a silhouette that flickered and jumped in the light of a guttering candle.

Realisation hit her, depriving her of yet more breath. She opened her mouth, gasping, trying to find air. Stiffly her hands clutched her chest as it tightened and stars started to swarm in front of her eyes. Black dots and silver flickered; she needed to breathe, now. Then, just as dizzy waves started to roll over her, air filled her lungs, sweeter than any bee's honey; she gasped it in, filling her lungs again and again.

'Lora!' Her mother's shrill voice brought her sharply back into the room, the house full of guests. Guests, she realised, that were completely unaware of what had just happened.

'I am sorry, Mother, I feel unwell,' Lora said, slipping from the room; she needed to see Rafe. Now.

Twenty-Nine
2013

The late September sun tried unsuccessfully to penetrate the chill of early autumn, and Regan snuggled deeper into her oversized chunky-knit jumper. She pulled the sleeves further still over her hands, until she had only the tips of her fingers free to turn the diary's pages.

The fog was particularly thick today and I sensed that something was amiss. I was still not fully prepared to fight with two of the witch's creatures, yet that is what I faced in the mist.

It was only with luck that I managed to kill both creatures by using the first to damage the second. When one was injured it was easy for me to kill and the other creature, cowering at the death wail, soon fell prey to my sharp knife.

I do not understand why the attacks have been more frequent recently, or why the creatures are becoming more vicious. I certainly do not understand why two of the creatures were out tonight.

It is nights like this that I really miss mother. If she was still alive, would she have the answers or would she not know what it meant? I do not know how she kept her hunting from my father, I find it more difficult each time I have to leave the house. Baby Elsie is so good, she settles down quickly. Violet promises me that if she wakes in the night she will settle her if I am not there, yet she too is so young to leave with this burden. Violet believes I leave the house to meet with a sweetheart. I pray each day that she won't tell father I go out.

'Regan,' called Katherine, 'I'm leaving now, are you going to come and keep an eye on Ashleigh?'

Regan put her bookmark back in place and rubbed her eyes. It didn't matter that she was becoming used to Elizabeth's elegant script, it still made her eyes ache to read it.

'Sure, coming Mum,' she said, unfolding her legs from under her and rubbing away the pins and needles. She rolled her shoulder where it still ached from her last encounter with the creatures and thanked God for the cooler weather and thicker jumpers she could wear.

The kitchen smelt of fresh bread and Ashleigh showed her the loaf Katherine had helped her make. 'It's hot still, but it will be great to have when we're watching the film, won't it?' she said, 'I've got loads of different things to put on top of it. Do you think Ella will like it?'

'It smells great kiddo, I'm sure Ella will love it. Go and check the sitting room's tidy, I'll just help Mum get Aunty Vi in the car.' She shooed Ashleigh off and tried not to roll her eyes at Katherine's long list of warnings — the same list she gave her every time she went to work and left Ashleigh in Regan's care.

'Are you sure this film is suitable for her? She's only eleven.'

'Mu-um,' Regan muttered.

'I know, I know,' said Katherine followed by, 'one day you'll—'

'—have children and I'll understand!' Regan gave in and rolled her eyes, 'Have fun at work.' Katherine gave her eldest daughter a well-practised resigned look and slammed the car door shut.

Just as she pulled away, Maeve's red sports car pulled up with Toni's yellow Honda close behind.

'Have you got the DVD, Toni?' she asked as the girl slammed her car door shut.

'Sure have, Robert Pattinson in all his vampire glory-ness! I can't believe you've never watched this yet!'

'Just cos you've watched it a million times, doesn't mean everyone else has,' said Ella, climbing out the passenger side. 'Guess what?' she asked in mock delight as they all headed to the house, 'she's brought the second film too, in case we really like it. Are you sure we can't watch anything else? A classic, a horror, an eighties film — paint dry?'

'It's not that bad,' said Maeve.

'And I really want to watch it,' said Ashleigh, setting the last of the snacks onto the coffee table.

'If you want to watch it, I don't mind,' said Ella, 'I could do your nails while it's on if you like?' Ella and Toni babysat Ashleigh on the odd occasions when both Regan and Katherine were at work; Ella especially had developed a very strong bond with the younger girl. It was her one redeeming feature as far as Regan was concerned, and the only reason she tolerated the snide remarks she was so fond of making.

'Cool,' said Ashleigh, 'I'm going to my friend Meg's party this evening; a glittery nail varnish would match my dress!'

'Well I tell you what, when the first film is finished how about we go and make your hair really pretty for the party?' Ashleigh beamed her answer and set up a manicure area in the corner of the room.

* * *

'Mmm,' said Regan, flicking off the DVD player and turning on the stereo, 'I'm going to dream of good-looking werewolves tonight!'

'I knew you'd love them!' said Toni, waving her hands to dry the nail varnish Regan had just applied.

Maeve looked up; her piercing green eyes looked straight at Regan and, raising one perfect eyebrow, she said, 'I suppose Nate's resemblance to the werewolf passed you by entirely, did it?' Regan felt the heat of a blush warming her face.

'He looks nothing like Nate,' she said, picking up an empty salsa pot from the floor, 'I just preferred his character …'

'Yeah, right. Pull the other one,' said Maeve, 'I don't think it's the werewolf you'll be dreaming of at all!'

'Maeve! Nate's just a friend, and *sshh*. Ashleigh might hear.' She packed away her nail varnish and tried to ignore the thud of her heart as an image of Nate crept into her head.

'Nah, she'll be upstairs with Ella getting her hair perfect for at least another half an hour,' said Toni, 'besides I want to hear about Nate too! My love life is boring — and for boring read non-existent — so I need to live vicariously through you! Plus, Sam has driven me mad this week. If it could annoy him, I'm all for it'.

'There's nothing to tell, and even if there was it would be nothing to do with Sam!' Regan insisted, doing her best to ignore the fluttering in her stomach at Nate's name.

'Really?' Maeve looked at her in mock disbelief, 'I know you said you had a teeny, tiny crush on him, but I can't help thinking that it's more than that. I mean, you do spend an awful lot of time together — every time I ring you're with him, he's at the pub every time you're working, he gives you lifts everywhere ...' she trailed off and looked at her friend. Regan knew the discomfort she was feeling must be showing on her face as Maeve said, 'I'm sorry Regan; it's absolutely none of my business! I love my manicure; this shade of red is my favourite and I have the perfect dress to go with it.'

Toni snorted, 'I never thought you'd give up so easily!' she said to Maeve.

The older girl shrugged and gave a small smile, 'It's none of my business really, is it. I was just teasing, Regan.'

Regan smiled — this is what she missed most about Ems. All of a sudden, she had an overwhelming urge to confide in her two new friends.

'Alright, I admit it. I do have a crush on Nate,' she buried her face in her hands, the smell of the nail polish drifting up her nose. 'It's awful; there's no way he feels the same. And he's so much older than me!'

'He's not *that* much older. What, three years?' Toni asked, putting her arm around Regan. Regan nodded miserably. It was the first time that she had admitted, even to herself, that her feelings weren't just hormonal.

'Three years isn't anything honey, and honestly, I already thought you were seeing each other!' Maeve said. Regan twisted her hands together. Words choked her throat. She wasn't sure she could admit to them what was really bothering her. Maeve perched herself beside her on Vi's old-fashioned settee and held her hand. 'What is it, Regan? You know you can tell us anything. Only if you want to, of course — I'm a great listener, I promise!'

'So am I,' said Toni, looking more solemn than Regan had ever seen her.

Thoughts raced through her head. Should she confide in them? Suddenly the need to blurt out what was on her mind overwhelmed her; she'd been here five months and she'd never really explained to anyone what had happened between her and Marcus. She checked the living room door was still shut and turned up the volume a little to make sure Ashleigh couldn't listen in.

'It's not the age gap as such,' she said, picking at a loose thread in the hem of her jumper. 'My last boyfriend was a few years older than me too.' Her voice cracked, too embarrassed to utter the next words.

'What is it, Regan?' Maeve frowned, concern etched over her features.

'My boyfriend, Marcus — well, I thought we were serious. You know, the real deal. But — I —' she twisted the thread harder, the stitching in her jumper puckering tightly. 'I wasn't ready to, you know, sleep with him …'

'And he didn't take it well?' Maeve interrupted, the look on her face showing nothing but concern for her friend.

'We broke up,' said Regan. 'I asked him if I could move in with him so I could stay in Brighton, but he came up with every excuse in the book. I sometimes wonder if he was with me for as long as he was because it was a challenge to try and get me into bed.' The thread pulled tighter, wool bunching up until it gave way and a small hole appeared. Tears welled in her eyes, threatening to fall. She hadn't thought about Marcus in weeks — well, since she'd met Nate if she were honest — but it did hurt how easily she had been dismissed.

'Oh, Regan,' said Toni, pulling her into a huge bear hug.

'Regan, honey,' Maeve passed her a tissue, 'I never met Marcus but I can tell you now he's an idiot. Breaking up with him was the luckiest day of your life. Honestly Regan, I know it sounds clichéd but if you're not ready then don't do it.' She grabbed Regan's hands and looked at her in earnest, 'It's not something to be thrown away; it's really important to wait until it's with the right person.'

Regan swallowed. 'But you've both done it, haven't you? I mean you're not virgins, are you? And Ella, I bet even she has.'

'If you could call it that,' said Toni, 'trust me, it's not all it's cracked up to be! Ella will tell you the same, and I know Sam was decent to her.'

Regan let this information process. So that was what the deal was between Ella and Sam.

Maeve frowned at her. 'I'm older than you honey. I tell you now — I wish I *had* waited for someone special. I know it's easy to say when you've done it. I don't want to sound like your mum Regan, but it is special — or it should be — and once you have given up your virginity you can't take it back. It needs to be with the right person or you'll live with the regret forever.'

Regan pulled a face, 'Well I don't think it's going to be too much of an issue in the near future. Nate only notices me when I'm—' she stopped short. *When I'm fighting beside him.* 'When I'm serving him in the pub,' she finished lamely.

'Now that *is* something I can do a bit about,' said Maeve, pulling out her make-up bag, 'Ella isn't the only one who specialises in make-overs!'

'Good idea,' Toni re-opened the bag of nail polish, 'we've got, what, two hours until you have to be at work?'

* * *

Her hand shook as she handed Nate his usual cola, newly manicured nails shimmering under the dim pub light. Embarrassed, she whipped it back quickly, hoping that he wouldn't notice. Though why he should she couldn't logically work out. It was just one of those things — now she had admitted to herself that she fancied him, she felt as though it was emblazoned on her forehead in permanent ink.

The girls had done miracles with her; even Ella had done something clever with her hair, twisted it into a sassy, shaggy ponytail. Toni had raided her wardrobe and found some tight black jeans and a fitted, low cut burgundy T-shirt. Regan had added the silvery scarf, vital if she wanted to hide the scratch marks just visible above her left shoulder. However, as good as she had felt about how she looked at home, it was now equalled by how embarrassed she felt here at work. She was convinced Nate would think she had dressed up for him. Which she had, of course. But she didn't want him to know that.

'So when are you going to ask the most beautiful barmaid in Norfolk out then?' Jim said, putting his empty pint glass down and winking at Nate. Regan felt the colour rise in her face and turned to the sink before anyone else noticed. Every shift one of the regulars would tease either her or Nate; usually she gave back as good as she got, but now she actually wanted Nate to ask her out she got completely tongue-tied.

Nate just smiled at Jim and took his drink to his usual table. Regan didn't know whether to feel hurt or relieved that he didn't notice her any more usual.

'He's a tough customer,' said Maeve in a low voice, 'but don't worry honey, by the time Toni and I have finished with you he won't stand a chance!' Regan smiled, but in the pit of her stomach she felt a leaden lump, a truth she had to acknowledge; she wanted Nate to notice her, but not if it took a lot of manipulation on her part. She wanted him to like *her*, the Regan he saw nearly every day. The Regan who joked with him, who researched with him. Who hunted with him.

'So what are you doing after work?' Maeve asked. 'I know Toni and Ella are busy now, but we could go out for a little while.'

'I'd love to Maeve, but I'm going round to Nate's.'

'Say no more,' Maeve winked, 'not still looking through those boring old diaries, are you?'

'Afraid so!' She wiped down the bar, trying to appear busy in case Nick looked over. 'I know you think they're boring, but honestly, they really are interesting. Lora …'

'Save it for Nate, honey. History is enough to put me to sleep. Though I can understand the attraction if it involves time spent with Nate!' Maeve grinned at her, eyebrows wagging up and down. Regan threw her dirty cloth at her friend and then caught Nick looking over at her, so she disappeared to the other end of the bar to serve one of the Barneys.

Thirty

Regan put her hand over her mouth, trying to hide her yawn. As much as she was fascinated by Elizabeth's diary, some of it was damn boring. As well as the entries written about the nights Elizabeth was out hunting, a lot of entries were concerned with the minutiae of daily life. And, frankly, Elizabeth's account of the comings and goings, affaires and disputes of the residents of Old Scytheton in the twenties wouldn't have been a contender for Hello magazine. Reading it at Nate's tiny kitchen table with his dimmed light bulb the only source of light didn't help either.

Flicking the page over carefully, she started to read the entry for 5th February 1922.

Today I read with excitement an entry in Catherine's diary that talks of thickening fogs and the increasing numbers of creatures she had to fight. She writes that she wishes Edward had not departed for America as she needs his help more than ever. The Hunter Edward believed he was following the trail of the creatures overseas and that activity in this area of England was decreasing sufficiently for him to depart. I was most astonished to read that Catherine believes the increase in familiars means that they are back under the control of a mistress. Her earlier entries had me wholly convinced, as was she, that the creatures hunted on their own and that witches were no longer in existence. The worsening and more frequent fighting conditions of which Catherine writes echo the conditions that I am experiencing. I am not sure I want to believe the possibility that Catherine has stumbled on the truth. That witches do still exist.

Regan's heart skipped a beat. Her hands trembled as she carefully re-read the entry. She skipped forward to the next and skim read it as fast as she could. Nothing. She pushed the book into the centre of the table, where the light was slightly stronger. Skipping pages, she flicked on and on through the diary trying to find what conclusion Elizabeth had come to.

'Careful with that, Regan,' Nate said. She looked up.

'I might have found something.' She explained what she had read, pausing intermittently as she tried to find out more. Nate waited patiently as she explained.

'Who's Catherine?' he said when she fell quiet, trying to read as fast as she could.

'I don't know,' she muttered, 'unless …' she paused in her reading, looking up. 'There were some other diaries in the pile with these two but they were rotted beyond saving. Could Catherine have written one of them?'

Nate got up and flicked the kettle on. Slowly, it began to boil as he spooned coffee into two mugs. 'That would make sense; it's such a shame they didn't survive life in the attic.' Regan was getting a headache trying to skim through Elizabeth's elaborate handwriting.

'Here, swap you,' said Nate, handing her a steaming mug of coffee and taking the diary from her hand. He sat back down at the table, scrutinising the diary. Feeling her knees cramp up from sitting, she stood and stretched them then walked to the window. The blackness of the night stretched out beyond the glass, but it was Nate's mirrored reflection the Regan found her eyes drawn to. His Bourneville hair was lost in the darkness of the night but she watched the familiar furrows etch across his brow as he concentrated on the diary. She watched his hands, so masculine — and handy with a hunting knife — delicately turn the fragile pages. His eyes devoured them at speed, his jaw clenching and unclenching as he tried to find relevant information.

'Listen to this,' he said, '*Today I saw a woman watching me. She was more beautiful than anyone I have ever seen before in my life. She was so delicate, with beautiful ebony dark hair in the latest London style. For a moment I wanted nothing more than to be near her, to be her. Then she smiled at me and it chilled me to the bone. I knew then that Catherine was right, witches do still exist.*'

Regan's brain raced. So Elizabeth — Elizabeth, the great aunt she had never met but with whom she shared a special bond — believed that, in 1922, she had sighted a witch.

'So, ninety years ago,' she said, 'Elizabeth believed she saw a witch.' Nate nodded, looking at her in anticipation, his dark eyes boring holes through her. When she failed to respond further, he rolled his eyes and went back to flicking through the diary. Regan felt the adrenaline surge through her body as she finally came to the conclusion she realised Nate had already reached. 'So if there was still a witch here less than a century ago, the chance is that there is *still* a witch here,' she said slowly. Nate nodded, his fingers still turning pages, eyes scanning back and forth. Regan shivered as a mix of fear and excitement coursed round her veins, a thrill she'd never felt before she'd moved to the fens. 'Do you think that the reason the familiars have increased and the fog has worsened is that there's a witch controlling them again?'

'I don't know, Regan. I mean, it's an easy conclusion to jump to, isn't it?' he said, marking his place and closing the journal. 'And even if it does mean that, why? Why then, why now?'

Regan shrugged, pacing around the floor, her head racing with a hundred unanswered questions. 'So why did you believe that witches don't exist anymore?' she asked, 'I mean, Elizabeth seemed to think the same before she read the entry Catherine had written. Catherine seemed to think the same or Edward wouldn't have left for America. Why?'

Nate pursed his lips, thinking. 'I don't know. I was just taught the tale of witches and the familiars. I was taught how to fight the familiars but the knowledge passed down to me was that there weren't any witches left.' She traced the wood grain of Nate's tabletop with her fingertips, her mind racing through the possibilities. She checked her watch; it was past midnight and she knew she should really be thinking about going home. As energy buzzed through her body, the last thing she felt like doing was going home to bed. And, she admitted to herself, like iron filings to a magnet she was drawn to Nate.

She looked up at him through her lashes, the outline of his chiselled jaw with its five o'clock shadow causing her breath to catch in her throat. He was thumbing through the diary again, 'This must hold more clues than that,' he muttered as he skimmed the pages. 'Here it is!' he said, speed-reading the page. His eyes darted from side to side, and then slowly a frown tugged at his forehead.

'What is it?' she sat forward, 'what, Nate?' she repeated when he didn't reply. He looked up at her, 'I know why we are fighting so many familiars,' he said. 'We have a serious problem on our hands.'

'What do you mean?' said Regan, pacing round Nate's kitchen again. 'What kind of *serious problem*?' Nate ignored her, skimming the diary as fast as he could. It was all she could do not to rip it from his hands and start reading it herself.

'Nate! What problem?' Frustrated, she used all her willpower to stop herself punching Nate on the arm. The seconds stretched like knicker elastic; just when Regan thought she actually *was* going to hit Nate, he said, 'According to this, via Catherine's diary, an increase in fog and creature activity is a sure indicator that there is a witch. Not only is there a witch, but she is getting ready to strengthen her powers. I'm summarising here but basically every century a witch will need to renew her powers. Catherine wrote that the witch she knew of — and apparently, they really are a rare breed — needed to renew her powers in the thirteenth year of every century.'

Regan interrupted, 'As in *this* year? 2013?'

'Yes, though this doesn't fit in with Elizabeth's disappearance in 1922. I think she was just unlucky one night. It could happen to any of us. I bet Elizabeth encountered her though.'

'So how are we going to find this witch?' She paused as a thought occurred to her, 'Are you saying that this is the *same* witch that was haunting Elizabeth a hundred years ago? *And* Catherine, however long before that?' she asked. 'That would make her …'

'Really old. Yes, it says here that the witch looks young and beautiful, yet she is older than anyone in town.'

'How is that possible?' Regan said, her forehead furrowing.

'I don't know, it's just what's written here. The thing is, Regan, I believe it. I also believe that our witch could be back.' He looked at her, 'And it says here that on December 21st she'll need a sacrifice in order to keep her powers strong.'

'That's less than a month,' said Regan; Nate nodded. 'What kind of sacrifice does she need?' Goats, sheep, pigs … various animals ran though Regan's mind. Maybe they could start watching farms that had animals, keep a tab on local smallholdings … her brain raced. Nate's next words stopped her heart though. 'According to this, the sacrifice she needs is an eighteen-year-old virgin.'

Thirty-One
1645

Hearing the creak of the stairs, Lora slipped under her covers and tried to look as though she had a headache. It wasn't as difficult as she'd imagined; her forehead was clammy and her skin pale grey, the colour of rags washed and scrubbed beyond repair. She had just pulled the cover up under her chin when her mother barged into the room.

'Lora, how very rude of you. It is most ill-mannered to leave in the middle of dinner.'

'I'm sorry Mother, my head … I feel so terribly unwell. I do not know why, it came on so suddenly.'

Concern crossed her mother's usually severe features. 'I have some boiled cottonweed. Try the vapours of that.' As her mother left to get the treasured treatment, Lora concentrated on looking feeble, her mind trying to focus on the problem of getting her mother out of the room so she could think.

Her mother soon came back and wafted the vile vapours under her nose. Acid surged in Lora's stomach, already weak from such a disturbed night's sleep. The aroma of the cottonweed was tempting the few bites of eel pie she had eaten to surge back up. After a short time had passed and Lora could bear it no more, she said, 'I feel much better Mother, I think some sleep will aid my recovery.'

'Are you sure, dear, you do not think a bleeding would work better?'

'No, Mother,' Lora felt a look of alarm cross her face — a bleeding was the last thing she needed; time to think was what she really required. Thankfully Eleanor Smith was anxious to get back to her guests, and her sense of maternal duty was easily mollified.

As soon as she was alone Lora sat up in bed. Sweat stuck her hair to her head, her hands were clammy and bile kept burning her throat. Her brain wouldn't work and the headache that had threatened all day, the one she had claimed to have already, was starting to clutch more tightly at the edges of her skull. Lora drew in slow, deep breaths and shook her head; she needed to think straight. At this moment the witch was sitting around the table with her family. And she knew that Lora knew who she was; Lora didn't know how, but she was certain that she knew.

Think, Lora, she told herself. She needed to get her family to safety — but how? If she went down and told everyone, would they believe her? She doubted it; every guest seemed as entranced by Cecily as she had been. If she bounded down there accusing her of witchcraft and sorcery, it would be her who they would cart off to the lunatic hospital. And there was no way of knowing how powerful Cecily was, what damage she could cause — the creatures she commanded were evil enough. Oh God, Mary was there with an innocent babe in her belly. Mother, Father, Uncle Stephen and Aunt Louisa … they hadn't known what Cecily was. It was all her own fault that all their lives were at risk.

A tear leaked down the side of her face and she wiped it furiously. The sound of laughter floated up to her room, the gentle hum of distant conversation. 'Do you not know how much danger you are in?' she wanted to scream, 'Can you not feel the evil at the table?'

Climbing as silently as she could from her bed, she knelt beside it, hands clasped together, head bowed. 'Dear Lord God, I know that it has been my ignorance and pride that has brought the devil into this house. It is not the ignorance of my family though, of the innocents sitting around my father's table. Please, dear God, help me keep my family safe. I will sacrifice anything to keep them from harm. I pray, dear God, that you guide me in this. Amen.' She rose again, her head clearer, her faith strengthening her.

Be careful what you wish for. Any number of times her old grandmother had told her this. She had never fully understood it before; nobody wishes for bad things, so how could a wish hurt? Now she understood with all too much clarity. She had wanted so much to put a face to her enemy, to know what she was fighting to rid the world of. But this was not what she had imagined — the devil's mistress dining with her family. Creatures she could hunt and fight, but this — this was beyond her capabilities.

A pretty laugh rose up through the floorboards, a soft lyrical sound. Her chest constricted and she absentmindedly rubbed it, trying to ease the tightness. Dark nights, and fogs; fighting in the marshes … they were easy to deal with. She couldn't go downstairs and take a knife to Cecily. The thought almost made her laugh. Family or not, they wouldn't just sit around and let her stab a dinner guest; she would be locked up for her own safety or hanged for that of others.

Finally, she let her brain take her where she had known it wanted to go all along — Rafe. She needed Rafe. He would know how to deal with this. She should have listened to him all those weeks ago, walked out of the fens and forgotten everything that she had seen. Before she knew it, she had grabbed her shawl and was creeping quietly back down the stairs. Heart thudding loudly, she shut the back door as silently as possible and, praying her mother wouldn't want to check on her, fled into the night.

Thirty-Two
2013

'Hallo gorgeous,' said Sam as he leaned across the bar, eyes twinkling, 'so, is tonight going to be the night I get you to agree to a date?'

Regan pushed the frothy pint she had just drawn across the bar towards Howie, added it onto his account, then looked over at Sam. She took a deep breath, 'I don't think it is, Sam — I mean, you could try and see, but I'm pretty sure the answer is going to be no.'

'Oh, you break my heart!' he said, the glimmer in his eye gleaming just a bit brighter. 'I'm not going to give up, Regan — you're single and only human. I'm pretty sure you'll give in to your natural urges sooner or later!'

'I wouldn't wish too hard Sam. You're lovely and all but …'

'You're not her type,' said Toni. 'Get a clue, Sam!'

Sam frowned a little, eyed Regan up and down, and muttered, 'Oh god, not you too,' cryptically, before sighing and taking his beer over to his group of mates in the corner. Regan and Toni exchanged glances.

'What the hell did *that* mean?' asked Toni.

'Oh, you know Sam. Probably can't believe someone is able to resist his advances,' said Ella.

Regan was about to agree with her when she noticed the look of anger on the other girl's face. Great, *another* reason for Ella to be pissed off with her. After the conversation she'd had with Toni and Maeve, it hadn't taken her long to realise that the dark-haired girl's problem with her was to do with Sam. After Toni had let it slip that Sam had been Ella's first love, it wasn't too much of a stretch to realise that she still carried a torch for him. Even if Regan wasn't half in love with Nate, she wouldn't take Sam up on his offer — she might not really get on with Ella, but she didn't want to hurt the girl if she could help it.

'Come on Toni,' said Ella; she took her friend's elbow and led her possessively towards a small table in the corner. Well away from Sam and his mates, Regan noticed. Not long after Maeve came in and, seeing Regan was busy, joined them. Glancing over, Regan gave a quick wave. Ella was giving Maeve one of her best dirty looks. Regan shook her head. Maybe Ella *was* just mean — Maeve had never even met Sam, so that wasn't the problem in their case.

The pub was nicely busy for a Thursday night. It was a fine evening so more customers had ventured out. The fogs were becoming a bit of a discussion point though. Once Regan had overheard some customers talking about strange cries they'd heard in the mist. Her heart had stopped for a second — a brief panic ensued, then someone else had replied about Muntjac deer and how they screamed sometimes. This seemed good enough for all those involved in the conversation. Fearful people, ready to believe in anything that could be safe Nate had said when she mentioned it later. They were both thankful that people were willing to believe benign reasons; the last thing they needed was a search party out in the fog, hindering their own hunt.

Regan grabbed the boxes of crisps and refilled the empty stands, then she did a round of the pub and loaded the dishwasher with the used glasses she collected. Next, she grabbed a cloth and scrubbed the length of bar clean, leaving the deep mahogany shining, before moving on to the tables. She hadn't stopped being busy since the previous day at Nate's house. She was either talking to people or working — anything to keep her brain from mulling over the latest revelations.

She wasn't sure what she was trying to ignore — the fact that witches could still exist, the fact that possibly a witch was looking for a sacrifice, or the fact that she could quite easily be exactly what that witch was looking for. She didn't know whether to be terrified or just laugh damn loud at the whole ludicrous situation.

Serving a couple of the regulars, she laughed along with their banter. Then Maeve wandered over, 'Hi honey, we're going to grab a take-away then go back to Toni's for a bit.' She leaned in close and whispered, with wide open eyes, 'Why didn't you tell me her brother was so *hot*? Apparently, him and his mates are grabbing a film for us all — any way you can slope off early tonight?'

Regan pulled a face, turning her lips down. 'No way, it's just me working really. Nick isn't officially here on a Thursday.' She looked down the bar to where her boss was chatting away, 'Of course, it seems it's impossible for him to *actually* stay away from the place. Mind you I bet if you're all descending on their house Cyndi will come and claim Nick for an hour or two.'

Just then the door swung open again and Nate walked in. Maeve turned at the sound then twisted back to Regan, mirth glistening in her green eyes, 'Don't worry honey, I won't ask again — the view is going to be so much better here for you.'

She waved goodbye to her friends, ignoring a wink from Sam — his eyes had turned to appraise Maeve before she had even got through the door, which made Regan chuckle.

'Let me guess — cola?' Regan asked as Nate took a seat at the bar.

'Thanks,' he said, settling onto a bar stool near her. She smiled and was about to ask if he'd given the diary entries any more thought when a customer caught her attention. By the time she'd finished serving him Nick stood in front of her, Cyndi by his side as predicted.

'We're going for some dinner; do you mind locking up and sticking the key through my door when you're done?' he asked Regan. She shook her head then, as her boss left, made her way back to where Nate was sitting.

So …' she started.

'Indeed,' said Nate. 'I guess you've not been able to think about much else either?'

'That has to be the understatement of the century!' Regan checked no-one needed serving and leaned against the bar opposite Nate. She tried hard not to notice the strength in his muscled forearms, or the smooth mocha of his skin, or the scarred fingers wrapped around the chilled glass.

'I'm trying very hard not to think about it; I don't know what it means, or even how we would begin to tackle hunting a witch. Familiars are easy money compared to this — we wait for the fog, turn up where it's thickest and fight the creatures we find lurking there.'

Nate laughed — a soft, sarcastic sound that sent shivers down Regan's spine. 'I can honestly say I've never thought of fighting familiars as easy money!'

Sighing she said, 'All in context, Nate. All in context. Have you had any brainstorms about what we should do?'

An unexpected smile flitted across his face, 'As a matter of fact I have. I think the best way to tackle finding the witch is by a process of elimination.'

Checking again that there were no customers waiting to be served, Regan lifted up her shoulders and said, 'Huh? Eliminate what?'

'Possible places that a witch could live. We figure out where she's most likely to be dwelling, most likely to be preparing for her *ritual,* and take it from there.'

'Oh well if I'd've known it was going to be as easy as *that* ...' muttered Regan.

'I'm not saying it's going to be easy, but at least it's a starting point,' Nate shrugged, 'do you have any better ideas?'

'You know I don't. So explain to me exactly how we go about finding where she lives.'

Nate drained the last of his drink and pushed the dirty glass back to Regan. She re-filled it and poured one for herself. The sweet taste of the soda was nice; she hadn't realised she was thirsty till then.

'I've been thinking about it and I think that the witch is likely to be close to where the familiars lurk. If they are her pets, and causing more mayhem because her powers are changing, then it makes sense they're nearby.' Regan nodded — it still didn't help her understand where Nate thought they should be looking though.

'So I thought about where we've had to hunt the most.'

'In the fens, mainly,' said Regan. 'A couple of times in the woods but generally just in the fens.'

'Exactly,' said Nate, 'and what better place to live than in the middle of the fens?' Regan was still a little puzzled.

'You know, out in the heart of nowhere — you live there, so do I.... Across even this small area of fenland there are hundreds of desolate properties. I know *The Fens* covers a wide area but we need to concentrate on this part, where the creatures seem to be strongest.'

'So you're saying I could have a witch as my next-door-neighbour?' Regan shuddered; granted, her next neighbour was about two miles away, but still. The thought was creepy. Actually, the thought was downright frightening. Especially when she thought of Ashleigh, her mum and Aunt Vi all at home together. Vulnerable.

'I'm afraid that's exactly what I am saying. The other option we have is to try and pinpoint who could be the possible target for the sacrifice.' He paused and looked Regan in the eye, 'But I think that's going to be pretty difficult.'

'Yeah,' said Regan, frowning and embarrassed. 'It's not as if we can hand out surveys!' She nipped down the bar to serve another customer, her heart pounding. There was no way she could admit the truth to Nate. She scooted back to finish the conversation, 'besides, even if we did find a way to do a survey, no-one would fill it in honestly.'

Nate shook his head, 'More's the pity. It's a real shame that girls are so desperate to appear cool they'll say anything ... and in some cases, *do* anything.'

Regan mumbled agreement — this conversation was taking a turn she really didn't want.

'So how do we go about eliminating possible lairs for old Winnie?'

'Huh?' said Nate.

'Winnie the Witch. She's a ... never mind. How do we find where she lives?'

'Well, the best way I can come up with is to actually go and search. I thought I could mark off the possible parameters on a map of the area, then literally drive each road, lane and by-way. The way I figure it, she ...'

'Or he!'

'Or he — but it was a woman mentioned in the diaries,' Nate's dark eyes burrowed into her, 'is not going to leave a traceable trail if possible. No internet searches to pinpoint her, for example. She's going to be off the radar.'

The door swung open as a large group of customers left. Ten fifty and only a couple of groups of regulars were still lingering. Regan left Nate and cleared up the empties; she pushed in the barstools and chairs and ran a wet cloth over sticky tables. As the hand crept past eleven she called, 'Time, gentlemen, please,' then waited patiently as the last few left. By the time she had locked the door and tidied away the last few bits, Nate had drained his drink and added his own glass to the dishwasher. Regan turned it on then realised that it probably wasn't the best idea to leave it running. Grabbing a bag of peanuts and one of pork scratchings, she pulled up a barstool next to Nate and offered him the choice. He took the peanuts.

Regan loved the pub when it was empty. The old building seemed to come alive when it was bereft of the noise of merry customers. The dark beams, virtually hidden by years of photographs, brasses and other general flotsam of public house life, seemed to suddenly ache with age. Creaks and groans unheard over the general hubbub seemed not frightening as one would think, but reassuring; an old building settling into the night, comfortable in its old bones. The ghosts of thousands of patrons hidden just a whisper away. Regan almost felt that if she listened hard enough, she would hear the sounds of those long-ago customers, their stories, their secrets, their warnings.

Until she'd moved to Norfolk she'd never been especially interested in history, but since discovering the diaries she had a burning desire to understand the characters of the past. Particularly Lora and Elizabeth.

'Do you think they were ever in here?' she asked Nate, out of the blue.

'Who?' asked Nate, not having been privy to her silent musings of the past few minutes. He shoved another handful of nuts into his mouth and sucked the salt from his hands. Regan's chest tightened at the thought of licking those fingers clean.

'Lora or Elizabeth,' she said, shaking the thought of his fingers from her head.

'It's quite possible, though perhaps more likely that Rafe was — I don't think women had quite the freedom they do today.'

This made Regan pause. 'I hadn't really thought about that,' she admitted. While she did sneak out sometimes, she knew she was allowed pretty much all the freedom she wanted. It hadn't really occurred to her that both Lora and Elizabeth would be in enormous trouble if they were found out. Now she was eighteen, she was pretty much able to come and go as she pleased and it was only courtesy that let her mum know where she was — or at least a slightly altered version of where she was.

'Wow, what they did — it was really brave. Especially Elizabeth, she didn't even have anyone fighting with her. I'd love to travel back in time to meet them — I bet they were generations ahead of their own time!'

'I bet,' agreed Nate, 'It does make you re-think the "problems" we have today, doesn't it?'

Swallowing a flippant remark about terrible broadband coverage, Regan nodded her agreement; how she would have survived in such restrictive ages, she didn't know.

'So, next on our "to do" list is to get a map and start looking for possible places our witch could live?' said Regan, slipping on the red cardigan she had stored under the bar. The heating went off when the patrons were kicked out and the autumn chill was creeping in fast.

'I've already got one, and yes, I plan to start tonight. Once I've dropped you off.' For once, Regan didn't start a disagreement by insisting that she come with him. As much as she was starting to want to spend every single spare second with Nate, it had been a long day and she was tired. Besides, an idea was tugging at the corner of her mind. She needed time alone to think it through.

Thirty-Three
1645

The night air was frigid and Lora's shawl was not adequate protection against the cold. Goose pimples sprang up down her arms and her breath billowed out in misty puffs. Fear at the knowledge that any moment Mother could check on her and discover the bed empty was only drowned by the dread of who — what — was breaking bread with her family.

The stars twinkled in the sky, jewels against an inky background. The moon shone brightly; it was almost full and lit the way near clear as sunlight. The smell of smoke from the town's chimneys made her wish for warmth as the cold air pinched at her nose. Forcing her feet to move faster, Lora was soon away from the town and heading into the fens towards Rafe's humble abode. An owl hooted in the distance and a bat swooped overhead. A rustling in the leaves on the side of the road caused Lora to hurry quicker still; without her knife she felt vulnerable. *Please, God, keep my family safe*, she prayed with each quickened step. There was no doubt in her mind that Rafe would save her, that he would know what to do, how to keep them all safe. Yet going to Rafe was a risk in itself. Had not Cecily told her that she knew *all* about their hunting expeditions. How could she have known? No-one knew but Lora herself, and Rafe....

Stumbling, Lora pulled herself to a halt. How had Cecily known? How had Rafe known who Cecily was? Could she trust Rafe? Standing alone in the cold night air, surrounded by the vast night sky with its million twinkling stars, she wasn't sure. Her family all at home, in danger beyond her imaginings, and Rafe — her saviour — now a possible threat himself, Lora suddenly felt very lonely. Despair shrouded her like a cloak; doubt tugged at her heart. Blackness enveloped her, a gloom invisible to the eye. Any fight she had left departed her — after all, what was the point? She was not powerful enough to fight Cecily; she was silly to want to try. Pulling her shawl tighter, she sat down. Maybe if she rested a while it would become clearer to her what she should do.

* * *

Time passed; soon Lora's hands were stiff with cold. Her shawl, even wrapped tight, was no defence against the icy fingers of the night. Tiredness radiated from her; sleep threatened to pull at her eyelids and shut them even in the frigid midnight air. She was trying to remember why she was there. Somewhere in her heart she knew she should be afraid, but she couldn't remember what of. And, if truth be told, she was just too tired to be afraid of anything. *In fact,* Lora thought to herself, *maybe just a little sleep would help clear my head.*

The ground was hard and stone-cold beneath her, but Lora didn't really feel it as she folded her legs under herself and wrapped the shawl closer like a blanket. Her lead-heavy lids slowly shut and her head fell heavily to her chest. Dreamless sleep invaded her body.

The moon lit the night bright, yet the raggedy pile of dark blanket in the shadows of the grass was not easily to be seen by unsuspecting human eyes. The air grew more frigid; a badger sniffed from a distance but trundled past on the other side of the road. A fox was braver and sniffed around Lora's sleeping body; a breeze blew and the whiff of hare caught the fox's nose. Hare was a meal much easier to take back for her cubs, so as the breeze blew again she fled silently into the night.

Whispers of freezing night air slid silently around Lora, covering her body in a frosty blanket. Her breathing became shallower. A spider zealously scurried over her face, spinning its web across from her nose to her frozen hair and to her chilly blanket. Backwards and forwards it weaved, busily making its silken lair. Lora slept on, completely oblivious of the spider at work, of the owls calling to each other in the distance. Of death soundlessly creeping in with the cold.

Thirty-Four
2013

The idea had been formulating in Regan's head ever since Tuesday night. Her discussion with Nate had got the cogs turning in her head. She liked his plan, it was logical and had plenty of merit. It didn't change the fact, though, that while he might think it best to find the witch, she wanted to take temptation out of its way. Just in case they couldn't find it. Of course, he had no idea she was still a virgin.

It hadn't been that long ago she'd had this entire discussion with Maeve and Toni. She might been holding on to her virginity like it was some sort of prize, but she felt sure there weren't many eighteen-year-olds who thought the same way. Nate had actually laughed out loud at the idea before suggesting that maybe they needed to check out local religious groups, see if there were any younger members who would fit the bill. Of course, apart from a small Anglican church in the next village, Upper Bridgeton, the middle of the fens wasn't exactly a thriving religious centre.

It was fine for Toni, Maeve and Ems to be sweet about it all, but none of them knew anyone else who was eighteen and hadn't done it yet. It was all very well for them to tell Regan she was doing the right thing wanting to wait. *They*'d all done the deed —

experienced sex, lovemaking, having a shag or whatever label they wanted to put on it. At the moment, Regan was finding it hard to remember why hanging on to her virginity had like seemed such a good idea. At the moment it seemed like the worst idea possible; literally, it could be a death sentence.

Checking the heat in her curling tongs, she set about adding some volume to her usually straightened hair. Tonight she needed to feel bolder, not quite like her normal self. And as she twisted a second strand around the tongs, she admitted to herself that she needed to look pretty darn hot. A lot was riding on this.

When she had finally let herself think about the idea that was playing hide and seek in her brain, she'd rejected it immediately. No way could she do this — she wouldn't have the guts. Then she'd decided to write down the facts. Her list had looked something like this:

She was an eighteen-year-old virgin, at a time when being an eighteen-year-old virgin could seriously damage her health. Ergo:

She needed to get rid of her virginity. To do this she could either:

Choose some random stranger from a club who she would never see again and just 'get rid of it'.

Choose someone from the pub — Sam for example — they were all nice chaps. It wouldn't be a complete stranger, but she would have to live with it every time she went to work and discourage any thoughts of a future relationship.

Seduce Nate. Someone she literally trusted with her life, someone she found attractive and someone she knew wouldn't want to take it any further. He was all about the business, but for god's sake he was still a red-blooded male — surely, he couldn't be a *complete* saint.

2+c = solution.

Of course, writing it down in a list and actually trying to seduce someone were quite different things, but once Regan made up her mind to do something, she never backed down. Or so she told herself as she applied some black kohl liner to her eyes and carefully smudged smoky grey shadow round them, making their ice blue colour stand out. A touch of clear gloss to her lips and somehow she'd achieved that look of vulnerable and sexy.

Of course, her dress had nothing vulnerable about it. It was one she'd seen Maeve looking at last time they'd gone shopping; as soon as she'd formulated her plan, she knew there was no other dress suitable.

It was emerald, green, long and made of satin. Completely backless, she couldn't wear a bra under it — one less obstacle for later — and it fitted her newly-toned body like a glove. As she looked in the mirror Regan gave thanks for the endless exercising of the last months — she'd never have dared wear a dress this revealing before. With her hair curled and tumbling down her back, a satin choker at her neck and some to-die-for emerald satin heels, she was ready to go.

When she'd been thinking through this plan, she'd thought the hardest part would be getting Nate into a situation when she could seduce him. The only times she ever saw him were after work, when they were training or doing research, or when they were out fighting together. None of those situations, she had concluded, were particularly conducive to seduction.

Then she remembered her birthday celebrations — or, to be more precise, her lack of birthday celebrations. Next week she turned eighteen — that magical age that launched her into adulthood and the 'perfect as a sacrifice' bracket. She'd dropped plenty of hints to Nate and when none of them had blossomed into him asking her out, she'd taken the bull by the horns and asked *him* out.

She'd laid it on thick, saying Aunty Vi was too ill for a party or for her mum to take her anywhere. That she was going to have a small celebration at home but she *really* wanted to try Giorgio's, the newest Italian restaurant in Lynn. In the end it hadn't taken long for Nate's chivalrous side to come to the fore, and he'd agreed to have dinner with her. Of course, she planned on totally rewarding him for his kind deed.

After all, dessert was her.

It wasn't until Nate pulled up outside in a car that Regan didn't recognise that she started to feel nervous. Twisting her blonde hair round her finger then giving the whole lot one last squirt with the hair spray, she slowly descended the stairs. Nate was waiting in the hallway with her mum; she studied his face carefully for his reaction — she needed to make an impression. She knew that in order for this to work, she had to show him that she was more than just Regan White, companion hunter — she needed to show him she was also Regan White, woman.

'Oh Regan, you look stunning,' said her mum, 'doesn't she Nate?'

'Thanks Mum,' Regan managed, her eyes never straying from Nate's face, searching it for any sign of approval. He stared, speechless for a second, until Katherine repeated her question.

'You look absolutely beautiful, Regan,' he said and Regan started to breathe again, not realising until that moment that she had been holding her breath.

'Thanks,' she replied, 'you don't scrub up too badly yourself.' This was perhaps the understatement of the century. She had never seen Nate in anything other than his training gear or his uniform of jeans, t-shirt and leather jacket. Today, though, he was wearing a black suit with a bright blue shirt underneath; a black tie and a fresh shave completed the look. He was positively gorgeous; even in a suit there was no disguising his broad shoulders and taut stomach. He wouldn't have looked out of place on the cover of *Vogue*.

'Are you ready?' he asked, offering her his arm. She managed a nod and said goodbye to her mum.

'Have fun,' called Katherine. Regan was pleased she didn't add the usual *don't do anything I wouldn't do.* Because tonight she couldn't promise to comply.

'Our reservation is for eight,' Nate said, opening the car door for her, 'that'll give us time to park and walk to the restaurant. Will a walk be okay in those?' he asked doubtfully, looking at her feet. She laughed and waited for him to slide into the driver's seat.

'Of course,' she said, 'I've had my high heels licence for a while now. Though I did have to get it down and dust it off today,' she added mournfully, trying to remember the last time she'd worn a pair of truly killer heels.

'So where did you get the car?' she asked, screwing up her nose at the faint odour of fags in the air.

'I borrowed it from Si,' he said. Si, she remembered, was his landlord. 'Sorry about the stench of cigarettes, I have cleaned it all out today but I can't shift the smell. I didn't think the bike would be appropriate transport for tonight.' They both glanced at her skin-tight outfit and reached the same conclusion — no way could she have gotten on the bike wearing that dress!

'It's fine,' she said, 'it was very thoughtful of you. So, are you hungry?' She was, she realised — despite the butterflies tangoing in her stomach. It was already dark and there was no sign of any fog, so she might even let herself have a drink tonight; a glass of wine with dinner might just be what she needed to calm her nerves.

'Yeah, I guess,' he replied, 'it's been so long since I've eaten out, I'm looking forward to it.' Regan smiled. She knew that his diet usually consisted of food simply for the purpose of fuelling his body. Like everything else in his life, food was another way of ensuring that he was the best hunter he could be. He treated his body as if it were a machine — it needed to be looked after and maintained purely so it could fulfil its purpose. Sadness filled Regan; Nate was such a wonderful person, any fool could see that. Yet he existed literally for one reason only and didn't allow himself any pleasure in life. If it didn't benefit his fight against the familiars — and now, of course, witches — then it had no place in his life as far as Nate was concerned. The only pleasure he had was his bike, and that was only because he considered it a useful tool in his fight.

'Why did you agree to come out tonight?' she asked suddenly, not sure how this date fitted in with Nate's hunter philosophy.

'Everyone deserves to celebrate their birthday,' he said simply, 'especially a landmark one like eighteen.' She thought about that for a second.

'So what did you do on your eighteenth, Nate?' she asked, twisting in her seat so she could look at him. The sight of him took her breath away again.

'That's irrelevant,' Nate shrugged, 'it was a long time ago anyway.'

'It was three years ago!' she said, 'and it isn't irrelevant, Nate. You're a person too, not just a hunter. You have a right to be more than that. What you do is important — vital even — but it isn't everything you are.' She stopped as Nate pulled the car into one of the free spaces along the riverfront. 'At least, it shouldn't be,' she added quietly to herself, realising with a shock that Nate's lack of self-interest and care really bothered her.

Like a gentleman, he opened her door and helped her out of the car. The musky smell of his aftershave wafted under her nose and she shivered slightly; he smelt as gorgeous as he looked.

'Are you cold?' he asked as he offered her his arm before walking her towards the restaurant.

'Not at all,' she said, 'everything is perfect.' Grimacing inside, she really hoped that didn't sound as cheesy as she thought it did.

Cheesy but true, she admitted to herself, looking around. The sun had set but the moon was bright and glinted off the water as it lapped gently against the riverside. It was impossible to see where the river washed out to sea, there was just a dark, empty nothingness that splashed beside them. The sky was vast and beautiful above, diamond pricks of starlight echoing endlessly in the black.

'I hate to sound like a broken record,' she said to Nate, 'but it really is so beautiful here.'

'It truly is,' he agreed, 'It's nothing like where I grew up, yet it manages to feel like home.'

They walked in silence alongside the river until they turned left down the cobbled street to Giorgio's. Nate tightened his grip on Regan's arm; however licensed she was, these cobbles were not designed for high heels. Excitement ran down Regan's spine and for the first time since she'd formulated the plan, she started to think it might be a good idea.

The restaurant was beautiful and they were seated within seconds of entering. Regan perused the menu, trying to decide which pasta dish she fancied the most. Anything with garlic was off the menu for tonight, obviously.

Settling for a simple creamy chicken and linguine she passed the menu to the waiter, waited for Nate to add his order to hers, and then picked up the conversation they'd been having on their way in.

'So where do you hail from then, Nate? You've been my best friend for nearly five months now and I know so little about you,' she said.

He looked at her, his dark eyes thoughtful, 'You know more about me than most people, Regan.'

'Nate, if that is true then it is really sad. I know about you the hunter, but I don't know you, who you are, what you like. What makes you tick, Nate Hunter?'

'You know what makes me tick. I'm here for one reason and I intend to fulfil that reason to the best of my ability until … well until it's not needed any more or until I die, I guess.' Regan looked at Nate and listened to the sincerity in his tone; tears choked in her throat for him.

What kind of life was this for him? What right had 'destiny' to take away his freedom and give him this prison sentence instead? He might not be enclosed in four walls, but his boundaries were just as rigid. In an age where very few people cared about duty so much, she felt she should applaud his dedication to the cause. But she couldn't. Everyone had the right to *live* his or her life, even taking responsibility into account.

'So? Where are you from?' she repeated, determined to get to know him better — ashamed that, after the hours they had spent together, she knew so little about him. He, on the other hand, could probably write an entire book about her. Far from being quiet and mysterious, she was more the 'wears her heart on her sleeve' type. Suddenly Regan wanted to know everything there was to know about Nate.

'Well …'

'Salem, Massachusetts,' he said, 'I should imagine you've heard of it.'

'The witch trials?' Regan asked, amazed; Nate nodded.

'Not a coincidence, I suspect. Rafael moved to Salem from Norfolk, and I'm pretty sure now that he was following Cecily. Between Lora's diary and his journal it's all starting to make sense.' Regan was intrigued; despite the resolution she'd made not to talk about hunting or familiars or witches, she couldn't help but be interested.

'And your family has been there ever since?' she asked, reaching across the table and touching her fingertips to his hand. The touch was brief, but a volt of electric shot up her arm; she couldn't believe that he hadn't felt it too.

'Pretty much,' said Nate, 'each generation has travelled — following the fogs, as we say — but we've always ended up back at home.'

'So all you men are destined to be hunters, but what about the women? What about your mother and grandmother, how do they fit into the story?'

Nate looked uncomfortable. 'It isn't nice for them,' he said, 'I know that. Their husbands and sons out fighting god knows what, never knowing when they will return home. Hell, never knowing *if* they will return home. I know my father hates the pain it caused Mom every time he went out to fight. The pain it causes her every time *I* go out to fight. I hate the fact that I break her heart by living halfway around the world from her.' He stopped and thought for a moment. 'But she did know what she was taking on when she agreed to marry Dad. So did my grandmom. Years ago maybe the women were kept in the dark, but these days they're given the choice — they know how it's going to be. It's a testimony to their love, I guess. Their love is stronger than their fear.'

Regan sipped her drink, the light white wine she'd chosen tingling nicely on her tongue. 'So what is your mum like then, Nate? Do you take after her or your dad?'

He chuckled, 'Oh I definitely take after my dad. Mom says I am a true Hunter to the core! Mom is …' he thought for a second, 'the word that springs to mind when I think of Mom is *laughter*. It's like if she can fill the house, fill our lives, with enough laughter then it will protect us.'

'Do you look like her?' Regan looked at his dark hair, his inky black eyes.

'Oh, I don't know. Mom is beautiful — Dad always says she was the only girl at Springs High worth a second look!'

'What about your dad, what's he like?' Regan was fascinated; this was the most relaxed she'd ever seen Nate. He was her best friend and she knew so little about him.

'Dad is the best, he's lived with this burden his whole life — spent all his nights hunting, practising, searching for leads of where familiars could be — but he still managed to be there for us. He's larger than life — every time he had to be away for our birthdays, or Thanksgiving, or Christmas, I know it hurt him more than us. And he made up for it as soon as he got back. I didn't realise until I was a lot older how exhausted he must have been.'

Nate fiddled with his drink and a sad look passed over his face. He tried to hide it, but it was too late. Regan had noticed.

'What is it?' she asked, then paused impatiently as the waiter brought their food. Her pasta looked delicious and smelt better, the creamy sauce was mouth-watering. Nate's steak, she was pleased to see, was far more well done than Maeve's had been. The waiter offered them pepper, asked if there was anything else they needed; as soon as he'd left, she repeated her question.

'What is it Nate? What is wrong?' she put her fork down, waiting for an answer.

'Nothing,' he shrugged. She stared at him and raised an eyebrow.

'Nate …'

He cleared his throat. 'I've always known what Dad did, it's not been a secret in our family. I also knew that I was the next in line and that it would fall to me to carry on hunting when I was old enough.' He paused and took a long sip from his water, the ice clinking against the side as he lifted his glass, and Regan was shocked to see his hand trembling slightly. He put his drink down and she reached across the table and took his hand. His eyes caught hers briefly and she glimpsed a pain in them she'd not seen before. He tightened his grip on her fingers and continued.

'We used to practise fighting, ever since I was a little kid; I used to love it, out in the yard with sticks — he'd always let me win. I was about twelve when he showed me the knives for the first time. We went to the local camping shop and I tried all different ones until I'd found the one that fit me perfectly. He showed me how to use one to start with, how to draw it out without cutting myself, how to turn it in my hand if I needed to stab backwards. Then we went on to two knives and we'd use the punch bags to simulate a real fight.' Absentmindedly, he stroked her hand with his thumb; a tingle ran all the way down her spine.

'I was twelve and a half when I saw my first familiar. He just wanted me to see what it actually was I would be fighting, then for the next three years I practised and watched Dad. I started to fight alongside him. I started to go out on my own.

'I used to play the guitar as well, me and some of my friends had a bit of a band going on. It was pretty much the only hobby I had that wasn't related to hunting. When I was sixteen my school had a dance — one of those ones when the girl asks the boy — and Jenny Taylor asked me. My friend Josh had also arranged that our band played a short set on the night. I wanted to go really badly.'

He gripped her hand so tightly that it started to hurt. She didn't ask him to let go though.

'What happened, Nate?' Regan asked quietly.

'Dad had a bit of a flu thing, it had been going around and he wasn't really right. The night of the dance was supposed to be a beautiful clear July evening but …'

'It was foggy?' Regan guessed. Nate nodded.

'I was having a shower and Mom came and told me. I lost it — shouted that it wasn't fair, why should I have to miss the dance, it was only one night, I had a chance to play in the band … well I'm sure you can guess, I was a real dick. So dad called upstairs, he said "don't worry son, I'll go, it doesn't matter, you should go to the dance." So I did. I had the most fantastic night of my life, the band played the best set they had ever done, Jenny Taylor was the perfect date, and I had my first kiss …'

Regan's stomach clenched; it took her a second to realise she was jealous of this unknown girl — Jenny Taylor — who'd tasted Nate's lips.

'What happened?'

'Dad shouldn't have been fighting. I should've been, he wasn't well enough. He was getting old. He got attacked — very badly attacked. He managed to get on his bike and get away, but he lost so much blood he fainted at the end of our street. I got home from the dance and there were blue lights everywhere. He wasn't supposed to make it through the night, but he's a tough old cookie. He made it.'

'That's good, then. It wasn't your fault, Nate. You were — *are* — entitled to a life too.'

Nate's gaze pierced right through her and the vice-like grip he had on her hand tightened so much she wondered briefly if the bones were going to break. He swallowed hard and said in a low voice, 'He's paralysed from the waist down. He's never walked since that day.'

Tension filled his face; his jaw clenched and Regan could see tiny movements where he was grinding his teeth. 'Nate,' she whispered, 'I am so sorry, but it wasn't your fault. He knew the risks, the same as you do every time you go out and fight. You're a hunter, it's what you do — but you're a person too. You were sixteen years old. Going to a dance wasn't a crime.'

'But if I hadn't, Dad wouldn't be stuck in a wheelchair. Mom wouldn't be nursing the man she loves for the rest of her life.'

'And if you *had* gone out hunting, you might be the one in the wheelchair. If you hadn't taken Jenny to the dance maybe she would have been out where the familiars were. If Rafe hadn't saved Lora, then maybe he would have been killed and you wouldn't exist, no hunters would — if, if, if ...' she took a sip of wine. 'We all make decisions, Nate. We all have things that we would do differently. There's nothing to say that, as horrible as it is, this destiny wasn't your dad's and that even if it hadn't been down to hunting, he wouldn't have ended up in a wheelchair anyway. It sounds cruel, but who knows what the fates have in store for any of us.

'If Lora hadn't met Rafe, would things have still turned out the same for her? I don't know. What I do know is that you can't save the world *and* all the people in it, no matter how much you want to.' She stopped and looked at her hunting companion. She understood, now, why Nate Hunter was the way he was.

'Is everything all right with your meals, Sir? Madam?' Regan jumped at the sound of the waiter's voice beside her. Stunned, she turned to him, aware that her dinner was getting colder by the second.

'Everything is fine, thank you,' she said, forking in a mouthful of pasta to prove her point. Nate nodded in agreement.

'Actually, this is delicious,' she said when the waiter had left, 'stone cold, but delicious!'

'I would recommend eating it hot, though,' he said, a small grin eventually tugging at the corner of his mouth. They ate the rest of the meal quickly and decided to pass on the dessert menu. Nate insisted on paying the bill and Regan didn't argue too hard. She wasn't prepared to waste her breath; Nate had quite an old-fashioned sense of honour, she realised.

'So where to now, birthday girl?'

'Follow me!' Regan led Nate out of the restaurant and they turned back towards the river. Her mum had told her about a small pub along here that she used to go to when she was growing up. It was the pub where she'd met Regan's father, and it was a place Regan had always wanted to see. For some reason, it seemed to fit perfectly with her plans.

The evening was cool and she shivered a little as the breeze blew over her skin. 'Come here,' said Nate and put his arm around her shoulder, rubbing her arm to keep her warm. Her whole body tingled and Regan didn't think she had ever been happier in her whole life. She had come out with a mission in mind tonight and she hadn't forgotten that, but she hadn't known she was going to connect with Nate in so many more ways.

The river path was quiet; not another soul was on it. The full moon was reflected in the ripples and waves of the river like streaks of silver. The air smelt slightly salty as a wind blew in from the sea.

'Where are we going, Regan?' asked Nate after about a half mile of walking.

'Just there,' she said, pointing as a small pub unimaginatively called The River's Side came into view. The River's Side was an old, not-quite-crumbling building, and Regan wondered if she'd made a big mistake coming here. After all, it was a long time since her mum had been there. As soon as she pushed open the door, though, she knew it was exactly the right place to come.

Light and warmth spilled out into the night, inviting them in. The bar was split into two, one side was bigger, wider — a more sociable area, an old-fashioned Jukebox in one corner. Considering how far out of town this place was, Regan was surprised to see it so full. Conversation buzzed, couples danced on a small dance floor and Regan could hear the sound of balls being hit around a pool table that she couldn't see.

The other part of the pub was made up of small, intimate areas; a huge fire roared in the grate, a welcome change from the chill autumn air. Only one couple were in this part of the pub. It was exactly as Katherine had described it to Regan years ago.

'Oh my god, how did you know about this place?' asked Nate, 'It's fantastic!'

'It's where my mum and dad met,' she said simply, finding a space at the bar and ordering herself a Bacardi Breezer and Nate yet another glass of water.

'So which side do you want to sit?' she asked, 'just be warned if we sit this side then we will be dancing!'

'Definitely that side then,' said Nate, leading her to a little red couch. A huge wooden pillar hid them from anyone else and the fire roared away in front of them.

'Perfect,' said Regan, slightly unnerved at the effect his thigh pressing against hers was having.

The Breezer was sweet and Regan took a long sip from the bottle.

'You're right you know. It wasn't my fault, I know it wasn't, but how can I see my dad in that chair every day and not wish I had done things differently?'

'Everyone has things they would change if they could,' said Regan, 'and as my mum would say, if wishes were horses, then beggars would ride.'

'I like that,' said Nate, 'you know you really are more than just a pretty face, aren't you Regan?'

'Oh gee, thanks Nate. I might be blonde but I'm not that dumb! I do know a little bit about life you know.'

'Do you really?' he said.

'I do,' she dropped her voice an octave and looked up at him through her lashes. She wanted him, she realised, and it had nothing to do with saving herself from being a potential victim. She just wanted him plain and simple. He was like no one she had ever met before, everything about him set her pulse racing. *God Regan, how has it taken you this long to realise that?*

The song on the jukebox changed and the old rock number 'Nights in White Satin' started to play.

'I love this song,' they both said simultaneously.

Regan looked at Nate. 'Dance?' she asked softly.

'Sure,' he replied, pulling her gently from the couch. He tugged her to him and she found her body fitted his perfectly. Laying her head on his chest, she felt his hands on the small of her back. His heart thumped loudly in her ear.

Then she realised he was singing, hot wisps of breath tickling against her ear. His voice was beautiful, low and husky, and he hit every note perfectly. Reaching up, Regan drew him to her and kissed him. His lips felt perfect under hers.

He hesitated — just for the briefest of seconds — and Regan's heart forgot to beat. Then suddenly he was kissing her back, each movement more wonderful than Regan could ever have hoped for. If she could freeze time, she would freeze it right now. Right now, when all her senses were filled with Nate — she could smell his rich musky aftershave; hear every breath he took; feel his heart pounding in his chest, matching her own, the way his chin scratched a little against hers.

His hands moved up her bare back, stroking the smooth skin there.

'We need to go,' she said, and he took hold of her hand. They walked silently out of the pub. The river walk that had seemed enchanting on the way there now seemed long and unnecessary. All Regan wanted was to feel Nate kissing her again, his hands on her skin, his body next to hers. Her body needed him as it had never needed anyone before. She stopped abruptly and turned him around to face her. His eyes smouldered and even Regan could see the lust in them. She licked her lips and stood on tiptoe to kiss him again. He offered no resistance.

'Nate,' she whispered, his name catching in her throat as he kissed her neck. She let her hands slide under his shirt and run over his fighter's body. The smooth contours could have been crafted from granite. He kissed her deeper, harder as she ran her hands up his back.

She wanted Nate. This passion that filled her body was a new, unknown sensation. She thought she would be shy — wary and hesitant — but every fibre of her sought Nate. Even this close was not enough; his thin shirt and the silk of her dress might as well have been concrete barriers.

'Nate,' she said again, more forcefully, 'let's go back to yours?'

Words she would learn to regret.

At the sound of her voice, Nate stopped and pulled back. He let his arms drop to his sides and looked away. When he looked back the professional mask he had worn when she first met him was firmly in place, and the words he said hurt more than any cuts the familiars had given her.

'I'm sorry.' He tried to look her in the eyes but she turned away. She was aware he was speaking again but the voice in her head drowned him out. *Sorry. He's sorry. Wrong girl, wrong time.* The desire that flooded her body was chased away by the humiliation of knowing she wasn't even good enough for a fling — a roll in the hay, a one-night stand. Silently she turned and headed back to the car. Tears threatened, but her stubbornness refused to let them flow.

The drive to her house was silent until they reached her drive. 'Thank you,' she said, her pride insisting on good manners, 'it was a very nice evening.' He tried to speak but she'd opened the door and made her way to the house before he had the chance. It wasn't until she'd shut the door behind her that she heard his engine start and he drove away. And it wasn't until she'd made it to her room and shut the door firmly behind her that the tears flooded over her cheeks. The night played over and over in her head until her brain, unable to take any more, fell into a restless sleep.

Thirty-Five
1645

Muffled footsteps quickened down the road; the thunk, thunk, thunk of soft boots on compacted mud travelled unheard into the dark blue night. Rafe's breath came in heavy billows of condensation, his eyes scanning endlessly back and forth. The town was asleep behind him, the fens awake in front of him.

Too far away from the water yet to disturb the eel fishermen as they checked their baskets for the snake-like fish so plentiful in the gloomy fenland waters, Rafe's passing did not go unnoticed. A fox bitch with her prey in her mouth slunk in the deep shadows lest he try to steal her supper. Slugs and snails oozed their slimy paths across damp fenland byways. An owl swooped ghost-like, a flash of white skilfully hunting its quarry. Night-time was a time for hunters, a time that usually belonged to Rafe. But not tonight. No-one noticed as he breathed deeply, trying to ease the panic that tightened his throat. Nobody saw that fear was his companion tonight, as unfamiliar as it was unwelcome.

Lora hovered in semi-consciousness, somewhere between sleep and beyond. *I feel so peaceful*, she thought, *cold, but peaceful*. In this quiet, silent place, cold was a welcome companion, a friend. Soon she'd get up again, but now — just for a while — she would rest a little.

She felt her face tickle and thought about scratching it. Her nose twitched a little but her arms were comfortable and she didn't feel like moving them right at the moment. The silence was so soothing; too much noise gave her a headache. Too much thinking gave her a headache; here in this quiet, cold place she didn't need to think, she could just … be. The noiseless world echoed emptily around her head — silence, serenity, calm.…

The loud screech of a bird of the night penetrated the quiet. Startled, she whipped open her eyes, wincing as the icy air stung them. Consciousness pooled in her brain, thoughts and memories gradually starting to filter back. The cold and the memories were equal in their sting; slowly, a tear trickled down her cheek. Anger flared, but when she tried to move her hand to wipe the tear away, she found she couldn't. Instead, a dull pain coursed through her limbs as she attempted to move arms that were numb and heavy with cold. Leadenly she pulled one hand up and started to clench and unclench her fingers, but even that simple movement was hard beyond belief. As she worked her joints, trying to loosen them, the realisation dawned that if she didn't move, didn't get up and get warm, she would die. Here, in the cold, alone.

Come on Lora, her brain was screaming to her. *Move.* It took all her effort to unfold her legs from under herself, to get up into a sitting position. Panting, she forced her legs underneath her and then swung her arms gently by her sides, trying to get herself warm. It was hard work and hard work usually meant heat — this time, though, the chill felt too deep to penetrate.

Placing her hands on the ground, she tried to push herself up. The cold hard earth bit into her palms, yet the pain barely registered compared to the tingling sensation in her legs. As if full of a million hot needles and pins, they prickled agonisingly from her thighs to her feet.

'Aaaggh,' she yelped, her quiet voice piercing the air.

'Hallo? Who's there?' A familiar voice echoed loudly across the countryside. 'Lora, is that you?' Her heart jolted and a sob choked in her throat.

'Mistress Smith? Lora, please …'

'Here,' her voice cracked; even to her own ears she sounded feeble. Coughing a little, she called again, 'I'm here. Please. Help me.'

Then suddenly there he was in front of her, her very own saviour. He bent and scooped her up, her tired, heavy arms managing to cling feebly to his shirt. The warmth that radiated from his body felt like a heatwave on her icy skin. He held her close and she could feel his long, loping strides as he walked, hear the pounding of his heart in his chest. *Or is it mine?* thought Lora, *I cannot say for sure.*

His stride quickened and his arms held her tighter. His hot breath tickled her neck and for a second Lora wasn't sure that she had not actually died. She breathed in his scent of warm spice and ale. Felt the strength in his arms as he cradled her to him, and the wanton longings of lust stir within her, so strong she forgot for a second the pain of the cold in her limbs.

'I fear I find myself in debt to you for my life once more, Master Hunter,' she said, her voice feeble, trying to distract herself from the unfamiliar stirrings.

'I'm not sure it would be wise to put your life at risk a third time, Mistress Smith. I cannot promise to be there to save you.'

'I do not plan to put my life in jeopardy again, of that you can be assured.' The effort of talking took the little strength she had managed to summon and once again she fell silent, letting her lids close and her head rest against the hunter's chest. At that moment, her doubts about him were forgotten.

* * *

The bed beneath her was harder than usual. *Yet it does not feel uncomfortable,* Lora thought hazily as she opened her eyes. She could hear the muffled sound of someone moving around and the flickering orange glow of a candle penetrated the darkness to reveal a small, familiar room. Rafe's room, she realised. She was at Rafe's home. She closed her eyes again and a heartbeat later opened them wide. If she was in Rafe's room, that must mean she was lying in Rafe's bed. Oh dear God, what sins had she committed? With haste, she tried to push herself up.

'Oh good, you're awake. Do not try to move,' said Rafe.

'But I must! I must get out of …' she couldn't bring herself to say *your bed*, '… of your house.' Another thought entered her head. 'Mother, Mary … Rafe, we must help them.… If she finds me gone …'

It was too much for her brain to process — she couldn't make sense of what she needed to do first. She pushed away the blankets and tried to get out of bed, but before her feet could touch the floor Rafe was there, gently pushing her back down.

'I have some lavender if you think it will aid your rest.'

Lora frowned — lavender? Was he mad? She needed to get to her family.

'Rafe please, my family …'

'Your family are fine Mistress Smith; I promise you; they are perfectly safe.' His hands, though gentle, forced her shoulders to the pillow. Lacking the energy to fight him, Lora lay her head back and felt a tear trickle down her cheek. The candle flickered softly, making shadows jump around the room.

'Please do not cry, Lora. Your family are all safe, I promise you. It is you who needs to mend.'

'But you do not understand, sir. The witch, she was there with us tonight at the dinner table.'

'I know she was, Lora. It was I who put her there.'

Thirty-Six
2013

Regan cranked open a window to try and rid the car of the smell of cigarettes. The chart on her lap slid as she moved and she shot a handout to catch it. As she did, her knuckles brushed Nate's and she felt the usual burn of fire lick across her skin; jerking her hand away, she looked out the window.

Four weeks had passed since her birthday meal and every meeting with Nate felt awkward, the conversation stilted. Her desire for Nate had not waned in the slightest, but her embarrassment at his brush-off was always at the forefront of her mind when she saw him. For his part he was polite, as interested in the diaries as ever and always fought with unfaltering skill and precision.

On the outside, nothing had changed — he still took her home after work, he still practised and fought alongside her, he was still researching the diaries and he still took her along on these mapping trips. But on the inside, everything had altered. Regan herself was tongue-tied and could only talk about hunting and related subjects. And Nate? After a brief but sincere apology the day after the date, he'd reverted to the business-only Nate she had first met. No other topics of conversation were open between them.

In a way, this was a relief to Regan. She took the shame of his rejection and buried it deep, only thinking about it in those quiet minutes just before sleep stole in. The pain in her heart she could just about bear — it was a reminder of the line she had tried to cross — but the look in Nate's eyes nearly broke her every time she saw it. It was distance and colleagues and hunter. It was business and chains and servitude. Nate had shut himself away; only the hunter remained.

Regan wasn't sure if it was the revelations he had given away that night or her own attempt at seduction that had closed him up, but whatever it was she knew it was a result of their night out together. The night that she had manipulated into being.

'There's one,' Nate said, breaking through Regan's daydreams. She squinted out of the dirt-splattered windscreen at a cottage hidden away down this long drove. It would be the perfect place for a witch to live, surrounded only by fields and waterlogged dykes. She grabbed the pen from behind her ear and marked a cross on the map.

'Okay, I think we've done all of this section. We need to turn left up here a bit, it's a small track, runs between two long ditches by the look of this map.'

'Okay,' Nate replied. No sarcastic retort, no witty observation, just 'okay'. Regan could have cried.

Shivering at the cold coming through the gap in the window, Regan looked at the map on her knees. It showed a 25-mile square area of fenland and was covered in tiny red crosses. This was their last trip out marking up potential spots; they'd methodically gone along every road, track and by-way sighting residences to mark on the map. They discounted nowhere — modern, old or derelict. They'd travelled down tracks so muddy the car had had to be abandoned halfway and through half gritted lanes that may or may not have been private property. They had been nothing less than thorough.

This was the last winding road they had to take. So far, they had detoured down two half-roads and marked off a couple of isolated buildings. Regan hoped that soon they would link back up to the road they started on and this job could be finished. She had never seen such a maze of by-ways. The fens truly were a warren and though she'd been driven around them enough, not least when she was on the back of Nate's bike following the fog, until they had started this mission she hadn't realised the sheer complexity of them. It was a good job she wasn't in the driver's seat.

'There's a turning on the right, Nate,' she said, suddenly spotting the muddy gap at the edge of a field, 'just there, before the line of poplars.'

Nate spotted the junction and, after a couple of seconds, pulled the indicator stalk down and made a right-hand turn. The way, as ever, was more of a track than an actual by-way, though rubble had been placed in several spots to stop the mud causing problems so it was obviously used. A small copse of birch trees appeared on the left-hand side; hidden just behind them was an old cottage.

'Wow, that's old!' exclaimed Regan, forgetting for a second that her and Nate didn't chat anymore.

She took in the higgledy roof, white rendering, and deep-set beams before marking another little X on her chart. Smoke was wafting from the chimney, a sign that this place was occupied, so they didn't linger for long. Nate carried on until the track petered out to nothing. Executing a perfect three-point turn, they travelled back the same way, Regan peering across the car to take in any further details.

As they approached the house again, another car came towards them. With no room for two moving vehicles to pass, Nate pulled over to the side. Regan squinted at the car, wondering what type of person lived this far in the middle of nowhere. Was it a witch? *I mean, what signs do I look for?* she thought, *a warty nose, a pointed hat, a cauldron full of frogs?* Wishing she could share her sarcasms with Nate, she stared harder, determined not to let the tears that threatened spill over. It was then that her heart missed a beat — as the car turned left into the yard of the house, she caught a glimpse of the driver. Of long black hair and a pale face. She knew the green eyes that sat in that face, the perfect lips — she'd been insulted by them enough times.

'Nate. It's Ella,' she hissed.

He turned to face her, 'Who?'

'Ella — Toni's friend! You know the one ...' she trailed off, realising she'd never really discussed any of the girls with Nate. She'd kept the different parts of her life separate. Intentionally or not, she couldn't say.

She ducked down in her seat as the driver's door of the car opened and Ella got out.

'One of the girls from the pub,' she hissed to Nate, who was watching the other girl. Slowly, he pushed his foot down on the accelerator and they pulled away.

'Yeah, I know who you mean,' he said.

Of course he did. Nate had observational skills Sherlock Holmes would be impressed with. Once again, silence descended. The last road produced no results and Regan was able to mull things over in her mind. Had she ever had any inkling that Ella had lived out here, in the middle of nowhere? Would she have given it a second thought if she had known? It was only when Nate suggested looking for remote houses that Regan had given the matter any kind of thought at all. Did it mean anything to her now?

Regan sighed and leant her head against the cold glass of the window. A cool breeze ruffled at her hair and she shivered, suddenly exhausted by it all. For the merest moment she wished that she could go back to a time before all this. Before hunting and familiars and witches, before eerie fogs, night-time expeditions and knife skills. Before worrying about the weather forecast was more important than worrying about shopping and friends and manicures. Before Nate.

A movement to her right caught her eye and she turned, catching the concern in Nate's eyes before he refocused on the road. Just that brief look, though, reminded her that she wouldn't change it, wouldn't go back, not to Brighton and not to ignorance. Yes, there was pain — both physical and mental. She was shattered some of the time but honestly, she had never felt more alive than she had since living here. She'd grown oddly attached to this strange countryside with its huge skies and flat ground. Adrenaline coursed through her as she defended unknown innocents, laughter and joy coursed through her when she was with her new friends, her family. She felt accepted in the village, in the pub. She belonged. And then there was Nate — he was here, at least for now, and that was something that Brighton had never had.

'I'm all right,' she said, 'it's just, you know, we're looking for a witch and is this what it's come to? Suspecting our own friends? I mean, who next? Toni? Mum?'

'Maybe,' said Nate, 'though I doubt it.' He closed his mouth and concentrated on navigating the winding road towards Regan's house. After some seconds of silence, he said, 'I didn't think you were particularly friendly?'

She turned, surprised, 'We're not — well, we're okay ... it's complicated,' she said, glancing at his profile. She thought she saw a hint of a smile pass over his lips, but she couldn't be sure. Relief spread over her as her house came into view. She'd be alone for a while until Toni dropped Ashleigh off, or Mum and Aunty Vi returned. She really needed to think.

'I'll have a look at this,' said Nate, holding up the map that had slipped from her knees as she'd gotten out of the car. 'I'll let you know tomorrow which places are the most likely locations.' She nodded in reply and went towards the house. She thought she could feel his eyes burning into the back of her neck, but she wasn't going to turn around and check. If they weren't, it would be fresh disappointment all over again.

* * *

Tucking her feet under her, Regan took a sip of hot chocolate and stared at the sky out her window. It was a study in grey — pale, pale ash painted across the whole sky, with stone flecks and stormy granite swirls moving rapidly across the frame of the skylight. It was like looking at a canvas of modern art, temperamental and evocative. It suited her mood perfectly.

Every meeting with Nate was both agony and bliss. He was nothing but polite, every carefully cultivated sentence from his mouth was short and precise, designed — she imagined — to try and make things as easy as possible between them, to make her as comfortable as he could. So why did she come home in more pain than if she had been attacked by the claws of the creatures they sought?

Seeing Ella in one of the remotest houses in the area had opened her mind to all sorts of possibilities she didn't want to think about. What if the witch was someone she knew? What if it was Ella? The worries she had had about her virginity suddenly multiplied with the thought. It was already a chain around her neck as far as she was concerned. Now it felt as though the chain was being pulled tight.

The chances of her being in danger multiplied greatly if you were looking at the whole thing from the angle that the witch was someone she knew — or more to the point, someone who knew her. A friend who knew everything about her, like the fact, for example, she was still a virgin. Oh, Ella hadn't been in the room at the time of the discussion, but Regan was in no doubt that she knew.

Of course, if she was willing to accept that Ella was who they were seeking, then she had to face the fact that Ashleigh had been left alone with her on several occasions. The thought made her sick to her stomach. The more she thought about it, though, the more it made sense — Ashleigh was kind of a bit obsessive about Ella. Could she have been bewitched?

Regan rubbed her hand over her eyes and sipped at her drinking chocolate again. The sugary sweetness was soothing. She tried to think logically and put her emotions to one side; this, she would have to admit, was not a strength of hers. She thought with her feelings — she was definitely led by her heart and not her head.

Ella's wasn't the only house in the middle of nowhere, not by a long way — the scrawls of X's on Nate's chart proved that. She couldn't remember exactly how many she had marked in, but even once Nate had pared them down to the most obvious choices, they would still be left with couple dozen to look into. She knew the next few days — maybe even weeks — would be a process of eliminating as many as possible, but they were still going to be left with several potential places. Then it was down to observation and research — finding out as much about the people who lived in them as possible. Ella, she assumed, lived with her family. At the very least, a parent. She frowned, raking through her memories of all the conversations she had had with or about the girl. She soon realised they were few and far between, that really all she knew about Toni's friend was that she didn't like Regan.

Untucking her legs, she drained the last of her drink and took the mug downstairs. After washing it she started some preparations for tea. Her mum had stuck a stew in the slow cooker, but the potatoes needed cooking and mashing and the dumplings needed to be made.

Her head was spinning, her thoughts doing a great big figure of eight; as she deftly peeled the spuds, she tried to find a beginning to them, something firm she could act on. She put the peeled potatoes in a pan and turned the hob on, then found the suet and followed the instructions on the back for dumplings. *Okay, firstly there is no way of knowing that it is Ella we're looking for — however, it could be, so it makes sense to take precautions. I need to do this without arousing suspicion, by her or anyone else. And I want to get her away from Ashleigh....*

It occurred to Regan then that this could be quite simply done — if she said to her mum she *thought* that she'd seen Ella smoking some weed, then her mum would be sure to find reasons to not allow Ella to be alone with her youngest daughter. Of course, it was a lie and it would make life a little more difficult for them babysitting-wise, but really, she would rather be safe than sorry.

Having made one solid resolution, Regan felt a little lighter. As she moulded the suet mixture into round balls ready to place on top of the stew, she thought about what other problems she could deal with. Her feelings for Nate? There was no way she could see that these could be resolved — how do you just turn off an attraction to someone? Unless she removed herself entirely from the situation — from Nate — there was nothing she *could* do other than cope with it, and she wasn't prepared to take herself away from him. Fighting was too important to her; though the skill had lain dormant in her until she had moved here, now the idea of not using it was unthinkable. It didn't define her in quite the way it did Nate — maybe because she had been lucky enough to develop a life away from all this, before the supernatural had been revealed to her — but it was still an integral part of who she was now. A part she needed to keep. So no, she was just going to have to suck it up as far as Nate was concerned.

Okay, now she was getting somewhere. Even if she couldn't change something, at least taking it out and examining it — determining the truth — helped her deal with it. Her job — as far as she could see, there was no need for a change there. If anything, it benefitted their cause. The Hunter's Rest was a hotbed of gossip, and anyone who said that women were the biggest gossips hadn't been in a pub full of men after a hard day's work. They could talk the lips off of any woman Regan knew. If anyone started to act suspiciously, if anything suspect came to light, The Hunter's Rest would be the place to hear it first.

She turned her thoughts to her friends. She needed to keep them safe, particularly Toni with Ella. The thing was, how could she break up their friendship without arousing suspicion? Toni and Ella had been friends for many years; thinking about it, Regan wasn't sure she actually knew how long they'd been friends. Maybe that was something she could find out.

As she filled the sink to wash up, it occurred to her that maybe driving Ella away completely was the wrong path to take at all. Maybe the old adage of keeping your friends close but your enemies closer was true. If Ella was near, then at least she should stand half a chance of knowing if she was up to anything. She dumped the washing up on the draining board and rummaged through the cupboard for some paracetamol — she was getting a headache.

'Frankly, Regan, you can't do anything about Ella at the moment and as you have no idea if she is a witch or not it's probably for the best,' she told herself.

Finally, as she dragged in the coal and lit the fire in the lounge, she let her thoughts drift back to her perennial problem: sex. Hundreds of teenagers up and down the country grappled with this dilemma every day, so she knew she wasn't alone. Her determination to wait for someone special was completely thwarted now — she'd found him and he wasn't interested. Yet she was still left with the problem of her virginity being a risk. How big a risk she couldn't be sure, but to get rid of it and to concentrate on finding the witch, keeping the familiars culled, was more important than some antiquated sense of a special moment, surely?

In an instant, she'd made up her mind — she would ring Maeve and see if she wanted to go clubbing. She'd have loved to ring Toni, but there was no way she'd be able to convince her to go without Ella. She felt as though a huge weight had been lifted from her shoulders. The decision had been made; now she just had to get on with it.

Thirty-Seven

The music pulsated, the heavy bass pounding the floor and sending vibrations up Regan's legs. Closing her eyes, she let the beat embrace her body. The club was packed and, above her own jasmine scented perfume, an assortment of aromas assaulted her nose: alcohol, both stale and fresh; a variety of perfumes; the unmistakeable smell of hot bodies packed tightly together on the dance floor. A pungent aftershave, overly sweet and heavily applied, suddenly blocked out all the others and Regan opened her eyes.

'Hi gorgeous, how about I buy you a drink and you join me over there?' A squat blond bloke tipped his head towards a crowded table and couch. Restraining herself from shuddering at his open shirt and hairy chest, complete with gold chain, Regan shook her head.

'No thanks, my friend's getting me one already.' She smiled quickly and averted her gaze, hoping the lothario would get the hint. He didn't.

'No probs love, your friend's welcome to join us too, especially if she's as good looking as you!' He leered at her and Regan felt her skin crawl — give her creatures of the night over class A creeps like this one any day of the week.

'I said no thank y—' she began, but as she took in his drink-glazed eyes that hadn't yet made it up as far as her face, she decided that this was no time for subtlety.

'I'm not interested thanks,' she said.

'But love,' he told her breasts, 'I could …'

'Piss off,' said Regan, spotting Maeve with their drinks. Not wanting to give him any further opportunity to speak, she stepped away from him and squeezed her way through the crowd to her friend.

'Thanks, Maeve,' she said, taking a long sip from her double gin and juice.

'Who was that maggot and what did he want?' Maeve asked. Regan turned and caught the end of an indecent gesture aimed at her, 'Nice,' she muttered, 'Oh, just the usual. I told him to piss off.'

Maeve chuckled, a low throaty sound that rang sexy even to Regan's ears, and a group of should-be male models surreptitiously looked their way. Showing no such subtlety herself, Maeve looked at the best looking one, smiled her most predatory smile, then grabbed Regan's hand and led her around the dance floor to the other side of the room. Grabbing a table for two beside the packed floor, they sat down and surveyed the club.

'Oh my god, they were gorgeous!' Regan said, 'We should have stayed over there — he was definitely interested in you!'

'But I'm here to have a good night out with *you*,' Maeve replied and Regan felt her face fall. As much as she wanted a night out with Maeve, she did have the ulterior motive of needing to get rid of her pesky virginity.

'Besides, they'll find us again, don't you worry.' Maeve's confidence was contagious and a couple more swigs of her drink helped Regan believe it.

* * *

'You look fabulous, Maeve,' she shouted above the music, the ice in her orange juice melting rapidly in the sultry heat of the club.

'You like?' she replied, standing and twirling to show off her strappy sandals, skintight snakeskin-effect trousers and silky black V-necked t-shirt. Her dark hair tumbled carelessly over her shoulders and Regan suddenly felt like Maeve's kid sister instead of her friend.

'Oh, I don't know,' said Maeve, 'I would die for your hair. In fact, you really look beautiful tonight — sexy but vulnerable. Not everyone could pull that off, you know!'

Regan glanced at one of the many mirrors that surrounded them and managed to single herself out from the images reflected there. The confidence she'd felt when she was getting ready came back and she took in the slate grey halterneck dress she was wearing. It shimmered very subtly in the lights; the halterneck gave her a great cleavage but the slightly ruffled edge and tiny pearl buttons somehow stopped it from looking slutty. The silky soft fabric caressed her gently without clinging and ended midway down her thighs.

Draining the dregs of her drink, she stood up. 'Fancy a dance?' she asked her friend, the pleasant buzz of alcohol fizzing her brain. She wasn't used to drinking and, despite making her last drink nonalcoholic, she could feel the effects coursing through her. Maeve followed her onto the dance floor and the chilled R n B tune vibed through her body.

Lost in the rhythm, Regan didn't pay much attention to her friend when she left the dance floor. The old skool tune playing was one of her favourites and she was entranced by its sound. How much longer it was that she began feeling thirsty she had no idea, but a quick look round didn't reveal where Maeve was hiding so she decided to get a drink just for herself. She squashed through the crush at the bar and tried to get the barmaid's attention. The tall, extremely good-looking man beside her was having much more luck.

'Four bottles of Bud please, and whatever the lady's drinking.' Both he and the barmaid turned towards Regan and she realised he was talking about her. About to turn the offer down, she suddenly remembered her mission for the night and, pulse throbbing, flashed her best Maeve-esque smile and said, 'Gin and juice thanks.'

'Hi, I'm Matt,' he said as she quickly appraised him. Tall and muscular, he seemed familiar … and then Regan realised he was one of the group that had caught their attention earlier.

'Regan,' she introduced herself, flashing another smile. 'Thank you for the drink.' She clinked her glass to his bottle and waited. The alcohol was giving her a false sense of confidence but she could feel her usual nagging doubts lurking. He was exactly the kind of person she was hoping to meet tonight, but there was no getting away from the fact that he wasn't

Nate. And she wasn't Maeve; if she had an ounce of her friend's confidence, she was sure he'd be wrapped around her finger already. Then she remembered that the Regan who had lived in Brighton had been confident — she'd known how to be just sassy enough. Somehow, the fens had made her care about more than where the next party was, or what the latest fashions were. Of course, Nate turning her down had taken away the confidence she'd had left. But tonight that would change.

'No problem, Regan, it's great to meet you,' Matt casually swept back a lock of hair from her face. 'Would you like to dance, or shall we take our drinks and get to know each other a bit?'

'I'd love to get to know you better,' she said, straightening her back and remembering how much fun it was to flirt.

They settled into a free couch tucked away in one of the corners. The dark leather felt tacky against Regan's exposed legs and Matt's proximity made her nervous, but she plastered a smile onto her face and sipped her drink, concentrating on appearing to listen intently to Matt's life story.

To be fair, her internal voice piped up, *he is interesting. Funny and not at all a slime ball.* She quashed the voice before it added that his only obvious flaw was not being Nate.

She swallowed a large gulp of her gin and orange and savoured the fuzziness in her head before making sure that every ounce of her concentrated on Matt.

'So how long have you been paramedic then?' She asked after he'd described a rather nasty RTA that he'd had to attend the day before.

'Oh, about three years. Since I came out of the army.' His voice hinted that he'd already told her this.

'Sorry, I don't normally drink!' she held up the offending glass as if it was proof that she rarely consumed alcohol.

'Yet you work as a barmaid …'

'Hmm, well there's not much call for drunken barmaids,' she grinned and inched closer. He placed a hand on her exposed thigh and ran his fingers over it; she looked into his hazel eyes, then looked away in a manner she hoped was demure. It was only when she blinked her eyes shut for a second and Nate's deathly dark eyes flashed into her head that the touch on her thigh sent shivers to her secret places. She sighed and Matt, taking this as a good sign, simultaneously moved his hand up her thigh and leaned forward to kiss her. Her brain registered that it was a very nice kiss — Matt clearly knew what he was doing. Her heart, however, couldn't help comparing it to the last time she'd been kissed and Nate's urgency and need.

Except, she reminded herself, *he hadn't needed her, he hadn't wanted her*. Remembering this, she kissed Matt back with full force and recalled that this wasn't just about want. It was about a lifesaving need, and who better than a paramedic to deliver that?

Regan tried not to flinch as she unstuck her legs from the sofa and leaned further into Matt's kiss. She placed her hand on his chest and the muscles he'd earned in the army were obvious even under his shirt.

He used his spare hand to caress the bare skin left exposed by the halter top of her dress. His fingers ran lightly up her spine and neck and teased the loose tresses of hair at her nape.

She pulled away briefly to catch her breath and caught the smell of subtly applied musky aftershave. He pulled her back into the kiss and she could taste the beer he'd been drinking. His kisses were expert, just forceful enough to be nice but not brutal. His touch was gentle. But every fibre of her knew that he still wasn't Nate. All her energy went into pushing the hunter from her mind, to remembering that she wasn't doing this for fun and — as unromantic as it sounded — it was something she really needed to do. Being a virgin was not at all good for her at the moment.

The DJ put some mellower sounds on and Matt drew Regan even deeper into the kiss. His right hand mussed up her hair, his stubble prickled her chin and his left hand stroked its way further up her thigh.

'Is this all right?' he asked quietly, his lips pulling away from hers only enough to speak.

She answered by leaning forward and kissing him again, her hand toying with the short hairs at the back of his neck. He, reluctantly, pulled away again, 'We can stay here for a while longer, or go for a walk. My place isn't far if you'd like a coffee …'

A coffee. Even Regan — young and, she was learning, pretty naïve — knew that coffee wasn't what he had in mind.

'A coffee sounds …'

'Regan, I wondered where you were!' Maeve. Regan had almost forgotten about her friend; she leapt back from Matt guiltily.

'Hi Maeve, this is — er — Matt,' she introduced him.

'Hi Matt,' Maeve said and his eyes bulged slightly; his restraint was good, but no red-blooded male could meet Maeve without some reaction. 'I'm just going to steal Regan for a couple of minutes, we need to powder our noses!' she said, reaching for Regan's hand and pulling her up. Regan shrugged at Matt, who said 'I'll be waiting,' as she followed her friend to the loos.

The harsh lights in the ladies' seemed to counteract the effect the alcohol and mellow lighting had had on Regan. Watching Maeve apply her deep red lipstick, she decided to top her up her own lip-gloss — Matt had done a good job of kissing the last lot away.

'Wow Regan, he's gorgeous! Make sure you get his phone number!' She looked intently at her friend in the mirror. Regan hesitated, then said, 'Well he's invited me back to his place for, uh … coffee.' Suddenly, abandoning her friend seemed very selfish. 'I'm sure you could come too,' she added, not sure at all really.

Maeve took a second and looked at Regan in the mirror, then she turned to her friend, 'Regan, I know you're not naive enough to think that an invitation to drink coffee means that he actually expects you to go back and drink coffee.' She paused, waiting for Regan's response.

'Damn it, Maeve, I know he doesn't want coffee.' She didn't know what else to say.

'Oh, honey. And this is what you want, right? I mean,' Maeve paused as if unsure how to word what she wanted to say, 'please tell me to shut up if it's none of my business but, well, after you told me about Marcus, I thought you wanted to wait.' Regan shut her eyes; she wished she had never said anything to Maeve.

'Yes, well, things change. Maybe I just got fed up with being the only eighteen-year-old virgin left in East Anglia.' She stared in the mirror, using her finger to adjust her eye make-up.

Biting her lip, she met Maeve's gaze, 'I'm not here to judge you,' her friend said, 'whatever you want to do is great. It just seems to me that if you're willing to invite me back as well then maybe — just maybe — you're not as ready for this as you think you are.'

'You don't think I'm an idiot for … not having done it yet?'

Maeve looked amazed, and a little hurt, 'Why would I think you were an idiot?'

Regan grabbed a paper towel and started blotting off her freshly applied gloss. 'I don't know, maybe because you're so experienced …'

Maeve chuckled, 'Well, when you put it like that! Honey, I'm older than you, and my "experience" tells me that waiting until the right time is the best thing. I'm not telling you to wait until you're married, or to become a nun. Just don't throw it away at the first chance you have.'

Maeve checked her refection over in the mirror once more, 'Why is it so important now? Is it something to do with this fight you've had with Nate? I know you said you only had a teeny crush on him, but I see you together all the time. It has to be more than just a passing fancy.'

Swallowing hard, Regan nodded. 'I do have feelings for him, but he's just not interested in me that way. He's only interested in work,' she added, a little bitterly.

'I'm sure that's not true, and even if it is, sleeping with someone to make you feel better — or make Nate jealous, or to get back at him — well, it just isn't a good idea. No one is going to feel better in that situation — not Matt, not Nate, and certainly not you.'

Regan acknowledged what her friend was telling her with a nod of her head.

'I think maybe it's time we left anyway,' said Maeve, 'you take these tickets and get our coats, and I'll tell Matt that you're not feeling so well and I'm taking you home, okay?'

Regan nodded, then glanced at her watch and said, 'You know what, Maeve, I'm going to go but you stay — you're having fun, I don't want to spoil your night out.'

'You're not! I want to make sure you're okay.'

'I'm fine,' Regan flashed her brightest smile, 'I just feel like a bit of an idiot.' She shrugged her shoulders, 'honestly, Maeve, I'll be fine.'

'Well, if you're sure.' Maeve hugged her friend, gave herself a quick once-over and headed back into the club. Regan looked at her own reflection again. Damn it, why couldn't life just be simple?

* * *

Holding her ticket for the cloakroom, Regan shuffled forward as the line inched slowly towards the desk. She didn't know whether to laugh or cry; she was sure she was on the verge of hysteria. Surely getting laid wasn't meant to be this hard — *mind you*, she thought, *I'm my own worst enemy. I could be back at Matt's now 'having coffee'.*

At least her integrity and self-respect were still intact. Just. Though what good either of those qualities would be when she was being used as a human sacrifice, she wasn't entirely sure. Wearily she took another step forward as a gang of lads left the front of the line and headed towards the stairs back into the club. It took her just a second to realise that the lanky blond leading the pack up the stairs was Sam. She started to call after him but realised that between the music blaring down from upstairs and the chatting of the queue of waiting clubbers, it was very unlikely that he would hear her.

She continued shuffling forward as the line slowly dwindled, her resolve to go home weakening with every moment. When she'd spoken with Maeve it had all seemed so simple and logical, but as soon as she was on her own, she found herself backtracking to her original conclusion. It was only the fact that she'd been gone for nearly three-quarters of an hour and she was sure her friend would already have spoken to Matt — given him her excuses — that prevented her from returning and carrying on where they had left off. It would reek of desperation and that was *never* attractive.

It was only when she'd handed over her ticket and her faded denim jacket was already being collected that the fact that Sam had just entered the club occurred to her. Sam. Sam, who'd been continually asking her out since the day they met. Sam, who was a friend, reliable, cheeky and, if she didn't start comparing him to Nate, pretty damn sexy. He was someone she could trust, someone she *did* trust. Relief flooded over her as she realised that tonight may still have some potential.

When the gum-chewing girl had retrieved her jacket, Regan nearly snatched it out of her hands before running back up the stairs into the club. Maybe this night wasn't going to be a total disaster after all. She reached the top and pushed open the door, peering through the crowds for any sign of Sam. *Or Maeve,* she thought. It may look slightly odd her being back, but Maeve was pretty chilled — she didn't get hung up on the little things like some people. Though running into Matt may prove awkward. Or not. She watched in partial disbelief as she caught him heading towards the door entwined with a tanned, leggy blonde. *Well that was a lucky escape,* she thought. She ducked out of the way before he noticed her, then carried on looking for Sam. The nineties dance classics were blasting out, with full on strobe lighting pulsing in time. It made looking for anyone nearly impossible.

She swept the place for him, more than once catching sight of tall blonds who, on closer inspection, weren't him. She glanced across at the bar, trying to see if he was in the queue there. No luck. Then she moved round so she had a better look at the seating area and she spotted him. She started to make her way over when she pulled up short. It was too late. He already had his arms around someone, and, as Regan watched, he drew them in deep, caressing the back of the girl's dark hair and stroking her face before gently kissing her. Regret coursed through Regan — if she didn't know better, she would have sworn she was a little jealous.

It took her a couple of seconds of staring before she realised that the dark hair and silky t-shirt of the girl were familiar. 'Shit,' she whispered as she realised Sam's new interest was Maeve. Clutching her jacket, she turned and sped out of the club as quickly as she could. She was pleased for Maeve; it would just feel a little awkward if she was caught gawping. At least, that's what she told herself.

Thirty-Eight

Regan stumbled and the familiar's claws caught the elasticised fabric of her top, shredding it instantly. She reacted, slicing its skin before the pain of its claws on her had even registered in her brain, but she knew it was only her sloppiness that had caused her to be got in the first place. Damn it, she had to do better than that. Her head pounded as she ducked down and struck from beneath, the blade in her hand splitting its belly.

As the creature's scream faded it disintegrated, vile and bubbling, until it mulched down like autumn leaves in a well-rotted compost. Regan knew she didn't have time to rest, to celebrate. Again they were fighting three creatures, and she knew Nate was struggling to keep the other two at bay. Ignoring the queasiness that was the aftermath of her night out, she leapt to Nate's side. Her hangover was causing her to be clumsy and adding further guilt to the burden she was carrying. She pushed all thoughts that weren't connected with killing the creatures from her mind and tried to get into her natural rhythm; to slip into the instinctive mode that fighting beside Nate usually took. But she was clumsy, as though every move was just a millisecond too late — she knew it, and she knew Nate knew it.

She ducked as a claw swept above her head; she swung her knife up and just caught the thing's arm —

not quite soon enough to stop the arc of its blow catching the hunter's neck. A muted groan escaped his lips but, despite having his back to it as he fought the other, he didn't falter once. One blade went straight through the creature in front of him and the other jabbed up behind, meeting just enough flesh to make the familiar stumble. Regan took her chance; both creatures shrieked as they died, the noise echoing across the fog-filled fields and penetrating Regan's painful head like shards of glass. She flinched once, then siphoned the pain to just one part of her brain. She deserved it — she'd just put them both in serious danger. It was unforgivable.

'What the hell was that about?' Nate rounded on her, his hand wiping furiously at the slash on the back of his neck.

'Let me look at that for you,' Regan offered, avoiding his question. She studied the ground, unable to look him in the eye.

'Oh, I think you've done enough today, Regan. You can fight way better than that! What is wrong with you?' he softened his tone a little, the spark of anger in his eyes replaced with one of concern. 'Are you ill?'

God, how she wanted to lie to him — to say yes, I've got a stomach bug, a migraine — hell she'd tell him she'd got her period if she could. But she couldn't. She'd fucked up and it could have resulted in her death and Nate's. The fact it hadn't was down to him; she owed him the truth.

'I'm sorry. I went out with Maeve last night … I am so sorry Nate, I promise it will never happen again …'

She watched as he processed this information. His eyes narrowed and he looked at her with disbelief, 'You went out. With Maeve. And you dare come and try and fight with — what, a *hangover*?'

She nodded, unable to defend her actions.

'How dare you! This is *not* a game.… I thought you knew that, Regan. If we don't get this right, lives could be lost. Lives *will* be lost — your life, my life …'

'I know, Nate. I'm sorry.'

'You're sorry? Maybe you don't care about me, or yourself. What about when it's your mom? Or Ashleigh …'

Tears prickled at her eyes and swelled her throat. She blinked and swallowed hard. She would not cry. She deserved it; every word was true.

'I *do* care, you know I do. I made a mistake …' she was unsure how to continue, unable to meet Nate's eyes. She could feel his stare on her face, sense him trying to figure it out. She glanced up and felt her soul tear in two; the disappointment in his face was unbearable.

'You made a mistake.' Nate's voice was so cold it cut her to the quick. 'Do you know what happens when we make mistakes, Regan? People die.' He looked at her, unspoken accusations in his eyes. 'How can I make you understand?' he asked. A smile flitted across his mouth; it didn't reach his eyes. Then he sheathed his knife and shed his jacket. Slowly, he pulled his t-shirt up and over his head; Regan started at the sight of his bare skin.

'This is what happens when we aren't careful, Regan.' He pointed to the ugly red and silver scars over the left side of his chest. Over his heart, Regan realised, confused. 'One for every person who has died because I wasn't vigilant enough,' he moved closer so she was right in front of him. Her heart pounded and she lifted her hand up and traced the scars with her finger. A bar of five and three little lines.

'Eight people, Regan. Eight people who have died because I didn't kill the monsters in time. Unknowns, vagrants, lost souls with no-one to know or care they'd gone — but I knew, and I cared. So I marked myself,' he drew out his knife and gently ran the blade down beside her fingers, mimicking marking a fourth line. Tears choked in her throat as she saw Nate slide away and the Hunter step back into place.

'And these?' she asked, her voice barely a whisper as she touched her fingers to the tattoo marks on the other side of his chest. Again they were bar tallies, neater and more plentiful than the scars; she estimated there to be close to fifty. Some, she realised, were new — the ink dark and neat, edged by raised red skin.

'One for every monster I've killed. Every killer taken away, never able to hurt anyone.'

She wanted to tell him to look how many more familiars were dead than people, to think about how many potential lives he had saved with the sheer number of creatures he had killed, but she knew it would be futile. The Hunter didn't believe he was a hero. To him it didn't matter — he did a job, beginning and end.

And she had let him down. She dropped her fingers from his chest and folded them into her fist, ignoring the craving to touch him again. Needing to try and explain, she started to talk.

'I needed to go out. I needed to …' she stopped, thought for a second and then looked Nate in the eyes. His face was blurred through her unshed tears; she didn't let them distract her.

'I needed to try and stop this in my way. If these creatures are here because of me, because of what I am, then I needed to take away what they wanted.' Nate frowned as he tried to decipher her words.

'They want me because I'm a virgin, or at least their owner, mistress, whatever does. If I'm no longer a virgin the problem is solved, she'll have nothing to crave. They'll go away.'

Nate blinked. For the first time since she'd known him, he seemed completely lost for words.

'You slept with someone — with a *stranger* — to make this *go away*?' Her heartbeat faster as repulsion crept into his face; humiliation washed over her.

'Well *you* wouldn't sleep with me! You might find the idea disgusting but not everyone does!' The tears spilled over in anger, running in rivulets down her face. Ignoring them she stared defiantly at Nate, daring him to carry on.

'And did it work? Did you —' the words seemed to swell in his mouth, '— did having sex stop the creatures?' His shoulders slumped and his voice sounded weary, 'As we've just fought more than ever, it would appear not. Was it worth it?'

'I didn't do it.' She could feel herself trembling, whether from fear, shame or the remnants of the alcohol, she wasn't sure. As ever, though, her pride was there to protect her. Straightening her back she said, 'I could have, but Maeve stopped me — made me realise that it wasn't worth it.'

'You've told Maeve about this?'

She shook her head, 'No, of course not. Look, what does it matter? I didn't do it. Maeve is a good friend, and I trust her. She makes sense. Take me home, Nate,' she said, exhausted. 'I need to get my arm looked at and I need to go to bed.' He opened his mouth to speak, and then shut it again. They'd both run out of things to say — accusations, excuses, whats, whys and wherefores, all lost in bone-wearying tiredness and confusion. Now was not the time to try and riddle it out.

Silently they climbed onto his bike, the comfort Regan usually found in wrapping her arms around Nate gone today, the frisson she felt at his touch quenched. She just wanted to get home. To be alone.

The night was clear again by the time they pulled up at the end of the lane. 'Do you want me to look at that?' Nate asked, trying to see Regan's injured arm.

'I'm fine,' she said, pulling away and heading into the house without a backward glance. She crept through the silent house, glad of its sleeping occupants. Stopping on the landing she looked out the window, making sure first that she was hidden from view by the shadows. Her eyes sought through the darkness to where Nate was; straining, they watched him pushing his bike further down the lane. He got on and started the engine, the sound barely audible from behind the thick walls of the old house. She watched as his taillight twisted and turned away from her, until it was a pinprick and then completely swallowed by the night.

As was becoming her habit, she made her way to her bedroom and lay on her bed, sobbing as silently as possible. She welcomed the pain from the wounds on her arm — it reminded her that she was alive, and of everything she could have lost tonight.

Thirty-Nine
1645

Breathing was difficult — her throat had closed and air couldn't get through. '*You* put her there? You risked the life of my family?'

Rafe leaned in closer to her, his lips inches from her face, 'Please calm down Lora, you are going to make yourself ill. Here, have sip of this,' he reached back and collected a cup of hot posset, 'you need to get warm.'

'Unhand me, sir,' Lora said, pushing weakly at the hand still restraining her. 'Unhand me! I trusted you.' Tears leaked from her eyes as her still-heavy arms tried to push Rafe away. Boiling drink from the cup spilled onto Rafe and he cursed under his breath.

'Sit still or I will be forced restrain you with rope!' One last push told Lora she wasn't strong enough to escape from Rafe and the look in his eyes let her know he was deadly serious. She bobbed her head, agreeing to his conditions. Accepting the posset, she took a small sip. It would at least help her regain her strength and feeling.

In silence Rafe cooled his scalded arm and then turned back to Lora.

'I promise your family is safe. I was there tonight; I was watching the witch and saw her meet with a man and a woman. I followed them to your house.

'She bewitched them. I saw her do it. I don't know how she did it but I saw it happen with my own eyes.' He sat on the hard chair beside the bed, hands in his lap. It was tempting to try and run but Lora knew that if she attempted to get up again Rafe would stop her before she could get one leg out from under the covers.

'Is the blanket sufficient?' he asked suddenly, 'I needed to warm you up, you were so cold it was leeching the life from you.' Rafe looked at her, his eyes full of concern, and Lora knew in her heart that he had not betrayed her. His gaze was so intense she could almost feel it burning her. Flushed, she looked down, remembering the musky scent of him and the strength in his arms as he had carried her. The break in his voice as he had called to her.

Some of Lora's tension eased. So many times they had fought together now, her wearing nothing more than a pair of men's breeches and a loose shirt. Rafe could have hurt her at any time. He could have taken her life at any point, yet she had never feared him. Her family was safe. She just had to pray that Mother wouldn't try and see her and discover that she was no longer there.

'It is fine, thank you,' she said as she pulled the blanket self-consciously closer, feeling suddenly very vulnerable. The rough wool scratched at her arms but it was bringing welcome warmth to her bones. Never had she felt so awkward around Rafe. Never so defenceless. Lying fully clothed under his blankets, she wasn't sure if it was Rafe she feared or her own sinful feelings. She forced the thought from her head.

'It was my aunt and uncle whom she came to the house with,' put in Lora, swallowing her drink. She watched Rafe carefully; his silhouette jumped as the candle burnt lower and a breeze made the flame dance. 'Her name is Cecily. She knew things that she could not have known,' Lora said, 'about us, about our hunting.'

'I took too many risks, spying on her, taking you to see her … it was foolish of me. It was my fault she was at your table. I would never have forgiven myself if anything had happened to you or your family.' Anguish was etched across his face, lines furrowing his brow. Lora longed to reach out and soothe them away.

'It was not your fault. I am headstrong, I have been told so all my life. I made you show me the witch. I am not stupid, sir. I knew the risks.' But even as she said it, she knew it to be a lie. Rafe had *told* her of the risks, but she had not really given them any thought. It was the excitement that had led her on, the adventure that was so different from her tedious daily life. 'Any fault lies solely with me. The question is, what are we going to do about it?'

Forty
2013

Sleep that night was fitful, to say the least.

Her arm ached, her head ached and her heart ached — not necessarily in that order. She was too embarrassed to see Nate, felt guilty about seeing Maeve and Sam, tense about seeing Ella, and as though she had too many secrets and emotions to hide from just about everyone else. Life was not about to let her get away with skulking in bed though. Sounds of daily life were coming from downstairs, and she knew she had to get up and paint on a face before her mum came looking for her.

She showered quickly, letting the steam soothe away some of her anxiety. She dressed her arm, then dressed herself — layers of cotton and wool to block out the early December chill. Gloomy grey light filtered in from her skylight and she had to flick on the lamp to see properly. She applied her make-up, carefully adding layers to her defence. When she finally faced the world, it had to have no clue that she was in turmoil.

Her mum needed to know she could look after Ashleigh, Nick needed to believe she was capable of her job, Nate needed to know she was a competent — no, an able, an equal — fighter. She needed the girls to see fun Regan, Sam to see flirty Regan and Ella not to have a clue she was on to her. She needed to get the Regan White show together and fast. There was no time for her to fall apart; no time to feel.

Finally, as ready as she would ever be, Regan descended the stairs and made her way into the kitchen. Ashleigh was spreading a thick layer of chocolate spread onto her toast at the kitchen table and her mum was making up a tray for Aunty Vi. She balanced a cup of tea and marmalade-coated toast on a tray and squeezed past Regan.

'Stay here, Regan, I need to talk to you before I go to work.'

'Sure,' Regan said, flicking the kettle back on and tipping a spoonful of coffee and sugar into a mug.

'D'you think Ella will come and do my hair on Friday?' asked Ashleigh, 'I've got my winter disco after school.'

'I don't think she can Ash, I'm pretty sure she'll be working,' Regan lied, carefully crossing her fingers behind her back. 'But hey, I can do your hair — I could straighten it, or curl it and put it up, whatever you like,' she said as Ashleigh's face fell.

'Okay, that could be fun,' Ashleigh replied, biting off a huge piece of toast.

'Ashleigh, you need to hurry up — really, do you need to have so much chocolate on that toast? Come on, Jenny's mum'll be here in a minute to give you a lift.' As her sister stuffed the last of her breakfast into her mouth and grabbed her school bag, Regan was filled with an overwhelming sense of love. She really hadn't paid much attention to Ashleigh lately — granted she was often at work when her sister was at home, but still, there was no excuse really.

'Hey Ash,' she called after her sister, 'Friday night — it'll be fun hey?' Ashleigh nodded her approval before clambering into the waiting Range Rover. Katherine and Jenny's mum took it in turns to take the girls to school. The two grownups had nothing in common, really — other than daughters who were friends — but the arrangement was convenient for both of them.

Sitting at the table Regan sipped her milky coffee, working hard to ignore the sharp stinging in her arms. It was nothing less than she deserved.

'I need to talk to you, Regan,' Katherine said, pulling up her own chair and pouring a cup of tea from the green teapot. 'In about three weeks the day centre is running a trip to a Christmas spectacular at Thursford and they've asked if I can work and be part of the trip.'

Regan looked at her mum blankly, not quite sure what this had to do with her.

'It's brilliant, I can remember going years ago, but it goes on quite late. Accommodation has been arranged overnight so we're not travelling back too late.'

Suddenly it was starting to make sense. 'Okay, so you're going to need me to watch Ashleigh?' she asked.

'Yes — I was going to ask Cyndi, but believe it or not she's got tickets for her and Toni to the same show! The trouble is I don't know if you'll be working or not.'

'I should imagine so,' Regan said grinning, 'I seem to spend most of my life there.'

'Yes well, that's a discussion for another day,' Katherine frowned and Regan changed the subject before a talk about her "career prospects" started. 'Hmm, even if I am at work, well …' she paused, thinking through the possibilities.

'I wondered if Ella could look after her?' Katherine said, 'Ashleigh is really taken with her; I'd be willing to pay babysitting rates.'

Regan's blood ran cold and she gulped at her coffee to hide her unease. Mentally composing herself, she said, 'Well, I actually wanted to talk to you about that. I, um, I'm pretty sure I caught Ella smoking something that wasn't legal the other day.'

At the look of horror on her mum's face, Regan backtracked a little — she didn't want to overdo it, just keep Ella away from Ashleigh. 'I mean, I think she was maybe smoking a little bit of weed, but I can't be sure. I'm just not certain that leaving her solely in charge of Ashleigh is a good idea, especially if Toni isn't there.'

Katherine's face was impossible to read; her forehead was creased as though she was trying to work out the best course of action. 'Don't worry Mum, we'll work something out. I mean Sam, or Nate, or Maeve,' she added as inspiration struck her.

Her mum looked doubtful. 'I don't think she'll want to stay with Sam or Nate and I don't really know Maeve. I mean I know she's your friend and I'm sure she's lovely but …'

'It's okay Mum, I understand. Okay what about her friend Jenny, maybe she could have a sleepover or something?'

'Hmm, that could work,' Katherine agreed, 'I'll see what I can sort out.'

She got up and rinsed out her mug, 'Well I'd better see how Vi is doing, then get in the car and off to the day centre I guess.'

'Sure Mum, I'll see you later — or not! Ships that pass in the night is us at the moment.'

Her mum smiled, 'I tell you what — I'll book a day in to see you Christmas day, if not before!'

Regan smiled and hugged her, 'Definitely Mum.'

* * *

Once the house was empty Regan found herself alone with her thoughts again, and she didn't like it. She needed to be doing something. She wanted to show Nate that last night was a mistake, that she was reliable and capable. She couldn't ring him, she just couldn't face him today. If only she had a car, she could go and do some surveillance on the houses they'd charted — they needed to find out who occupied where, and time really was running out.

There was nowhere she could walk to — the houses were spread over many miles, all in the middle of the most desolate fenland. She wondered if there was anyone she could borrow a car from ... unfortunately most of her friends knew she didn't actually have a driver's licence. Just a minor point really as she could drive perfectly well. Before her dad had gone off with Trish, he'd spent hours at a local track teaching her to drive — cars were his passion.

The only person who she could think of who might not know — and might lend her a car — was

Sam. But every time she thought of him, an image of his limbs entwined with Maeve's popped into her head and she felt the stirrings of something she didn't want to dissect in her stomach. She wandered around the house, trying to tidy it a little, but her heart wasn't in it. Eventually, she settled with Elizabeth's diary and a cuppa, but after a couple of pages she found her mind wandering so much she hadn't taken a single word in. Images of the club — Matt, Maeve, Sam — all kept fighting for headspace with the memory of Nate's face when she'd admitted she had been drinking. She couldn't even let herself think of his disgust when she'd confessed her reason for clubbing; that sword just went too deep.

If she could just prove that Ella was — *or wasn't*, she told herself — the witch, then she would feel as though she had made a positive contribution, that she would raise herself in Nate's estimation again. Putting the diary back, she made her decision. She would ring Sam. Toni was at college on Mondays, Sam biked his course as a postman and Ella had the first day of the week off — no other day would be as perfect as today to do it. Of course, if Sam wouldn't lend her his car then she was stymied, but as her mum was fond of saying, she'd cross that bridge when she came to it.

Grabbing her mobile before she could change her mind, she flicked through the phonebook and found Sam's number. She pressed the call button and waited for him to answer.

'Lo, Regan, how are you gorgeous?' Sam greeted her. It felt wrong — normal, as though the past two days hadn't turned her whole world upside down.

'I'm good, Sam,' she hesitated, 'Sam, I was actually ringing to ask you a favour …' She trailed off, trying to assess his mood.

'You ask away, beautiful. Of course it means you'll owe *me* a favour!' He laughed, the sound twisting in her gut — why did Maeve have to kiss him? He was *her* friend. Illogical and selfish, she knew — especially as she didn't want Sam to be more than a friend (or a convenient bed buddy for one night). She blushed, glad he couldn't read her thoughts.

'I wondered if I could borrow your car, Sam?' she pushed the guilt at this being completely illegal away — the roads were perfectly safe, pretty much deserted, *and* she was a totally safe driver.

'Sure thing, chick,' he said without hesitation, adding to her guilt. If he'd questioned her or guessed she was unlicensed it wouldn't be so bad. Except it would be. Lying to your friends was never going to be easy. She resisted the urge to elaborate the pretence; it was only likely to catch her out in the end.

'How about you meet me in the village in half an hour and I'll give you the keys then? I've just got to finish sorting the letters before I start my round.'

Regan agreed and wrapped herself up against the December chill before she set out. The fresh air was lovely and even the biting wind didn't bother her; it all helped her stay away from the thoughts twirling in her head. Black clouds scudded across the sky, dead leaves leftover from Autumn whirled at her feet as the wind gusted. The fields were no longer a patchwork of bright colours, but squares of brown - mahogany, cocoa, tan — all in uniform furrows. The ploughs were gone for now, it seemed.

She pulled her hands up into her sleeves, the cold biting at her fingers even through the red gloves she wore. The road, dusty and dry in the summer, was muddy and she was glad for the new thick leather boots she had on. More practical than beautiful, they symbolised to her more than anything how much she had changed since she had left the bright lights of the south coast. With her head crammed full of thoughts all vying for attention, the walk to Old Scytheton passed by in a flash and she was almost surprised when she found herself in front of the little shop and post office. Sam was waiting, his bike laden with letters and parcels; December really was a nightmare month for the postal service.

'Here you go,' he jangled the keys in front of her, 'I'm fully comp so you'll be covered, it sometimes sticks in reverse but just shove it hard and it'll go. You've got my number if you have any problems, sorry to rush but this lot is going to take twice as long as normal to deliver!' He nodded to his over-laden basket and jumped on the bike. 'Laters.'

'Yeah, see you Sam. I owe you!' She could just make out the grin that stretched across his face as she turned to go back to his place to pick up the car.

Forty-One

Thankful Toni and Cyndi were both out, Regan swallowed back her guilt when she reached Sam's house and unlocked his car. It took a couple of attempts to get the thing in reverse but she pushed heavily on the gear stick and eventually it clonked into place. She slowly backed out of his drive, nerves kicking in as she realised this was the first time she had driven in several months.

By the time she was out of the village and on the winding fen roads with no-one else around her, though, her confidence had grown. Man, she loved to drive — how could she have forgotten this feeling? Then she remembered the tingle that ran up her arms as they wrapped around Nate and the thrum of the bike between her legs. Oh yeah, that was how. In an effort to stop this line of thought she leaned forward and pressed on the CD player. She was pleasantly surprised when Def Leppard blared from the speakers and not some dance album like she was expecting. There weren't many things she could thank Marcus for, but a love of this old rock group was one of them.

Singing along to *Love Bites*, she searched the skyline for anything to give her an indication she was heading in the right direction. A line of poplars looked familiar — but she knew from experience that these sentries often edged fields. She passed over a small bridge she recognised and searched her memory to recall if it was the last trip out when they'd gone over it. Pretty sure it was, she continued and it was only when she had driven past a turning between two long ditches that she remembered pointing it out to Nate before. Executing a — frankly scary — three-point turn, she carefully made her way back and pulled down the narrow turning. She followed the trail onto a winding road and kept her eyes open for the muddy track she knew was just a little way down it. She spotted it just before another line of poplars and indicated right. It wasn't long before the copse of trees came into view in the distance, and it was then the nagging doubts surfaced in her mind.

Ella would recognise Sam's car if she saw it; she would wonder what he was doing out this way. Or worse, what if she saw Regan at the wheel? She'd know that she was onto her. Anyway, exactly what was it she was going to be looking for? Signs that someone other than Ella lived there, she supposed. How she was going to do that from the inside of the car was anybody's guess though. She slowed and pulled over; maybe she'd be better off on foot from here. After all, Ella's house was surrounded by a thick copse of trees.

Pulling the car up she turned it around, ready to go if she needed to, then edged it behind a rather sparse hedgerow. Not perfect, but the best she could do. She debated leaving the keys in the ignition and the door open or having them as a make-shift weapon. As it wasn't her car, she decided on the weapon option. It hadn't occurred to her 'til then she may even need one or she'd have brought her knife.Of all the badly thought through plans she'd had recently, she was beginning to think this would take the top spot. Still, stubborn as ever, she pulled her hat down low, opened the door and climbed out. At least the day was clear. Fricking freezing, but clear. No signs of the familiars the witch used as her pets. It crossed her mind that at least they would have been a foe she knew how to handle … until the cuts on her arm burned a reminder that she didn't *always* know how to handle them.

Using the scant hedgerow as cover, she made her way as close to Ella's house as it let her. A small patch of open land was between her and the trees; checking that no-one was in sight, she ran across it, thankful that her fitness levels were a hundred percent improved from this time last year. A tall oak was the perfect hiding place and she leaned against it, finally trying to formulate some kind of plan. Edging as close to the property as possible, she supposed, was a good place to start.

Using the shrubs and trees as cover, she moved as close as she could to the house. The garden was open — no fences were in place as the trees formed a natural border. Crouching close to the ground behind a holly bush, she realised she was at the back of the property on the right-hand side. She could see across the empty back garden, full of mulching leaves and overgrown grass, and down the side of the house to the corner of the driveway. The back end of Ella's car was just in her vision and her heart started to thump as she realised this meant Ella was home. Now what?

There was no way to get across the yard without being seen as she was unable to tell if Ella was looking out any of the windows. Suddenly, Regan felt deflated; all the adrenaline that had been pumping through her suddenly drained right out. So, she'd got here and seen Ella was home. This information was going to impress Nate exactly how? She'd already known it was likely the girl would be at home, seeing as it was her regularly scheduled day off. She knew exactly zilch fresh information — and for that she'd used an illegal mode of transport to get here and scuttled along in the undergrowth like some kind of criminal.

Not wanting to give up, she skirted round the back of the garden, always keeping the trees as a safety barrier. As she moved, she eyed the garden for any signs of other people living there. No washing on the line, no boots at the back door, no stack of bicycles … the back garden obviously wasn't the hub of this household.

Settling into place on the other side of the house, she watched as a thin spiral of smoke started twisting from the chimney. Then the back door opened and Ella appeared with a bucket full of ash in her hand. She deposited it beside the back doorstep and disappeared back into the house. *Definitely home then*, Regan thought. As she sat there watching it occurred to her that maybe a covert operation wasn't actually necessary. If she could just think of a valid reason then she could quite easily walk up to the front door and speak to her — after all, she was a friend. The loosest classification of the word ever, but nonetheless she would have no reason to suspect that Regan thought anything suspicious about her.

Of course it would mean going back to the car. Ella would never believe she had walked all this way. As she contemplated this angle, wracking her brains for some excuse to use, the sound of an engine cut through the air. The adrenaline that had subsided started to pulse again; she used the conifers that edged this side of the house for cover and moved as far to the front of the building as she dared. The sound grew louder and it struck her that she recognised it … with a sickening thud she realised it was the sound of a bike engine and, though she was no expert, she could have sworn it was Nate's bike. Her heart raced. Damn, now she wasn't only trying to stay out of sight of Ella, she was trying to stay out of sight of Nate too. She checked she couldn't be seen from the road and hunkered down. Working on the assumption that, like her, Nate had come to observe the house and work out what he could about its occupants, she sent up a silent prayer that he wouldn't choose to hide in the same place that she had.

The ground was cold and hard beneath her, yet she barely felt it as she flattened herself as far into it as possible. Her ears were pricked, listening to the sound of the thrum, praying it was just a biker passing by; in her heart she knew it wasn't. She had trained herself to listen for the sound of Nate's bike months ago. Her heart thudded as the bike slowed; it hadn't yet reached the house — what was he doing? *God,* she prayed, *please don't let him find me.* She was honestly more scared of being found by him than by

Ella. Though fuck knows what she'd do if Ella started casting spells at her. She knew she was relying on ignorance — hers or Ella's she couldn't say. It frightened her a bit, but more than that, it angered her. Nate discovering her though, seeing the disappointment in his eyes again ... that struck fear to her very core.

A sudden silence made the thoughts echoing around her head sound as loud as shouted words. She wished she could see more and slid forward on her stomach like a soldier in warfare. A little in front of her was a thick evergreen bush; carefully, she wedged herself under it. The rotted earth was wet and squishy under her stomach and she shivered as the cold started to chill her, but she had a partial view of the driveway and was pretty sure she was hidden from view. She strained her eyes and ears, trying to work out what was going on. The sound of wheels splashing through a puddle reached her ears and, listening as hard as she could, she could just make out the squelching of heavy boots through mud.

Then, in a heart-stopping moment, Nate came into view. He was pushing his bike and his helmet dangled from his hands. He was wearing his usual uniform, though he had a scarf round his neck too; shame surged in Regan as she realised it was probably to cover up the cuts to his neck. He propped his bike up at the end of the drive and walked towards the front door. He glanced around as he walked and, for one unnerving second, his ever-vigilant eyes scanned past the shrubbery where she was hiding. Regan froze, sure he could hear her heart beating, but he carried on moving until she could no longer see him.

A couple of seconds later the sound of his knuckles rapping echoed to where she was hiding, and Ella opened the door.

'Hi, I'm sorry to disturb you but my bike has just conked out. I wondered if I could use your phone?' came Nate's familiar drawl. There was a pause and then, 'my cell has no signal.'

'Er, yeah, sure,' Ella said, then there was the sound of a door clicking shut. A small pause and it re-opened, Nate thanking her for the phone. He dialled a number and then came in view again, phone pressed to his ear, waiting for someone to answer. After a few seconds he cussed, softly but loud enough for both girls to hear him.

'Is there a problem?' asked Ella and she too came into view.

'Hmm, yeah, my mate isn't answering his cell.' Facing Ella, he handed her back the phone and thanked her.

Before he could leave, Ella said, 'Aren't you Regan's friend?' At the question Regan's head sprung up and she banged it on a branch of the bush. She clamped her mouth shut, refusing to yelp.

'Yeah, I am,' said Nate, and Regan hoped so much this was still true.

'Hi, I'm Ella. I'm, um ... an acquaintance of hers. We're both friends with Toni?'

'Toni?' said Nate, 'Oh, hang on — is she the girl with pink hair at the moment?' He sounded convincingly unsure — even to Regan, who knew he was perfectly well aware of who Toni was.

Ella laughed and said, 'For this week!'

'I know who you are,' he said, smiling, 'I've seen you in The Hunter's Rest, haven't I?'

'Yeah, Toni and me are usually in there. Can I give you a lift or help you out? I've got some tools if you know what's wrong with it.' Regan almost swore aloud. Never in all the time she had known Ella had the other girl sounded so friendly with someone she didn't know. More to the point, Ella knew how she felt about Nate — how could she not, she'd been there when Toni and Maeve had pumped her for information, teased and advised her about him. It crossed Regan's mind that Ella was maybe playing tit for tat — Sam flirted with Regan, so Ella was going to be friendly towards Nate.

'Some tools would be fantastic,' said Nate, breaking into Regan's thoughts.

'No problem,' Ella said, disappearing from view again.

Regan shifted a little; the ground was starting to feel really uncomfortable and dampness had started to penetrate her many layers, causing her to shiver. Nate made his way up towards the house until he was out of view and long minutes stretched coldly in front of Regan as she wondered what they were both doing. Just as she was just contemplating whether it was worth risking trying to get back to the car, the rare sound of Nate's laughter sounded — with the even rarer sound of Ella giggling back. A few seconds later he was at his bike, fiddling with some spanners as Ella stood drinking something steaming from a mug.

Nausea blossomed in Regan's stomach that had nothing to do with fear and everything to do with jealousy as she watched Ella hand over a spanner. They were talking together again, too softly for Regan to hear. She hated it and prayed that Nate would just fix the damn bike and go; she couldn't cope with him flirting in front of her, even if he was unaware she was there. It wasn't long before the recognisable purr of the engine filled the air, yet for Regan she may as well have been stuck under that bush for a week. She surely couldn't have been more miserable.

Not long after, Nate climbed on board and, waving to Ella, rode away. Regan waited for the sound of his bike to fade into the distance and retraced her earlier steps. She kept well away from the house, hidden by the woody trunks and branches of the copse. She ran back to Sam's car behind the hedgerow, brushing the damp mud from her front and hoping that she hadn't completely ruined her clothes.

She didn't turn on the music on the way back. Not even her favourite songs were going to dislodge the thought of Ella giggling at Nate from her head. The resolve she'd found this morning was rapidly dissolving, yet she knew she had to find some strength to face Nate later. And her mum, Toni, Maeve, Sam and, oh god, Ella. Thankfully no one was at Sam's when she dropped the car; after stuffing the keys through his letterbox she walked home again. The fates had obviously taken pity on her; she made it home, got showered and changed and put her dirty clothes in the wash before the rest of the household made it in.

Forty-Two
1645

In time, Lora managed to fall asleep again. Her arms and legs ached a little still, but the warmth had helped to take most of the pain away; despite her sinfulness, God must have been watching over her tonight to send Rafe to her. *At least*, she thought as sleep stole in, *I hope it was God and not the devil.*

Rafe woke her early and she stepped outside in the still-dark morning, her feet crunching on the hoarfrost that had settled in the night. Icy spiderwebs hung like jewels, glinting in the lowering moonlight. The ground crunched underfoot as they made their way in silence back to the town and Lora's house. Lora had prayed that God would keep her family safe and she had prayed that he would keep her sinful thoughts hidden. She was ashamed that she hadn't prayed that he take away the lustful feelings she was having, but the tingling she had felt all over when Rafe leaned close, when she remembered the strength in his arms or had breathed in his musky odour, was just too pleasant.

Knowing that she had asked God for a lot over the last few hours, Lora just *hoped* that her absence had not been discovered instead of praying for it. As they walked, the black sky in the east started to show the merest hint of purple. The stars and moon were fading and the dark outlines of trees and hedgerows could just be made out.

'It's only going to get harder,' said Rafe suddenly, his voice husky from lack of sleep, 'the witch knows who we are now, and she knows your family. I have never been in this situation before. I can fight her creatures day and night if I have to — I have used their pets to destroy them before — but I have never fought the devil's servants when they have known who I am.'

It is an impossible situation, Lora thought, *I have put those I love at risk because I wanted an adventure. I will put this right.*

'We will put this right, Rafe,' she said.

Stopping at the edge of town lest they be seen, Lora said goodbye. 'I will work this out, Lora,' promised Rafe, '*I* am the hunter. I will not be caught by my prey.' Noticing the dark circles under his eyes and the weariness etched in the lines on his face, Lora clasped his hands in hers. 'I know,' she whispered, 'I trust you will always keep us safe.' He loosened a hand and stroked his fingers gently down the side of her face. His tired eyes were trying to tell her a thousand things, things she wouldn't let herself hear. He moved his head forward a little, pausing, asking for permission. *Yes*, screamed her heart, *please, yes*. Before she could regret her actions, she unclasped her hand, shook her head, and turned away. Walking without looking back, she refused to let the tears fall. He was not hers to have; she was betrothed to another. She had a family to keep safe.

Whether it was God, luck or chance Lora would never know, but she was able to slip into the house unnoticed. Collecting some wood she set a fire ablaze and quietly started her morning chores. Not long after, her mother bustled in; Lora noticed her eyes were red from crying as she prepared to say goodbye to Father. Today he joined James in their fight against the cavaliers. Lora remembered with shame that she hadn't felt so bad letting James go to war; it had been much harder leaving Rafe this morning.

Forty-Three
2013

Work that night had never been so awkward; it was getting harder and harder to keep a game-face on. But she had to — the only person who knew the world had tilted on its axis was Nate, and life around him had been pretty damn uneasy for the last few weeks as it was. What was one more problem to add to that mix? She was going to have to face him later anyway. A thick fog had already gathered outside.

It made her uncomfortable knowing that Nate would patrol on his own until she was off work, but it was impossible to leave mid-shift. Impossible if she wanted to retain her job. Impossible if she didn't want to arouse suspicion, especially now she suspected Ella. If Ella had any misgivings about her, wouldn't she be sending the familiars and watching if Regan left to fight them?

Laughter rose from the table Toni, Ella and Sam sat at. It echoed round the nearly-empty pub and Regan wondered what the joke had been. She felt left out; oh, she could have walked over there — she wasn't exactly run off her feet — but she found herself unable to. So she watched them surreptitiously as she meandered around the bar, trying to keep herself busy. Sam, she noticed, kept glancing towards the door. *Curious,* thought Regan. The boy was usually surrounded by a group of mates and hardly ever stayed with his sister and her friends. As she rearranged bottles in the fridge it occurred to Regan that he was waiting for Maeve. Almost as if he'd read her mind, when she next looked up Sam was waiting at the bar, his long arms resting casually across the top of it, easy smile in place — yet, Regan noted, it was not quite as easy as usual.

'Hey Sam, what can I get you?' she asked, standing up and dusting down her jeans.

'The usual thanks,' he said, pushing his dirty glass across the bar top. 'So Regan, is your friend going to be in tonight?' he asked. His tone was casual, but Regan could hear the interest behind the question. She was sure she would have heard it even without witnessing the floorshow at the club. She shrugged, damping down the jealousy that threatened to swell in her stomach.

'I'm not sure, she doesn't always show up when the weather's bad. It's not so easy to get out from her place,' she said, neglecting to add that she hadn't replied to any of the three texts Maeve had sent since Friday night. 'Did you need her for something?' He shook his head and Regan found herself delighting at his discomfort. It was good to know someone else was feeling at least a little bit of the misery that she was. The feeling was short lived as the door swung open and Maeve came in, followed closely by Nate. Any jealousy that she'd felt at the thought of Sam and Maeve together multiplied a hundredfold as she saw Maeve lean in and whisper something to Nate. Her throaty laugh followed and Nate's lips turned up a little at the edges.

'Well I guess that answers your question,' she said to Sam, glad to see a little of the green-eyed monster rising in him too. To give him credit, he blinked and it disappeared, replaced by his usual grin and twinkle. Maeve raised her hand and waved; both she and Sam returned the gesture and her friend smiled. Regan just wasn't sure who at. Grinning wildly, Sam made his way back to his table.

'Coke please Regan,' Nate made his way to the bar for his usual order. Silently she pushed the nozzle into the glass and filled it up. Her brain was racing for something to say. She settled on an apology. Again.

'I'm sorry about the other night Nate. I know I was out of line, I promise it won't happen again.' She wanted to carry on — to try and explain, to make him understand how serious she was — but, thankfully, her pride stopped her.

He looked at her, molten eyes assessing and judging. She felt naked, sure he could see into the very core of her soul. She wanted to avert her gaze, hide the truth from him, but she couldn't. If she looked away now he would never trust her again, and too much depended on them for that. Finally, he nodded — whatever he'd been looking for, he'd found. Relief coursed through her. She couldn't take back what she'd done, she couldn't make him forget, make the facts go away, but she hadn't lost — *they* hadn't lost — not yet. They still had a chance.

'It was foggy, I couldn't get away,' she said, knowing he understood.

'It was a little. I couldn't find anything; it was just a normal fog.' He drank from his cola. 'I think they'll be out later — I've never known them to resist it when the weather is in their favour anyway.'

'Why only at night?' asked Regan, 'I mean, I'm not complaining. It's terribly convenient!' she tried to joke.

'I really don't know,' Nate shrugged, 'I think that today there is never any stillness in the world — people, phones, traffic, music … I think they thrive in the quiet, the dark. They feed on fear and worry. We're all too damned conditioned to a little fear these days, too many films and too quick to explain away strange happenings. That noise upstairs? It's the house settling, not a monster under the bed and hey even if it is a monster under the bed it'll be friendly really. It's amazing what people are able to close their eyes and ears to.'

Regan blinked. It all made sense. Heck when Lora — even Elizabeth — was patrolling these watery lands, the devil was a very real entity. Good and evil existed. Now good was celebrity and fame, and evil was reserved for tabloid newspaper headlines; it was bankers and M. P.'s and Europe. It was broken, drug addled parents too sick to care. It *was* child abuse, stabbing, loss of innocent life. It wasn't witches, familiars or any of the things that were passed off as supernatural. Belief in good and evil in the traditional sense had passed. Gone. Unfortunately, evil hadn't actually disappeared. It was just better hidden, and good was struggling to keep up.

'Hmm,' she said and nodded her head in agreement. This was the most Nate had spoken to her since *that* night. She really didn't want to blow it.

'So we've got less than three weeks, Nate. How are we going to find our witch?'

'I'm on it,' he said, pulling up a bar stool. 'I've been out over the last couple of days and assessed most of the houses. I think I may have a possibility.'

'You do?' asked Regan; her heart thudded. 'Who — I mean which house? Why do you think that?' Involuntarily, she glanced across the room towards Ella, then looked away when she caught the girl's glare.

'It's not her,' Nate said quietly, 'at least, I'm pretty sure it's not.' Regan looked up, shocked. She didn't realise until that moment that she had convinced herself it *was* Ella.

'How sure?' Regan couldn't resist asking; she had invested so much thought in the idea it was Ella, she couldn't just shake away the possibility. Not without firm proof.

'I went out that way and checked it out. I guess it's more a feeling than anything else. I have to trust my instincts a lot, Regan, and at the moment they're telling me it's not her.'

'So who do you—' Regan stopped when Toni appeared at the bar.

'Hey Regan, long time no see,' she said.

'It's been, what, like a week?' Regan asked laughing as Nate took his soft drink and found a table on his own.

'Well yeah, but I haven't seen Ash for even longer. I miss that little shrimp.'

'You really wouldn't, not if you lived with her,' Regan raised her eyebrows, knowing this to be untrue; she'd miss Ashleigh tons if she didn't see her every day. 'You'll have to pop round — tomorrow maybe, after school? I'm sure she'd love to see you. Maybe we can watch some more films or something. It was fun last time.'

Toni leaned across the bar and hugged Regan, 'That sounds like a plan, I'm sure I've got something we can watch. I'll tell Ella — what time is good, about four-ish?'

Regan's eyes strayed to Ella as soon as Toni mentioned her friend's name and for a second the breath stopped in her throat. Maeve was talking to the girl but she was paying no attention. Instead she was watching Regan, a look on her face of pure malice.

'Er, um, actually Toni, I'm really sorry but I've remembered I promised Ashleigh I'd take her … Christmas shopping after school — she was really looking forward to some sister time.' She smiled what she hoped was a sorrowful smile, her heart pounding. Nate's instincts were completely off this time, she was sure of it. Ella was the witch. But what the hell she was going to do about it she didn't know.

* * *

The rest of the evening passed in a blur. Maeve came to talk to her but she couldn't really remember what her friend said, though she did watch as she left with Sam. Toni and Ella left not long after, and the next time the door swung open Regan noted the fog recurring outside. As if her instincts had honed themselves, she knew this wasn't nature; the smell of it was evil.

Nick let her go not long after — nervous glances at the door as people left and the odd comment about the fog was a ploy she'd used before, to leave early when she needed to fight. Nick of course thought it was all his own idea, compassionate father-figure that he was. If she didn't know that what she was doing was damn important, she might have felt guilty at manipulating him.

She nodded to Nate, who finished his drink and grabbed his jacket. Outside a thin mist veiled the streets; with the ease of a hunter tracking his prey, Nate sped his bike through it, following the misty air to where it grew thick and potent. Wordlessly they jumped off the bike, the weak beam of its headlight having little effect in the fog. The air was freezing but Regan felt nothing but warmth as energy raced through her veins. She took her stance and sensed Nate behind her in his. As a disgustingly phlegmy noise penetrated the fog, Regan raised her knife. Adrenaline surged and then she was fighting. Fighting to make up for last time's error. Fighting because she needed to. Fighting to save their lives.

Forty-Four

By the time Nate pulled up to Regan's house, it was 3am and snowing gently. She shivered as the adrenaline left her body and a chill set in.

'You need to go to bed, get some sleep,' said Nate as he walked her to the front door. For a moment she pretended everything was normal, that she was just a girl being dropped off home by a boy. Then he looked at her and she could see the unspoken worry in his eyes and she remembered this — it, she — was anything but normal.

'I'll try,' she sighed as she fished in her pocket for her key, 'I'm not sure how successful I'll be though. Time's running out, Nate, and are we really any closer to finding out who the witch is?' Even as sleep tugged at her brain her mind started to worry at the knotty confusion of thoughts that was never far from the surface.

She shrugged and turned away from Nate, unlocking the door as quietly as she could and making her way to bed. She lay down without bothering to brush her teeth or wash her face, convinced that sleep wouldn't come. Exhaustion overtook her though and her lids grew heavy. Glad to escape the pain of thinking, she slept as if she was dead to the world.

* * *

'Pass the tape then, Ash,' she asked her sister as she folded back the corners of the wrapping paper. The snip of scissors sounded and Ashleigh passed over some Sellotape so Regan could seal the parcel.

'Here kiddo, that can go on Mum's pile.' She chucked the present to her sister who added it to the growing mound of red, green and gold beside her.

'Okay, what's next?'

Ashleigh pulled a face as she held up an 80's compilation CD. 'This. Honestly, I don't know why you bought her a CD, that's so last—'

'Don't say it,' Regan warned as she cut a strip of gold paper to size, 'Trust me, Toni's going to love it.' Ashleigh grinned at her, looking anything but convinced. 'Ooh, shut up you little rat bag,' Regan said, throwing a scrunched-up bit of paper at her sister. Ashleigh was the perfect cure for her tired brain, even if it only worked for a short while.

The sound of knocking came from the back door and Regan frowned; she was too tired for company today. 'I'll get it Ash, you wrap this for me,' she pushed the present and paper across the table. Rubbing her eyes and yawning, she opened the door; Toni, effervescent as ever, hugged her and let herself into the kitchen.

'Wondered if you were busy,' she said waving a DVD in front of her, 'as it's December I'm officially allowed to watch Christmas films!' Smiling despite herself, Regan peered at the title.

'*Santa Claus the Movie*. Really?' she asked.

'Hey, it's my favourite Christmas film! It was the first film I saw at the pictures.'

Regan let her raised eyebrows do the talking for her. 'So what do you think, up for it?' Just as she was about to say that yes, maybe a cheesy film and a mince pie might be what she needed, Ella appeared at the back door. Regan felt her smile slip and watched the grin appear on Ella's face as she noticed.

'I told you she wouldn't want me to watch it,' Ella said to Toni.

'Nah, Ella, you're being paranoid,' Toni's bright grin turned towards Regan. Tiredness slowed her reflexes and she couldn't hide the scowl she was wearing.

'I'm sorry Toni, I'm busy right now,' she said, 'maybe another time?'

'Another time what?' asked Ashleigh, coming into the room.

'Christmas films,' said Toni waving the DVD at Ashleigh without taking her eyes off Ella.

'Oh cool, we can watch that can't we Regan? You can't come into the sitting room yet though,' she pouted at Toni. Toni ignored her as she narrowed her eyes at Regan. Guilt swelled in Regan's stomach as she reiterated her previous statement.

'I'm sorry. We're busy Ash, we've got to get this done before mum gets back.'

'But they could help,' Ashleigh's pout turned from funny to serious. Her little sister didn't throw a strop very often but Regan could feel one brewing. Her patience was starting to wear thin. She looked out the window at the rain that had turned last night's snow to slush already. She took a deep breath.

'I'm really sorry but we need to get this done. Another time Toni, I promise.' She couldn't resist a look at Ella; hatred swirled in her stomach as she took in the girl's twisted sneer of enjoyment. Toni followed her eyes.

'And will Ella be welcome when you're free to watch it,' Toni asked as comprehension slid onto her face.

'Of course,' stuttered Regan, not sounding at all convincing even to her own ears. Ashleigh gasped.

'You're lying!' she yelled, 'What's wrong with Ella, Regan?'

'Yeah Regan, what's wrong with Ella?' Toni's voice was cold, her lips drawn in a thin line, the happy-go-lucky grin she always had completely gone. Regan stuttered and stumbled.

'Nothing's wrong with Ella, you guys can come back another time and watch the film, it's just not a good time now.'

'You're so mean,' Ashleigh cried, running from the room. Regan's heart sank. Could she have made any bigger hash of this if she'd tried?

'Ashleigh,' she called as the sound of her sister's feet thumping up the stairs echoed down into the kitchen.

'Look Toni, I'm really sorry, you're—'

'Save it. If Ella's not welcome then neither am I.' She'd slammed the door shut before Regan could work up to lying again.

'Fuck, fuck, fuck,' she said before punching the nearest available surface. It didn't make her feel any better and she only just had the common sense to shove her hand under the cold tap before it started to swell and bruise. A fat lot of good she'd be wielding a knife with a swollen hand. 'Fuck it,' she said again for good measure, wondering if things could actually get any worse.

* * *

The last place Regan felt like being that evening was work. She'd spent an afternoon trying to get Ashleigh to talk to her but the most she'd gained was a silent partner helping her wrap presents — and that was only after emotionally blackmailing her (it *was* only fair to help Mum).

She'd sent several texts to Toni, none of them replied to. Her head was pounding, the snow had started again and she really felt like seeing no-one. The temptation of pulling a sickie was really strong, but as she already had a day off booked soon — the 21st of December, etched in her brain like a hallmark in silver — she couldn't do it to Nick. Or Nate. So, reluctantly, she'd come in. And sitting at their usual table defiantly ignoring her were Toni and Ella. Nick looked at them, then at Regan; he opened his mouth to say something, but Regan flashed him a warning look and he shut it again. He walked off mumbling about teenage girls and Regan coolly served the next customer.

It was a long shift. Nate came in and sat at his usual table, talking jovially to Old Sid about Christmas plans and what he'd done for thanksgiving (nothing). Regan wanted to scream at him. *What the hell are you doing here, shouldn't you be out observing houses, watching for witches?* After a time it dawned on her that he was here because Ella was. The lying bastard, he *did* think it was her. She slammed down the pint she'd just pulled, spilling half of it on the wooden bar. The splash of beer snapped her attention to what she was doing.

'God, sorry Joe,' she whisked the pint away and poured another, slipping the money into the till from her own purse to cover it.

What's up with you?' asked Sam as he sat down at the bar. 'Anything to do with why my sister's in such a foul mood?'

'I'm fine,' she snapped, 'there's just been a misunderstanding.'

'A misunderstanding that involves Ella, by any chance?' He sipped the lager she'd drawn him, his grey eyes watching her knowingly.

'Why, what's she said?' Regan asked in spite of herself. She studied Sam as he sat there grinning at her.

'Sam …' she warned.

'Nothing, she hasn't said a dickey bird. But I'm not stupid. She's been stomping round the house all afternoon and Ella looks like the cat that got the milk.'

'Cream. It's the cat that got the *cream*.'

'Milk, cream, whatever, it doesn't take a genius to work it out.'

'Work out what?' Regan asked through gritted teeth. Her patience was stretched further than it had ever been stretched before, and Sam was drawing it out even more. Goddamn, she had a knife under her shirt and at this rate she was going to be using it before she'd left the pub.

'That Ella's finally got what she wanted.' Sam sipped his drink and Regan glared at him until he put it down. Sighing, he said, 'She's got you out of the picture. It's all she's ever wanted since day one.' Regan could feel the look of bewilderment on her face. Sure, she'd guessed that Ella didn't like her, but for it to be so obvious that Sam noticed too … well, what was the girl's problem?

'Oh crap,' said Sam, putting down his glass, 'if I tell you this, Regan, you take it to your grave, right?'

She could feel herself nodding, bewilderment finally cooling her anger. She glanced at Nick; he was safely chatting to a regular and wouldn't care if she was talking too. No customers needed serving, so she turned back to Sam. 'Come on then Sam, spill it. I'm sick and tired of this. I mean, we're not at primary school, are we? Toni is allowed to have more than one friend.'

'She's jealous of you, Regan …'

Regan snorted, 'Yeah right, she's way better looking than me!' She looked at the girl's long dark hair and creamy skin. 'What the hell has she got to be jealous about?'

'Toni and you being friends. She thought she was going to lose her to you.'

'This isn't reception class, Sam. A girl can have more than one friend.'

'Yeah, not when you're in love with that friend and are absolutely petrified that anyone new on the scene is going to take them away.'

'Yeah, well I— what ... huh? In love — Ella's not gay! Neither is Toni!'

'Toni isn't, I agree. Ella ...' Sam shrugged.

'But she's ... you've ...'

'Slept with her. Yeah, I know. I was the nearest thing she could get to Toni. It doesn't do much for a man's ego when the girl bursts into tears at the end of the act.'

Regan blushed; this was getting too close to her own secret for comfort. 'Yeah, well I'll take your word for it.'

'Trust me, she's in love with Toni — or at least thinks she is — and she's terrified that anyone new is going to come between her and her chance with my sister.'

'That just doesn't make sense. If Toni is straight, she's never going to want to be like that with Ella. Why doesn't she go out and find herself a girlfriend? Who's *also* gay?'

Sam downed a mouthful of beer, 'Because nobody apart from me, and now you, knows. Think about it, Regan. Maybe in Brighton it's easy to come out, gay bars on every street, but here, in Old Scytheton ...'

Regan shrugged. She could see it was harder, but living a lie? Pinning all your hopes on something that was never going to happen? No. She'd rather take her chances and be out, thank you very much.

'Easy for you to think,' said Sam, his grey eyes never leaving her face. She blushed at his perception. 'It's different when all you've known is the back of beyond. I may love it here, but not everyone is exactly open minded.'

'I suppo—'

'Hi you two, you look like you're having a deep and meaningful,' Maeve interrupted, slipping her arm around Sam. *Her arm around Sam,* Regan thought, *this is more serious than I realised.* One look at the smile that spread across Sam's face was more than enough proof that there was something more than a two-minute fling going on here.

'Never mind me,' she stared pointedly at Sam, then Maeve, 'I think you've been holding out on me.'

Maeve dropped her chin to her chest, a shy smile playing on her lips. 'Yeah, I guess I have,' she said. Sam's grin just grew wider as he pulled Maeve in closer. 'Later,' her friend promised Regan as she collected her drink and made her way to a quiet table with Sam.

Shortly afterwards Toni and Ella left; even the sad look on Toni's face didn't stop Regan from feeling relieved. She did a round of the pub collecting the empties that had accrued on the tables, her mind running over what Sam had revealed. Could it be true? Was all Ella's hostility just because she was in love with Toni? It seemed so absurd that Regan was quite sure it was possible. But where did that leave her — was she the witch, or were Nate's gut instincts correct?

'If you're right about Ella, who are you thinking it is?' she asked Nate as she wiped a rag over his table. He didn't look surprised at the random question.

'I don't know who, but there is one house we passed and when I went back to it, it just had a feeling about it. It felt evil.'

'A house felt evil. Nate, we can't pin everything on a house that feels evil!' He shrugged, and Regan noticed for the first time how tired he looked. She'd been so caught up in her own problems she hadn't realised the pressure Nate was under. Her heart thudded; she wanted nothing more than to draw him into her arms and rub his back, whisper in his ear that it would be okay, they'd figure it out. But it wouldn't be okay, she reminded herself. Not until the witch was stopped.

'So who lives there? Is she a likely candidate?'

Nate looked down at his drink, 'I don't know. I've stood outside that house for hours at a time and haven't seen anyone come or go. It's as if … as if whoever lives there knows I'm watching.'

'You don't *know* who lives there. We're hanging an awful lot on a feeling, Nate,' Regan knew it was mean, but she had to say it.

'I know,' tiredness emanated from him and she wondered just how long he had spent outside, watching, waiting.

'Let me go — tell me which house it is, I'll be lookout,' she offered, 'you're going to be no use to anyone like this. You look awful Nate.'

'Gee, thanks,' he smiled wearily, his dark eyes brightening slightly as they crinkled at the corners. 'It's fine, Regan. I'm fine.' His tone was final; Regan knew he wouldn't listen to any argument she came up with. Besides, she still had to figure out what she was going to do with Ashleigh on the 21st. She may not be working, but she couldn't leave Nate to face whatever the hell it was by himself.

'We need to talk properly, Nate. I need to know what the hell is going on,' she said before she made her way back to the bar.

Forty-Five
1645

'I disagree, Rafe. I think it is the perfect idea,' Lora said, crossing her arms in front of her and setting her mouth into a firm line. 'For three weeks we have tried to work out how we are going to rid the town of the witch and her creatures. Matthew Hopkins is the perfect answer — extracting the truth is what he does!' She paced the floor of Rafe's home, trying to think of another way to persuade him she was right.

She had awoken in the middle of last night, her dreams plagued as ever by images of Cecily. Her brow had been warm despite the freezing October air and she had opened her window to cool herself down. A crowd of drunken young men, thrown out of The Hunter's Rest, were singing in the streets. Two doors down another window had been flung open and Old Bess called out for the raucousness to stop. 'I know where you live, Matthew Carpenter,' she yelled, 'and you, young Rory …' Lora had quietly pulled closed her shutters, a memory slowly surfacing. The name, Matthew … then she had remembered the men speaking about a Matthew the night that Cecily had dined at their house. Matthew Hopkins, Witchfinder General. For the rest of the night she had mulled the idea over until she was convinced that it was the perfect solution. The *only* solution.

'All we have to do is convince the town that 20 shillings is a price worth paying,' she said, 'and it is!' She stopped pacing and sat down, her hands fiddling with the edge of her cloak as she organised her arguments in her head.

'The townspeople will be easily persuaded,' she said earnestly, 'James Butcher for a start; he cut off his thumb last week. He's been cutting meat for the town for two and ten years and never so much as pricked his finger. Folk would easily believe it was the work of a witch!'

'It was just a terrible accident, Lora. He's getting old and had been frequenting the ale house more and more.'

'I know, but he doesn't want to admit that. He would easily be swayed to believe that it was witchcraft.' She barely paused for breath, 'Henry Farmer lost four pigs this year, and I heard he has already muttered that it was the devil's work. Charles Pounder's wife died in childbirth … we don't even have to suggest it ourselves! A word or two in the right ears and the town will convince itself that it needs the services of Matthew Hopkins and John Stearne.'

Pausing in her pacing, Lora knew from the look on Rafe's face that he didn't agree with her. His brow creased and he rubbed his hand across his face. He had increased the number of hours he was patrolling at night, Lora knew. He didn't always tell her he was going, but she was round often enough to see the telltale signs — yawning when he claimed to have been here asleep all night, mud on his boots when no rain had fallen that could only have come from the swampy fenland. The fact that she had seen him guarding her house on more than one occasion. She herself had found it increasingly difficult to get away since father was not around to occupy her mother's time.

'It is too risky; the witchfinder puts innocent women on trial. He finds a town willing to pay and he listens to the gossip and the tales and then he accuses an innocent woman of witchcraft and tortures her until she confesses to the crime. Ofttimes he will torture her more so she names her companions. Innocent women all of them, of that I am certain, put to death for the sum of twenty shillings.'

This could not be true, Lora knew, 'But torture is not lawful, sir.'

'That it is not, but it gets the Witchfinder his money and that is all that concerns him.' She tried a different tact, 'Nobody would admit to something of which they are not guilty …'

'The words of someone who has never been tortured!'

'And no one would name members of their family and friends as witches if it was not true, sir!'

'Trust me, Lora. When you are tortured it takes a strong soul not to say what the torturer wants to hear. A very strong soul. Most of the accused women are old or frail; they have not the strength to withstand the pain.'

'In this town though Rafe, it would be obvious to any witchhunter who the real magic-caster is. We were able to find her with little trouble!'

'It is what I do, Lora — I am the Hunter!' Lora looked straight at him. She took in his tired, haggard appearance; took in the exhaustion that had etched itself onto his face. She understood that he needed her to agree with him, though she was utterly convinced that should Matthew Hopkins come to the town he would have no problem at all singling Cecily out.

Boldly she took his hand, raised it to her lips and kissed it softly, her heart breaking. 'I concede your point, sir. I will think on it no more,' she lied.

Forty-Six
2013

The snow was falling hard and fast outside and Regan wiped the condensation from the windowpane so she could watch it. It was idyllic, really — less than a week until Christmas, and a thick layer of snow was hiding the flat, empty fields. Any other year — in fact every other year — she would have prayed for a white Christmas, but now there was a chance it may actually happen, it was just an added complication to contend with. Turning, she watched Nate at his kitchen table. He was focused, eyes scanning endlessly as he scrolled down page after page on Google. He looked more drained than she had ever seen him and, despite his denials, she was convinced he was barely sleeping. Though there had been a surprising lull in the number of creatures out on the fens, he'd been splitting his time between trying to identify the witch and finding out how to stop her.

'Have you found anything?' she asked, convinced that he wouldn't. 'I told you, I've trolled through pages on Google and, apart from the religious and the downright mad, I couldn't find anything of use. If we could just kill her it would be so much easier.' A shiver ran down her spine and she wiped her hands across her face wearily. 'Forget I said that, I know we can't. Whatever she is, she's still human.' Nate grunted, not looking up from his research.

Sitting twiddling her thumbs had never been Regan's strong point. Sighing, she pulled out the spare chair and opened Elizabeth's diary. She'd skimmed through it as best as she could given the old-fashioned writing and found nothing of use. But even re-reading was better than nothing; better than sitting there feeling useless, helpless. She shifted to try and get a better view of the diary under Nate's dim light bulb. Her knee hit his under the table and the unexpected contact sent a searing heat through her skin. Pulse beating, she glanced at him; nothing, nada. He was still searching the internet, trying to find something that might help.

She felt a scream swelling in her throat and swallowed it back, buried it down with her feelings. She had to accept that Nate had no interest in her, other than as companion hunter. She thought she'd got her need for him under control and she had, for the most part. When she knew she was going to see him, she could prepare herself. When they were fighting or at work she could concentrate on the task at hand. But this — just sitting there watching him as he was devoured by the hunter — it was hard. Unexpected contact sent frissons through her that reminded her she was alive. But it hurt too, knowing that these moments, that made every inch of her hyper-aware, went unnoticed by him. It hurt a lot.

'Nothing. There's nothing,' Nate said suddenly, sighing and pushing the lap-top away from him. 'The best I've got to work with is Dad's advice — take away her tools.'

'Her tools?' Regan asked, visions of hefting a toolbox out of an unknown garage entering her brain. 'How is that going to help?'

'The tools of her witchcraft. Dad sent a list of what they use. Here, I'll show you …' he opened up his e-mail and turned the screen to Regan.

To: nate@yahoo.com
From:TJHunter@google.com
RE: Witches
Hi son,

I've searched for the information you asked for and I'm afraid to say I'm drawing a blank. I did find a list of tools they need to perform their magic — supposedly; how much can you trust the world wide web? — I've enclosed it below. My best guess would be to try and remove these items before she needs them, it sounds as though she needs this ritual to strengthen or maintain her power, if you take away her tools, weaken her, hold her captive until December 21st, maybe it will be enough to stop her.

I know you don't want to think about it son, but maybe you have to consider the other possibilities.

Stay true,
Dad.

A 5-sided star (Pentacle) — to protect her power — possibly jewellery
13 candles — 12 red, 1 white
Rope for binding
Herbs/incense/roots for burning or use in magic particularly: dragon's blood & wort, fennel,

hellebore, hemlock, rue, aletris root, avocado, blackberry
A vase, urn or bowl for burning above
A knife

'What does he mean, consider other possibilities?' Regan asked, her voice quiet, scared.

Nate caught her gaze, his deep eyes shadowed, not quite able to disguise the worry. 'He means killing her.'

'But I thought we'd agreed we couldn't do that. She's not a creature — she's human.'

'I know Regan, I know. If I kill her it will be a last resort. I'll do everything in my power to stop her before it comes to that. Dad is just reminding me it's a possibility.'

Throat constricting, Regan spoke, her voice barely a whisper, 'But what if I have to do it? I … I don't know if I'll be strong enough.'

Nate's head shot up, his mahogany eyes fixed on Regan, a look of pure bewilderment on his face. If she wasn't so damn scared, she might have laughed out loud at him. 'Regan, you're going to be nowhere near *her* when it happens, I thought you understood that.'

Unable to stop it, her pride swiftly came to the fore. 'What do you mean I'm not going to be there? Of *course* I'm going to bloody well be there — I'm the hunter's companion, you can't do this alone!'

His eyes flashed. 'You are not going to be there. You are going to be as far away from there as possible.'

'Easy for you to say, we don't even know where *there* is yet! Hard to stay away from a place that we don't know where it is.'

'You'll be at home; I thought that was why you had booked the evening off.'

'I booked it off to help you.' Ice dripped from every word. She sat up, her back rigid, not noticing this time when her knee scraped across Nate's. 'I thought we were partners.'

Nate slumped, his face pleading with her to understand, to not fight him. 'It's too dangerous, Regan. You'll be in danger.'

'No more than you.' She watched him, waiting for his reply. The expressions on his face told a million stories. She could see him running through every argument in his head. She could see point and counter-point, reason and disagreement all written on his face as clear as day. His eyes clouded over for a millisecond as he looked at her, a hint of apology in the draw of his brow. Then they cleared, his gaze fixed with a resolve that scared Regan. As he opened his mouth to speak it dawned on her what he was going to say, what argument he knew would work. A blush tainted her cheeks, her head warm and her hands clammy.

'You *are* in more danger than me. You know what she wants — you're everything she wants and needs.'

'It's still not too late to change that, you know,' she said, her voice strangled with restraint, tears welling in her eyes that she refused to let fall. Nate started to speak, then stopped. His face flushed with anger and he turned away, took a breath. His shoulders were rigid, his jaw tensed. He walked to the sink, poured some water into a glass and took a sip. Regan watched, the tears still blurring her vision, humiliation welling in the pit of her stomach.

'If you go and sleep with someone to 'solve' this, Regan, I swear to God … I'll not be responsible for my actions. I'll kill him,' his voice shook, the words barely audible. Heat blazed through Regan; hope, cruel mistress that she was, flared for a second — hope that he was jealous, that he wanted her. But realism set in, leaving nothing but a familiar ache in the very core of her.

'Don't worry, Nate. You already have one potential death on your conscience, I won't leave you with another.' She picked her jacket up from the back of the chair and slipped it on, 'Take me home, please.'

Forty-Seven
1645

Old Scytheton was not a big town, but it did boast a few good shops. A baker's did good trade, as did a haberdashery full of both practical and pretty fabrics and ribbons. A twice-weekly market was held in the centre of town; it was renowned for being the best market for miles. The butcher's had been very popular too, before James Butcher had had his accident. Now it was the centre of suspicion and many customers travelled a little further, to New Scytheton, for their meat.

Autumn was wearing its colourful dress of red, orange, yellow and brown today, and whilst the wind whipped at Lora's ankles as she fetched some shopping for her mother, it had not the icy bite of a few nights before. As she walked her mind was racing. Since her conversation with Rafe, the idea of the Witchfinder General swooping into town and ridding them of Cecily seemed more and more perfect. It tugged at her heart that he disagreed with her, but her stubborn nature refused to yield; she knew she was right. She had thought of nothing else for the last three days, until she had formulated a plan to bring him to town.

By chance her mother needed some fabric from town, and Lora had offered to collect it. As the breeze playfully tugged at her bonnet, she let herself hope that in town today she would meet at least one of the many gossips of Old Scytheton. Everything hinged on her managing to say a few choice words in the right ear. Old Scytheton had more than its fair share of gossiping women, both young and old, and Lora felt it would be very bad fortune to not bump into one today, when she most needed to.

It was important, she knew, not to appear to *be* gossiping; there was nothing a gossipy hag could abide less than another gossip. It was her plan to appear as innocent as possible and just let a few words slip into a listening ear.

There was a fine line between planting the seed and ruining the plant; she had to say just the right words to the right person for the idea to grow on its own. And fortune, it appeared, was for once on her side. As she entered the haberdashery she noticed that not only was Father John in there, but also Ivy Beeston, a close companion of Tess Pounder who had died recently in childbirth. She was, Lora knew, a woman of a naturally suspicious nature and a most fantastic lover of others' ills to boot.

'Good day to you, Mistress Beeston,' she said, shutting the door behind her, 'that ribbon will look grand on a new bonnet.' She eyed the length of cotton the old woman was fingering. The pinch-faced lady frowned at Lora through narrowed eyes. 'New ribbons on bonnets are a frivolity that God-fearing folk do not need, Mistress Smith,' she sniffed, her hand immediately pushing away the forget-me-not blue ribbon.

'Without doubt Mistress Beeston, God-fearing folk like yourself know better than to spend money on unnecessary adornments, no matter how much they might suit them.' She watched as a small flush of pleasure flicked across the older woman's face at the flattery. 'Of course, I consider myself of good fortune to have such moral guidance from the elders around me.' Mistress Beeston nodded her head and Lora knew she had not gone too far. 'I said to myself not a clock's turn ago how lucky I was — why, I saw a young lady in here, maybe of just four and twenty, trying four different ribbons against her complexion to see which suited her more.' Lora looked around and lowered her voice conspiratorially, 'and guess — it was only my Aunt Louisa's new companion!'

Feeling she had just about planted the seed, she decided it was time to take her leave and let Mistress Beeston's inclination towards eavesdropping and gossip take over. 'I'm afraid Mother bid that I collect her order as quickly as possible, good day to you,' she said, inclining her head before making her way to the haberdashery counter.

As she waited her turn behind Father John Simpson, an opportunity beyond what she had dared hope for presented itself to Lora. While the old man behind the counter was finding the fabric the reverend needed, Lora bade the vicar good morning.

'Good morning to yourself, Mistress Smith, and God's blessing to your family.' The Reverend turned back to the counter, but Lora needed to keep him talking for just a moment more. Doing her best to look a little scared, she once again spoke to the clergyman in front of her, 'I beg your pardon for interrupting your contemplation Reverend, but I did have something on my mind. I prayed to God that he guide me with this worry and, well, on the very morning I offered my prayers I have had the fortune to meet you.' She paused and to her delight could see the old idiot was swelling with importance. 'It is, I fear,' she lowered her voice, 'a topic which truly frightens me.'

The reverend smiled a smile of false modesty. The hideous man had always acted as if he was God and not just preaching about him. Lora tried to arrange her features to look like a scared young girl — anything to bolster his feeling of superiority. 'Of course, child. It is God's will that I look after the sheep of his congregation,' he said, 'pray tell me your fears.'

'Well Reverend, I am afraid I overheard a conversation betwixt my uncles. I know that to eavesdrop is a sin but truly it was not my intention, merely an accident that I overheard their words.' The reverend nodded sagely — advisement of the sin of eavesdropping could be dispensed at any moment, so Lora hurriedly carried on. 'It was the words I overheard that have me afeared, Reverend — words of witches and witchfinders!' Lora paused and looked down, a show of contrition that was actually hiding her desire to laugh at the goggling eyes of the pompous pastor. Controlling herself, she carried on.

'My uncle said there had been suspicious acts and that mayhap a Master Matthew Hopkins ought to be appointed by the town.'

'And what acts did your uncle feel warranted the concern of the Witchfinder General?' Father John asked, his beady eyes widening at the prospect of scandal.

'Well sir, he mentioned the butcher's terrible accident, the awful death of Mrs Pounder and her newly born babe. I might have misheard but I believe he said that the wheat crop had failed this summer and that, in the orchards, apples were down in number …'

'Tis true all these things have happened of late,' the reverend muttered to himself. 'It is not for you to worry about, child, but the concern of more important men; it is a sorrowful thing that you overheard your uncles, though wise words they were repeating.' He all but patted her head, 'It is bad to listen to the words of others without them knowing; I suggest you pray to the good Lord for forgiveness tonight as you kneel by your bed.' He turned himself back to the long counter, dismissing Lora, but not before she recognised the glint of self-importance in his eye. The reverend collected his parcel and left with Lora not far behind; the look Mistress Beeston gave her as she passed told Lora all she needed to know. The seed was well and truly planted; she just needed to let it grow.

Forty-Eight
2013

'Maeve, you truly are a life saver,' Regan said, hugging her friend, 'Ashleigh, are you sure you're going to be okay? You don't mind going to Maeve's house?' She wound a scarf around her little sister's neck and tucked it into the front of her coat. Snow was still blowing sporadically, but the old saying it's too cold to snow wasn't ringing true this evening; it was literally freezing outside.

Saturday December 21st was already proving to be the worst day in history as far as Regan was concerned. It had been over a week since she'd spoken to Nate. They'd exchanged words, he'd given her lifts home from work, but no actual conversation had taken place. Toni had yet to speak to her, neither she nor Ella had been near the pub again since their disagreement and Regan had had no response to the texts she had sent to either girl. If it wasn't for Maeve, Regan would have gone completely insane.

Her friend had popped round on Tuesday to dish the gossip on her and Sam. Regan had led her up to her attic bedroom and closed the door and, before Maeve could say one word, had promptly burst into tears. Her friend had put an arm around her shoulders and let her cry until the tears would come no more. She'd fetched tissues for her, told her Ella was a bitch and that Toni would come round in time, and barely mentioned Sam at all.

'I'll tell you about him another time,' she'd said.

'Maybe you can come round on Saturday? I've got the day off and I'm looking after Ashleigh,' Regan had asked. Maeve had agreed and the week was suddenly looking up. It hurt — burned — that she couldn't go with Nate, but even she had accepted that sneaking around to try and join him was just too dangerous. Having Maeve round *might* help distract her.

Katherine and Aunty Vi had left this morning, then at lunchtime Nick had rung and asked her to work. He said he was too ill to open up — and as he'd had to stop talking to throw up Regan didn't doubt him. Very reluctantly, she'd agreed, her mind planning on stowing Ashleigh in the pub kitchen for the evening. Ashleigh was not impressed; her normally placid, easy-going sister was on the verge of a temper tantrum. They'd barely patched up their differences since the whole Ella debacle and Regan was tearing her hair out trying to decide what to do. When Ashleigh suggested that Maeve look after her, it seemed like a possible, workable solution. A phone call later and Maeve was ready to collect Ashleigh — for an evening of fun and fashion, apparently.

'Okay, well I'll come and pick you up after work tonight and drop you and Ashleigh home,' said Maeve as Regan gave Ashleigh a hug.

'You're a life saver Maeve — and you behave yourself, squirt,' she said, ruffling her sister's hair then plonking a hat on her head.

'I'm not two, Regan,' Ashleigh complained, 'I do know how to behave.' Regan smiled as she shooed them out the door; she'd worry about how to explain Maeve babysitting after all to her mum at a later date.

Double checking her make-up in the mirror, Regan decided she'd have to do. She chose her warmest coat and scarf. She checked her phone before putting her gloves on, not knowing whether to hope Nate had sent a message or not. The message screen was blank, her inbox proclaiming *no new messages*; her stomach knotted as the thought of what Nate might have to do tonight came unbidden to mind. She pushed the thought as far into the crevices of her brain as possible; there was nothing she could do about it except accept that if she'd never moved here Nate would be facing whatever he was going to face alone anyway. It was no different, she couldn't help. He didn't want her to. He was alone. She couldn't think about what she would do if anything happened to Nate. She wouldn't think about it.

Wiping a tear from her cheek, she grabbed her keys and left the house. She was barely off the driveway when Sam pulled up.

'Maeve called and said you'd need a lift,' he said, grinning; she climbed into the car, glad of its warmth and the distraction of Sam.

'I've got strict instructions to make sure you're okay tonight,' he turned his head to her, 'what's the matter, not still upset about Toni are you? She'll come around soon, she's already missing you.'

Regan did her best to smile at Sam; she wanted to get this mess with Toni sorted out, but it really wasn't top of her priority list at the moment. He parked the car, then walked her into the pub and plonked himself down on a stool in front of the bar. Regan raised an eyebrow at him.

'Boss's orders. I'm to keep you company and help out if needed.'

'Which boss?' Regan asked, 'Maeve, or Nick?'

'Both,' his grin widened, 'Maeve wanted me to make sure you were okay and Nick said if it gets too busy to help you out.'

'Great,' said Regan, 'so it's take pity on Regan day, is it?'

'Hey, there's nothing wrong with being helped out by a friend,' Sam patted her hand and warmth spread through her. A friend was always good.

* * *

The pub was busy soon after she'd opened the doors. This close to Christmas, people were celebrating, relaxing, getting in the Christmas spirit. Regan did her best to serve everyone with a smile on her face. Busy worked for her, it gave her little time to think; any lull in serving and cleaning and fear started to creep its way in. At times she found her eyes straying towards Nate's usual corner. The place was packed, but it seemed empty without him there. She missed his presence with a physical ache that started in her knotted, clenched stomach. She couldn't let herself think about what he was doing, so she made sure she always had something to do.

It was nearly twenty past ten when her world fell apart.

'Here you are Tony, and your change,' Regan said, pushing a pint across the bar. Just about to serve the next customer, she felt the phone in her pocket vibrate. 'Sam, can you take this order?' she asked as she fished the phone out. Her gut clenched as she ducked into the back room, barely daring to check who it was.

Maeve calling flashed across the screen. 'Hi Maeve, how's things? Is Ashleigh okay?'

'Oh God Regan, you need to get here, Ashleigh's had a fall …' Her stomach squeezed harder, threatening to bring up the sandwiches she'd eaten earlier. Her mouth dried out, her brain scrambled as too many thoughts, too many images all burst into her skull at once.

'Regan? Regan?' Maeve called, a frantic edge to her voice that Regan hadn't heard before.

'I'm here, I'm coming, what's happened? Is she alright?' Her brain raced and she tried to signal Sam as she was listening to Maeve.

'She's slipped on the ice, she has a huge crack on her head, I've called an ambulance. Oh god Regan I didn't know what to do!'

Regan felt her own head clear as Maeve's voice grew more panicked. She began giving first aid instructions down the phone as she finally caught Sam's attention.

'Sam I'm leaving, Ashleigh's had an accident and I'm going to Maeve's. You'll have to manage the pub for me. Ring Nick, get him in if you must, I don't care.' She walked towards the door then felt a tug at her shoulder.

'How are you going to get there?' Sam asked.

'I'll get a taxi, I'll walk, whatever it takes — I'm going.'

'Give me two secs,' said Sam. She ignored him and carried on out the door. She hung up on Maeve reluctantly and dialled for a taxi. An empty echoing was ringing in her ear as Sam grabbed her again and bundled her towards his car.

'I've left Old Sid and Tony in charge. I told them it's an emergency. If Nick has a problem, I'll deal with him.' A modicum of relief wiggled into her stomach; it hadn't occurred to her until she got in the car that she actually had no idea where Maeve lived.

Forty-Nine
1645

'You will never guess what Sarah heard at the market yesterday,' said Mary, rubbing the small of her back where she had been feeling pains for the last few hours. Wind rattled the windowpanes, letting in a small draught. Lora watched leaves swirling across the ground outside, but the fire in Mary's kitchen had been blazing for hours and the room was pleasantly warm.

'How are you faring, Mary?' Lora asked, concerned. She put down the apple she was paring for her sister. 'Is it time for the midwife to be fetched?'

'Not yet Lora, no. These pains are but the normal aches of being with child. Besides, Aunt Louisa will be here soon and I must be prepared.'

'If you are certain, sister,' Lora returned to the bowl of apples, 'so pray tell me what your maid heard in town!'

She had wanted herself to visit town, to hear if any rumours were yet spreading, but her concern for Mary had kept her at her sister's home for the past week.

'Sarah came back from the market when you were outside collecting the apples, and she had the most extraordinary news,' said Mary as she settled into a chair. 'Ooh, that's better. It would seem the gossip about town is that the Witchfinder General is himself coming to Old Scytheton! Imagine!'

Lora's pulse started to race and she could feel a flush of excitement creeping into her cheeks. It had worked, it had truly worked! She hadn't dared to hope that it would, and her stomach clenched at the thought that Cecily would soon be stopped.

'Here, let me get you a cushion,' Lora said as her sister twisted in her chair, the babe in her belly making it impossible for her to get comfortable. She picked up an embroidery-covered cushion and placed it behind Mary's back, trying to ease her sister's discomfort. 'Oh do not fuss so, Lora. It is just the pains of the babe, I had as much with Eve.' She returned to the conversation, 'According to Sarah, who heard it from several sources, Father John persuaded the members of the town guild that witchcraft was apparent in the town and that Matthew Hopkins was the very person we needed to find the witch. Or witches!'

'Oh, just one, surely? We would not be so unlucky as to have ...' she trailed off as her sister's face grew pale and perspiration beaded on her forehead.

'What is it, Mary? Is it time?' she asked, ignoring a knock at the front door, 'shall I fetch the midwife yet? Or send for Mother?'

'No, Lora! I am fine,' Mary said, though Lora grew uneasy as she watched her sister bite down the pain. Regaining her composure, Mary continued, 'According to Sarah, Father John feels we must have nigh on a coven of witches in Old Scytheton with all the maladies that have occurred! It makes me feel queer to think of those ladies who are practising the devil's magic!' The brief moment of joy in thinking that she had succeeded disappeared immediately and Lora's blood ran cold; this was exactly what Rafe had feared.

'Surely there has not been that much ill; one witch, if she was powerful enough, could cause much mayhem. I think it is best we pray that Master Hopkins is wise in his witch finding!'

'Mistress Little, Mistress Smith, Louisa Hammond and her companion have arrived,' announced Sarah, appearing at the door of the kitchen, 'would you have me show them to the parlour?'

'There is no need for that, Sarah. I am family and if Mary is comfortable here in front of the fire, then we will find the kitchen as convenient a place to be as any.'

'Lora, dear,' said Aunt Louisa, bustling into the kitchen. 'Now Mary, you are looking pale. Are you sure your time has not come?'

'No Aunt, it is near to be sure, but not yet time.' Mary said, trying to push herself out of her chair. 'I can't receive visitors in the kitchen, it is unseemly.'

Her sister's dark eyes looked huge in her unusually pale face and Lora was relieved that her aunt was here to aid her with Mary's needs.

'It is just I and my companion, Cecily,' Louisa said, and it was only then that Lora noticed the witch standing behind her aunt. Bile rose in her throat as she realised once again her family's sanctity and safety were at risk. 'I hope you do not mind, Mary — Cecily has knowledge of herbs that could be of use to you as your time is near.' Louisa bustled around the room but Lora stood frozen, words choked in her throat.

'Don't worry, Lora,' Louisa said, smiling kindly, 'Mary is in pain, but it is a wondrous gift from God bringing a babe into the world.'

Lora tried to smile. It felt forced but seemed enough to fool Aunt Louisa. Cecily's presence in the room had taken all the air from Lora's lungs. She moved closer to Mary and fussed at the cushion easing her sister's back while her aunt chattered away.

'I believe I heard you discussing Matthew Hopkins himself gracing our small town with his presence. It is indeed an honour!'

'The Witchfinder General will certainly be able to rid the town of any malignant women,' said Cecily in her soft, seductive tone. Lora was sure she alone heard the edge to Cecily's voice — the voice that had haunted her dreams and scratched at her soul as painfully as claws would scratch her skin. She thought frantically of a way to get Cecily from the house. Then a terror that ran even deeper struck as Mary moaned in pain.

The noise was not loud but low, guttural and far more frightening than any sound Lora had ever heard. Below the chair on which Mary rested was a pool of her waters, red and shiny with blood. The fire behind her flickered and danced, its reflection making the blood look as though it had come straight from hell. Aunt Louisa paled and said, 'Tell Sarah to fetch the midwife and tell her to hurry.'

Fifty

Unable to take her eyes from the liquid pooling under the chair, Lora stood frozen on the spot. 'Lora, fetch Sarah now!' She heard the words, somewhere in the back of her mind, yet still Lora found she could not move. 'I will tell Sarah,' Cecily said, disapproval at Lora's lack of action flitting across her face as she left the room.

Mary moaned again but Lora, transfixed by the ruby drops adding to the watery pool below, found herself unable to speak. Firm hands gripped her shoulders and shook them and she re-focused her gaze on her aunt's angry grey eyes. 'You are either going to help me move your sister to her bedroom or you are going to leave. God save us child, I need your help!' Mary's moans of pain penetrated and Lora wrapped her arm around her sister, mirroring her aunt; between them, they helped Mary stand.

Her sister's fist bunched the stiff cotton of Lora's dress, her knuckles grinding painfully into her back. Lora barely noticed. Taking as much of Mary's weight as possible, she followed her aunt's lead and between them they slowly stood Mary up.

'The stairs will be too much for her,' Lora told her aunt. 'Maybe if we take her to the parlour? I can make a bed on the floor in there.'

'No, let me sit.' The words were uttered so quietly, so lifelessly, that Lora had to strain to hear her sister.

'Is there straw in the yard?' asked Aunt Louisa decisively, 'go and fetch armloads of it, get one of the servants to help. Quickly, child.'

Soon a thick straw bed was made on the floor, covered in sheets and pillows, and Lora and Louisa had helped Mary down on to it. The bleeding had not stopped and Mary was alternating between deathly quiet and long, agonising moans that tore Lora's soul in two.

Sarah was not yet back with the midwife and Louisa had moved aside to let Cecily take control, 'She is practised in the old ways, herbs and medicines,' said Louisa in explanation.

Lora's panic doubled at the sight of the witch standing beside her sister. 'Aunt Louisa, I am sure Mary would be happier with you assisting her.' Lora did not care who helped Mary; truly, she just wanted someone to make her better — to bring the babe into the world and give the colour back to Mary's cheeks — but Cecily did not save lives. She stole them.

'Do not be so silly, child. Cecily is much more able than I am!'

'Please Aunt Louisa, please help, at least until the midwife arrives.' Lora moved forward towards her sister. 'Tell me what to do.'

The raven-haired witch moved to the side, letting Lora next to her sister. 'I am sorry,' Cecily said, addressing Louisa, 'I was only hoping to help. Lora is quite right — this is a time for family. I will wait outside for the midwife to arrive.' She turned towards the door and Lora felt a little relief as she reached for Mary's hand.

Before she had time to offer words of reassurance, another throaty moan emitted from her sister. As she groaned more of her life's force pooled out of her to the straw-strewn floor. *Surely there should not be so much blood.* Lora tried to remember Eve's birth five years earlier. She had been just twelve at the time, but she could not remember so much blood. *Nor the deathly pale of Mary's face. Screams, I remember screams and Mary panting like a dog.* The low, guttural sound coming from her sister frightened Lora much more than the screams had. *It's as if she has not enough life to give voice to the pain.*

Five of Mary's servants were in the room; banned from helping by Louisa, they were all asking God in their own way for his guidance. On bended knee with heads bowed or upright and arms outstretched, the servants all offered their prayers to the Lord.

Outside Mary's husband Oliver had been told the babe was coming; Lora knew that he and his manservants would be offering prayers too for the child's safe delivery.

God, please hear their prayers. Please God, keep Mary safe … the words ran over and over again through Lora's mind. Vaguely, she was aware that she had once promised God *any* sacrifice if he kept her family safe on that night. *But not Mary, Lord. It would be too cruel of you to keep her safe to then take back her life.*

'Uuuurr,' Mary called, her exposed stomach hard as her body tried to eject the baby from inside it.

'Mary!' cried Lora, 'Louisa, please help.' She felt so helpless — not knowing what to do, she dabbed ineffectively at the splurging blood with a cloth. It made no difference so she exchanged it for a clean, damp one and tried patting her sister's head instead. The relief she had felt when Cecily had left the room had faded completely; all she could see was Mary, losing life with every ragged breath she took. She looked around at her aunt, pleading her to save her sister.

'It is not me you need, Lora. I cannot save your sister. Cecily is the only one that can help.' She nodded to one of the servants, who quietly left the room.

'No Louisa, please not Cecily — she cannot help Mary.'

'Cecily is the only chance your sister has, child.' Lora started at the sharpness in her aunt's tone and Mary whimpered again, her belly hard and round.

Lora dropped the damp towel she was holding and held her head in her hands. 'I need to think,' she said.

'I can help Lora, if only you will let me,' Cecily's soft voice came from beside Lora, the servant Louisa had sent to fetch her once again praying for Mary. She pulled Lora's face round so she was looking straight in her eyes. The greenness of them entranced Lora, made her dizzy. 'I will do the best I can for your sister,' Cecily said, her voice barely more than a whisper. 'I cannot promise to save her — too much time has passed — but I will try.' Nodding, Lora stumbled back, making room for Cecily beside Mary. Shaking her head a little she tried to remember why Cecily should not be near her sister. Then Mary moaned again and she forgot to try.

'You are doing well, Mary,' Cecily said, 'grip Louisa's fingers in your own when the tightening comes.' Mary's head moved just a little in acknowledgement. Lora stood stock still, once again frozen to the spot.

Another contraction seized Mary; her body curled forward, her brow creased and dripping, and with laboured breathing she let out a long, hard grunt. When the feeling had passed she flopped back, her eyes closed, barely aware of Louisa's supporting hand or Cecily's soft words.

'It's coming now Mary, I can see the top of its head,' said Cecily, 'keep pushing, gentle pushes, that's it.'

Not yet, it's too soon, Sarah has not returned with the midwife. Lora stood watching Mary's agony and she felt cold to the bone. She wanted to look away, or hold Mary's hand and comfort her, or help Cecily bring the child into the world, but she couldn't move. She couldn't stop watching. Couldn't stop seeing the colour in Mary's face become paler each time her body went into spasm and pushed out more blood. At one end the bright, lustrous complexion was fading to grey to white; at the other the old grey sheet she was lying on was becoming more and more scarlet, the colour coming alive in the dancing flames of the fire. The contrast was stark and it sickened Lora, yet she could not draw her eyes away from it.

'Get a swaddling cloth Lora, the babe will need to be wrapped,' said her aunt. Lora looked around, confused. 'Here Mistress Lora,' said Sally, passing her a blanket, 'this is what you need.' She took it wordlessly, watching horrified as the babe's head appeared between her sister's legs. Mary was lying back now, her expression glazed, unseeing. She didn't move as her body contracted again, spewing out the body of her baby.

Cecily clamped down the twisted blue lifeline that stretched between mother and child and rubbed her hand across the babe's face to clear it of the blood and mucus there.

'You have a son, Mary,' she said as a small mewling came from the child and then she handed him to Lora. Somehow, and Lora wasn't quite sure how as she refused to let her eyes stray for long from her sister's ashen face, the babe was wrapped in its swaddling blanket and Lora held him in her arms. He mewled again, softer, quieter. Lora wanted to look at him, she really did. She wanted to worry about Cecily being so close. She wanted to hold the baby, tell Cecily to leave and look after her sister herself. But fear crippled her as she watched the life slipping slowly away from Mary.

Fifty-One
2013

The winding fenland lanes blurred past the window as Regan tried to get through to Maeve. The call went straight to voicemail; she pressed the red button then dialled again. Once more she got the voicemail message. Regan spoke frantically into the phone, 'It's me, Maeve, where are you, what's happening? Is the ambulance there yet?' She hung up and redialled. Still no answer.

'We're nearly there,' said Sam quietly, 'try not to worry Regan, Maeve will be doing everything she can for Ashleigh.'

'I know. I shouldn't have left her, I shouldn't have said I'd work, I shou—'

'Ripping yourself apart now is not going to do any good. It's not going to help Ashleigh at all.' Regan nodded, acknowledging the sense in his words. Snow started falling again, heavier than it had earlier, and Sam slowed the car a little. The muddy by-ways were already a slippery, dangerous mess.

Regan turned her attention back to her phone and sent a text to Nate. She wanted him to know what was going on in case he needed her, but ringing him could put him in further danger.

She pressed send and immediately dialled Maeve again. 'Can't you speed up a little?' she snapped at Sam as he slowed for a sharp corner.

'Not if I want to get us there in one piece,' he said, his voice calm as he negotiated yet another bend. Regan sighed; every fibre of her being wanted to jump from the car and run to Maeve's house — at least she'd be doing something. Logically, though, she knew this would not help in the slightest. She pressed Maeve's number again and raised the phone to her ear, leaning her head against the cold glass of the window. The snow swirled around outside, dancing in the headlights and coating the trees and fields, turning the known into an alien landscape. Regan was blind to it all, images of Ashleigh unconscious and bleeding leaving no room for anything else.

'It's just down here,' said Sam, breaking into her thoughts. She peered into the darkness, searching for house lights, or better still red-flashing ambulance lights. She could see nothing; visibility was decreasing by the second. Then a dark shape loomed on the left, a house softened round the edges by snow.

'Here,' Sam said, turning into the drive of an old but large house. He stopped the car and before he had turned off the engine Regan had flung open her door and run up the path.

'Ashleigh,' she screamed. Her words echoed through the night, fading into the ether like snowflakes in the warmth. She rushed to the front door, banging loudly. No answer. Turning, she made her way round the back of the house, searching for another entrance. The snow was falling into her hair, into her face. She rubbed her hand across her eyes, probing for any sign of anything. Then she was at the back and the door was opening. A dim light spilled into the garden and Maeve was silhouetted at the door.

'Oh Maeve, thank God, where is Ashleigh, how is she, I need to see her Maeve.'

She felt, rather than heard, Sam come up behind her. She was aware of him speaking to Maeve but didn't listen to the words as she pushed her way into the house, seeking for any sign of her sister.

'Where is she, Maeve?' Her friend put an arm around her, 'I'll take you to her. Sam, you wait here.'

Regan let herself be guided through Maeve's kitchen and into the hallway. Maeve had already shut the door behind her when a recognisable stench assaulted Regan's nose. Confusion crowded her head — that smell. It shouldn't be *here*. She gagged as the odour grew stronger, tendrils of it reaching into her nose, pulling at her stomach. Wrapping her hand around her mouth and nose she realised the darkened hallway wasn't just dark, it swirled and fogged around her. Panicked, she turned to Maeve, opened her mouth to speak — then realised it wasn't her friend who stood there.

Oh, it looked like Maeve — the same hair, figure, clothes — but the smile on her face, the gleam in her eyes, the coldness that coated her, the evil that radiated from her ... that was not Maeve.

Bile rose, fear clenched, terror tore through her. 'You,' she whispered, 'no, it can't be you.'

'Oh but it can be, honey. You have made me laugh, you and Nate, searching, seeking and all the while I was right here, right beside you.'

'Where is Ashleigh,' Regan hissed, her hand seeking the knife she'd wedged in the back of her trousers, the knife she'd had no intention of using today.

'I'll take you to her, but before I do there are some rules you need to understand—'

'You can forget your rules, I'm taking my sister and I'm going. You'll be lucky if I leave you alive tonight!'

'Now Regan, talk like that is only going to ensure that Ashleigh does not make it through the night living. I suggest you leave that knife alone and listen to me good and proper. It is entirely in your hands whether your little sister makes it home to your mum or not. I can't promise that *you* will get out of here — in fact I can pretty much assure you, you won't. But Ashleigh — I don't need her anymore. *She* still has a chance.'

Regan's hand loosened on the knife's handle. Her head cleared; she had to get Ashleigh out. Nothing else mattered.

'I'm listening,' she said.

'Okay, honey. Firstly if you scream or warn Sam in any way then Ashleigh is ...' she drew her fingers across her throat. Regan got the message loud and clear. 'Secondly, in a moment I'm going to ask you to make a decision. It's not going to be an easy decision, I'll give you time, *but* you need to listen to the question when I ask it because whatever answer you give is the answer I will work with. You cannot change your mind.' Regan nodded.

'Good. Follow me then,' Maeve walked down the hallway to the door at the end and opened it. Regan followed, then took an involuntary step backwards.

Fog spilled out of the room, expanding and twisting, seeking space. The smell made her retch and acid burned at her throat. Tears stung her eyes and she made herself step forward into the room. Ashleigh's prone form was lying stretched out on a small sofa; Regan muffled a scream and ran to her. She scooped her sister into her arms, tears falling freely down her face.

'Ashleigh? Ashleigh, please wake up!' The younger girl lay still, her chest rising and falling as she breathed gently in and out.

'What have you done?' Regan asked, moving her eyes to Maeve's face. She recoiled at the predatory, feline smile there.

Maeve laughed, a sound that Regan had always found so appealing, so delicate; now it sounded cruel, as if it could shatter glass and cut you with the pieces.

'So naive. You know Regan, if I didn't need you so much I might even have actually tried liking you. Just for the novelty factor, you understand. Don't worry, she's just sleeping — for the moment.'

Beyond even trying to understand, all Regan's instincts told her to turn and start running.

'Oh Regan, I wouldn't do that if I were you.' The iciness in Maeve's tone pulled her up short. Fear thumped with every beat of her heart as she turned back. She watched, confused, as Maeve walked across the mist-filled space, pulled a key out of her pocket and unlocked the double doors at the other end of the room. Unable to move, she stood transfixed as they swung open. As her eyes adjusted to the darkness of the room fear clawed her throat and her heart sank. In the middle of one wall, arms tied and suspended from an iron bar, was Nate. His feet were shackled. He was blindfolded and gagged. His naked torso was criss-crossed with jagged, bloody lines. Regan's world collapsed.

Fifty-Two
1645

'I need towels, many,' said Cecily, the urgency in her voice unmistakable. Lora looked on, almost unaware of her nephew tiny and helpless in her arms. 'Here Mistress, let me take him,' said Sally, trying to take the bundle, but Lora just pulled him closer. She hadn't looked at the babe yet, she didn't want to see his tiny helpless eyes; she didn't want to see a miniature replica of Mary's face.

Over and over Lora kept up a silent monologue: *please Lord, keep Mary safe. Please Lord, keep Mary safe.* She could see Cecily taking the towels the servants brought and replacing the blood-soaked ones, she could see the servants taking the ruined ones away and bringing hot water. She could see the afterbirth being tugged out and disposed of, and Louisa holding Mary tight, talking to her, rubbing her to try and bring some life back to her. But all she could hear was her own internal voice, *please Lord keep Mary safe, please Lord keep Mary safe.* Lora stared and stared at Mary; if she took her eyes away it would be too late. She hugged the newborn closer, tighter. Cecily was trying to stem the bleeding; Louisa was trying to get Mary talking. Lora watched.

Suddenly the air around Lora went cold, so cold and she watched as her sister's skin turned to alabaster. She watched the life slip away from Mary, as clear to Lora as if she had seen Mary get up and walk out of the room. Still Louisa and Cecily worked, trying to save Mary's life. *She's gone,* Lora screamed, her voice so loud inside her head.

Only then, when she saw her sister had left, did Lora look down at the new life she was holding and bile welled up from her stomach as she realised that she wasn't holding life at all, only death.

Fifty-Three

Lora looked at her nephew, blue and unmoving in her arms. Then she looked at Mary, waxen in her scarlet bed. Then her nephew, then her sister. Blue, white, red. Lifeless, waxen, still. She tossed and pulled at her sheet, kicking it off, half-awake but not quite. The same mid-sleep state she had occupied in the weeks since the deaths. Time had passed in a blur, a muddle of days and nights. Her father had been summoned back from Cromwell's army, the funerals had taken place. Friends and neighbours had offered their grief-stricken prayers. Their well-meaning platitudes. Words from the Good Book — some a comfort, some not.

'Lora,' her name was softly spoken and at first Lora thought it was in her dreams. Then it came again and a gentle hand pushed her. 'Mistress Smith, please, do not be scared.'

She started, recognising Rafe's voice, and sat up in her bed. 'Rafe! What are you doing here?' she said, her voice lowered, terrified her mother or father would hear.

'I learnt of your sister's death, and that of the baby. I had not seen you; I needed to tell you how sorry I was for your loss. I —' he hesitated, then strode across the room to her bedside, 'I needed to see how you were. If there is any help I can give you —'

'There is nothing you can do, sir,' said Lora dully. 'Unless you are able to bring Mary back to me.' She hated the bitterness she heard in her voice.

'I did nothing, Rafe. I stood there and did nothing. *Cecily*,' she said, the name leaving a bitter taste in her mouth, 'Cecily did more than I could. I couldn't even keep the baby alive.' Rafe clasped her hand. 'It was not your fault that this happened, that Mary and her son died. Women die in childbirth every day — it is not our place to question why God calls them home.'

'It is my fault, though, that God reclaimed Mary. I promised him any sacrifice if he kept Cecily from killing my family the night she came to dine. *Any sacrifice*. And he took his payment!'

'God does not make deals, Lora. It is the devil that does that. It was simply her time passed.' A small flame of hope flickered in her chest. 'Do you really believe so, Rafe? Do you truly believe that the blame isn't mine?'

'I know the blame isn't yours.' He stopped abruptly and bit his lip. Lora frowned, 'What is it, Rafe?' she said, knowing him well enough to understand there was something he was withholding.

'Cecily,' he said, 'what was she doing there?'

'She came with my aunt. It was not her fault, she did everything she could, she was much more use than I,' she paused, trying to think of what to say. 'Maybe we had it wrong, Rafe. Maybe she is not the witch at all. She tried so hard to save Mary — I watched her, she kept trying and trying …'

'Maybe,' he said, but Lora could tell he was unconvinced. She wanted to explain further but exhaustion suddenly washed over her. Sleepless nights and wake-less days were taking their toll and she felt her eyelids grow heavy, forcing themselves shut.

'I will go now, Lora,' Rafe said, 'Take good care of yourself. I promise you that I will find the witch, whoever she is. I will not rest until I have done so. But you are not to fight with me until your grief has dimmed and you are well enough.' He placed a soft kiss on her forehead and a feeling of warmth flooded her as she drifted back to sleep.

Fifty-Four
2013

'Nate ...' the word tumbled from her mouth; she felt unable to function, unable to move. She hugged Ashleigh closer; the dead weight pulled at her arms, but she refused to put her down. She raised her eyes, not wanting to look at Nate yet unable to turn away.

'Maeve, what have you done?' she whispered as he suddenly started struggling against his bonds. His arms, stretched above his head, were drained of blood but he still fought. Each jerk of his biceps pulled the ropes tighter. Terror clawed at her insides and she knew she had to do something, anything, to save him. She moved towards him, wanting to reassure him; if she could just untie him then they would stand a chance.

'Stay there,' Maeve snapped, 'if you move one foot forward, I'll damage him some more.' Horrified, Regan watched as Maeve picked up Nate's own hunting knife and moved closer to him. Slowly, deliberately, she ran the blade down his torso. The pin-sharp tip slit the finest of scratches from his throat to his groin and a line of fresh red blood oozed to the surface and trickled downwards.

A tear ran down Regan's face as she watched Nate tense against the knife.

'Oh, Nate. Now that Regan's arrived you don't seem to be enjoying it so much,' Maeve murmured. 'I thought having two beautiful girls here would add to your fun ...'

'Maeve, I don't understand,' Regan said, trying to distract her from Nate. 'What do you want? Let him go and I'll do anything.'

Again Maeve laughed, the sound — so beautiful — rendered vulgar by the look of pure evil in her brilliant green eyes. 'Oh Regan, dear, you need to be careful what you say. I told you that you were going to have to make a choice. Well this is it. This here,' she indicated the lacerations across Nate, 'this is just a bit of fun for me, a mere amusement, shall we say?'

Not daring to move as Maeve again teased the knife against Nate, Regan stood rooted to the spot, desperately trying to understand the situation. All the training she'd done with Nate. The fight against the creatures, the familiars. She thought she was ready; she knew that either of them could get hurt — that death was a possibility — so why was this so hard to make sense of?

'Shall I help you out, honey?' Maeve asked, circling Nate. The knife never left his skin, its razor-sharp blade carelessly catching and cutting as she moved. 'You've got a decision to make. I'll let you have one of them. One of those most precious to you gets to walk away from here — no, don't speak,' she spat as Regan started to interrupt, 'if you don't listen carefully you'll make the wrong choice and that will be something you regret for the rest of your life.' She laughed, a dry, mirthless sound. 'Of course the rest of your life isn't going to be very long, but still. Best not to have regrets, hey?'

Regan nodded numbly, her arms straining under the pull of Ashleigh's weight. 'Put your sister down, honey, I promise not to hurt her. Unless of course she is your choice.' Regan shook her head, holding Ashleigh in her aching arms as tightly to her as possible. Never, never would she let anything happen to her sister. She concentrated on not thinking what that would mean.

'Okay Regan, in a minute I want you to give me a name. I want the name of the person you want me to kill. *Not* the person you want to save, so you be careful what you say. The name you give me is the person who will die.' The world spun and Regan collapsed onto the chair behind her, her sister dropping into her lap.

She chose Ashleigh to save, it would always be Ashleigh, she was innocent, young, her sister. But she didn't choose Nate to die. Nate was her heart. She couldn't say his name, couldn't tell Maeve to kill him.

'You have me Maeve, you can let them both go. I'm who you want, what you need.' Maeve smiled and pressed the blade into Nate again. Her eyes lit up in delight as Regan gasped. Blood spurted from under Nate's ribs and he moaned — a low, pain-filled sound, barely muffled by his gag.

Maeve finally moved away from Nate, her blade leaving one last deep cut on his stomach trailing down to his groin; Regan turned away, unable to look at the pain his tensed muscles proclaimed.

'Put Ashleigh down. Come and sit next to me,' Maeve said in a tone Regan didn't dare disobey. She placed her sister on the seat, let Maeve take her by the hand and lead her to a matching stylish leather couch.

She patted Regan's hand. 'Don't worry honey, you can save one of them, I promise,' she smiled conspiringly. Nate started thrashing, making as much noise as his gag would allow.

'I need you to make the decision, Regan. I need to hear who you choose to die.'

'I can't choose who will die, Maeve,' she whispered, 'I just can't. Let them both live. You have me.'

Another muffled sound came from Nate and she turned to him, watching as he thrashed against his bonds. The temperature in the room was dropping and Nate was less visible than before as swirling grey obscured him. The underlying rotting smell became more pungent as a familiar came into view. Her heart pounded; the creature looked so out of place in this room. Its long, disfigured limbs moved clumsily about, the vapour trailing from it searching out every gap, every space. She followed it as it came further into the room, her eyes straining as if trying to see through dry ice. It moved towards Ashleigh and she stood up. 'No,' she cried running to her sister, pulling her knife out.

Maeve cocked her head to one side, paying no attention to her *pet*.

'Stop,' she said, and her creature stopped. Regan moved towards it, trembling, her knife hand shaking. 'Oh, I wouldn't do that, honey, if I were you. It would make me mad and there are two people you love at risk from me. Well, it's your choice I guess,' she shrugged her shoulders as if she didn't care.

'Now, time is ticking on. Sam won't wait forever, you know, and I don't want to have to kill another of your friends. I need you to choose, honey. It should be easy. I want to kill Nate anyway; he and his kind have been hunting my creatures and me for years. But,' again that catlike smile played softly across Maeve's lips, 'but I have Nate to thank for you, for your sweet, pure, innocent blood. If he'd given in to your advances, well we wouldn't be here now, would we? And for that I might let him live, but only if you give me Ashleigh. It's your choice.'

Fifty-Five
1645

A sharp knock sounded at her front door. A spasm of dread ran down Lora's spine, though she could not say why. Maybe it was the look that passed between her mother and father, maybe it was the irregularity of visitors calling at this time of day. Or maybe it was just a heightening of the emptiness that had settled within her since the death of her sister and nephew.

Once more the knock came and Lora's father left the hall to answer it. Did his normal loping stride seem more stilted — slower — or was it just her imagination? Muffled voices could be heard, then footsteps coming back to the hall. An unfamiliar man stood there, an arrogant look on his ugly face. Beside him, another smaller man and two women, their looks of disdain betraying their superior attitude.

'I am Matthew Hopkins. I have come with permission to take you, Mistress Lora Smith, for interrogation.' The arrogant man spoke in a haughty voice, 'I lay before you the charge that you are a witch, that your conspiracy with the devil did cause the loss of two of God's children, three weeks past, your sister Mary and her newborn babe.' Lora's throat constricted and her hands started to shake. 'You were given a babe, witnessed to be alive by many, yet he was dead when you handed him back. You have been seen unaccompanied in the presence of a man on more than one occasion. With this as evidence I am to seek further proof that you are a witch, or indeed to prove your innocence.'

Befuddled, tired from Rafe's night-time visit and her grief-ridden sleep, Lora glanced at her father, waiting for him to interject. Her protector, though, just stood to the side, a look of hate in his eyes that chilled Lora to the bone. Her throat tightened further as she slid her eyes sideways to her mother, waiting for her to contradict the man — to tell him how ridiculous he was being, to demand an answer to such nonsense. Tears ran down her mother's face, but her eyes were fixed firmly on the ground.

Sweat beaded on Lora's shaking hands and she wiped them on her dress. Her stomach clenched and her mind raced. The numbness that had been with her the past three weeks, which had been vital in deadening her grief, left her. She remembered the whispered conversation last night and clarity returned. *Cecily.* It could only be Cecily.

Terrified, Lora turned to her parents, 'Mother … Father … please! I promise you, I am not guilty of witchcraft.' Neither of them would look at her. Tears leaked from her eyes but she rubbed them away. 'I miss Mary so much it as if my soul is torn in two, I would never have harmed her. Mother …' But though big, salty tears dripped down her mother's face, she refused to look at Lora.

Her father regarded her with the chilling detachment of a stranger. 'You could have helped to save Mary's life; instead you left it to an outsider to try. The babe was handed to you alive but less than an hour later he, too, was dead. I have no daughters now.'

The man looked to his companions, 'Seize her,' he said.

Lora forced herself to step forward, 'That is not necessary. I will come with you.' Refusing to let the seed of fear in her stomach bloom, she stood still while the two sneering men held her arms and led her out of the house. Lora's neighbours stood outside their homes, all eagerly watching the drama unfold. Old Bess from next door spat as Lora was pushed past and others followed her example; Lora kept her gaze fixed forward, every part of her being concentrating on keeping the maelstrom of fear and shame that threatened locked inside of her. She understood they were afraid. They might be friends and neighbours, yesterday they might have passed the time of day happily with Lora, but to acknowledge Lora now was to potentially be the witchfinders' next victim.

Rain soaked through her woollen dress as she was paraded through the streets and it rubbed at her skin. Her thin, indoor slippers were soon caked in the mud that splattered up her legs as she walked. The small group moved through the streets, not in a rush but at a slow, steady pace. The gossips of town had been hard at work; aware that Matthew Hopkins was soon to make an arrest, they had whispered a word here and dropped a hint there. Men sipping ale in The Hunter's Rest jeered as she walked past. Women stood in their doorways, their silent recrimination harder to bear than the bawdy cheers. Humiliation seeped from every one of Lora's pores though she kept her head held high, her stubborn pride refusing to let her be cowed.

In the middle of town they came to a simple stone shed that the witchfinder had been given use of. As a strong hand pushed her in, Lora barely had time to take in the bars on the windows, the uneven stone floor and the heavy oak door before it slammed shut behind her. Matthew Hopkins himself slid the bolts shut, locking Lora and her captors in the room, and as he turned to face her Lora felt the fear she had been hiding start to leach through her body.

'Please sir. I haven't done any witchcraft,' she said. Would naming Cecily make her seem guiltier or prove her innocence?

'I have heard many accounts to the contrary,' the witchfinder's mouth twisted up, 'or do you deny your presence at your sister's death?'

'I was there,' said Lora, 'but so were many other people.' Trying to think of her best defence caused her stomach to clench and she swallowed back the bile that had risen in her throat. She could see no way to prove her innocence; every warning Rafe had given her echoed around her head. 'I am not a witch, but I know who is. Her name is Cecily Kashshaptu,' she said again in a voice so soft that she wasn't sure if she was telling the witchfinders or herself. The name had no effect; it was as if they hadn't heard her. 'Cecily Kashshaptu,' she said again, louder. Still they didn't react. The certainty that it was Cecily who had put her there filled Lora like milk filling a jug. Against every instinct in her, she clenched her teeth and lowered her gaze to the floor; it was too late for Mary, but the rest of her family were still alive.

'You know what to do,' Matthew Hopkins said and without hesitation the two women in his group of followers descended on Lora. They twisted her arms back and forth, up and down, tearing off her layers of clothing one at a time. Soon she stood there naked, her pride the only thing that kept her from screaming. As soon as they let go of her arms she moved them in front of her, trying to cover her small breasts. Her hands lowered to hide her more intimate areas.

Staring straight ahead and looking at no one, she shivered at the chill that caressed her body. Fear was a feeling with which she was familiar; it wasn't pleasant but since that long-ago day and her encounter in the fens she had learnt to deal with it. It was an enemy she knew. But now, exposed and vulnerable, she felt ashamed; this was a new foe, and it was one she had no idea how to conquer.

The humiliation of nakedness, though, was nothing compared to the fingers that started to probe her. She could take it no longer. With great care she folded herself away, shutting herself up and locking her soul into the deepest recess her mind offered. Deeper and deeper she locked herself away until only the body of Lora stood in the room; the essence of Lora was following Rafe through the paths of the fens, following the trails of evil that lurked there. The strangers prodded and pinched, feeling, stroking and searching her naked skin, leaving not even the most secret parts of her alone, but Lora followed Rafe. It was the time she was happiest.

Fifty-Six

'The mark is well disguised, sir,' one of the women muttered to the witchfinder.

'Then I will have the men bring the razors; you know what you must do. All her body hair must be removed and you will search some more. And use your pins to look for invisible marks.'

Lora didn't cry, she didn't think, she just let emptiness fill her head and stubborn pride fill her soul. Her eyes stared blankly forward as the women pricked at her body with knives and pins. No part of her was sacred. Somewhere, deep inside, she was aware of the scratching at her skin, on some level, well hidden within, the pain of each tiny incision registered. The women worked hard, searching meticulously for a part of her that would not bleed when it was pricked.

Still Lora stood strong.

'You can confess any time, witch,' sneered Matthew Hopkins, his voice penetrating the busy silence of the women. 'I will prove you are in league with the devil. You have been seen by many liaising with men alone at night.'

An echo of his words quietly wormed its way into her mind and a picture of Rafe briefly entered her head; she hoped he could keep her family safe. She hoped he could keep himself safe. She hoped he would kill Cecily.

At last the women stopped their pricking; not an inch was left on Lora's body that wasn't covered in blood and painful nicks and scratches. Yet not one single tear had fallen from her eyes. As if waking from a long sleep Lora found herself aware of what was happening again and as the women moved a step back, she dared let a little relief creep into her stomach. Despite the sharp stinging pain that covered her body, despite her shame, she let herself hope. They had found nothing. Surely they must let her go soon. No proof she was a witch; hope bloomed. But hope, Lora discovered, was often the cruellest of mistresses.

'Nothing?' said Mathew Hopkins, an undisguised look of joy fleeting across his features. He nodded to his group of helpers before adding with a smile, 'Then we will walk a confession from you.' Lora flinched, his words hurting more than the needles and knives. Heedless of the pain of the cuts they had already inflicted, the witchfinder's crones grabbed her arms and forced her to walk, still naked, around the room.

The cold November air whirled around her body; soon she was covered in goose bumps and shivering uncontrollably. She tried to retreat back into her unthinking haven but wasn't able, no matter how hard she tried to shut down. Each step was agony as her feet, bruised and cut, were forced up and down the uneven flagstones, backwards and forwards, tripping and stumbling. By some small mercy the frigid flagstones soon numbed the pain to her ankles.

Lora had no idea how long she was forced to walk around the room. After a time the women who dragged her 'round changed and fresh legs dragged her, for a start with renewed vigour. Every now and then the silence was punctuated by insistence of a confession.

Darkness fell outside and oil lamps were lit but Lora was still dragged back and forth. Tiredness seeped slowly through her body; her legs refused to walk but she was pulled up time after time. Her eyes tried to shut, tried to seek a little sleep, but she was forced to keep awake. To keep walking. The same demand repeated constantly: *you can confess anytime, witch.*

Still she refused to speak.

Still she refused to shed a tear. Eventually, exhaustion ensured that Lora returned to the hiding place deep in her head and she no longer heard the demands.

Hours passed and the soles of her feet were worn raw from parading across the hard, unforgiving floor. Her body was covered in dried blood and scratches. She was exhausted and death was a welcome thought to her. But she would not confess to something she was not. She would not cry; this was a high price but she needed to protect her family. She needed to protect Rafe.

'We will duck her tomorrow,' was the eventual command. 'I have no doubt that she will float.' As she sank to the stony, icy cold floor, she drifted in and out of sleep. Too exhausted to stay awake, she was too cold and in too much pain to ease into the deep sleep her body craved.

Fifty-Seven

As soon as the first weak light of dawn filtered through the barred windows, Lora's cell was once more filled with people. 'Wake up *witch,*' said one of the women from yesterday, her shoed foot kicking Lora's exposed back. Lora opened her eyes and tried to roll over, the stone floor bitter and hard under her bruised body. A dress was flung at her and she pulled it on, welcoming even the meagre warmth it offered her frozen self.

'Are you ready to confess yet?' said the woman. 'It will be all the easier for you if you do.' Lora shook her head, unable or unwilling to speak she was not sure. *Would it matter if I did speak? Rafe had the right of it, I did not know how cruel torture could be.* The night had been long and cold. In moments of lucidity between bouts of sleep she had felt almost ready to confess. Her hips, young as they were, ached upon the floor, constant pain caused by the icy flagstones that refused to warm up beneath her body. She had rolled this way and that to try to get away from the chill. Too exhausted to sit and, with feet torn and crusted in half-dried scabs of blood that were too painful to stand on, she could find no relief from the hurting that surrounded her.

The witchfinder entered the room and the woman shook her head to an unasked question. 'Then we take her to be ducked,' he said, a smile almost visible on his face. Once again she was paraded down the street, an army of people following, all chanting and calling her wicked names, accusing her of any bad luck that had happened upon them in the recent months.

The compacted mud road ripped the scabs from her feet and the soft grass near the pond was almost a relief. Until she fully comprehended what was about to happen. *No,* she screamed inside her head, panic stealing her voice as she was strapped up by Matthew Hopkins himself. All the while he was tying her, he asked for her confession. *Confess witch, confess, witch, confess …*

Lora tried to retreat back into herself but the taunts from the crowd made it impossible. *Child murderer, sister-killer, harlot, whore.* The words echoed round her head as tears choked in her throat and stung at her eyes. 'Do you perform witchcraft?' Matthew Hopkins asked one final time. Biting her tongue, she refused to answer. She pushed the panic away; she refused to cry. Her right thumb was bound so tightly to her left big toe that blood seeped from the wound. It was the indignity of it that nearly broke Lora, though. The indignity and the humiliation. She felt vulnerable and threatened by voices in the crowd that she recognised — neighbours, friends. Though, she thanked God, not family. Tears burned painfully behind her eyelids but she refused to let them fall. Stubborn pride was the one thing that was hers to hold on to, and she was determined not to relinquish it.

As soon as she was bound she was thrown in the pond, the frigid water robbing her of any feeling. Murky pond water blanketed her, weed, insects and mud wrapping themselves around her, filling her nose, her eyes, her ears. She held her breath — drowning was not how she wanted to die. Then she realised that if she just breathed in under water her lungs would fill, her inevitable death would come quickly and she would be pardoned; they would know she wasn't a witch. Her family would not have to bear the humiliation of her accusations. They could all lead the lives they were destined to.

She opened her mouth, ready to draw in breath, and was yanked from the water. Coughing, she choked out the water that had filled her mouth, her nose ran with snot and her eyes smarted from the filthy muck.

'This wanton witch floated, she repelled the water of the holy spirit, given to her during baptism. I have given you the proof you require, and the date for her execution should be set.' Matthew Hopkins spoke to the crowd, but Lora wasn't listening. She stood as tall as she could, aware the crowd was taking in the witchfinder's words and her bedraggled appearance. Her soaking dress clung to her body, water dripped from her shaven head. She fixed her gaze into the distance, her chin held high.

Then her heart stopped, for on the other side of the pond stood Rafe, a look of vulnerability on his face that tore her apart. The tears she had held back for so long started to flow. Lora longed to shout his name, longed for him to come to her, to rescue her. But she knew it was impossible. As the tears streamed the mob cheered — another witch was soon to be struck from their masses. She blinked the tears away, yanked an arm from Hopkins' iron grip, wiped at her eyes and looked back over at him, but he had gone. With that, Lora's hopes died.

Fifty-Eight
2013

Regan looked at her sister asleep on the couch, her face serene. Pure and innocent.

She looked at Nate struggling against his bonds, ripped, bloodied and broken. Two parts of her heart. She felt warm tears leave tracks down her face as the ache in her chest grew. It grew and spread and twisted and finally split her apart as she whispered, 'Nate. I choose Nate.' She choked out a sob, wanting to take the words back. Wanting to not have to choose. Wanting to be anywhere but here.

'Good choice,' said Maeve, 'now let's get Ashleigh out of here. I'm going to tell Sam to take her, I'm going to tell him to look after her tonight and tomorrow to tell everyone he found her wandering around. You'd left her alone while you went to work and now you've disappeared.'

'Sam will never say that — even if he did lie he'd buckle under the pressure eventually,' Regan said, her voice thick with tears as she picked Ashleigh up again.

'Oh don't you worry about that honey, Sam and Ashleigh will remember exactly what I want them to remember. After all I *am* a witch, aren't I? Now don't try anything or you'll all die tonight. As it is, half of you are going free. I think I'm being very generous.'

Regan nodded; her vision blurred from her falling tears. She hugged her sister to her as she made her way to the kitchen.

Sam rushed forward, 'Are you alright Regan, is Ashleigh okay?' he asked, concern lacing his voice.

'They're both fine, Sam,' Maeve moved towards him and put her arms around him. 'Sam, I need you to do something for me. Look at me, listen, you're going to take Ashleigh home, you are going to …' Regan zoned out Maeve's voice as she watched her sister sleeping in her arms. Salty tears dripped down onto Ashleigh's peaceful face.

'I love you Ashleigh, I love you and Mum. I'm so sorry. Please forgive me,' she murmured softly, wanting her goodbye to be between her and her sister and no one else. 'Please forgive me,' she repeated as Sam took the girl from her arms, gave a cheerful 'See you later,' and walked out into the snow. She stood, desperate to scream and run, desperate to fight and kill. But Maeve still had Nate, and if Regan could save him, she would.

'So it's just the three of us then, honey,' said Maeve. Regan could feel her watching but she kept her head lowered and let the tears continue falling. Her brain raced and she waited.

She heard Maeve sigh, she felt a coolness enter the room, tendrils of it reaching her legs and winding round her; she smelt the fetid smell of the creatures and still she stood with her head dropped. As soon as she heard the engine start and the car pull away, she moved. Her hand reached back for her knife as she swung a kick up to the first, nearest creature. As her fingers closed around the hilt, she felt her boot reach the creature's centre, heard the howl of it. She brought her hand and weapon round and stabbed up and hard then smacked her head forward in a Glasgow kiss.

Claws raked across her back and she yelled in pain but didn't stop. The oily substance at the core of the creature exploded into the kitchen; instantly she swung her freed weapon behind her, aiming for the other one. She caught its hide and it wailed, she aimed a kick at Maeve as she swirled back to finish the familiar off.

'STOP!' Maeve commanded and before she could blink she found herself pinned to the wall, Maeve's hand around her throat.

'Go,' the witch said, speaking to the long-limbed creature behind her whose claws were poised to rake at Regan's skin. It moved an infinitesimal amount as Regan tried to draw breath. The hand at her throat was strong. Stronger than Sam, stronger than Nate and most certainly stronger than Regan. She scrabbled at it, trying to pull it away so she could breathe. She needed air. Black spots swam in front of her eyes, the room crowded in, blood swirled in her ears. Her throat ached; her lungs burned. Darkness came, it enclosed her slowly, so slowly. She longed for it, begged for it. It covered her like a blanket; she stopped trying to breathe, stopped needing air.

Then she was dropped and cold air found its way in. Now she needed it again. She needed more and more. She pulled in great, gasping breaths; cold and fetid though they were, they were the sweetest she had ever drawn.

'Finished?' asked Maeve, any drop of warmth gone from her voice. 'We can do this the easy way or the hard way, Regan. I suggest easier would be better all round. Now get up and follow me. If you disobey, I'll make the end as painful for you as possible.' The creature crowded behind Regan and she felt compelled to follow Maeve. As soon as they were back in the sitting room Regan spat at her former friend.

'Do what you want to me Maeve, I don't care. I'm not going to sit cowed and just surrender to you, I'm going to die anyway and I will fight you. I promise you, this is not going to be easy.' She struck her fist back at the familiar behind her and turned, other fist clenched, when a muffled but agonised scream tore through the room.

She stopped and turned. Maeve was standing beside Nate, a fresh line of ruby red glistening from his torso. It was deeper, Regan could see that even from where she stood across the gloom-filled room. Pain was etched across his hollow, pallid face.

'Now I have your attention.' Maeve held the knife gently at Nate's stomach. 'If you don't care about yourself, I know you care about Nate. I guess this will prove how much. I was going to kill him first, make you watch, but I've changed my mind. I need him as a guarantee that you're going to behave. If you do then I promise once I've killed you his death will be quick and painless. If, however, you cause me any further *problems*, then I promise you I will make sure his end is not fast and most definitely not pain free. In fact, I promise you it will be the slowest, most painful death ever. Do you understand?' Regan nodded numbly. She could handle whatever Maeve had planned for her, but she couldn't bear to see Nate in any more pain.

'I knew you'd see it my way,' said Maeve, clapping her hands together as if Regan had agreed to go to a party with her.

Maeve gave an order and a familiar took up position beside Nate. Tendrils of vapour emanated from its body and coiled around his suspended form. Its stoat-like head was barely visible through the mist that cloaked it, but its long limbs and extended talons were clear to see. Regan knew the pain they could cause and Nate's body was already so broken and lacerated.

She recoiled as Maeve linked their arms together; suddenly, breathing was hard. She wanted to retract her arm, move as far away from Maeve as possible, but she wasn't able to. The creature that lurked next to Nate, with its claws extended, would do anything its mistress commanded and Regan couldn't, wouldn't, be the cause of that.

Tears blurred her vision as she was led into the room. She wanted to stop, pull back, run, scream — but Nate hanging helpless prevented her. They were a team, hunter and companion, and she wasn't going to leave him. She couldn't leave him, she loved him. She held on to the belief that they could still get out of this; that *he* would still get out of this. It was only her that Maeve needed, after all.

'It's a beautiful room,' she said, sniffing back the tears, trying her best to gain some time.

'Thank you,' said Maeve, looking genuinely pleased at the compliment. 'It's really the only room I have that reflects me.'

Regan looked at the dark crimson walls and deep mahogany furniture. A large table dominated the space but it was a cupboard full of herbs, its top covered with bowls and surgical instruments, which caught her eye. Hope started to stir.

'This is a really unusual picture,' she said, walking to the other side of the room from Nate, where an enormous oil painting hung on the wall. A scene from hell — naked bodies writhed in orange flames while Satan lounged on a throne of red and gold, watching. Minions, other-worldly creatures, also watched, delight gleaming in their eyes. Torn, broken bodies lay strewn around in blood and guts and gore.

'Isn't it just,' said Maeve. Regan looked at it without seeing, her brain whirling nineteen to the dozen trying to figure a way out of this.

'So, honey, if you could get on the table, I'll just change into my robes and we can get started.'

'Sure,' said Regan and turned towards the table as if climbing on it was her intention. Her brain raced; the cabinet caught her eye — she paused. 'So, er, Maeve, what exactly is going to happen? I mean, I know you need a sacrifice who is … er … well, like me …'

'Pure. Yes Regan, you really are like a gift from God. You are a gift, from my Master. I have hunted your family down through the centuries. I've got you all. Lora, she started it,' Maeve's eyes gleamed as she remembered. 'Oh honey, it was so much fun watching her trying to figure it all out. She thought she was so clever, she thought she could outwit me. I showed that bitch. But then her niece grew up and started fighting my creatures and once I killed her, her daughter started and … well, you get the idea. So all the hunters had their companions. They all thought they could defeat me, but they couldn't. I showed every single one of them exactly how good they were. And now there is you, my perfect sacrifice.'

Regan bit her tongue to stop from yelling and nodded as though interested. She moved towards the cabinet of herbs and said, 'Well, I know you need a sacrifice, but the diaries weren't really specific about the details. I mean, do you need these?' She spread her arms towards the plants in the cupboard. Maeve twisted from where she was donning a dark purple velvet cloak, then shook her head, 'No, not for tonight.'

'So, what do you need?' Regan asked, moving nearer the bowl of scalpels and knives. 'Do you need these?' she asked, picking up the bowl and facing Maeve.

'PUT THEM DOWN,' Maeve roared and the air in the room became frigid as the creatures that were guarding Nate sprung to life. Fog extended from them like a sixth sense, trying to feel its way to Regan.

'Sorry, sorry …' Regan turned to put them down and, praying her fingers were quick enough, that she wouldn't fumble, used her turned back and the fog to slip a scalpel up her sleeve.

'I'm sorry, Maeve,' she said, raising her hands to show they were empty. She felt the icy metal of the instrument slide up her arm and bent her elbow to halt its progress. A sharp nip told her the blade had found her skin and she winced. 'I'm just curious, I guess. I mean, it is me you're doing it to — am I to be burnt … what?' She took a deep breath, swallowing back the vitriol that rose — it was only hiding terror anyway — and didn't let herself think about what she'd just asked.

'I need to cut your heart from your chest before midnight,' said Maeve in the same voice she used to describe her favourite nail colour. 'And time is getting on. Come on Regan, onto the table. I need to bind you to it.'

Regan couldn't stop the tear that rolled down her face then, couldn't stop the fear that felt all-consuming. 'Can I at least say goodbye to Nate? Please Maeve, I'm doing this for you. Please let me have that one thing'.

Maeve looked at her, the deep purple robes fastened at her neck, her long dark hair flowing over the collar.

'Please Maeve, with you and your … creatures … here I'm not going to be able to do anything. I just want to say goodbye.' A smile crept onto Maeve's face.

'Oh honey, of course you can say goodbye. It's so romantic, really. Kind of like Romeo and Juliet.' Regan couldn't see the connection.

'Thank you,' she said. *Think Regan, think,* she thought as she moved across the room towards him.

The familiars moved closer; Regan shivered at the chill.

'Maeve, please,' she said, looking imploringly at her ex-friend. Maeve observed her with cool green eyes, not saying anything, assessing. Regan held her gaze and prayed that she wouldn't give anything away. 'Alright,' said Maeve, 'they will move away, but if you try anything I fucking promise you'll be begging me to kill you both.' Regan nodded and moved closer to Nate.

She stood on tiptoe and looked at him, 'Can I move his blindfold?' she asked. 'Just for a minute.'

'Oh honey, take it off. I think I'd quite like him to watch this anyway; he deserves to see that I am so much stronger than he is. Stronger than you both.'

'Thank you,' Regan choked out as she reached up with one arm to pull off his blindfold. His eyes were filled with pain, just echoes of their former watchfulness remained. The ache in her chest grew. She realised there was no way she could slip him the scalpel, his hands were suspended from an iron bar that stuck out of the wall and curled back on itself; if she reached up, Maeve would see instantly what she was doing. Yet she couldn't risk holding onto it. She could see how Maeve had planned on tying her; if it was found, it would all be over. Instead, she hugged Nate, aware that her touch would be agony on his injuries and dropped the instrument onto the floor behind him. It fell silently into the thick, blood-stained carpet.

Then she reached both hands up to his face, 'I'm so sorry,' she said, 'I love you, this is all my fault, if you'd never met me, if I'd let you carry on hunting alone, none of this would be happening.' She talked and talked, her words just as much for Maeve as Nate. She hoped and prayed that her words would be enough distraction from the fact that her feet were unhooking Nate's from the bar to which they were attached. Her boots were clunky and she wished her feet were bare, easier to feel what she was doing. Hell, if she was wishing, she wished they weren't there and she had never met Maeve. She kept up the chatter and eventually felt the binding attaching Nate's feet to the iron bar moving forward. She flexed the muscles in her calf and eased his feet slowly towards her. It wasn't easy, but as she couldn't undo the bindings it was the best she could come up with.

As she fought with her foot, she kissed his chest until finally she felt his feet slide free, 'I love you,' she repeated and looked into his eyes. They sparked alive and he nodded at her, like he was saying *I know,* but Regan knew it meant he understood. Suddenly, she had hope again. Tears started to fall as she kissed him one last time and moved across to Maeve. There wasn't much hope, but at least there was some.

Fifty-Nine
1645

The rope was rough and uncomfortable around her neck and Lora wished she could loosen it a little, but her bound hands made it impossible. She wanted to close her eyes, to shut out the crowd, but she needed to see if he was there. Seeking his face was the only small comfort she had. Then she saw him, her Rafe. Unblinking, his gaze held hers. The look on his face was like nothing she had seen before. It gave her the strength not to scream or cry.

The man beside her was speaking but the crowd in front of her was so noisy even she could not hear the words he spoke.

The words of the hangman.

Then silence fell and an insane calmness stole through her as the stool beneath her feet gave way to air.

As the life choked out of her she saw the fens, saw Cecily smiling sensuously, Mary, the baby, blood, too much blood, her mother, father, Eve.

She saw Rafe; fierce, vengeful, silent.

Then she saw no more.

Sixty
2013

Regan moved to the table where Maeve was waiting. This was it; she'd done all she could think of. She could try and fight Maeve but she knew the witch was so much stronger; even if she got out, she would have to leave Nate and that was something she couldn't live with. The table was smooth under her as she slid back on it. Nate moaned and even through the gag Regan could hear the pain in it. She couldn't stop the tears falling from her face to the sheer surface.

'I'm doing it,' she muttered to Maeve, 'leave him alone.'

'Oh honey, we're not touching him,' Maeve said. As soon as Regan had laid down, Maeve grabbed her hands and then her feet, tying them to the strips of cloth at the corners. Soon Regan lay spread-eagled across the table, unable to move.

'I don't need you now,' Maeve dismissed her creatures, 'go out, make the fog, take as many as you like. But don't let anyone near the house — when I am done you can have their remains. Don't worry, Regan. Nate will have gone before they come back for your bodies.' It was a cold comfort.

As the icy fog drained out of the room Regan took one look at Maeve. Her beautiful, evil face held a look of pure joy. She let herself think of Nate — for a second, she allowed herself to think of how much she loved him, how she longed for every arrogant piece of him. She heard Maeve moving about, the clanging of the surgical instruments. She was so afraid, her heart raced; her hands sweated and she wanted to scream. Instead, she closed her eyes and continued to think of Nate. When she was with him, she was happy.

She was in the pub serving him a Coke; being ignored by him. The way it felt on the back of his bike. She thought of how it felt to wrap her arms around him, to feel his strong body as they twisted and turned with the machine. She thought about his deep dark eyes, usually so serious but how, when he smiled, they changed completely — how they crinkled at the edges and were warm and carefree. She remembered mirroring his moves in the rundown buildings outside his place, how in sync they were; she hoped this was still true. It was all she had left. She thought of *that* night and how his lips felt on hers, his stubble, his scent, the taste of Coke and Nate. She reme—

'Aargh …' a burning sensation on her chest forced her eyes open. Maeve loomed over her, chanting words she didn't understand. Her eyes were drawn to a flickering light and she bit back another scream as hot wax dripped from the candle Maeve was holding onto her chest. She squirmed, trying to move out of the way as burning pain seared through her.

She widened her eyes as she realised her top had been slit open and her chest was exposed. More wax, more burning. Maeve's strange words. Then it stopped and Maeve moved away. Regan wanted to turn, to look for Nate, but she forced herself not to —

she didn't want to draw attention to him. Instead, she closed her eyes and tried to escape back to her memories. The room she was bound in was red and dark; her memories of Nate were bright, light and happy. Strange really, since half the time they'd been together it had been night-time and fighting devil-like creatures.

Then all the air went out of the room. Regan bit down on her lip, a sharp pain and then the metallic taste of blood in her mouth. She focussed on that. She screwed her eyes tightly shut; water leaked from the corners and trickled tickly paths down the sides of her face. But she couldn't escape to her memories this time. The sounds in the room were keeping her trapped and aware — she had to look, to see, even though it was the last thing she wanted to do. Metal clanging on metal and chanting, footsteps padding across the thick carpet and Maeve was beside her again. The hood she wore cast a shadow across her features. She raised her face up and her eyes were fixed, they looked right through Regan, her lips still moved around unfamiliar words. As she chanted, she lifted her hand into the air and Regan lost the ability to breathe. A scalpel glinted in the flickering candlelight. Her eyes followed it as it lowered to her chest. She summoned the air in her lungs and started to scr—

— she was outside, somewhere unfamiliar. The air was muggy and thick with gnats. A girl in front of her swatted them away as she smiled prettily at the men walking past. Their clothes were centuries old, hers

poor and tattered, but nobody noticed as her face was so beautiful ...

... She was at a river; it was cooler. The girl was there, washing clothes against an old stone. Gossiping women were talking not too far away and Regan could hear snatches of conversation.

'A face so beautiful must be devil-made.'

'Aye, the menfolk turn and watch where e'er she goes. It is surely a sin.'

'May God have mercy on her and save her soul.'

'Time will not be kind. The devil may have given her beauty today, but time will take it away. Then she will have nothing.'

She felt a pain then, an anguish that wasn't hers ...

... She was in an old stone cottage — one room, strewn with rushes, a fire in the corner, an all-pervading smell of animal everywhere. The girl stood, talking to a shadowy figure. Regan tried to focus on the figure but she couldn't. Her eyes strained but every time she thought she had it in focus the edges blurred some more. It was like trying to look through glasses of the wrong prescription ...

... 'I promise you eternal beauty Cecily, eternal beauty and power. I ask only a sacrifice one year in one hundred. I give you creatures, familiars to share your burden. Power and beauty and friendship and riches for all eternity. What your heart desires the most will be yours. One in one hundred years Cecily, that is all I ask.'

The girl spoke, her voice small, quiet, scared, 'But what if I fail?'

'Then time will take what is mine.'
'And what if I wish never to agree to this?'
'Then you will forget our meeting. But time will take what belongs to it, and what will become of you? One in one hundred Cecily, it is all I ask …'

… Time flashed; red and screams and creamy skin and dark hair and blood and shrieks and pain and beauty and friendship and money and outfits — many outfits of beautiful colours — and dancing and balls and joy and pain and blood and pain and cold, fog, fear, blood, pain …

'Aarg—' she strangled back the cry before it left her mouth. The pain in her chest was deepening, worsening. Maeve's dark hair and purple cloak loomed above her, the scalpel biting into her skin.

She heard a quiet sound and her eyes flew to Nate. Somehow, he had managed to fray one part of the knots that bound him. The sound came again, a quiet grunt of air as Nate pulled himself up and bit at the worn edge. Maeve hesitated, a glitch in her chanting. Regan knew she had to prevent her from turning round. Nate had a chance — was giving himself a chance — and she would do everything in her power to ensure he used it.

She groaned again, letting herself feel the pain of the scalpel. She shrank away from it and Maeve stopped her chanting. 'Shut up, bitch,' Maeve hissed and Regan tried to obey. She knew that if only Nate could get free, he could save himself. Biting her lip, she tried to escape from the pain of the scalpel as it dug deeper and deeper. Pain blinded her and she was unaware of anything but the cutting of her flesh.

Pain — red, dark and all-consuming — tore at her. Everything was pain. Blinding agony. She strained against her bindings. Her back arched; her throat burned from the scream issuing from her mouth. She couldn't stop, couldn't draw in air. A sharp sting across her face paused her for a second, then the knife and the hurt and she screamed again.

Then suddenly it was gone. An ache stayed but the all-consuming, biting pain disappeared. He eyes shot open just as Maeve slammed into the wall opposite.

Nate sliced the bonds on one of her wrists, gave her the scalpel and turned to fight. Maeve sprung at him hissing; she pounced, catlike. Regan sawed at her remaining bonds, ignoring the pain from her chest and worrying she wouldn't get free in time to help Nate. She already knew how strong Maeve was.

But Nate fought as if he were possessed. Arms that shouldn't be able to move hit and punched and thumped again.

'It's nearly time, you fucking bastard,' screamed Maeve as she launched herself at Nate again. A stream of nonsensical words left Maeve's mouth, a chant, an intonation. She repeated them again and again as Nate hammered blows home. Frustration etched itself on the witch's face and her voice grew higher, more frantic. It wasn't working; the words weren't slowing Nate down. She shut up and hit back harder, faster.

Finally the last thread broke on Regan's ties. She scrabbled from the table and stabbed Maeve. Fear hid and adrenaline kicked in. She could rule the world. She stabbed and stabbed, attacking anywhere she could reach, aiming, when she could, for the face. Nate kicked and punched too, but Maeve fought back. She was possessed, screamed and fought. They both attacked but still Maeve kept on coming. It didn't matter how hard she was hit, how fast the volleys were, she just kept coming back.

The world was red and black and blurred limbs. Pain and energy combined. Power. Force. She hit then snapped her arm back and hit again. The scalpel glinted in the flickering candlelight, cutting, slicing, carving. Nicks and scratches and deeper wounds.

Regan could feel Maeve's frustration; it was palpable, almost a physical presence between them. From the thwarted magic grew hate, it grew and ballooned and became sharper kicks, stronger punches. It was darkness and it was growing. Regan felt her own blows becoming futile. A glance at Nate and she could see him waning — not much, but enough. Maeve's strength grew, fed by their hate. Hair wild, she fought; two on one was nothing. Regan and Nate were losing.

Tiredness started to claim Regan, a fatigue grown from exhaustion and defeat. She carried on fighting, but it was a token gesture. Death was close, she could feel it's breath on her neck. Without looking she was aware of Nate's energy draining too. He remained defiant, refusing to stop, but Regan could feel the triumph growing in Maeve, the power stolen from their bodies.

Then the clock struck. Twelve times the gong sounded through the house. Twelve peals. And

Maeve stopped. Her face grew pale, her eyes wide. She clasped her hands to her mouth.

'No,' she whispered, 'no, it's too late.' Her hands scrabbled at her face; she didn't seem to notice the cuts and bruises. 'No, you've ruined everything.' And she turned and fled.

Sixty-One

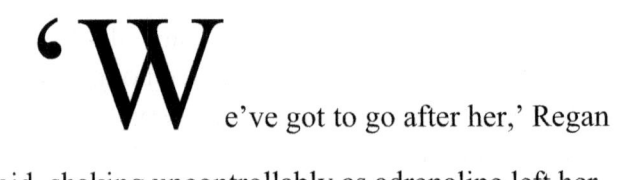

'We've got to go after her,' Regan said, shaking uncontrollably as adrenaline left her body. As it seeped away, she became aware of the pain in her chest and looked down. She saw the congealed blood that covered her left breast and the air went out of the room. The world spun and she collapsed.

When she came round, she was laying on the table again, Nate wrapping a torn shirt tightly around her cuts. 'We need to get out of here,' he said, 'are you strong enough?' Regan nodded. Nate held her as they made their way outside. She'd found her coat and put it on over her ripped clothes; Nate's jacket covered him a little against the snowy outdoors.

Nate hugged her to him and led her round the side of the house to where his bike rested. 'Will you be okay? Just hold on to me and I'll get you home.' Regan nodded, not sure if she trusted herself to speak. She climbed onto the bike and leaned into Nate; she borrowed her strength from him, from the knowledge that they were — for the moment — both still alive.

'Ashleigh,' she whispered, 'I need to get Ashleigh.' Nate nodded, not arguing with her. He started the bike and drove slowly into the chilly night. Time passed and she realised they were outside Sam's house. She climbed off the bike and ran to the front door, knocking as loudly as she could. Sam opened the door, wearing the clothes he'd had on earlier.

'Regan, what the hell are you doing here?'

'I want Ashleigh, Sam. I'm going to take her home.' She pushed past him into the house.

'She's asleep — can't I just bring her back in the morning?' He didn't seem at all confused as to why Ashleigh was there or why Regan was barging into his house to collect her sister at past midnight.

'I need to take her now,' she said, then muttered, 'oh damn.' Looking at Sam she said, 'I know I'm taking the mickey but can you please give us a lift back to my place?'

Shrugging, Sam gave his usual grin. 'I don't see why not, nothing much else going on.' Regan turned to get Ashleigh and bumped into Nate, who was standing directly behind her. 'I'll fetch her,' he said, 'and follow you.'

'So, you two finally got it together, huh?' asked Sam as he searched out his car keys. Regan just nodded wearily. She was fading fast and needed to get her and Ashleigh home and safe. Half an hour later, that's exactly where she was. She waved Sam off and opened the door for Nate. Ashleigh woke while she was being put into her bed. 'Oh, you're here, Regan. I didn't say goodbye to Maeve.'

'Don't worry about that, Ash. You go back to sleep,' Regan tucked her up and just about made it downstairs. She sat down in the kitchen and started to shake. Her arms trembled, her body shook, the pain in her chest was no longer bearable and she started sobbing. Relief and fear erupted together and she couldn't stop. Nate's arms surrounded her, warm and strong and comforting, and she cried into his jacket, snot and tears covering it. She didn't care; Nate just held her, let her cry. His hand rubbed gentle circles on her back and his lips muttered reassurances in her ear.

Eventually, she stopped. The panic had lifted and no more tears would fall. Her left breast ached so badly that soon this was all she could focus on. Reluctantly, she pulled away from Nate and touched her hand to the makeshift bandages.

'Are you ready for me to take a look at it?' Nate asked softly, his dark eyes glistening with understanding. 'I could take you to the hospital — *should* take you, but it would mean a lot of explaining — and the police, and waking Ashleigh …'

Regan shook her head, 'No, I want to stay here.' She didn't even feel embarrassed at the idea of Nate tending to such an intimate part of her. After all they'd been through, all he'd seen, everything they'd shared, it really didn't seem important.

He asked for a first aid kit and Regan directed him to it. He gave her some painkillers and a glass of water. 'This is going to hurt Regan, I'm sorry.' She took off her top and he gently unwrapped the bindings; as soon as the air hit the wound, the pain increased and Regan couldn't stop from wincing. She gripped the side of the chair as he cleaned the wound. 'Fuck, fuck!'

'I'm sorry.'

She closed her eyes and shook her head. 'It doesn't matter.' He washed and dressed the wound, placing a careful line of steri-strips along it, holding the edges together. Then he bandaged it all with fresh crepe bandages.

'How is it?' he asked as she re-dressed.

'Painful, but I expect *that* will get worse before it gets better. I think the pain killers are starting to work, they've taken the edge off.' She got up and put the kettle on. 'Where do you think she is?' she asked, not wanting to think about it but knowing she must.

Nate sat down and rubbed a hand across his face. His eyes were drawn, worried and edged with dark smudges. He looked as if he'd aged ten years in one night and Regan suddenly noticed how tired he was, how weary he looked. He shifted in his chair, his movements awkward and pain-riddled. It was only then Regan remembered she was not the only one who'd suffered injuries that evening. She'd been so caught up in her own pain that she'd paid no attention to Nate, forgotten his suffering and relied on him to be her rock.

'I don't know, but I don't think she'll be back tonight — she's weak,' he said at the exact same moment she said, 'You're injured Nate, I am so sorry. Let me look at them.'

'I'll be fine,' he said, reaching for the coffee she put in front of him.

'I'm looking at them,' Regan's own pain had suddenly faded; whether it was due to the painkillers or the realisation she wasn't the only one hurt, she wasn't entirely sure. She stood up and peeled Nate's jacket off. One look at the lacerated skin in front of her and her vision blurred as tears filled her eyes. She wiped them away.

'Oh Nate, how can you even be standing?' She had one wound, deep though it was; his front and back were criss-crossed with cuts and scratches. Blood, crusted and congealed, covered any bare patches of skin, making it difficult to see the exact extent of the damage.

'They're not that bad, Regan. Mostly scratches, not as deep as what she did to you.' He shifted a little and a small drizzle of blood made its way down his back as a scab tore.

'I've got to clean these up first,' she told him as she filled a bowl with water. As gently as she could, she bathed his back and then his front. A whole roll of cotton wool soon lay in an empty carrier bag and the water was changed and re-changed as it turned rusty brown. Eventually she could see the extent of his wounds. Most of them, as Nate kept protesting, were shallow scratches. One or two were deeper and Regan steri-stripped them shut.

'So,' asked Regan as she carefully applied another butterfly stitch, 'how exactly did you end up there, like that?'

Nate winced, 'You mean how was I stupid enough to get caught?' He sighed, 'I was watching the house, I saw her pull up — it's the first time I've seen who lives there. Suddenly it all made sense. Then I saw she had Ashleigh with her.' He stopped, lost in his thoughts. As eager as she was to know what had happened, she carried on tending the cuts on his back. The hunter wasn't used to failing. 'I knew I had to get Ashleigh; I nearly called you but then you'd have been at risk too.' He uttered a mirthless chuckle. 'So I followed them in. I didn't want to frighten Ashleigh but I knew I had to get her away. Maeve left her to go and get a drink, obviously with some sort of sedative in it, and I tried to grab her, get her to come with me, but she started screaming. I thought it was because I was trying to take her, then I got clubbed on the back of my head. The next thing I knew, I was strung up and I could hear your voice. I was stupid, reckless, I—'

'You did everything you could,' Regan said, quietly feeling for a lump on his skull. Nate dodged away from her touch, 'It's fine, I promise.'

'I need to look at the cuts on your front now,' said Regan, leaving the back of his head alone. He turned around and Regan tried not to gasp. The wound that ran clavicle to navel was the worst. Shallow in parts and pretty deep in others, Regan knew it must be extremely painful. Nate disagreed and refused any painkillers. 'I can't, it'll skew my judgement, my wits — I don't need it, Regan.'

'You'll have to stand,' Regan said as she tended him. The shallow parts she made sure were clean, the rest she slowly steri-stripped. The deepest parts she covered with a dressing. She was so caught up in what she was doing that it wasn't until she'd pushed the edges on a dressing beside his belly button that it occurred to her how close to Nate she was — how intimate tending his wounds was — and she felt a hot flush creep up her skin. The panic of earlier had gone and she remembered her words in Maeve's dining room. Remembered telling Nate she loved him. Her hand trembled and she paused her ministrations.

'Regan?' Nate asked, 'Are you alright?' She nodded and stuck the last edge down. She moved to tidy away the medical supplies, but before she could Nate caught her wrists. He took the dressing from her hand and placed it on the table behind him without turning.

'Regan,' he said again and his hand caught her chin and moved her face upwards.

'I am so sorry,' he said, 'I should have realised it was her. I should never have let you get in that situation.'

Regan let out a snort, '*You* should have realised? I'm the one who spent all that time with her — I'm the one who could have, *should have*, worked it out.'

Nate's hand stroked her cheek, sending electric pulses through her body. 'It was part of her magic, she was able to control the thoughts of those who cared for her.' Regan nodded, remembering how Sam had agreed with Maeve in the kitchen, how he hadn't found any of it strange.

'Oh fuck — Sam,' she said, 'what have we let him go back to? What if she goes after him?'

'I don't think she will,' said Nate, 'she needed the sacrifice before midnight; we denied her that. I don't know what will happen, but if she still had her strength then she'd have stayed and carried on fighting. She wouldn't have run.'

Regan shook her head, 'I can't take the risk, I've got to warn him.' She took out her phone and dialled Sam's number. He answered nearly straight away.

'Don't you ever go to sleep?' she asked.

'Nah, some ... mates called round,' Sam said and Regan heard a soft giggle in the background. *Mates my foot*, she thought. 'Okay, I just wanted to thank you again and tell you to take care, but it sounds like you're already doing that.'

'Always do sweetheart, always do.'

'You won't be alone tonight, will you Sam?' Regan knew she sounded like a mother hen but she couldn't help it.

'No Regan, I won't be alone.'

Relief swept over her, 'Okay. I'll see you tomorrow then.'

'Sure thing, laters,' and he hung up. Regan turned off her phone and put it down.

'It's okay; I think he has company — the kind he wouldn't want Maeve to find out about, so he won't see her tonight.'

Nate frowned, 'How on earth did he hook up with someone at this time of night?'

Shrugging, Regan said, 'Who knows with Sam. It's a talent he has.'

A shadow crossed Nate's face. Something unreadable appeared in his eyes. He took hold of Regan's wrists again and pulled her close. 'And did you ever receive any of his *talents*?' His voice was gruff, his eyes fixed on hers. *He's jealous*, thought Regan, almost unable to believe it.

'Of course not,' she said, her voice low, 'if I had I'd have been no use to Maeve today, would I?'

Nate grimaced, 'Maybe it would have been better if you had been with Sam.' He stroked her face, her hair.

'Or maybe it would have been better if our date had ended differently?' Regan said, her heart thumping so loudly she was sure he could hear it. 'I'm not interested in Sam, Nate. I never have been.'

'Good,' said Nate as he closed the gap between their faces and placed his lips on hers. Heat rushed through her body and she leaned into the kiss, letting his mouth gently caress hers. His stubble scratching her skin, his breath warm on her face; it all reminded her of what she had nearly lost tonight. She moved her mouth more firmly, parting his lips. He responded with longing; his hands held the nape of her neck, his mouth seeking, searching against hers. Months of yearning led her. She was hungry for him, she needed him, she wanted him. Her fingers ran through his hair and smoothed over his cheeks. He pulled her closer and deepened the kiss. She lost herself in it. Thoughts and worries disappeared, everything was Nate. Taste and touch and smell; it was all Nate.

After a time — time that could have been five minutes or an hour or longer — he pulled away. He held her face in his hands and looked straight in her eyes.

'I love you, Regan. I love you and I am so sorry. I will *never* let anyone harm you again.'

Warmth exploded through her body, every nerve tingled. 'I love you too,' she managed to reply before he kissed her again. *I love you too,* she thought before she could think no more.

Sixty-Two

Regan squinted at the red numbers on her alarm clock. She rolled over, into Nate's embrace.

'Nate, it's six o'clock — I'm sorry, we've got to get up. I don't know what time Ashleigh will wake up.'

He opened his eyes, looked at her and smiled. 'It wasn't all a dream then?'

'A nightmare,' said Regan rubbing sleep from the corner of her eye.

'A nightmare,' agreed Nate soberly, 'but not all of it.' He pulled her forward gently and kissed her. She ignored the ache in her breast; it was better than the pain she'd had in her heart. The pain that had only eased last night. He'd kissed her and he'd told her he loved her. They had spent the night — well, the three hours of sleep they'd gotten — wrapped in each other's arms.

Neither had been ready to move it further last night; it was a big step and Regan wanted it to be perfect, not a reaction to events. She didn't doubt for a second it would happen though. He kissed her again and she sighed. She didn't even care that they both had morning breath. Time was so short, could be snatched at any moment; she was not going to get hung up on the small stuff.

'How are your injuries?' she asked as she pulled away from him and slipped out of bed. She wrapped her housecoat round her and shoved her feet into her slippers.

'Absolutely fine,' said Nate as he slipped on the jeans he'd worn yesterday and borrowed an oversized band t-shirt Regan used to sleep in. He looked down. 'One Direction? I will never live this down!'

'Sorry, it's all I've got — unless scooped-necked or frilly is your style?'

He smiled, 'I'll take my chances with the boys, I think.'

Downstairs she made a pot of tea and put toast in the toaster. 'So,' she started, 'what happens now?'

'Now we track her down and kill her.' His eyes glinted darkly. 'She tried to kill you; I will *never* forgive her for that.' Regan shuddered.

'So what do we tell Mum and Ashleigh? And Sam and Nick …'

'We'll keep it simple. Sam is our biggest risk, we're not going to know exactly what he remembers. I think we tell your mum you were called in to work; you left Ashleigh with Maeve because you don't want her in the pub. Then you got a call to say Ashleigh felt unwell so you left the pub and picked her up. In fact, I think that's what we tell everyone and we stick with it.'

'But what about …' She shushed as Nate put his fingers to her lips.

'Keep it simple and as near the truth as possible. Just keep telling the same story; no-one is going to suspect anything near the truth, so why wouldn't they believe you?' Regan nodded as she spread honey on her toast. It made sense, so she put thoughts of apologies and explanations away and concentrated on Nate. Mum and Ashleigh, Toni and Ella — they could wait, for now.

'Okay. What do I tell them about us?' she asked, suddenly nervous about the answer.

'You tell them the truth there as well,' he said, leaning forward and kissing her softly, 'you tell them I finally opened my eyes and saw what was right in front of me. You tell them I'm your boyfriend.' Regan smiled as his lips found hers again.

A creak on the stairs told her Ashleigh was awake. 'I'll be back as soon as I've showered and changed,' said Nate, 'we'll figure this out, I'm not leaving you alone again, I promise.' He kissed her once more then silently left by the back door. She heard his engine start just as Ashleigh came into the kitchen.

'Morning, Ash. How are you today?'

'I'm good. I had some really horrible dreams though.'

'Oh, Ash,' she said, scooping her sister into a hug, 'it's because you didn't feel well, I had to come and collect you from Maeve's. But you look much better this morning. Here, have some toast.' She put Nate's uneaten bit onto a plate for her sister.

'Yeah, I think I remember that,' Ashleigh said, frowning. She collected the chocolate spread from the cupboard. 'What time is Mum coming home?'

'About dinner time,' said Regan, looking at the clock. A warm glow spread to her stomach when she thought that Nate would be here before then. Her hunter; her boyfriend; her love.

Sixty-Three
2014

The witch studied her complexion in the bathroom mirror. She fingered the tiny crow's feet that had started to appear. She stretched her mouth wide open to try and iron out the little creases that were starting to show in the corners. She wanted to frown, but that would only create more lines.

'Are you ready, gorgeous?' came a familiar voice from the bedroom. She tried to cull the anger that flared at his words. Was he blind not to see what was going on? Could he not tell she was aging? If this is what happened after just three months, what would happen after six? Or twelve? She couldn't afford to find out. She needed to rectify the situation, and to do that she needed a sacrifice. The time might be wrong but she'd suffered, these very lines were proof of that. Surely her master would forgive her this once — grant her his gifts, even though hers was late? So, she must find another suitable sacrifice. And then she would find Regan and kill the bitch. But not until she'd suffered. Not until she'd seen those she loved suffer. No. Regan was going to pay.

'Maeve, my love, are you nearly ready?' he called again.

'Won't be a minute, Sam,' she called to him, pouring as much honey into her voice as possible. Three months with him was starting to wear on her nerves; she might have to dispose of him soon. She shook her head at the thought. No, he was useful. He was a link to *her* — even though he hadn't been in touch since that night. He hadn't thought of his family or friends once. She'd made sure of that.

'Okay honey, are you ready to go?' she asked, reaching for her handbag and opening the door into the city night. Tonight she was hunting, searching for the sacrifice that would bring her strength. Sam was the passenger, oblivious.

'Oh Sam, we're going to have fun tonight!' He smiled blindly at her, not caring about his previous life. If Maeve was the cat, then he was the mouse. And he was well and truly caught.

To be continued …

Dear Reader,

Thank you for reading The Hunter's Companion. This book has been a long time in the writing and a real journey of discovery for me; I started off an avid reader and became an enthused writer. So many lessons were learnt along the way (though I thank Lynda Lamb for her editing skills, because properly placed commas is not a lesson that wants to stay in my head…)

For me, self-belief, tempered with a good dose of reliable advice has been the most significant lesson. If *I* didn't believe in my story, in Regan and Lora, who else would? I wasn't pig-headed enough to believe that I'd written a perfect story straight off the bat though. Hilary Johnson's critiquing service gave me things to think about; without their input, Sam, Toni, Ella and Cyndi would not have existed and this tale would have been quite different.

My sister, Lynda, and my Unicorn friend writers – Nash, Nico, L, Sara – all helped me improve my writing by being nicely critical, if not of this story of my writing in general. Reviewers too really help me. *All* readers' thoughts and opinions, whether praise or criticism, result in my improvement.

I feel privileged to live in the fenland of East Anglia. Where many see desolation, wide open sky and endless flat fields, I see inspiration and stories that just need uncovering. To stand outside away from the masses and just to listen, is to hear the stories the land is trying to tell. In these once boggy by-ways is history… and fantasy and a million hidden tales just waiting to be heard. It's in the wind that rustles the acres of crops; it's in the poplar trees that stand guard so solemnly; it's in the earth, both rich and dark, or wet and clay like. The echoes of people past, and perhaps those to come, can be heard if you just stop and listen a while. Without this as my muse who knows whether Regan and Lora's stories would have been heard.

Thank you, reader, for taking this journey with me. I hope you join Regan and Nate in the next part of their tale.

Love

Lori Powell x

Books with romance, books with sex,
Voodoo books & books with hex,
Fantasy, mystery, humour & crime,
Young adult, adult adult & kids from time to time,
In all their shapes & all their sizes,
I love books in all their guises.

Since I read Enid Blyton's Famous Five series as a child, I've been enamoured by books. Books have let me fall in love a thousand times and taken me on adventures to places I've never actually been. They've let me solve mysteries and figure out crimes and interact with the supernatural... and I can fit it all in around my daily life.

With two amazing children, one perfect (for me) husband and a shelf full of books, I have everything I could wish for. The crazy cats are just a bonus.

My writing is an extension of my love of reading - all that daydreaming I was told off for at school is put to good use! It's a wonderful world of fantasy in my head, and I love sharing it with you all.

Take care,

Lori x

Printed in Great Britain
by Amazon